GEORGIANA

THE AUTHOR

Brian Masters is the author of books on
numerous subjects ranging from Molière to
EF Benson. He has also written studies of
true crime including those on Dennis Nilsen
(which won him the Golden Dagger Award),
Jeffrey Dahmer and, most recently,
Rosemary West. He lives in London.

ALSO BY BRIAN MASTERS

Molière
Sartre
Saint-Exupéry
Rabelais
Camus – A Study
Wynyard Hall and the Londonderry Family
The Dukes
Now Barabbas was a Rotter: The Extraordinary Life of Marie Corelli
The Mistresses of Charles II
Dreams about H.M. The Queen

GEORGIANA

BRIAN MASTERS

a&b

This edition published in Great Britain in 1997 by
Allison & Busby Ltd
114 New Cavendish Street
London W1M 7FD

First published in Great Britain in 1981 by Hamish Hamilton Ltd

A catalogue record for this book is available from the
British Library

ISBN 0 74900 269 7

Printed and bound in Great Britain by
WBC Book Manufacturers Ltd
Bridgend, Mid Glamorgan

CONTENTS

To Andrew and Debo

ILLUSTRATIONS

Illustrations in the text

ACKNOWLEDGEMENTS

I should like not merely to acknowledge, but to proclaim my debt to Their Graces the Duke and Duchess of Devonshire, who made available the entire archive in the 5th Duke's collection, including many hundreds of letters never before published, and allowed me to pursue my work in the comfort of their home. I was assisted on many occasions by the librarians at Chatsworth – Mr Peter Day, Mr Michael Pearman, Miss Christine Tyndale, and the late Tom Wragg – to whom I should like also to express my gratitude. I am similarly indebted to Mr George Howard for permission to consult the archives at Castle Howard, and to the archivist Miss Judith Oppenheimer, who guided me through a mass of largely uncatalogued papers. Mr Richard Page Croft kindly allowed me to see the letters of his ancestor, Dr Croft, who delivered Georgiana's son, thus enabling me finally to confirm the legitimacy of the birth. Dr. A. N. E. Schofield of the Manuscript Department in the British Library was most helpful in showing me the Melbourne (Lamb) Papers the very minute they became available for public scrutiny.

For permission to see the archives of the French Foreign Ministry in Paris, I am grateful not only to the staff at the Ministry, but to those who helped bring me into contact with them, namely Lord Nicholas Gordon-Lennox and Monsieur Michel Huriet, Cultural Counsellor at the French Embassy in London. The Secretary of Brooks's Club allowed me to have a photograph taken of their portrait of Lord Hartington, and Professor Ivan Hall has graciously given me use of his own photographs of furnishings at Chatsworth. Lord Hampden generously allowed photographs to be taken of the miniature of his ancestress, Eliza Courtney, and of the pendant which Charles Grey gave to Georgiana, now in Lord Hampden's possession.

In tracking down the history of Corisande de Gramont, I was given ready assistance by her descendant, the Hon. Ian Bennet, and by the present representatives of her family, the Duc de Gramont and the Duc de Polignac, to each of whom I am most grateful. Mr Bennet also enabled me to consult his family papers (Tankerville) at the Northumberland County Record Office. I am likewise eager to thank the University of Nottingham (Portland Papers), the Royal Academy of Art (Lawrence Papers), the William L. Clements Library at the University of Michigan (letters to Comte Perregaux), for their willing co-operation.

A number of Georgiana's letters have sentences obliterated by a later hand. Many attempts were made to reveal the hidden sentences, all of which failed owing to the fact that the ink used was of the same chemical composition as the ink of the original writing. Nevertheless, I am deeply grateful to the laboratory staff and officers at Scotland Yard and the Public Record Office for their untiring efforts with the most sophisticated equipment.

Diana Steer, as usual, patiently made a respectable typescript out of an untidy manuscript, and Mr Roger Machell made many helpful suggestions for amendment to the finished text, all of which I happily and gratefully adopted.

B.M.

FOREWORD

I have lived with Georgiana for more than fifty years. She is in our drawing room, my little sitting room, and the library. Sometimes she moves into the Great Dining Room. These constant reminders make Georgiana's presence at Chatsworth almost tangible.

None of the many portraits we have of her show a classic beauty, not even those by Lawrence, Reynolds, Gainsborough and Downman. Her son, the 6th Duke, wrote of Maria Cosway's large canvas that 'the head ... is very like my mother and it is almost the only likeness of her that reminds me of her countenance'. It was impossible to capture her charm on canvas and from all contemporary accounts I imagine her appearance must have been what the French call *journalière* – changeable, with good days and not such good days. But everyone who met her fell under her spell.

It is perhaps her letters more than her portraits which bring her most vividly to life. Two tall bookcases removed from old Devonshire House in London are crammed full of them. They tell of her feelings in her own words and in her own hand to her intimates: her mother, her sister, her children and friends.

Georgiana was married on her seventeenth birthday to a silent, lethargic husband. Her loyalty to him never faltered but his coldness and lack of interest drove her to a frenzied search for happiness, living 'in a continual bustle without having literally anything to do'. She was the centre of fashionable society, filling her houses with the most eminent politicians and writers of her day; she developed a fatal addiction to gambling, and was haunted by debts to the end of her days.

With the appearance in 1782 of Lady Elizabeth Foster, the story of the Devonshire household becomes extraordinary. Were it not for the evidence of the family's letters, those of contemporaries and the existence of the children, legitimate and illegitimate, it would be impossible to believe. All the accepted rules of human relationship were shattered. From then on Georgiana's story is bound up with that of Elizabeth, and their abiding love for one another, with the Duke as the third of the trio. The intimacy and lack of jealousy between the two women, which continued until Georgiana's death twenty-four years later, makes their tale unique.

Brian Masters not only reveals the truth behind their convoluted human relationships but also weaves into it the day-to-day life of the family, almost as interesting to me as the story itself. Their travels, as the two women, in emotional turmoil, went abroad to have their babies, Paris at the time of the Revolution, electioneering – all are vividly recreated. Now, after two hundred years, the 5th Duke of Devonshire, Elizabeth, their friends and, above all, Georgiana, are brought back to fill the drawing rooms at Chatsworth once more.

Deborah Devonshire

Chapter One

AMIABLE, INNOCENT AND BENEVOLENT

Sarah, the redoubtable Duchess of Marlborough, was especially fond of her grandson John Spencer, the second son of her daughter Anne. Of course, there were times when they quarrelled, for Sarah quarrelled with everyone sooner or later, but their relationship was on the whole warm and, as we shall see, fruitful. The cause of their temporary rift was a bright, witty remark which John made at his grandmother's expense on the occasion of a grand dinner party which she gave for all members of her family. Referring to the assembled guests as 'a great tree, herself the root, and all her branches flourishing round her', she beamed and looked proud, until gusts of laughter from the other end of the table soured her pleasure. John Spencer had turned to his neighbour and said that 'the branches would flourish more when the root was underground'. Sarah asked for an explanation of the merriment, and when John himself repeated his joke, she not unnaturally took umbrage.

Still, they were reconciled in time, and the day eventually came when John should consider getting married. It was of the first importance to Sarah that her grandson should choose well and carefully, so she prepared for him a list of suitable young ladies and bade him make a selection. He avowed that he would be happy to marry anyone who met with her approval, and since in the manner of the day it mattered little whether he loved the girl, he thought that to save time he would take the first one on the list. The names were arranged in alphabetical order, and at the top was a name beginning with C. Thus it was that John Spencer came to marry Georgiana Carteret, a daughter of Lord Granville.[1]

Sarah was evidently delighted with this display of common sense, for she made John the principal benefactor under her will, enabling him to inherit the manor and park of Wimbledon, which she had built. Furthermore, although he was only the second surviving son of his father and ought normally to be neglected in accordance with the strict rules of primogeniture, he profited accidentally from a detour in the descent of the Marlborough line, inheriting the paternal estates as well. As the great John Churchill's only son had died of smallpox when a child, leaving him with four daughters, an Act of Parliament stipulated that the dukedom of Marlborough should pass first to his eldest daughter Henrietta (who was thereby Duchess of Marlborough *suo jure*), and thereafter, if Henrietta had no male heir, to the eldest son of his second daughter Anne. Anne married the 3rd Earl of Sunderland, head of the Spencer family, and when Henrietta's son died without issue, the title and estates of Marlborough duly passed to Anne's son, who thereupon became 3rd Duke of Marlborough as well as Earl of Sunderland. It was his younger brother, John Spencer, who was grandmother Sarah's favourite and who found himself heir to his father's property of Althorp in Northamptonshire and Spencer House in London, it being thought that the Blenheim estates were quite enough for the senior Spencer to inherit. With the death of Sarah in 1744, John also received Wimbledon Park, as promised, with a typically eccentric condition attached by old Sarah, to the effect that if he or his sons were to accept any office under the Crown (apart from the fairly innocent rangership of Windsor Great Park), he would forfeit all claim to benefit under the will as completely as if he were dead.

While the senior Spencers went on to continue the Marlborough line (and change their name to Spencer-Churchill), lucky John Spencer set about founding an entirely new branch of the family at Althorp. Both branches continue to this day.

The Spencers had originally been husbandmen in Northamptonshire and Warwickshire, who rose by diligence to positions of some prominence under the Tudors. Sir John Spencer of Wormleighton and Snitterfield, Co. Warwick (now a little village a few miles from Stratford-upon-Avon), was knighted by Henry VIII and bought Althorp in 1508. His descendant, Sir Robert, gave further evidence of the Spencer wit when challenged in Parliament by Thomas Howard, Earl of Arundel, who, during a debate on the Royal Prerogative, taunted him with the remark, 'When these things were doing, your ancestors were keeping sheep', to which Spencer replied with spirit, 'When my ancestors were keeping sheep, your lordship's ancestors were plotting treason'. Arundel was so excited that he had to be committed to the Tower of London to calm him down, and was released only when the customary Howard irascibility had subsided sufficiently for him to apologise to Spencer.

The earldom of Sunderland was created for the Spencer family in 1643, and stayed with them for ninety years until it was absorbed into the dukedom of Marlborough in 1733, leaving John Spencer happily ensconced at Althorp. Although the choice of his bride Georgiana Carteret was somewhat haphazard, he managed fairly promptly to produce a son ten months later, who became M.P. (Whig) for Warwick at the age of twenty-two. After first flirting with a daughter of Sir Cecil Bishop and raising hopes of a match which came to nothing,[2] the younger John Spencer lighted upon a fairly obscure but rich young lady called Margaret Georgiana Poyntz, daughter of Stephen Poyntz. In spite of being the son of a mere upholsterer, Stephen had moved in the very highest circles, becoming first tutor to George II's son the Duke of Cumberland, and then a Privy Councillor. Most important of all, from our point of view, he had been a life-long friend of the Duke of Devonshire's family. When his daughter married Spencer in 1755, she brought with her this highly desirable Devonshire connection, which was to prove her most significant contribution to the marriage. (Being a Whig, Spencer presumably knew the Duke of Devonshire already, as he was the recognised leader of the Whig faction, but Miss Poyntz it was who brought the two families together in intimacy; her aunt Louisa Poyntz had already been wooed unsuccessfully by Devonshire.)

This Spencer marriage, like his father's, also had its unorthodox aspect. The wedding took place in secret at Althorp, in a dressing-room. Considering there were five hundred people dancing in the great house at the time, and that none knew a wedding had taken place until the following day, this was no mean achievement. It was observed that the new Mrs Spencer wore diamonds worth £12,000.

Spencer was raised to the peerage in 1761 as Baron Spencer of

Althorp, and then further elevated as Viscount Althorp and Earl Spencer in 1765. His wife must henceforth be known as Countess Spencer; it is with this name that she assumes one of the cardinal roles in the present book.

The match would prove to be a whole-hearted success. Many years later the bride told David Garrick, 'It will tomorrow be one and twenty years since Lord Spencer married me, and I verily believe that we have neither of us for one instant repented our lot from that time to this.'

Lady Spencer was a woman endowed with great strength of character and many virtues, principal among which was a deep unshakeable piety. Her religion was the mainstay of her existence, yet it was not a religion which battled for supremacy with ambition or pleasure; on the contrary, it was allied to these perfectly laudable pursuits. Not for her the unbridled undignified ecstasy of the mystic, or the emotional hysterical pose of the convert. Such extravagance was a reprehensible insult to the quiet decent flow of life which God ordained. Lady Spencer neatly illustrated the prevailing eighteenth-century attitudes of the aristocracy in religious matters, all refinement and common sense, polite and practical, eschewing the waste energy which speculation would encourage, and devoting oneself instead to the nurturing of fine ethical conduct. Religious education of one's children consisted in teaching them how to behave, not how to think or feel about metaphysical questions, which were not the province of man to examine. Provided you did good acts, knew your duty towards your fellows and especially your dependants, gave of your time towards those less fortunate than yourself, and heeded God's precepts in all things, the Almighty would see that you rose in the world according to your just deserts. It was a healthy religion, not narrow, and not particularly heartfelt. It enabled you to develop your personality to its full potential and embrace all the joys which life had to offer without fear of capricious retribution. 'Christianity as taught in the Gospel', Lady Spencer said, 'has nothing formidable in it; the end and design of it is not to sour but to sweeten life.'[3] She spent a great deal of her time doing her duty and exhorting others to do theirs. She was said to have the art of 'leading, drawing, or seducing people into right ways'.[4] Such a sensible, elastic attitude was to meet its severest test in dealing with her children.

The Countess was also well read and intelligent, with a firm respect for the delicate refined use of language and the worthwhile occupations of the mind. She despised extremes in all things, welcomed social intercourse, provided it was restricted by well-kept rules, thought politics were not a proper subject to interest a lady, and elections were 'vile things', admired love as long as it was decently trammelled by the proprieties, and deemed that any thought or emotion which had no practical application was to be discouraged above all.

And she had one worrying weakness. She could not resist the gaming-tables. This she inherited from her mother Mrs Poyntz, who played at cards from morning to night,[5] and it caused her much perturbation of spirit. For a short period she kept a diary which was meant to help record her struggle with the demon and thereby exorcise it. 'Enable me O God to persevere in my endeavour to conquer this habit as far as it is a vice', she wrote, implying that it would not be vicious if only it could be contained in moderation. Again she wrote, 'Played at billiards and bowls and cards all evening and a part of the night . . . nobody acts so constantly inconsistently as I do. It is a bad account of myself but may I at least make the best use of it, by learning to make universal allowances for others.'[6] The fault in Lady Spencer's pragmatic view could be turned to advantage by practical endeavour.

Two years after the Spencers married, there was born a daughter destined to lurch beyond all those extremes which the mother so assiduously avoided. She was the great-great-granddaughter of Duchess Sarah, and she was christened Georgiana.

*   *   *

The world into which Georgiana was born was solid, calm, self-assured. The great house of Althorp, already two hundred and fifty years old and one of the colossal establishments from which England was governed, predicted a life of ease and agreeableness for the little girl as a matter of course. With its majestic drive sweeping to an imposing entrance, its lush womb-

like park, regiments of servants, and rooms great and small constantly busy with talk of hunting, of people, of manners, of
affairs of great moment, Althorp managed to combine formality
with cosiness, graceful style with an unceremonious manner,
entertaining on a baroque scale with an unfussy delight in the
pleasures of home life. Though prodigiously impressive, there
were other houses that were more so, and the inhabitants of
Althorp were not burdened with any self-conscious idea of
their own importance, still less any coruscating ambition. That
they *were* important went without saying and was therefore
unworthy of comment. They occupied a place close to the
summit of a well-ordered hierarchical pyramid, and yet within
their own circle of acquaintance, which meant a few dozen other
families similarly placed, they had friendly social intercourse on
a footing of equality. The rigid ritual of precedence and stern
inhuman straitjacketing which were to characterise the Victorian period had not yet touched them. They were above all
relaxed, charming, and honest. Georgiana would inevitably
absorb all the benefits of this harmonious existence, grow into a
well-mannered spontaneous girl, make a fine marriage, and
produce offspring to continue the tradition of graceful living.
That much was certain. What could not be known was that she
would add to the recipe a dash of sprightly delinquent
originality all her own.

Georgiana Spencer was born on 7 June 1757, to be followed
by a brother in 1758 (soon to be known to family and strangers
alike by the courtesy title of Lord Althorp), and a sister, Harriet,
in 1761. Georgiana and Harriet were not just sisters, but
devoted companions, sharing the same frolics, learning
together, planning their futures with that earnestness which
infants bring to their deliberations, and enjoying the spacious
freedom of the big house which was their domain. Of course,
they had to be educated to take their place in the world, and it
was right and proper that their mother should personally
oversee this very important, perhaps *most* important, element in
their upbringing. It was their good fortune to have a mother so
superbly fitted to the task.

We have seen that Lady Spencer was the embodiment of
eighteenth-century womanhood, well bred and self-contained,
always in command of her emotions, religious without being

meditative, orderly and practical. It was her intention that her daughters should inherit good sense and judgement, and to this end she set about controlling their lives with a respect for discipline which would equip them to cope with all of life's vagaries and enable them to be mistresses of their destinies.

Lady Spencer believed in the supremacy of method in regulating the day, and in the virtues of simple country life. At half-past five in the morning she would be out of bed, would dress, say prayers, and for well over an hour read some passages of the Bible. After breakfast at nine, she went for a bracing walk, taking plenty of fresh air and pausing perhaps to watch the shearing of sheep or some other farming occupation according to the season. She dined at three in the afternoon, having answered all her letters as soon as they were delivered and read, and had supper at nine in the evening, to be in bed by ten. In winter, she would rise slightly later, at seven o'clock, and dine a little later in the afternoon, so as to enjoy the maximum amount of daylight. Such was the salutary regime imposed on the young Georgiana.

Georgiana was taught that idleness was the besetting sin, that occupation was praiseworthy. Hence much of the day was spent making one's clothes and mending one's boots. Visits to the poor were a duty to be welcomed; still more so was the education of poor village children, who thus enjoyed the peculiar distinction of having their tables taught by the grand Countess. Georgiana herself put in some hours at the village school, both as pupil, when she was forbidden by Mama any airs which might discountenance the other children, and later as teacher, though she was still only a girl. Georgiana also learnt to be frank and open at all times, to eschew intrigue and contrived feelings, to respect the honourable intentions of everyone. 'Avoid mystery in everything', wrote her mother, 'and consider a late confidence is always mortifying to a person to whom an early one is due.'[7] Lady Spencer had trained herself in sagacity, and quite naturally hoped to bequeath to her daughters the benefits of her accumulated wisdom. Her one mistake was to be a trifle too forceful in her endeavours, with the result that both daughters would feel a blessed lifting of weight when they were free of her fretful influence, though the umbilical cord could never entirely be severed. That she never understood this is illustrated by her

regrets, many years later, that she had not been more firm in in-
hibiting her daughters' conduct.[8] Yet her grandchildren would
always turn to her for advice, even if they were slow to heed it.

Unlike many of the great Whig ladies who were complacently
philistine in their artistic tastes, admiring the epigrammatic and
decently architectural expression to the exclusion of anything
more robust and original, Lady Spencer was a learned woman.
Of course, there were the standard works of literature and
history, Greek and Roman classics, Bossuet's sermons and
Paley's *Principles of Moral and Political Philosophy*, all of which
Georgiana was required to study, as well as to learn the
obligatory French which was the *sine qua non* of every aristocratic
young lady's educational baggage, but Lady Spencer had a
reputation for scholarship above the ordinary and was
frequently seen to dip into modern works whose worth had not
yet been established by custom. It is on record that she wrote to
the strange reclusive William Cowper asking for the privilege of
an interview,[9] and her grandchildren were later to look to her
rather than to anyone else for a reading-list. Lady Spencer's dis-
ciplinarian attitudes might have appeared despotic, but
Georgiana happily submitted to them in the knowledge that her
mother's carefully nurtured experience was a gift to be
cherished. Throughout her quixotic career, Georgiana's admiration for her mother's more stable intelligence never left
her, and she passed this conviction on to her own children. Fifty
years later, Lady Harriet Cavendish wrote to her grandmother,
'Do you know how much you are loved, admired and honoured
by every person who has the least connection with you?'[10] This
was already a just statement when Georgiana was growing up at
Althorp.

Then there was the constant stream of visitors, whose
company and conversation represented an education in
themselves. Statesmen, writers, poets, actors, scholars, all
descended on the house at one time or another, giving their
erudite opinion in cleverly turned phrases, endowing the
dinner-table with the best wit and sparkle of the day. In the un-
generous opinion of one of her relations, some part at least of
Lady Spencer's reputation was derived from the company she
kept rather than innate ability. She did not possess quickness of
understanding, says this correspondent, 'but she had taken

great pains with herself, had read a great deal, and, though herself far from brilliant in conversation, had lived in the society of clever people.'[11]

One visitor in particular stood out above all others, not because he was brighter or more intelligent – indeed, his conversation was markedly dull and his company on the whole burdensome – but because he was quite simply, in the eyes of a Whig family who did not toady to royalty, the most important person in the land. This was the adolescent Duke of Devonshire, head of the mighty Cavendish family and proudest mascot of the Whigs. It has always been thought that the young Duke did not meet Georgiana until 1773, when he was twenty-four and she sixteen, but letters among the Portland Papers reveal that he was a frequent visitor to Althorp long before this. A cursory glance indicates that he spent some time there in 1765 and 1766, when he was a lad of sixteen or seventeen and little Georgiana a charming ebullient sprite of eight.[12] As Lady Spencer had known him since he was a boy, there is every reason to suppose that he was in Georgiana's company even before this. (There is a letter from Mrs Spencer, as she then was, to the 4th Duke in 1760, when Georgiana was three years old). It is not known at what point in their respective childhoods the possibility of their marrying was first mooted, nor whether they were themselves consulted in the matter until after decisions had been taken, but it was clearly a splendid idea from almost every point of view: the union of two Whig houses, the alliance of money and style, the connection of two young people who had known each other all their lives and got on well together. They might not be in love, but that would come in due time. Meanwhile, Georgiana was marked down as a possible future Duchess, and groomed for the role by her assiduous mother, tactfully and quietly, without postulated glory being allowed to fill the girl's head. First, however, all three children had to undergo the statutory Grand Tour of Europe, and so the whole family set out from Wimbledon in 1722, when Georgiana was fifteen, her brother fourteen, and Harriet eleven.

* * *

The 'whole family' meant not five people, but maids, cooks, butler, and other servants necessary to alleviate the toil of travel

by horse and carriage over primitive roads. Memoirs of
travelling through Europe at this time in such conditions always
tell us where the travellers went and what they saw but never,
alas, what it was like to spend hour after hour in a bumpy
carriage nor how they contrived to occupy their time on the long
journey. Little Harriet kept a diary of this trip, and she was no
exception. They went from Calais to Brussels and the
fashionable watering-place of Spa, where *everyone* went sooner
or later, and where they met the Duchess of Northumberland
and Princess Esterhazy. Harriet noted that the Duchess was 'very
fat and has a great beard almost like a man.'* Mama and Papa
also played at faro, the notoriously chancy game which was later
to bring both daughters to the point of despair.

From Spa they went to Liège and took part in a boar-hunt,
Georgiana and Harriet following on gentle ponies. The kill was
'very shocking', but not half so horrid as the scenes they were to
witness in France. From Lille they continued to Senlis and Paris,
staying at the Hotel Radziville, and meeting many of the
grandest people. There was old Madame du Deffand, now blind
and sitting like a concierge in a porter's chair, and Marie-
Antoinette, 'so fair and so handsome, it is impossible not to
admire her'. But there were more of those shocking sights, of
bodies broken on the wheel, or dangling and rotting from a
gallows.

The journal becomes interesting when it allows us a glimpse
of Papa, for Lord Spencer has ever been a figure drawn only in
outline compared with the full portrait we have of his wife. We
know that he was admired for his sincerity, and feared for his
bad temper, but little else.[13] Harriet tells us that he was much
concerned lest his daughters should be spoilt. At many an inn
the girls had to sleep rough, wrapped up in a blanket on the
floor, because 'Papa says girls of our age should learn not to
make a fuss but sleep anywhere'. Nor did he want them to be
squeamish. Visits to gallows and boar-hunts were undertaken at
his instigation in order to accustom the girls to unpleasant
sights. At Toulouse they went deep into the dark vault of a
church where dead bodies hung in grisly positions, there being

* Lady Betty Seymour, daughter of the Duke of Somerset, married Sir Hugh
Smithson who was later created Duke of Northumberland. They are ancestors
of the present Duke.

no room to bury them in the churchyard. Georgiana and Harriet were told not to be frightened – 'papa says it is foolish and superstitious to be afraid of seeing dead bodies'.

In Montpellier Lord Spencer fell ill and had to undergo a serious operation, which was well-timed in so far as Montpellier boasted the most famous medical school in Europe. The surgeon told Georgiana and Harriet that their father had submitted to the ordeal with exemplary stoicism, never once flinching under the knife. 'Les filles d'un héros ne doivent pas pleurer,' he said. They later visited the beautiful Roman aqueduct at Le Pont du Gard (still one of the most glorious sights in the south of France), and the little port of Cette, to be celebrated over a century and a half later in Paul Valéry's most famous poem. Lord Spencer thought it proper that he should give a ball on the Queen's birthday, he being the most prominent Englishman in the town, on which occasion poor Lady Spencer had to forgo her frugal habits and stay up until six in the morning.

Every experience was used by Lord Spencer as a further brick in the construction of his daughters' education, and some of his wisdom is manifest in the observations which Harriet assiduously recorded. Talking of the antipathy between Catholics and Protestants, 'Papa bids us observe how much persecution encreas'd zeal for the religion so oppress'd, which he said was a lesson against oppression, and for toleration.'

They started their journey north again in April 1773, passing through Lyons and on to Paris, where they saw Marie-Antoinette once more and were carried into the theatre at Versailles. A highlight was the visit to the Convent of Saint-Cyr, where they saw the room to which Madame de Maintenon retired after the death of Louis XIV, and where it was pointed out that if they were to ask permission for the nuns to be allowed to talk, it would be granted. Lady Spencer did so, and was astonished at the clatter.

In June they were back in Spa, and shortly afterwards returned to England, having been absent for fully twelve months.[14] Georgiana's education was now complete. She was sixteen years old, pretty, of lively disposition, quite unaffected, and totally disarming. She had created a very good impression in France, where comments had been made approving her beauty and character, to the detriment of Mrs Crewe, the other English *belle*, whose features were found less impressive upon closer examination. As for 'Georgine', wrote Mme du Deffand, on 12 June, 'sa taille, sa physiognomie, sa gaîté, son maintien, sa bonne grâce ont charmé tout le monde.' She needed only to curb her enthusiasms by a settled maturity, and no doubt the responsibilities of marriage would see to that. She was ready.

*   *   *

Or was she? Lady Caroline Lamb would say that her aunt had not been at all interested in being married, had been ignorant of everything, and would have been quite content to continue hunting butterflies; the housekeeper, she said, had to break a lathe over Georgiana's head before she would take the matter seriously.[15] Mama was certainly anxious lest Georgiana's giddiness might not be sufficiently under control before she left home. She told her friend Mrs Henry in January 1774, 'My dread is that she will be snatched from me before her age and experience make her by any means fit for the serious duties of a wife, a mother, or the mistress of a family.'[16]

Clearly, Georgiana was not responding to her mother's careful grooming with quite that weight of solemnity which should become a young lady, and the Countess observed many signs of flippancy in her daughter which alarmed her. She took to sending her reproachful nagging letters even before she was married, in a tone half-apologetic for being such a nuisance as to lecture, and half-sermonising. She hoped that Georgiana would not receive admonitions 'with a fretful kind of impatience, and think a parent unreasonable for being always preaching'. The fact that she needed to say so was evidence enough that Georgiana had given her that impression in the past. This is the most dangerous period in your life, the Countess went on,

> when you are so near entering into a world abounding with dissipation, vice and folly, and where your conduct for the first year or two will in great measure determine whether you shall be rank'd among the idle, giggling, despicable set of women who crowd up all assemblies and public places, or

amongst those who, by their accomplishments, the modesty of their behaviour, the sweetness of their disposition and the goodness of their hearts, are the ornament of their country, the delight of the society they live in, and are lov'd and respected by everybody.[17]

The Countess wanted more than anything to avoid haste, but by the Spring of 1774 it was too late. Georgiana had received some proposals of marriage, which she had rejected no doubt on Mama's advice, and to her own relief. But now the Duke of Devonshire himself had requested her hand, and as he was the greatest catch of all, and not a man used to having his will thwarted, there was nothing for it but to let Georgiana go, and pray God she would find resources of stability within her. The Duke and the Earl had agreed the alliance, Lady Spencer had to succumb to powers greater than her own. She confided once more to Mrs Henry her fears that the marriage was premature:

[Georgiana] is indeed to be taken from me much sooner than I think either for her advantage or my comfort, as I had flatter'd myself I should have had more time to have improv'd her understanding and, with God's assistance, to have strengthened her principles and enabled her to avoid the many snares that vice and folly will throw in her way. She is amiable, innocent and benevolent, but she is giddy, idle, and fond of dissipation.[18]

Rarely can a mother have watched her daughter's entry into marriage with such sore misgivings, but on the basis that Georgiana would immediately assume, as Duchess of Devonshire, the first place in society and be thrust to a pinnacle of responsibility second only to that of royalty, where her every gesture would be noticed, recorded, and commented upon, Lady Spencer's anxiety was understandable. Devonshire wanted the marriage to take place as soon as possible, while Georgiana was still sixteen (he was now twenty-four), but since Lady Spencer was equally hopeful that it could be delayed as long as possible, a compromise was reached. The wedding would take place on her seventeenth birthday.

On 4 June, three days before, the Duke partnered Georgiana

at a ball given in honour of the King's birthday. Probably because rumours of the impending match were already circulating, it was decided then that the ceremony should take place the following morning, in the greatest secrecy, to avoid the attention of crowds and gossip-mongers. Not even Georgiana was informed until she woke up and found herself being dressed in great haste to be packed off to Wimbledon Parish Church, where, in the briefest, quietest ritual sandwiched between two ordinary church services, she duly became the Duchess of Devonshire. The only guests were her grandmother Lady Cowper,* the Duke's sister the Duchess of Portland, and his brother, Lord Richard Cavendish. Georgiana's uncle, the Rev. Charles Poyntz, officiated.

The first days of married state were spent at Wimbledon Park with the Spencers, where Mama could keep a close eye on Georgiana's behaviour. The Duke did not much care for all that early rising and those sensible meals, and took his bride with a certain ill-disguised relief to his own place at Chiswick a few days later. Even there, Lady Spencer's interfering *soucis* were despatched by post. There was the important matter of the *levée* to attend to, followed by Georgiana's presentation at Court. 'I send this to Chiswick for fear the Duke of Devonshire should not yet be up', she wrote, 'that you may put him in mind of the Levée for which I have some fear he will be too late, and that will make your presentation tomorrow very awkward.'[19] We are not informed how the Duke took to being ticked off by his mother-in-law.

In the event, the presentation passed off extremely well, Georgiana a vision of youthful radiance to attract every eye. The Duke was content, the Spencers proud, and the new Duchess an immediate success. Her position as the leader of society was assured from the first. Everyone marvelled how natural and spontaneous she was, how easy it was to be with her. She was a creature to fascinate and beguile, and she gave every cause to expect the marriage would prove an unmitigated success.

The next day, Lady Betty Ponsonby wrote to congratulate Georgiana and to express her belief that the Duke was a very lucky man. 'The justice the world does to your Grace's person

* Earl Spencer's mother, Mrs Spencer, had taken as her second husband the 2nd Lord Cowper.

and character', she said, 'leaves no room to doubt that he will experience every felicity that this life can afford.'[20] And Papa wrote his own word of encouragement: 'You are married to a man whose temper, disposition and good sense put it in your power to be happy.'[21]

Chapter Two

CAVENDISHES AND THE WORLD

The disposition and good sense of the Cavendish family were never in question, and the man whom Georgiana had married possessed by heredity, qualities of probity and integrity which distinguished him from many of his contemporaries. Whether he also had the makings of a cosy husband was quite another matter.

William Cavendish, 5th Duke of Devonshire, descended from that most amazing Elizabethan, Bess of Hardwick,* who had married four times and was four times a widow. Each of her husbands adored her so much that he left her every penny he had, and with the accumulated booty she spent her entire life building great houses with a passion that bordered on the obsessive. She breathed the dust of masonry, being responsible not only for Hardwick Hall, that most perfect of Elizabethan mansions, but Chatsworth and Welbeck as well. Her second husband was Sir William Cavendish, close adviser to Henry VIII and one of the architects of the dissolution of the monasteries. It was the Cavendish good fortune that this was the only one of the four marriages which gave Bess any children, with the result that all her wealth and estates passed by inheritance to the Cavendish line. To her first surviving son, William Cavendish, she bequeathed Chatsworth, Hardwick and Oldcotes, all in Derbyshire, while Welbeck went to another son, who is the ancestor of the Dukes of Portland.

In recognition of his pre-eminence in the county of Derbyshire, William Cavendish was raised to the peerage first with the rank of baron (in 1605) and then with the earldom of Devonshire in 1618.† For this privilege he was said to have paid

* Elizabeth Hardwick, later Countess of Shrewsbury (1518–1608).

† There is no foundation for the belief that the scribe made a spelling

£10,000. His son and grandson, the 2nd and 3rd Earls, established the family preference for solitary intellectual pursuits, the 2nd Earl being educated by none other than Thomas Hobbes, and the 3rd becoming one of the earliest Fellows of the Royal Society in 1663.

The story of Cavendish supremacy among the Whig radicals began with the fourth Earl, who supported the Exclusion Bill and was one of the seven signatories inviting the Prince of Orange to assume the Crown of England. He had indeed been one of the engineers of the Whig party, hatched at Southampton House (the London home of the Russell family) by a few men dedicated to reform and the limitation of royal power, and responsible in the end for the Revolution of 1688. Gratefully, William III bestowed the dukedom of Devonshire upon him in 1694, on the same day that his colleague and political ally Russell was created Duke of Bedford.

The dukedom pursued its course in the eighteenth century, gaining distinction and yet more property along the way. The eminent 4th Duke who was Prime Minister for six months in 1756–7 in a caretaker capacity, married a daughter of the Earl of Burlington, thereby acquiring Burlington House in Piccadilly, Lismore Castle in Ireland, and the charming country mansion of Chiswick. Poor health played havoc with the family in the decade from 1754 to 1764, like 'a plague fixed in the walls of their house',[1] taking the Duke's sister and four of her children to an early death with a mysterious sore throat which the doctors were unable to diagnose. When the Duke himself died in 1764, the entire weight of the title, carrying with it ten great houses, all staffed and kept permanently ready for occupation, huge wealth, vast estates and overwhelming responsibilities inherited from generations of men admired and respected, fell upon his sixteen-year-old son William. As the boy had lost his mother at the age of six, he had not only to assume the burden of his title prematurely, but to do so alone and unsupported. The prospect might have terrified anyone but a Cavendish, but while there was nothing in the family genes to produce fear in the young man's breast, there was plenty to encourage complacency, and

mistake in writing Devonshire when he should have put Derbyshire. The patent in the Public Record Office reads quite clearly *comes Devon* for the earldom and *Dux Devon* for the dukedom.

to these influences, inherent in his blood, he was easily to succumb. This was the youth who grew up to take Georgiana Spencer as his Duchess.

Had the 5th Duke pondered the characteristics of his ancestors, he would have been in every way able to understand the springs of his own personality, for the Cavendishes were, and still are, remarkably faithful reproductions of each other. There are few noble families whose members are so consistently alike through the generations. Many of them had been distinguished by real achievement, though always unobtrusively, and without publicity. They desired to be left in peace, and if circumstances or talent propelled them into positions of esteem, they hoped that little fuss would be made. The 4th Duke's brother, Lord John Cavendish, acquitted his task as Chancellor of the Exchequer with quiet efficiency, while the Duke himself had to be coerced by his friends into taking the helm of the Government because Pitt refused to serve under the outgoing Prime Minister – the Duke of Newcastle. He acquiesced without enthusiasm, returning afterwards to his Homer and his Plutarch with obvious relief. George Cavendish had written an excellent *Life of Wolsey*, Thomas Cavendish was the renowned navigator. In many ways the most accomplished of them all was also the oddest, the eminent astronomer, mathematician and geologist Henry Cavendish, a contemporary of the 5th Duke though seventeen years his senior. Living as an eccentric recluse in a villa overlooking Clapham Common, Henry Cavendish abhorred human contact and would leave his laboratories only to visit the Royal Society, where he listened rather than talked. He took with him enough coppers for his meal, and no more, in spite of his being so immensely rich that he left a fortune of over a million pounds, which eventually found its way to the Devonshire coffers.

Henry Cavendish exemplified the shyness of the Cavendish character and its reverence for intellectual distinction above worldly gain. He was also typical in his dislike of conversation, though he may with justice be said to have carried this to extremes. 'He uttered fewer words in the course of his life than any man who ever lived to fourscore years, not at all excepting the monks of La Trappe,' said Lord Brougham.[2] If anyone approached to speak to him, he would slink away in fear. Another contemporary advised that the way to talk to Cavendish was 'never to look at him, but to talk as if it were into a vacancy, and then it is not unlikely you may set him going'.[3]

A Cavendish was not disposed to chatter. He should be pictured in his library, left to the calm serenity of his own company, unwilling to be bothered with problems or difficulties which intruded upon his peace; there were others to deal with such matters. If pressed, however, a Cavendish would always give the benefit of his wisdom after careful reflection and due consideration of all the circumstances; he would show enviable clarity of judgement and incorruptible integrity in his deliberations. Hobbes paid tribute to his pupil the 2nd Earl of Devonshire 'whom no man was able either to draw or jostle out of the straight path of justice', and Walpole, who did not care for the Cavendish family, spoke generously of the virtue of the 4th Duke.[4] Burke was later to make a most eulogistic reference to 'the temperate, permanent, hereditary virtue of the whole House of Cavendish'.[5] Everyone knew that a Cavendish could not be bribed. Had not the 1st Duke taken William III to task in utter disregard of the honours which the King had bestowed upon him? When William had shown signs of immoderate religious bias, Devonshire had reminded him that he had come to England to protect Protestants, not to persecute Papists.

Honesty of purpose, probity of mind, unflustered temperament and love of tranquillity, and withal a powerful sense of duty, all these are quiet, cerebral qualities. Yet they were alloyed to a certain earthiness which made the Cavendish men vulnerable to the attractions of love. When they could be prised from their habitual torpor, they were roused if not to passion, at least to a regular, orderly satisfaction of libido. Even the sensual side of their nature was subject to habit, and the 1st Duke in particular gained a reputation as a ladies' man simply because women snatched at him and he could see no reason in the world why he should not profit by it.

They were, finally, prone to lethargy. Their political influence was great, but it was prodded into life by others. They tended to guide events from behind, leaving their associates to wave banners and shout the slogans. They did not exert themselves more than was necessary, and it is to their credit that they could utter more sense when requested than many who were more overtly energetic and who actively sought to achieve the influential status which seemed to come to the Cavendishes as part of the air they breathed in Derbyshire. Had they not been constantly brought to the front of the stage by virtue of the respect they enjoyed, they would have been perfectly content to remain in private, with their books, their wives, their mistresses and their acres. In almost every regard, the young 5th Duke of Devonshire was the quintessential Cavendish man.

In the first place, he was spectacularly lazy, so much so that he could scarce be bothered to write letters. The correspondence which survives from this period contains astonishingly little of the Duke's letters, not because some vandalising hand has extracted or destroyed them, but because he simply didn't write them. In many of the letters he did bring himself to write, his reluctance is manifest, his desire to get it over and done with palpable. He refers to 'many complaints made that I never wrote any letters', and having begun, it is with difficulty that he can stay the pace to the end of the page. Still, that is the best he can do, and 'I don't care for the trouble of writing a fresh one' he says.[6] To receive such a letter must have been a questionable pleasure. Lady Spencer lost no time at all in reprimanding him, and within a few months of the marriage we find the Duke excusing himself to his mother-in-law thus: 'You are mistaken in thinking that I am too lazy ever to write letters.'[7] Georgiana would have many occasions to regret her husband's negligence in this regard, however, for he appeared to assume that his intentions should be known without his having to suffer the tedium of imparting them. His indolence was deplored by everyone, not least his wife, who was to watch a potential political career go to waste simply for want of effort. Activity was tiring – all that rushing about, *doing* things – and the Duke was much happier if life could be made to proceed at a measured, dignified amble. 'All his ideas arose in his mind with very gradual progress', commented one contemporary.[8]

Such a man was very easily bored. Half way through a letter he would suddenly declare, 'I am so tired of this narration', or apologise for the dullness of the prose, which petrifies his hand as he writes and even manages to make him yawn. 'I warn you not to be surprised at my letters being tiresome and foolish', he tells his sister, 'for this punctuality will certainly make each letter have less news and be less worth reading if possible than ever.'[9]

He spoke of his capacity as 'somewhat too low and grovelling' to understand the subtle attractions of the arts. He did not care for the opera, and when he played the piano it was with a total lack of musical sense.[10] Yet he was extremely well read in the classical literatures. There was something endearingly professional about a man who knew his Cicero but could not master the new-fangled waltz.

In an age when all fashionable people kept late hours, the Duke of Devonshire was no exception. He would play cards at Brooks's Club until four in the morning, then call for a supper of boiled mackerel.[11] It was hardly surprising, then, that he was rarely out of bed until well into the following afternoon.

With a cold, shy manner and an intensely reserved nature, the Duke found it virtually impossible to show his feelings. Those around him had to guess what emotion might disturb his phlegmatic exterior, for he never gave way to any open demonstration of affection, anger, distress, or disappointment. His calm even temper permitted kindly feelings and generous acts, but the touch of ice rendered any effusion of gratitude unwelcome. Many were those who lamented his serene but grave detachment from the normal coils of human involvement. He once watched a house being looted with as much concern as if it had been a sedate auction.[12] On another occasion, when he was woken to be told the house was on fire, he turned over on his other side and observed that someone had better put it out. Taciturnity set his features in wax. Had he only been able to free himself from the imprisonment imposed by congenital timidity, affection would have fallen like an avalanche upon him, for he was a decent, good man whose gravity unhappily repelled any display of warmth. It is doubtful that he was even aware of the power he had over the feelings of others.

Conversation with the Duke was a perilous exercise. Even his men friends found him uncommunicative, and inquisitiveness was particularly abhorrent to him. He never spoke about himself, and had no time at all for the kind of talk which analysed motive or speculated upon the hidden sources of human conduct. To know what he was thinking, his family would have to wait for a tiny hint dropped as he was leaving the room, or the lightest feather of an idea from which to construct a comprehensive point of view. If he could dispense with talk altogether, he would have been content, and was especially fond of the Rutland family because they were so busy chattering that he was spared the need to utter a word.[13] When he did talk, the experience for his interlocutor was akin to being cross-examined before a judge, as this normally silent man released his words sparingly, to the point, with no waste.

Uneasiness with people was intensified when children were around. On the whole, the Duke preferred to avoid them, but if this could not be assured, he would decline a game of Hide and Seek, and treat the young with a stern civility they found quite foreign.[14]

Adults, too, would on occasion be mystified by his curiously marmoreal responses. He was clumsy, but not embarrassed by his clumsiness, which had to be accepted along with the rest of him. He broke two of Lady Spencer's best wine glasses and did not appear even to notice.[15] Once he managed to knock over a beautiful crystal lustre, and when the crash and tinkle had subsided, looked indifferently at the floor and said, 'This is singular enough!'[16]

Like many who feel uncomfortable with people, the Duke was inordinately fond of dogs. Before his marriage, he spent much of his time with pets called Turkibus, Pigg and Sophy,[17] whose welfare and progress he cared for with a deeper commitment than he ever willingly revealed for a person of his acquaintance. With his dogs, this humourless, passionless man would frolic and giggle like a child, able at last to relax the iron conventionality of his behaviour. Years later, his daughter commented, 'his love and admiration of this race is quite extraordinary and I quite rejoice at having one in my possession, for it is a never failing method of calling his attention and attracting his notice'.[18]

The brightest jewel of the Duke's inheritance was of course his solid immovable integrity, to which all who knew him paid tribute without a single dissentient voice. An anonymous pamphleteer, regretting the Duke's reputation for pusillanimity, admired 'the serious, tranquil, composed cast of character which he possesses', and congratulated him on the lack of 'those flashy talents' which were of no use to Society. 'He has been endowed with an understanding which has been cultivated with wisdom . . . an understanding that is subject to regulation but not to caprice.'[19] Others praised his rectitude, his indifference to flattery, his incorruptibility. 'As neither bribe nor power could have moved him to one act contrary to his principles of integrity', wrote Lord Avondale, 'so neither danger, fatigue, nor any personal consideration could have deterred him from that which he considered as the business and duty of his life.'[20] Dr Johnson praised the Duke's 'dogged veracity' in more vivid terms, and speaking of his father said, 'If he had promised you an acorn, and none had grown that year in his woods, he would have sent to Denmark for it.'[21]

To conclude this introduction to Georgiana's bridegroom, we cannot do better than give the word to the estimable Wraxall, who as usual is able to capture the man's character in an exquisitely wrought miniature:

> Constitutional apathy formed his distinguishing characteristic. His figure was tall and manly, though not animated or graceful, his manners, always calm and unruffled. He seemed to be incapable of any strong emotion, and destitute of all energy or activity of mind. As play became indispensable in order to arouse him from his lethargic habit and to awaken his torpid faculties, he passed his evenings usually at Brooks's, engaged at whist or faro. Yet beneath so quiet an exterior he possessed a highly improved understanding, and on all disputes that occasionally arose among the members of the club relative to passages of the Roman poets or historians, I know that appeal was commonly made to the Duke, and his decision or opinion was regarded as final. Inheriting with his immense fortune the hereditary probity characteristic of the family of Cavendish, if not a superior man, he was an honourable and respected member of society. Nor did the somnolent tranquillity of his temper by any means render him insensible to the seduction of female charms.[22]

As someone else rather wittily put it, 'he lacked *spring* rather than *sense*',[23] which lent him rather uncomfortably a personality precisely the opposite of that possessed by his new wife who, by all accounts, had plenty of spring, and despite her mother's endeavours, not much sense.

✻ ✻ ✻

'You know I have always thought *le mariage* a very serious thing, where characters agree it may be the happiest of states, but else it must be the most miserable, I think.' So wrote Lady Harriet Spencer when she was contemplating a union with Lord Duncannon in 1780.[24] It is not impossible that she had in mind the early years of her sister's marriage, for rarely can there have been a more striking instance of 'characters' not agreeing.

Shortly after the successful presentation at Court, Georgiana was made to recognise this disparity of personality in particularly brutal fashion. In the presence of her mother and sister, she gaily hurled herself on to the Duke's lap and threw her arms around his neck in an access of girlish affection. Horrified, he brusquely removed her and walked from the room without a word.[25] It was explained to her that tenderness in public was firmly against the rules, and while it might be excusable in a young girl, it was not proper conduct for a Duchess. Alas, Georgiana was both; the situation inevitably called for conflicting responses which her impulsive nature was unable to bring into harmony.

Where the Duke was inhibited and introvert, she bubbled with unfettered enthusiam, where he was deliberate, awkward and reflective, she was spontaneous, natural and instinctive. In his view, it was her business to show herself a dutiful unobtrusive wife and to bear him children. He did not attempt to discover what kind of person she was, nor to understand that she was blessed with an ebullient assertive character of her own which needed to find expression in a stream of activity. Her bright intelligence was to him an irrelevance, her quicksilver energy an embarrassment.

Mama discerned the danger early on. Try to stay at home as much as possible, she counselled her daughter, find little things to share with your husband and give him the impression that you value his company above all other, which is 'a very essential point towards that *mutual* happiness which is alone to be enjoyed in the married state, separate interests, separate afflictions, or to any degree separate happiness can never be experienced by a

husband and wife who are fond of each other'.[26] Not that she
should strive to be stiff, that would do more harm than good,
but she might be well advised occasionally to check 'some
favourite inclination': 'consider my dearest girl no conquests
are so desirable and in the end so satisfactory as those that one
gains over one's passions'.[27]

Georgiana sought to reassure her mother, but the formality
of her language suggests that she was hedging. 'I have been so
happy in marrying a man I so sincerely lov'd, and experience
daily so much his goodness to me that it is impossible I should
not feel to the greatest degree that mutual happiness you speak
of.'[28]

It was odd that Georgiana did not mention the Duke in letters
to her mother, which arrived at Althorp at least twice a week,
unless Mama raised the subject first. 'You do not say anything of
the Duke,' she enquired anxiously. 'Does he employ and amuse
himself? Does he seem pleased and satisfied with you, and do
you ever pass any part of the day together in riding walking
reading or musick?'[29] Once more, Georgiana wished her
mother would not worry so. Of course he is contented with me,
she said, he is attentive and always trying to please me; things
just could not be better.[30] Nevertheless, Lady Spencer received
the unsettling impression that her daughter needed to try harder
to make the marriage work. She wisely forbore to write to the
Duke because she did not want to be 'troublesome' to him, and
indeed the deferential way in which she spoke of him indicated
that he was so massively important in everyone's eyes that he
must be handled with supreme tact and his wishes gratified in
every regard. All the compromises would have to be made by the
Duchess.

Lady Spencer then set about pouring advice on Georgiana's
head in a flow of long admonitory letters. First of all, if the
Duke was not communicative, then she must needs use her imagination to discover his will:

> where a husband's delicacy and indulgence is so great that he
> will not say what he likes, the task becomes more difficult, and
> a wife must use all possible delicacy and ingenuity in trying to
> find out his inclinations, and the utmost readiness in confor-
> ming to them. You have this difficult task to perform, my

dearest Georgiana, for the Duke of D., from a mistaken tenderness, persists in not dictating to you the things he wishes you to do, and not contradicting you in anything however disagreeable to him. This should engage you by a thousand additional motives of duty and gratitude to try to know his sentiments upon even the most trifling subjects, and especially not to enter into any engagements or form any plans without consulting him.[31]

Furthermore, Georgiana should make quite sure that she does not mix with the wrong people, for 'health and reputation are two of the most valuable blessings in life; do not trifle with them'.

You must learn, my dearest Georgiana, to respect yourself and the world will soon follow your example; but while you herd only with the vicious and the profligate you will be like them, pert, familiar, noisy and indelicate, not to say indecent in your language and behaviour, and if you once copy them in their contempt for the censures of the grave, and their total disregard for the opinion of the world in general, you will be lost indeed past recovery.[32]

Strong words. As if aware that her rebukes were harsh, and that her daughter might now be growing up and not want them, Lady Spencer reminded her that she always used to be grateful for advice, and confided that 'I have sometimes frighten'd myself with the idea of your becoming like one of those many flippant daughters to the imperious mothers that glide about the world together and give one so detestable a notion of parental affection and filial duty'.[33] Even Grandmama, Lady Cowper, joined the assault on poor Georgiana with her own un-solicited advice. 'I would have you lively but not frivolous', she said, 'your evenings allotted to amusements, your mornings to improvements . . . the D. of D. appears to have so much intrin-sic worth in him as to observe your utmost endeavour to make yourself always an agreeable companion to him.'[34] Lady Cowper signed off 'your humble servant', for Georgiana was now, after all, her social superior.

The young Duchess no doubt found all this somewhat trying, especially when she was told that she had to be complacent even if the Duke appeared to be less than strictly obedient to the marriage contract.[35] Do you never write any little verses for him? asked Mama. (Georgiana's letters to her mother were sprinkled with poems in English and French.) How absurd! Why, she was living with him; what need was there to write him verses?

All Georgiana could do for the moment was to make the correspondence more cheerful by writing jolly notes to her mother full of childish endearments, and expressed still in a hand that belonged to a girl. She told Mama how good she was, how indulgent and affectionate, how much gratitude she felt, and so on. 'Our letters are the most charming of conversations', she wrote, and again, 'I think I may look upon our letters as kind of visits we pay one another.' Turning to French, Georgiana said, 'Grâce à mon aimable mère, ses lettres ont l'art d'adoucir tout.'[36] Still Lady Spencer could not resist telling the Duchess that she should learn to write more closely, and to begin at the very top of the page.[37]

* * *

We do not know at what point the Duchess of Devonshire discovered that her husband was unfaithful, nor how deeply the knowledge affected her. It was a lot to ask that she should meekly accept instructions on how to space her letters on the one hand, while on the other she had not only to assume the responsibilities of her exalted rank, but to understand and reconcile herself to the peculiar moral attitudes prevalent among the members of that rank. Not for her the gradual easy progress from childhood to maturity; Georgiana had perforce to grow up like a hothouse plant.

The Duke's mistress was an obscure young lady who by coincidence bore the same surname as his wife – Charlotte Spencer. According to the gossip of the day, which is not entirely reliable, she had been the daughter of a poor country curate, upon whose death she had come to London to seek work as a milliner. There she had quickly fallen victim to the predators of the city, was hoodwinked by a kindly old lady who turned out to be a 'madam' and turned her over to a nobleman who seduced her. With pregnancy the legacy of this experience, Charlotte willingly accepted the protection of an old lecher who had enough money to set her up in her own milliner's shop in Mayfair. It was here that she was spied by the young Duke, who further advanced her fortunes by housing her in a handsome villa at his expense.[38]

Although the affair was not made public until some years later, everyone who mattered knew of it at the time, and we may be sure that one of that number was Lady Spencer herself. That this intelligence did nothing to blacken the Duke's reputation in her eyes, in spite of her strict adherence to principle, gives a very clear indication of the small importance attached to fidelity in that age. Charlotte Spencer bore the Duke a daughter some time between 1773 and 1775, either just before or just after he took Georgiana as his wife. Even if Georgiana knew of Charlotte's existence, she probably knew nothing of the baby, although later this child was to assume her role in the complex drama which unfolded under the Duke's roof as the years passed. As Georgiana herself, and her sister, her daughters, her friends, were all to partake of this delightful gavotte which permitted love affairs to proliferate without apparently disturbing the equilibrium upon which society was based, it is important we understand the rules as they themselves understood them and not perceive the events of the last quarter of the eighteenth century with the emotional prejudices of the twentieth.

It is doubtful whether the elegant ladies and gentlemen of Georgian England would appreciate what we now mean by a love-match. That a marriage should be founded on something as unreliable as the momentary preference of one human being for another would have seemed to them the ultimate folly. Marriage was far too serious an undertaking for that. It was essential that rank should be protected, so that a liaison between a peer's daughter and a footman was perfectly all right while it remained the satisfaction of lust or romance, but totally inconceivable if it threatened to become a life partnership. Once the purity of rank had been assured by a proper marriage, the next essential was to produce an heir. That done, almost anything was permissible. Sexual promiscuity was commonplace. The Duke of Richmond had three daughters by his housekeeper Mrs Bennett, and another by a Miss Le Clerc. The Duchess of Gordon found it difficult to place her fourth daughter because the man who proposed to take her hand had second thoughts on hearing that there was madness in the

Gordon family. She was able to deal with this simply by assuring him that there was not a drop of Gordon blood in her daughter's veins, and this was an answer which satisfied everyone.[39] A lady of pleasure such as Nancy Parsons could be the mistress of the Dukes of Dorset and Grafton in succession, then marry Lord Maynard and take her place in society; she had not offended against the rules by confusing marriage with romance – there was a proper time for each.

Nobody illustrated better how to benefit from careful application of the rules than Lady Melbourne. She maintained a position of the highest respect while being as bold as a Covent Garden whore behind the scenes. Of her six children, only the first was indisputably fathered by her husband, yet no one thought the worse of her for that, as she took the greatest pains never to place her husband in an embarrassing light, never to offend convention. She knew that loyalty to the accepted code of society was the path to happiness, and loyalty to the spouse's bed a silly aberration of the ethical instinct. She used to say that anyone who braved the opinion of the world would sooner or later feel the consequences of it;[40] the opinion of the world was acquiescent as long as discretion was maintained.

Lady Spencer was as aware of this code as anyone else. If she thought it whimsical or undignified, she certainly did not say so yet, but the time would come when her tolerance would be stretched to breaking-point.

The Duke of Devonshire had a mistress. Well and good! That was a circumstance in every way irrelevant to his marriage. Georgiana must learn to condone and not condemn, and one day she too might have the freedom to flirt. She would first however have to produce an heir, and despite the five months confined at Chatsworth, there was no sign of that. By January 1775, it was time for the Duke and Georgiana to move to London and take their place at Devonshire House, where life was destined to be crisply different from the relatively casual measure of Chatsworth.

'Dear, beautiful Chatsworth',[41] which Caroline Lamb was to regard as Paradise against the Hades of Hardwick Hall, had been a perfect venue for the honeymoon. Husband and wife had been able to spend as much time together as they wished, she had persuaded him to use the chapel more, and she had brought music to the sombre rooms, inviting the great violinist Giardini to spend his holiday there. The gentle pace of life seeped in to the skin and made one happy to be alive. Already, Georgiana's influence was felt. She had become enormously popular with everyone she met and was cherished by the poor for her genuine sympathy and generosity. She arranged for the old people in the village to receive proper medical attention, visiting them regularly and chatting cheerfully. Her civility and good humour endeared her to people who had been used to stiff inhuman formality at Chatsworth for years, and her laughter ricocheted from the dull old walls of this 'antique maison', bringing a gaiety which the house had scarcely ever known. Mrs Isabella Poyntz expressed the general feeling when she said that 'Chatsworth, like every other place where you are, is cheerful and happy'.[42]

Once a week, on Monday, there was a Public Day, when the Duke and Duchess received local clergymen, attorneys, and such like, together with their families, and entertained them to dinner. These were trying occasions, for the Duke because he was obliged to talk, for Georgiana because she was on display all the time and had to make sure she behaved. The whole morning was spent in dressing and getting ready for the event (for it was part of the treat that the ducal pair should be resplendent in all their finery), and the whole evening in recovering from it. It was common enough for the clergymen to get drunk. In a very short time, Georgiana was able to sail through the Public Days like a conqueror, putting the awe-struck guests at their ease and leaving them begging for more.

Now it would be seen if the effervescent Duchess could inject the same transformation of atmosphere into Devonshire House, the austere London home from which feminine influence had been missing for a generation.

London society revolved around a few impressive mansions. There was Lady Melbourne at Melbourne House; Carlton House, with the Prince of Wales as its pivot; and two houses in Piccadilly belonging to the Duke of Devonshire – Burlington House and Devonshire House. Burlington House had become Devonshire property in 1758, when the Duke was ten years old. At first it was intended to be demolished or sold, as a superfluous addition to the estate for which the Duke had no obvious use, but in 1770 it was let to his brother-in-law the Duke of Portland, after the removal of some furniture to Devonshire House, including a bedstead 'very full of bugs'. Portland was to stay there on and off until 1807.*

Just along the road was Devonshire House itself, built in 1733 for the 3rd Duke and designed by William Kent, whose finest achievement it was acknowledged to be. (There had been Berkeley House on the site until 1698.) It was set back from the road and approached through splendid wrought-iron gates leading to a wide drive up to a white-pillared portico. The exterior was strangely modest, leading a contemporary to compare it unflatteringly to an East India Company warehouse. There was a conspicuous lack of ornamentation on the windows, and those on the bedroom floor were quite obviously too small. But there was a spacious, peaceful garden behind, from which the noise of Piccadilly was entirely banished, and on the ground floor were some of the most magnificent reception rooms in London, perfectly suited for entertaining on a sump-tuous scale. There was a staircase in marble and alabaster, a fine library, the Kent Salon with its ornate ceiling, and picture-galleries stuffed with Titians, Tintorettos, Rubens and others. In such a setting was Georgiana to erect her throne.†

The whole was enclosed by a wall so forbidding that the house was virtually hidden from view, and moreover deprived those within of a view to Green Park. 'Would it be credible that a man of taste, fashion and figure would prefer the solitary grandeur of enclosing himself in a jail, to the enjoyment of the first view in Britain, which he might possess by throwing down this execrable brick screen?' So wondered one writer of the time. But the wall served a purpose, for beyond the gates, it was a very different picture. The London of 1775 was noisy and dangerous. Stepping into Piccadilly you would immediately be assaulted by the clatter of iron-clad wheels as the horse-drawn carriages bumped along the road, flinging mud at the unprotected

* The Elgin marbles were in the grounds of Burlington House until 1816, when they were removed to the British Museum. The house is now the Royal Academy.

† Devonshire House was sold in 1918 for £750,000, and demolished in 1924. The ornamental gates, surmounted by urns and bearing the Devonshire coat of arms, were moved across the street to Green Park, where they still stand.

pedestrian. Your nose would be attacked by a foul smell issuing from an open rut in the road, and you would be besieged by gangs of street vendors selling everything from apples and hot bread to cat's meat and medicinal turkey rhubarb. Then of course there were the dustmen, the knife-grinders, the sweeps and beggars, pitiful rotting creatures whose welfare was no one's concern.

The immediate surroundings of Devonshire House were not strictly part of London proper, but of the City of Westminster, which included the parishes of St Margaret's Westminster, St Martin-in-the-Fields, St George's Hanover Square, and St James's Piccadilly. And since the King held his Court at St James's Palace, the whole of government and society operated within these few square miles. The population of the entire urban complex which made up 'London' was about a million, but 'society' – those families who socially and politically controlled the refined existence of the other face of London – consisted of about three hundred.

The city was vastly overcrowded in spite of a death-rate which exceeded the birth-rate by two to one. Labourers were attracted by the prospect of work to leave their pleasant villages in exchange for a disease-infected slum. In 1771 Arthur Young had complained that men were tempted to 'quit their healthy, clean fields for a region of stink, dirt, and noise'.[43] The houses were poorly constructed and liable to tumble upon your head, ruthless property speculators quite as contemptible as their modern counterparts could get rich in no time at all (a Mrs Farrel was supposed to have built up a fortune of £6,000 by letting rooms at twopence each), and if you survived those you would probably succumb in the end to influenza, typhoid, small-pox, or any one of the rampant diseases which flourished in such squalid conditions. The average life expectancy of the poor, that is the great majority, was twenty-five to thirty years, and one child in every three died before the age of six.

Small wonder, then, that crime was widespread. The cry of murder could be heard in the streets any night of the week, and the incidence of brutish violence was excessive by modern standards. If a Member of Parliament is nowadays attacked in broad daylight, the event warrants a headline in every newspaper, but in 1775 he took his life into his hands simply by making his way to the House of Commons. The Prime Minister could be dragged from his coach and abused, while the coach was mindlessly destroyed. The Prince of Wales only just escaped when his carriage was attacked, the door flapping wildly as it sped off. Fox was set upon by a crowd and rolled in the gutter. Robberies were a daily event, and no house was safe without heavy bolts on the door and grilles at the windows. Punishment was dictated by the principles of retribution rather than deterrence, and was often extreme, so that it comes as a shock to discover that the sensitive and intelligent inhabitants of the grand mansions were on the whole indifferent to a penal system which allowed over two hundred offences to be punishable by death. In 1777 a fourteen-year-old girl was condemned to be burnt alive for having collected and concealed farthings (then the smallest coin of the realm); the Secretary of State intervened at the last minute to reprieve her.[44]

The French Ambassador, Comte d'Adhémar, was horrified by what he saw and heard, frequently departing from strictly political intelligence in his despatches to the French Foreign Office to give a vivid impression of the danger of London life. One daily risks having one's house invaded by the mob, he said, and robbery was so widespread that, even if you travelled with an armed escort, you took your life into your hands as soon as you left the confines of London proper. 'Les carosses sont arrêtées la nuit dans Londres même.'* D'Adhémar thought the authorities were cowardly in not taking vigorous action against offenders, yet he noted that the poor lived in lamentable conditions, and that there were not enough gallows to hang the excessive quantity of those condemned to die. 'Ce matin encore l'on a pendu douze misérables.'†[45]

The fact that the aristocrats in their seeming callousness were not massacred by the hundreds was due largely to the tolerance of the mob rather than the enlightened understanding of their masters, for the London crowd, in spite of the cruel conditions of their lives, were essentially good-natured and good-humoured. They might roll Fox in the mud, but a French crowd would have cut his head off; they could turn a man upside down and write something wicked on his boots, but they would

* Carriages are held up at night in the centre of London.
† This morning another twelve poor wretches were hanged.

hesitate to cut his throat. Apart from the Gordon riots of 1780, which anticipate our story by a few years, the regular upheavals of the populace were little more than a rowdy release of frustrations; from the filigreed interiors of Holland House and Devonshire House they were considered a wretched nuisance.

> It was this indignation – this comic fuming at the 'disgraceful' behaviour of thousands who could easily have torn them limb from limb – this refusal to believe in the destructive capacity or in the seriously ill intentions of such amiable helots as surrounded them, which saved the English aristocracy from the guillotine. They refused to have the sense to realise that they were in danger, and the Mob, for lack of being taken seriously, remained comic.[46]

Georgiana's impact was immediate. The sweet good-natured little girl had blossomed into a magnificent Duchess who seduced with her charm all who came into contact with her. Indeed, as Fanny Burney remarked, the word 'charming' might have been coined for her. The trouble with that elusive quality is that it is felt only in personal encounter and escapes all attempts at definition in words. Her letters cannot hope to tell us what fun she was to be with, nor can any record of her life recreate for us the amazing power of her presence. All those who were lucky enough to meet her fell totally under her spell and agree with one voice in praising the delight of her company. In the history of the English aristocracy there have been many women admired for their beauty, their intellect, their influence, their character, but there has been none more universally liked than the Duchess of Devonshire, none whose personality so enriched the lives of those about her. It is this inexpressible likeableness which renders her position unassailable and alone explains how she was able to gather about her in Devonshire House the most brilliant, sophisticated, clever and talented society that England has ever known.

Georgiana was not especially beautiful in the classic sense. She had fair hair, with a tinge of red in it, sparkling eyes, an unremarkable face, and was rather too tall to satisfy the demands of fashion. Elizabeth Sheridan said that when the Duchess entered a room there seemed a little too much of her, as if she

were larger than 'full length'.[47] Every contemporary reference
feels bound to point out that she was surpassed by others in
beauty, but it is a measure of her amiability that none felt
inclined to disparage her on this account.

When Walpole first saw her, he described her simply as 'a
lovely girl, natural, and full of grace'.[48] A few months later, he is
verging on the ecstatic: 'The Duchess of Devonshire effaces all
without being a beauty; but her youth, figure, flowing good
nature, sense, and lively modesty, and modest familiarity make
her a phenomenon.'[49] The cynical Dr Johnson, too, was en-
tranced. 'I have seen the Duchess of Devonshire, then in the first
bloom of youth', wrote Nathaniel Wraxall, 'hanging on the
sentences that fell from Johnson's lips, and contending for the
nearest place to his chair. All the cynic moroseness of the
philosopher and the moralist seemed to dissolve under so
flattering an approach.'[50] The actor David Garrick met her in
September, and felt weak with admiration. 'Her Grace of
Devonshire is a most enchanting, Exquisite, beautiful Young
Creature', he told Henry Bate, 'Were I five and twenty I could go
mad about her, as I am past five and fifty I would only suffer
martyrdom for her.'[51]

Mrs Delany, then an elderly woman whose long experience of
life might be expected to sharpen her critical guard and make
her less susceptible to the ephemeral attractions of youth, met
the Duchess a few days after her first arrival in Devonshire
House and was left floundering. 'So handsome, so agreeable, so
obliging in her manner', she wrote enthusiastically to Mrs Port,
'that I am *quite* in love with her . . . I can't tell you all the civil
things she said, and really they deserve a better name, which is
kindness embellished by *politeness*. I hope she will *illumine* and
reform her contemporaries!'[52]

One can without much effort picture the ancient Mrs Delany
in colloquy with adorable Georgiana, all attentiveness and kind
enquiry, smiling, soft-spoken, occasionally bubbling with
laughter. The smile and the kindness, apparently such
manageable tools in social intercourse, were everything with
Georgiana, for they were genuine. In an artificial age, she was
unstudied, natural and good. Her mother was constantly imploring her to be more selective upon whom to bestow her

smile; she really must learn not to be so nice to *everyone*! Wasted words. It was simply not possible for Georgiana to feign or contrive.

Fanny Burney has left us a complete word-picture which comes close to recapturing that warmth and well-being which the Duchess engendered. 'I did not find so much beauty in her as I expected', she wrote, 'but I found far more of manner, politeness, and gentle quiet. She seems by nature to possess the highest animal spirits . . . there is a native cheerfulness about her which I fancy scarce ever deserts her. There is in her face, especially when she speaks, a sweetness of good humour and obligingness, that seem to be the natural and instinctive qualities of her disposition; joined to an openness of countenance that announces her endowed, by nature, with a character intended wholly for honesty, fairness and good purposes.'[53]

It is a miracle that none of this turned Georgiana's head, for we may assume that these admirers did not withhold their comments entirely for posterity, but complimented the eighteen-year-old Duchess in person. Yet towards the end of her life she would recall that of all the nice things said about her the one she cherished most was the compliment paid by a drunken Irishman, who asked to light his pipe by the fire of her beautiful eyes.[54]

For an account written not in the excitement of the moment but with the cool accuracy of retrospection, we must turn again to Wraxall, in whose memoirs we find Georgiana's extraordinary fascination once more confirmed. She was,

one of the most distinguished females of high rank whom the last century produced. Her personal charms constituted her smallest pretension to universal admiration; nor did her beauty consist, like that of the Gunnings,* in regularity of features and faultless formation of limbs and shape; it lay in the amenity and graces of her deportment, in her irresistible manners and the seduction of her society. Her hair was not without a tinge of red, and her face, though pleasing, yet had it not been illuminated by her mind, might have been con-

* Elizabeth and Maria Gunning.

sidered as an ordinary countenance . . . [she possessed] an ardent temper, susceptible of deep as well as strong impressions; a cultivated understanding, illuminated by a taste for poetry and the fine arts; much sensibility, not exempt, perhaps, from vanity and coquetry.

And Wraxall finished with a sentence which more than any other has the felicity in its elegant expression to make us envy anyone who had the good fortune to meet Georgiana: 'Her heart may be considered as the seat of those emotions which sweeten human life, adorn our nature, and diffuse a nameless charm over existence.'[55]

Nevertheless, something is missing. The picture assembled in these harmonious reports by different witnesses is vivid, beguiling, but too near to perfection. To discover the subterranean streams which soured Georgiana's life, we must listen to hints from Miss Burney and Mrs Delany. In the enthusiastic account of Fanny Burney quoted above, two phrases are omitted. 'She seems by nature to possess the highest animal spirits', she said, 'but she appeared to me not happy. I thought she looked oppressed within. . . .' Mrs Delany, two months after the rapturous letter to Mrs Port, wrote again to the same correspondent and confessed the danger which she spied on the horizon:

> *I am sick of this bad world*, when I suffer my imagination to wander among the multitude; it would be more supportable could one select a number of any considerable magnitude *not* affected by the great whirlpool of dissipation, and (indeed I *fear* I may add) *vice*. This bitter reflection arises from what I hear *every* body says of a *great* and *handsome* relation of ours just *beginning* her part; but I do hope she will be like the young actors and actresses, who begin with *over* acting when they first come upon the stage . . . but I tremble for her.[56]

The unhappiness which Fanny Burney discerned was no fault of Georgiana's; it arose from the neglect her affectionate nature suffered from being constantly crushed by the iciness of her husband. Devoid of both envy or self-pity, Georgiana would not inflict her moods upon her friends; though inwardly disconsolate at times, she remained sunny and unaffected in company. A few years would have yet to pass before she could pour out her abundant affection without fear of reproof.

As for the whirlpool of vice deplored by Mrs Delany, this was a danger far more insidious than emotional discontent, and it must be admitted that Georgiana, for all her ability, was hopelessly imprudent. An instinctive being, she would act first and think afterwards. Mrs Delany hoped that she would 'illumine and reform' her contemporaries. Alas, she was not made of such stern stuff. With merry abandon, she would embrace all the delights which life hurled at her, and leave illumination and reform till tomorrow.

Chapter Three

DISSIPATION

'Dissipation' is a word which occurs again and again in Lady Spencer's letters to her daughter, and is scattered throughout the memoirs and journals of the eighteenth century. If it means the squandering and waste of energy in the pursuit of diversion or amusement, then it undoubtedly describes the prevalent mood of the Whig aristocracy at this time, a mood which reached its loftiest expression within the walls of Devonshire House. There, in the words of one writer, 'dissipation was carried almost to the pitch of sublimity',[1] and 'Devonshire bustle' was an expression coined to describe the relentless coming and going of folk engaged in frolic of one sort or another. Georgiana was often chastised for being busy all day long doing nothing at all, and her insistence that what she most longed for was a quiet domestic life must even now be greeted with a smile of disbelief.[2]

The smart set who established the tone of society life was appropriately called the *ton*, and Georgiana, having been quickly absorbed into their number, as quickly assumed ascendance above them all. The *ton* kept ridiculous hours, drank and ate to excess, gossiped, intrigued, watched each other, and gambled like lunatics. The new Duchess was more than ready to fling herself headlong into such a giddy life.

'The pretty Duchess of Devonshire', so Lady Sarah Lennox tells us, 'who by all accounts has no fault but delicate health in my mind, dines at seven, summer as well as winter, goes to bed at three, and lies in bed till four: she has hysteric fits in the morning, and dances in the evening; she bathes, rides, dances for ten days and lies in bed the next ten: indeed, I can't forgive her or rather her husband, the fault of ruining her health.'[3]

Her husband was hardly the man to remonstrate with her, for

he spent most of the night at Brooks's Club, walking up the road to Devonshire House not much before five in the morning, and letting himself in with his own key. He regularly passed a cobbler who had a stall on the corner of Jermyn Street, to whom he bade good night. 'Good morning, your Grace,' the cobbler would reply.[4]

Breakfast was normally served at ten or eleven, and dinner not before six. After dinner there was the theatre, usually at seven, though it was fashionable to appear late, tardiness reaching such a summit of absurdity towards the end of the century that the real '*ton*' was to arrive after the performance had finished. Then there were balls, masquerades, gambling parties, and supper in the dead of night.

Working politicians were not discouraged from keeping such hours, for the House of Commons did not sit until the end of the afternoon, and would carry on all night if it felt so disposed. Burke commented wryly upon the performance of Charles James Fox in debate. 'No wonder that my friend Charles is so often more vigorous than I in the House', he said, 'for when I call upon him in my way thither, jaded by the occupations of the day, there he is, just out of bed, breakfasting at three o'clock, fresh and unexhausted for the contentions of the evening.'[5] Charles James Fox was soon to be one of the luminaries of the Devonshire House set, whose hours suited him to perfection.

Of course, Lady Spencer retained her reputation as an early bird in stark contrast to Georgiana's habits, which gave Walpole the cue for a witty remark in one of his letters to Lady Ossory. 'I must rise with the lark to receive Lady Spencer at breakfast', he said, 'but as the Duchess of Devonshire is to come with her, I suppose they will not arrive till moonlight, and then they will think it is the painted glass that makes the house gloomy.'[6] Georgiana was definitely of the opinion that 'early to bed and early to rise Makes a man surly and gives him red eyes'.

Great quantities of food were consumed in meals which could last up to five hours. A visitor from France, the son of the duc de Liancourt,* confessed that he found dinner the most wearisome of English experiences. The first two hours, he said,

---

* François-Alexandre-Frédéric de la Rochefoucauld, duc de Liancourt, descended in the female line from the Duc de la Rochefoucauld of the famous *Maximes*.

are spent in eating, and you are compelled to exercise your stomach to the full in order to please your host. He asks you the whole time whether you like the food, and presses you to eat more, with the result that, out of pure politeness, I do nothing but eat from the time that I sit down until the time when I get up from the table.

The same witness gives an amusing account of the formalities which prevailed on these occasions. Having noted that you can come down to breakfast as shabby as you like and no one will even notice you, let alone talk to you, by the evening, you must, he says, be well-groomed and washed. 'The standard of politeness is uncomfortably high – strangers go first into the dining-room and sit near the hostess and are served in seniority in accordance with a rigid etiquette. In fact for the first few days I was tempted to think that it was done for a joke.' The food consisted in various boiled or roasted meats, and fish, and of joints weighing twenty or thirty pounds. The Duke of Norfolk used to get through several huge steaks every evening, one after the other. The almost complete lack of vegetables made scurvy a common complaint even with the rich.[7]

These formalities described by the French visitor were only partially observed at Devonshire House, where diversion counted for more than regulation, and talent became the distinguishing feature of the company more than an acquaintance with the rules. Indeed, the tone set by Georgiana was one which gloried more often than not in breaking the rules and generated an atmosphere which in later years would allow Lady Caroline Lamb to be carried in to dinner concealed under a silver dish cover, from which she emerged stark naked. On another occasion, the same exuberant young lady was to jump on to the dining-table to demonstrate visually to the butler how she wished the centrepiece to be arranged.[8]

To return to the impressions of our Frenchman. After dinner, he said, drink is consumed in alarming measure, and when thirst is no longer an adequate reason for opening more bottles, then toasts are called up to provide an excuse. 'Sometimes conversation becomes extremely free upon highly indecent topics – complete licence is allowed and I have come to the conclusion that the English do not associate the same ideas with certain words that we do.' In this he was mistaken. The Georgians knew what they were saying, but valued frankness.

One consequence of these daily gargantuan feasts was that an inordinate amount of time was spent in dressing and preparing for them, a task as demanding for the men as it was for the women. 'Prince' Boothby, a member of the Devonshire clan, eventually grew so weary of dressing and undressing that he shot himself in despair.[9]

The Rev. Dr Warner, a friend of Selwyn, described a dinner at Devonshire House in which white wine and port were followed by claret, burgundy, and cherry brandy, after which he parted 'in a tolerable state of insensibility to the ills of human life'.[10] This was by no means unusual. Ten men once locked themselves in a room with a hogshead* of claret and finished it within a week. Two friends of Sir Philip Francis drank ten bottles of champagne and burgundy between them at a sitting; John Mytton drank up to six bottles a day, beginning with his morning shave. Dr John Campbell told Boswell that he had drunk thirteen bottles of port on one evening, which, even if we remember that port then was not fortified with brandy as it is nowadays, is a colossal achievement. Dr Johnson thought it was possible as long as you allowed one glass to evaporate before drinking the next, and he himself admitted to three bottles of port without feeling any ill effects. Claret was for the boys, he said, port for the men, 'but he who aspires to be a hero must drink brandy'.[11]

With so much liquid to be consumed, measures had naturally to be taken for its release. The sideboard was usually furnished with a number of chamber pots, and the French visitor assures us that 'it is common practice to relieve oneself while the rest are drinking; one has no kind of concealment and the practice strikes me as most indecent'.[12]

How could Georgiana, the toast of the town, be expected to heed Mama's imprecations to look after herself? There were so many parties to attend, so much fun to be had! Naïvely, she assured Lady Spencer that the balls did not affect her, and anyway she did not go to *all* of them: 'There is a ball tonight at Lady Beauchamps. Tuesday Lady Lucan's (I GO upon PARTICULAR invitation), Wednesday Prince's, Thursday d'Adhémar's, Friday

* 52½ imperial gallons.

Mrs Poole (who was Miss Forbes), Saturday, the Prince, and Monday the survivors dance Scotch reels at the Dss of Gordon's.'[13]

Inevitably, self-indulgence on such a scale took its toll, and the effects of the London season had to be mitigated by a dose of medicinal waters at one of the fashionable resorts. Troops of gouty lords and fattening ladies went to Tunbridge Wells, to Bath, or across the Channel to the best of all, a holiday in Spa, where for weeks at a stretch the combined societies of London and Paris would assemble to make themselves feel better. Much as the *cognoscenti* flock to modern 'health farms' ostensibly to lose weight and regain a sparkle to the eye but in reality to have a good time, so in the eighteenth century they cheated appallingly. At Spa there were balls and suppers and casino parties, in which the Spencer family as well as the Duke of Devonshire had been regular participants. The restoration of health was but an excuse for more merriment, and most would agree with Lady Mary Wortley Montagu that the best cure was not 'the drinking of nasty water, but gallopping all day, and a moderate glass of champagne at night in good company'.[14] Georgiana's grandmother Lady Cowper was equally unimpressed. 'The young ladies by their manner of living will soon be *old* ones, and no *wash* will ever make them appear well,' she said.[15]

The regime was rather more strict at Bath, yet still the central occupation of the patients was to prolong the agreeableness of life, which meant to see everyone and talk about them afterwards. 'The great trade of all the inhabitants is to watch and be watched [which] makes one alarmed, and ought to make one cautious.'[16]

Tunbridge Wells was appreciably more democratic, in that the great families found themselves elbow to elbow with lesser mortals who goggled and stared and asked silly questions. This was fair enough, as long as those outside the set could be kept at some distance, for after all the main pleasure of exclusivity is to be derived from seeing those excluded. The guileless Georgiana was often caught out not making the proper distinction and had to be reminded by Mama that she must learn to be less affable and familiar with *some* people. One such was Lady Frances Marsham who, though the daughter of the Earl of Egremont, had married the second son of a mere baron, and worse still, was one of those hypocrites who could smile and smile and be a villain. Georgiana encountered her at Tunbridge Wells:

> I believe I am growing very deceitful [she told her mother] for I take great pains to get into Lady F. Marsham's good graces and yet I detest her vastly, but my reason is that I hear her abuse everybody so much the instant they have turn'd their backs, that my vanity is peaked to *concilier* myself her suffrage. She is an odious creature of notable ill nature and she puts me into ten thousand passions because she always talks to me as if she thought I had not my five senses like other prople. You cannot conceive the astonishment she exprest on my saying I walked very often in the garden at D. House; I am sure you know the kind of person I mean, who, because I was dissipated and what they call the *ton*, imagine that I scarcely breathe like other people.[17]

Mrs Montagu was of the firm opinion that it was safer to stay in London and avoid such contacts. 'I love London extremely', she said, 'where one has the choice of society, but I hate ye higgledy-piggledy of the watering-places.'

          *　　 ✻　　✻　　✻

Of all the people who clustered around Georgiana in London, the most astonishing, because the most unlikely, was Lady Melbourne. She was also to prove the most enduring friend. We have already seen that Lady Melbourne maintained a rational, not to say cynical, approach to marital fidelity; she understood the social machine perfectly, and was ruthless in operating it to her own ends. But there was much more to her than that. The fact that she had become the leading lady of London life at the time of the Devonshire marriage was a considerable achievement against heavy odds.

She had been born Elizabeth Milbanke, the unremarkable daughter of a Yorkshire squire, Sir Ralph Milbanke. Before she was seventeen, she had married Sir Peniston Lamb, the rich son of a lawyer, and had positioned herself in his lovely Piccadilly mansion ready to conquer London. The mansion stood on the site now occupied by Albany, next to Burlington House and half a mile from Devonshire House. In spite of her having the house

decorated with magnificent taste and flinging the doors open to
the best in the land, she was initially spurned by the older
families as a *parvenue*; her marriage had brought her wealth, but
without solidity – the Lambs and the Milbankes were too
obscure to secure entry into the highest circles. Within a very
short time, Elizabeth had changed all that.

She was moved by ambition to a degree which swept all
obstacles aside. Her husband was completely bemused by her
intense activity, but once she had given him a son and heir,
Peniston, in 1770, he was happy enough to occupy a subsidiary
place a few steps behind her. He was the domestic partner, she
the full-blooded career woman. Had it been possible for women
to rise in the world in their own right, she would undoubtedly
have done so, but as it was, she had to push her husband into the
limelight in order that the glow should fall upon herself.
Worldly, artful, and shrewd, she had a man's instinct and a
man's intelligence. She knew how to dominate events by
calculated judgement, and was unerringly correct in her assessment of her chances. She used men to advance her aims,
pragmatically dealing with them as an equal when occasion
demanded, with vigorous attack and cunning, or flattering them
if such would produce better results. Lord Egremont was in love
with her to distraction, so she gave herself to him and took from
him what influence could achieve. Her second child, who grew
up to be William Lamb, the great Lord Melbourne, was universally considered to be fathered by Lord Egremont, who was so
besotted by his mistress that he never married. Elizabeth had her
husband created Baron Melbourne, and by 1775 her Ladyship
had become the leading hostess of those Whig families who had
earlier looked at her askance.

When Georgiana came to Devonshire House early in 1775,
Lady Melbourne realised that if she was not to be eclipsed by
her, she must needs cultivate her friendship, for Georgiana was
obviously the person made by nature and marriage to occupy
the position which Lady Melbourne had so assiduously fought
to obtain for herself. Because she had feminine tact as well as
masculine single-mindedness, she made straight for
Georgiana's innocent heart and smothered it with attention.
Lady Melbourne was a perfect listener, Georgiana the most ingenuous talker. Should the Duchess have problems of any sort,

Lady Melbourne would advise, counsel, beseech her not to worry. In appearance, she was the wise disinterested friend for whom nothing was too much trouble; in reality, her ambitions to dominate society could only be protected if she and the wild young Duchess could avoid being considered rivals. In any contest, Georgiana would win, however clever and collected Lady Melbourne contrived to remain. And so, rather than allow rumours of rivalry to spread without discipline, she welcomed them, acknowledged them, and told Georgiana of them so that they could both laugh together at such absurd ideas. 'The Duke of Richmond has been here and told me you and I were two rival queens', Lady Melbourne wrote to the Duchess from Bath, trembling with indignation, 'and I believe, if there had not been some people in the room, who might have thought it odd, that I should have slap'd his face for having such an idea. . . . How odious people are, upon my life, I have no patience with them. I believe you and I are very different from all the rest of the world as from their ideas.'[18]

Lady Melbourne was adept at manufacturing the timely crisis to excuse herself from a situation which threatened to become complicated. Other women fainted. Here she is in the midst of an attack, which in her case is called something else: Lady Jersey is writing to Georgiana from Brighthelmstone (i.e. Brighton):

> Do you know that Lady Melbourne has been mad? She is quite well again now. The other day she found herself ill and was going up to her maid when she met her on the stairs and talked very wildly, she carried her into her room and it was half an hour before she came to her senses. They called it an indigestion.[19]

Though essentially a man's woman, and with such attractions as would ensnare even the Prince of Wales, Lady Melbourne appreciated the need to get on well with women. 'I find she is liked by everybody, high and low, and of all denominations', wrote a contemporary, 'which I don't wonder at, for she is sensible, pleasing, and desirous of pleasing.'[20] With Georgiana, she exerted the influence which her more robust nature and her greater years rendered quite irresistible. It was not to be an influence for the good.

Georgiana was soon to bestow a nickname on her friend,

calling her 'adorable Thèmire', and to declare that her tender feelings would finish only with her life. She also admitted, 'I believe I have been a *little afraid* of you', as well she might. The name Themire is significant. Themis, the goddess of justice, daughter of Uranus and Gaea, was celebrated for her wisdom and reliable counsel. Judges gave their verdicts according to her advice; she protected the innocent. In the most serious crisis of her life, a few years hence, it is to Lady Melbourne, adorable Themire, that Georgiana will turn for direction on what to do, and it will be Lady Melbourne alone, not Lady Spencer, who will hold her secrets.

Another friend was the dazzling Mrs Crewe, the woman whose beauty had been compared to Georgiana's in Paris in 1772, to Georgiana's advantage. Most would have disagreed with the French and given Mrs Crewe the edge, for it was generally recognised that her looks were flawless. Sheridan, who had himself married the beautiful Miss Linley, generously admitted Mrs Crewe's superiority at the end of his life, when he reflected that 'in truth she was the handsomest of the set'.[21] Fanny Burney said 'the form of her face is so exquisitely perfect that my eye never met it without fresh admiration. She is certainly in my eyes the most completely a beauty of any woman I ever saw'. She was also witty, warm-hearted, and fun-loving, a much cosier and less daunting presence than Lady Melbourne. Like Georgiana, she exuded kindness, and like Georgiana, she had no enemies. 'Instead of a fine lady, she is a comfortable kind of a creature,' said Charles Arbuthnot.

Born Frances Anne Greville, the daughter of Fulke Greville, she had married John Crewe, of Crewe Hall in Cheshire, whose income of £10,000 a year enabled her to preside over a salon in Grosvenor Street where she entertained lavishly the same set of friends as frequented Devonshire House. In addition to Crewe Hall, there was also a lovely villa in Hampstead to which the *ton* repaired for weekend parties. That she was as prone to 'dissipation' as the Duchess is evident from many little hints in letters of the time. Georgiana noted her imprudence and her capacity for getting into scrapes all day long; 'scrapes' was Georgiana's euphemism for huge liabilities incurred in hours of abandon at the gaming-tables. It is an expression she would have cause to use hundreds of times throughout her life. Mrs Crewe had about her such a look of baptismal innocence that one could not imagine her so foolish as to get into 'scrapes' of any kind. Georgiana called her innocence 'idiotism' and suspected it was contrived.[22]

Mrs Bouverie, wife of Edward Bouverie, M.P., was another of the *côterie*, also famed for her beauty (Reynolds painted a wonderful portrait of her and Mrs Crewe together). Lady Diana Beauclerk gained admittance to the Devonshire House set by right of birth, for she was a cousin to Georgiana, being descended from the first Duke of Marlborough and having Spencer as her maiden name. Her husband was the wild and witty bibliophile Topham Beauclerk, great-grandson of Charles II and Nell Gwynn and beloved friend of Dr Johnson (Lord and Lady Spencer had been the only witnesses at their wedding). Lady Diana was an accomplished artist, and indeed it must not be forgotten that these ladies were not merely beautiful and hedonistic, but talented as well. Mrs Crewe, Mrs Bouverie, Georgiana herself, wrote verses which, if not brilliant, required some study and application. Lady Di (as she was called) drew a fine portrait of Georgiana which was engraved by Bartolozzi, notwithstanding Dr Johnson's view that portrait painting was an improper pursuit for a woman. 'Public practice of any art, and staring in men's faces, is very indelicate in a female,' he said. Mrs Montagu and Mrs Vesey were two more prominent hostesses drawn into Georgiana's circle, both with pretensions to intellectuality, though in the latter case insufficiently convincing to impress Boswell. Lady Di gave her opinion that Mrs Vesey was an idiot, causing Boswell to defend the good lady with the reflection that she was less than an idiot than he had thought. Lady Di responded, 'I think she is bad enough, if that is all a lawyer can find to say for her, that she is only less an idiot than he imagined.' Mrs Vesey had the disconcerting habit of making her guests sit in little groups of three with their backs to the rest of the company, forcing conversation to be invented; there was none of this at Devonshire House, where talk flowed freely throughout the room and found its own centre.

To complete the gallery of Georgiana's friends there was Mrs Damer, daughter of Walpole's closest friend Henry Seymour Conway and through her mother's side a member of the Duke of Argyll's family. She had made a foolish and tragic marriage with an unenterprising fop called John Damer, which was already failing in 1775. On 15 August of the following year Damer shot himself dead at the Bedford Arms in Covent Garden. The widow devoted herself to literature and the arts, becoming in time a sculptress of considerable skill. Her conversation was learned and informed, but lacking, if we are to believe Lady Sarah Lennox, in humility: 'She is too *strictly right* ever to be beloved.'

It should not pass without mention that there was one particular lady of sharp intellect and lively mind who should have been, but was not, counted among the select visitors to Devonshire House. This was Mrs Thrale, Johnson's friend, whom Georgiana uncharacteristically considered 'vulgar'.* The epithet was both undeserved and ungracious, for Mrs Thrale was from a good family with a long history. That Georgiana should not like her is perhaps understandable, for Mrs Thrale was most certainly not the *ton*, being far too impatient of humbug to waste her energies in conforming to fashion, but that such a term of abuse should escape Georgiana's lips is surprisingly out of character. We may charitably suppose that the word carried less force than it would now.

Of the men who passed through the gates from Piccadilly, a faithful list would be tedious, for everyone of talent and intelligence was included and the resulting *mêlée* provided for the most stimulating drawing-room in London, where politicians, writers, journalists, the noble and the common, the refined and the coarse, could eddy round each other in a whirlpool of spirited conversation. Dr Johnson was admitted. Boswell, however, like Mrs Thrale, was not. Johnson's ungainly manners and indelicate habits were tolerated rather than applauded, Georgiana remarking that he did not shine so much in eating as in conversing, 'for he ate much and nastily'. Nor was he shy of bawdy. 'Pleasure, sir', he exclaimed, 'there is no pleasure like emission.' It was commonly known that Johnson reported conversations outside the walls of Devonshire House; Charles James Fox made it a rule not to speak in his presence, for he did not choose to figure in a reported conversation which would later be published.[23]

Of the older generation, Horace Walpole was welcome,

* 'Mrs Thrale seems certainly very clever, and she entertains me very much, her fault is having a vulgarity about her that seeks to be fine' (20 October 1778).

though never really an intimate, for his acerbic wit was never far removed from malice and his dislike of the Cavendish family made him an untrustworthy friend. George Selwyn, who was reputed to be always asleep in the House of Commons, woke up when at Devonshire House and entertained everyone with his wit. Colonel Fitzpatrick, Secretary of State for War, was another who combined the hard talents of political life with the more mellow virtues of poetry and gentle satire; he was nicknamed 'Fitz'. James Crauford was given the name 'Fish' to remind intimates that he was more selfish than the rest of them. He spent most of the time deploring the vexations and torments which encumbered his life: 'I wish he would mourn over them anywhere than at Devonshire House,' Harriet Cavendish would say. Bob Spencer, a son of the 3rd Duke of Marlborough and therefore Georgiana's cousin, was a cheeky, dissolute, congenial soul who achieved little but whom everyone liked. Mrs Bouverie liked him more than most, and bore him a daughter. On the death of Mr Bouverie in 1811, she duly became Lady Robert Spencer.

Yet another of the set was later to be caught by romance within the walls of Devonshire House. John Townshend, son of Lord Townshend, knew as much Shakespeare as the Duke of Devonshire and talked politics with Charles James Fox. 'An amiable young man,' said Georgiana, who was no older than he. Townshend fell in love with Mrs Fawkener, Georgiana's cousin on the Poyntz side, and eloped with her, bringing upon himself duels and intrigues, and culminating in a Fawkener divorce by Act of Parliament. The Devonshires were naturally in the thick of the scandal, which nonetheless ended happily with the couple's marriage.

No one was able to bring such laughter to the drawing-room as James Hare, an acute, dry man of the world whose humour was iconoclastic and bitter-sweet, and who most enjoyed the elegance of paradox. 'You cannot conceive anything so truly entertaining as he is,' said Georgiana. 'His kind of wit always surprises as much as it pleases one.'[24] Sir Augustus Clifford (who comes into the story later as one of the children of Devonshire House) described him as 'the tallest, thinnest man I ever saw, his face like a surprised cockatoo, and as white'.[25] He sat habitually with his long, spider's legs crossed, observing like a praying mantis. Hare's taste for playing the fool concealed the very real judgement he possessed, and the Duke counted him among his best friends because wit and sagacity played equal parts in his character, the one at service to, but never subservient to, the other. On one occasion he was one of 14,000 people assembled at Vauxhall Gardens for a celebration of the Prince of Wales's birthday, when the crush and tedium were intolerable. Hare said he would never have believed that any public amusement could have had the power to make him so completely miserable.[26] He was also remorselessly mischievous. Georgiana's sister Harriet pictured him thus: 'He sits ready arm'd in the great chair, book in Hand, with the other extended ready to discuss and pull to pieces any unfortunate Author that falls under his look. I very often attempt arguing with him more for the pleasure of provoking some of his sparkling flashes and of hearing his opinion than to defend my own. He told me the other day he wish'd I had been born a Man and made a special pleader, that I should have made the fortune of all my clients, for that I had more shifts and turns and ingenuity in supporting a bad argument than any body he ever met with. I told him that with all my ingenuity I could not find out whether this was most abuse or compliment.'[27]

When Harriet was so embarrassed by a remark at the dinner table that she went red in the face, Hare pounced upon her with relish. 'Heaven be prais'd!' he said, 'Once in my life I have seen a woman blush. I thought it was a poetical fiction, and never could happen in real life.'[28]

But for all his mischief, Hare was a supreme friend. In the end, this was the quality which counted for most in Devonshire House. The intimates were amusing, learned, respected, significant in one way or another, but the bond which united them, the one trait they had in common, was loyalty. They appreciated and fostered the quality of friendship, which made their assemblies much more than a glittering constellation of acquaintance. When Hare died, Fox remarked, 'One can hardly be sorry he is released; but an intimate friendship of upwards of forty years and not once interrupted must make one feel.'

Four of the leading characters are missing from this brief list of *dramatis personae*, simply because they are to play such a prominent role in the events to come that they must await a suitable entry on to the stage. They include Georgiana's sister Harriet, approaching womanhood in the 1770's, the dramatist Richard Brinsley Sheridan, who was to capture some of the *éclat* of Devonshire House in his play *The School for Scandal*, the politician Charles James Fox, in whose election to parliament Georgiana was to play the part which gave her a footnote in history, and the Prince of Wales himself.

Gatherings at Devonshire House were unlike others in London in their gaiety, their informality, their unselfconscious rejoicing in the pleasure of amiable company. While other houses celebrated ordered, rational discussion, wherein the subject was announced before anyone began to speak, and guests took their turns to contribute a word in strict succession, Devonshire House preferred the wild scramble, and was thereby the more sympathetic. 'The characteristic conversation of the Devonshire House ladies was "tête-à-tête", in a secluded boudoir, or murmured in the corner of a sofa amid the movement of a party.' It was glamorous, yet cosy, glittering, but personal. And above all, furiously active. There was always something going on. Life there 'passed in a dazzling, haphazard confusion of routs, balls, card parties, hurried letter-writing, fitful hours of talk and reading'.[29] 'Every thought was there uttered, and every feeling expressed: there was neither shyness, nor reserve, nor affectation. Talent opposed itself to talent with all the force of argument. . . . Opinions were there liberally discussed; characters stripped of their pretences; and satire mingled with the good humour, and jovial mirth, which on every side abounded.'[30]

In the midst of all this, the Duke was a silent, imperturbable host. The Duchess, on the other hand, was thoroughly enjoying her emergence as the first lady of London at the age of eighteen.

*   *   *

In the summer of 1775, the Spencers and Devonshires all went together to Spa, braving the difficult journey in return for a few weeks' 'relaxation'. Georgiana and the Duke returned to England in July, leaving the Spencers behind to lose more money at the tables. Little Harriet wrote to her sister with the innocent confession that Mama could not heed her own precepts; she thought she had discovered the magic formula to win, and proceeded to lose every penny.[31] The Spencers then continued to Paris, mainly to see what were the latest fashions, which caused Lord Spencer to comment irritably, 'I suppose all our fine ladies must as usual follow all the nonsense of this place.'[32] It seems they ascertained that the only colours which would excite admiration were *dos de puce* and *ventre de puce*.

The real excitement of the summer was Georgiana's first pregnancy, giving rise to more than usual concern on the part of her parents. She felt faint and sick on the journey back from Spa, but the Duke, in a rare footnote to one of his wife's letters, assured Lady Spencer that his physician, Dr Denman, diagnosed mere tiredness. However, it was not to be. At the end of September, the Duchess miscarried. Her father ascribed the mishap to 'all the racketting which did you a great deal of harm last year' and implored her to be more prudent in future. Lady Clermont wrote in mock-scolding tones, 'What possess'd you, child, to miscarry? Don't let me hear of such a thing again.[33]

The following Christmas was spent at Althorp, while the list of Georgiana's debts accumulated. Her allowance of £2,000 a year would not be sufficient to cover all her liabilities, there being £1,600 owing to tradesmen alone, not counting her debts at cards. Mama undertook to do some sums and help the Duchess see her way towards careful management of her affairs. 'For heaven's sake think anxiously of these things,' she besought. Intuition (and self-knowledge?) warned Lady Spencer that this was the tiniest cloud which heralded a mighty storm in years to come.

On this occasion, the Duke was able to rescue Georgiana from embarrassment without too much fuss, and after another hectic London season of balls and theatres and parties, the summer was spent at Chatsworth. Moments of levity and drama both interrupted the gentle flow of country life. On 1 August the Duke and Duchess attended the wedding of Lady Mary Bellasis, Lord Fauconberg's sister (the first Earl of Fauconberg had been one of the signatories inviting William of Orange to take the throne of England in 1688, hence the family was well viewed by every Cavendish). Georgiana gave an account of the bride to her mother: 'She is very old and ugly but seems a very good kind of woman, I thought the Duke would burst out laughing when she came in, it seemed such a joke her being a bride.'[34]

A few days later, Georgiana fell from her horse when out riding and suffered such serious injury that there were fears she would lose her life. With an eye on her audience, Georgiana wrote to Mama from her sick-bed a letter with the kind of sentiment which she knew would earn approval.

> I feel that I am unfit to die, but trust that I may become ready for death, and therefore fitter to live.[35]

In fact, she recovered by the following day. Lady Spencer's relief was not so great that she could resist the temptation to chide. 'Can you reflect without shuddering', she said, 'on the possibility of having been snatched so suddenly out of a world, where you have so much power of doing good and setting a glorious example, which you do not, I fear, often study to do.'[36]

She further seized the opportunity to chastise Georgiana for the wasteful hours she spent in bed; idleness, for Lady Spencer, was the most lamentable sin:

> Do try to bring yourself to the habit of getting up earlier than you do . . . nothing can be of such material consequence to your health, as weaknesses of every kind are frequently brought on by nothing but lying too much in bed.[37]

Lady Clermont was more abrupt: 'I really wish child you would not lie so long, come get up this moment.'[38]

As usual, the ladies were of course quite right, and the same advice today would carry as much weight and doubtless receive as little attention. Georgiana excused herself in French (Mama was always pleased when her daughters showed how clever they were in foreign tongues). 'Je ne crois pas que sans avoir commis un vrai mal on puisse avoir été plus imprudente que je ne l'ai été', she wrote.[*39]

To her credit, Georgiana nursed no illusions about the recklessness of her character, even if she showed herself less and less able to do anything which might correct it. 'With a heart not bad (I humbly trust) I have an instability of nature that is sometimes madness,' she confessed.[40] Self-knowledge afforded her little joy, however, for she was destined to see her mistakes and follies multiply rather than diminish as she got older. Lady

---

* Without doing anything terribly wrong, I don't think anyone could have been more imprudent than I.

Spencer was beside herself with frustration at her daughter's incapacity for improvement, so that one can scarcely blame her for treating Georgiana as an errant child long after she reached maturity. 'Your motives in everything are generous and benevolent', she told her, 'but you have never accustomed yourself to any degree of order or regularity, on the contrary you rather hold it in contempt.'[41] This was to be after Georgiana's forty-fourth birthday, but it was a refrain which accompanied her entire journey. Whenever she tried to draw herself into line, the attempt was overtaken by fresh opportunities for self-indulgence. 'I do not like to make promises', she told her mother, 'as I am used to fail'.[42]

* * *

One of the guests at Chatsworth that summer was the man whom Lord Ossory fulsomely described as 'one of the most extraordinary men that ever existed',[43] the power of whose personality was to exert a considerable influence upon Georgiana for the next thirty years. This was Charles James Fox, a prodigious character of the sort that English political life occasionally produces without quite knowing what to do with him; he was regarded with mingled awe and discomfort as a giant among men, whose undisciplined originality made him sit uneasily with his fellows. On the whole, the English distrust originality in politics, conferring popularity in preference upon the man who can express ordinary ideas with clarity; there was nothing ordinary about Charles James Fox.

Here is Georgiana's first recorded impression of him at Chatsworth on 14 August 1777:

I have always thought that the great merit of C. Fox is his amazing quickness in seazing any subject, he seems to have the particular talent of knowing more about what he is saying and with less pains than anyone else. His conversation is like a brilliant player at billiards, the strokes follow one another piff puff – and what makes him more entertaining now is his being here with Mr Townsend and the D. of Devonshire, for their living so much together makes them show off one another. The chief topic is Politicks and Shakespear. As for the latter, they all three seem to have the most astonishing memorys for it, and I suppose I shall be able in time to go thro' a play as they do.[44]

At this time, Fox was twenty-eight years old (eight years older than Georgiana), but had already lived the life of six normal men and was assured his place in history had he retired from public life the next day. He had been in Parliament since the age of nineteen, had been a Junior Lord of the Admiralty at twenty-one, then Junior Lord of the Treasury, was an orator of such attraction that he could fill the House of Commons, possessed massive erudition in five languages, and had frittered away a quarter of a million pounds at a time when noblemen were considered rich on £5,000 a year.

Charles James Fox was the third son of Henry Fox (later Lord Holland) and Lady Caroline Lennox, daughter of the second Duke of Richmond. His paternal descent was remarkable for the immense fortune which his father had accumulated as Paymaster-General, while from his mother's side he inherited royal blood, the Duke of Richmond being the grandson of Charles II by his French mistress Louise de Kéroualle. Both the Richmond marriage and the Fox marriage had been marked by adventure. Richmond had been married off to Lady Sarah Cadogan when he was eighteen and she thirteen, to settle a gambling debt between their fathers. They disliked each other immediately. The bride was sent back to school and the bridegroom packed off to Europe for the obligatory Grand Tour. Three years later he spent his first evening back in England at the opera, hoping to avoid the wife of whom he retained such unpleasant memories, and spied in a box opposite a young lady who attracted his romantic attention. This turned out to be his wife, whom he wooed with such success that one might say they fell in love at second sight. She bore him twelve children and was pregnant no less than twenty-eight times. The marriage was universally regarded as idyllically happy, as the two could scarcely keep from touching and kissing each other wherever they were.

When their eldest daughter Caroline wanted to marry Henry Fox, however, they were not at all pleased and refused their consent, so Henry and Caroline eloped and were secretly joined at the house of Charles Hanbury Williams, causing a mighty stir in the town. It was many years before the Duke and Duchess were reconciled to their daughter's choice, finally recognising that she was as happy in the conjugal state as they had been. They had four sons of whom the third, Charles James, was born in Conduit Street on 24 January 1749.

From the first, the young Charles was accustomed to hear talk of politics as a daily event and no attempt was made by his father to exclude him from these discussions. He received in some ways the best education a boy could have, with a parent who delighted in fostering his reasoning faculty and spent many hours conversing, arguing, disputing with him on a variety of subjects. In other ways it was the worst, for Lord Holland believed that a bright child should be indulged in everything, should never be thwarted or reprimanded, should receive no instruction which threatened his happiness. 'Let nothing be done to break his spirit', he said, 'the world will do that business fast enough.' When Charles pointed out that he had been promised he could see a wall demolished at Holland House and that the wall had disappeared in his absence, Lord Holland ordered the wall to be rebuilt forthwith so that his son could watch it collapse again. 'Young people are always in the right, and old people in the wrong,' he said.

At Eton, Charles had the additional good fortune to fall under the influence of the Headmaster, Dr Barnard, who valued the arts of rhetoric and disputation; whenever an interesting debate was promised in the House of Commons, the boy was regularly given permission to absent himself from school to hear it, and his own performance in debate at Eton was so accomplished that there was no doubt among his schoolfellows that he was destined for a distinguished political career. Furthermore, his knowledge of classical literature was profoundly rooted in genuine scholarship, enabling him to summon passages of Cicero, Tacitus, Juvenal or Virgil at the apposite moment and commit vast tracts to memory. He early formed a deep appreciation of Horace, whose poetry he carried in a pocket edition all his life.

At the age of fourteen, his father whisked him away from Eton to join the fashionable crowd at Spa, where Lord Holland determined that his education should include a swift introduction to the vices of his elders. For four months he was provided with five guineas a night to lose at the gambling tables, throwing himself with such energy into the task that when he returned to Eton of his own accord he managed to convert that establishment into a gambling den and his name was soon a password for dissipation. Yet his reputation for eloquence and his popularity as a congenial companion were sufficient to allow his sins to be forgiven.

Not by all, however. There were some who viewed the Holland progeny with alarm, including Chatham himself, who said that Lord Holland 'educated his children without the least regard to morality, and with such extravagant vulgar indulgence, that the great change which has taken place among our youth has been dated from the time of his son's going to Eton'.[45]

That his mother Caroline was not as content as her husband to watch Charles slide into 'dissipation' is attested by a letter he wrote her in childish hand apologising for causing her uneasiness. 'The reflection that I have behaved in many respects ill to you is almost the only painful one I have ever experienced', he wrote, adding that dissipation was not as bad as all that anyway, and he would not be ready entirely to give it up.[46]

At fifteen, Charles had outgrown school, where the tasks submitted were inadequate to test his intellectual powers. His teachers implored him to do less work, advising that application of such magnitude required some intermission. 'I am afraid', he said, 'that my natural idleness will in the end get the better of what little ambition I have, and that I shall never be anything but a lounging fellow.' He would never be free from this conflict between the seduction of lounging and the satisfaction of labour.

After two years at Hertford College, Oxford (during which time he was said to have walked in one day from Oxford to Holland House in sweltering heat and pawned his gold watch at Nettlebed in return for cheese and wine), he went at seventeen to Paris and Italy, learning to speak both French and Italian fluently and developing a twin passion for Italian literature and French fashions. He spent £16,000 in ten days at Naples, and travelled from Paris to Lyons for the sole purpose of buying some silk waistcoats. Lord Holland heard of all this but would do nothing to temper his son's excesses.

Charles Fox brought back to London the extravagant male fashions then popular at the French court – blue hair powder, hats with feathers, red heels on his shoes, frilly velvet, lace and brocade, extensive cosmetics. This was the uniform of the 'Macaronis', generously regarded as outrageous fops and dandies by the indulgent, at a time when it was common for male clothes to be called 'pretty', and less kindly considered by the prudish as passionless neuter animals without the virtues of either sex. At nineteen, Fox was the acknowledged leader of the Macaronis, which was no small triumph in itself, considering his unwieldy appearance; few people could have been less disposed by nature to be arbiters of fashion. He was corpulent, graceless, unaesthetic, clumsy and burdensome in movement, heavy in repose. Dark shaggy eyebrows (bequeathed by Charles II to many of his descendants) dominated his face, giving Georgiana the excuse to nickname him simply 'The Eyebrow'. Decidedly, he was an incongruous dandy, but so disdainful of opinion in such matters that he followed his own ebullient course. The great rotund face would break into the broadest of smiles and issue the loudest of laughs so that one forgave everything to share the boon of his jovial company.

In 1768, Lord Holland purchased the borough of Midhurst for Charles, and he took his seat in the House of Commons while still eighteen months below the regulation minimum age. His fame was sufficiently acknowledged for the House to make his case exceptional and to welcome him as a phenomenon. Within no time at all, he took the House by storm, astonishing all with the brilliant spontaneity of his speeches, which shone effortlessly above the studied prose of his elders. Fox did not care to prepare a speech, preferring instead to let it explode in sparks of genius from his fertile brain. He said that he would sometimes think about what he was going to say as he was travelling to the House, but more often than not his best performance was in unrehearsed reply. It was said that in all its history Parliament had never known such a master of ingenuity and improvisation. It must also be said that he was bumptious and insolent, for he did not descend to feign respect for experienced parliamentarians whose inadequacies were all too apparent. His Macaroni appearance was a further impertinence which he obviously enjoyed. Nevertheless, he never bored the House, his arguments were always shrewd and presented with the clarity of a judge, his eloquence was compulsive.

In his early days, Fox was openly contemptuous of the 'voice of the people'. 'It is our duty to do what is proper', he said, 'without considering what may be agreeable: their business is to choose us . . . I stand up for the constitution, not for the people: if the people attempt to invade the constitution, they are enemies to the nation. Being therefore, Sir, convinced that we are here to do justice, whether it is agreeable or disagreeable to the people, I am for maintaining the independency of Parliament, and will not be a rebel to my King, my country, or my own heart, for the loudest huzza of an inconsiderate multitude.'[47] It was shortly after this, in 1771, that Fox was pulled from his coach by the mob and rolled in the mud.

Later, he modified his view and became the champion of the people, supported the American war, discarded his peacock clothes to don the buff and blue by which Washington's army was recognised, and so neglected his appearance that he came to look very shabby indeed. 'His bristly black person, and shaggy breast quite open, rarely purified by any ablutions, was wrapped in a foul linen night-gown and his bushy hair dishevelled.'[48] In this guise, he became a bosom friend of the Prince of Wales, exciting all the wrath of the King, who already despised him for every possible reason. Fox epitomised the aristocratic vices which the virtuous George III hated to distraction. 'That young man has so thoroughly cast off every principle of common honour and honesty', said the King, 'that he must soon become as contemptible as he is odious.'[49] The judgement was unfair, but since Fox nursed a robust enmity towards the King, who knew of it, one can hardly blame his intemperate language. Fox, for all his bonhomie, could be vindictive.

The French Ambassador, whose job it was to interpret Fox's wayward character to his government, thought him a popular and dangerous libertine, who squandered public money 'pour séduire un jeune Prince qu'il a soulevé contre son propre père'.* When, later, d'Adhémar had to deal with Fox in his position as Secretary of State for Foreign Affairs, this serious and solemn French aristocrat was perplexed by Fox's apparent vulgarity, and finally exasperated by the way in which Fox toyed with him.

* In order to seduce a young Prince whom he has set against his own father.

'Il est bien fâcheux d'avoir à traiter avec des gens qui n'ont ni plan, ni principes', he said. 'Je vous assure que M. Fox me met à des épreuves cruelles.'* In his interviews with d'Adhémar, Fox would affect an insouciant bonhomie, rarely keeping to the subject, using slang expressions, telling jokes, and leaving the poor man confused. He is indeed the strangest Foreign Secretary, thought d'Adhémar, and when he has lost his popularity, very little will be left. 'I will not send you an account of all the opinions and jocularities of the Secretary of State', he told his government, 'as the tone would compromise the dignity of my despatches.' Once, when Fox referred to a bitter pill to swallow, d'Adhémar winced and pompously remarked, 'Assurément il n'y a rien de moins noble que le style de ce secrétaire d'Etat', while paying due tribute nevertheless to the prolixity and fluency of his talk. As he knew that Fox was very sensitive to his reputation as an orator, d'Adhémar was careful to sprinkle words of praise in those despatches which he knew Fox would have opened, reserving his more critical remarks for the secret letters. The French Foreign Minister, Vergennes, responded to these unflattering assessments with the conclusion that Fox knew nothing of the business of his department and was an amateur playing at being a politician. 'Je le regarde comme incorrigible.'† This is precisely what Fox wanted him to think.[50]

In 1774, the year of the Devonshire marriage, Fox's father, mother and brother all died. Another two years, and he was dismissed from office in unpleasant indifferent fashion. The Prime Minister, Lord North, wrote to him, 'The King has ordered a new commission of the Treasury to be made out, in which I do not see your name.'[51] Thus, when he formed a friendship with the young Duchess, Fox was a frustrated star blinking in the shadows. Deprived of work with which to harness his abundant energies, he gave way easily to his books and his gambling. Had he poured all his available time into the enjoyment of his worthy scholarship, all might have been well, and his influence upon Georgiana for the better. She would certainly learn from him. Homer, Demosthenes, Ariosto, Dante, he knew all their works intimately, and could discourse with charm upon them. 'What

* It is very annoying to have to deal with people who have neither plan nor principles. . . . I do assure you that I am sorely tried by Mr Fox.
† I consider him incorrigible.

can one suggest that he does not know and must have thought?'
asked Walpole despairingly.

Alas, Fox spent as many waking hours gambling at Almack's
(later Brooks's) Club, where he lost unbelievable sums of
money, as he did reading. Everyone appeared to be gambling
to excess, but Charles James Fox outdid them all. It was said that
had he confined himself to games of skill, such as whist or
picquet, he might have made a comfortable £4,000 a year. But
he was unaccountably addicted to games of chance and daft bets
placed on anything under the sun: against Turkey being a
European power, against Lord Northington swimming a mile in
the Thames, and so on. At faro he would play for hours on end,
until he fell asleep at the table, on one occasion at least playing
Fitzpatrick for eight unremitting hours, with a waiter at hand to
tell them both when a change of deal was called for, so comatose
had they become. Another account has him playing for twenty-
two consecutive hours, losing £11,000 by the end. He was even
reduced to borrowing money from the waiters to pay back the
moneylenders who stood in wait for him in a small room at the
club which he called the Jerusalem Chamber. Still, his vigorous
spirit would not be crushed. A friend followed him to his
lodgings in St James's Street after an especially disastrous night,
expecting to find him in despair and in need of comfort; instead,
Fox was calmly reading Herodotus. What else can a man do, he
asked, who has lost his last shilling?

For once, this standard remark was no picturesque exaggera-
tion. In 1773, Lord Holland had had to come to his son's rescue
with no less than £100,000, after Charles had lost his income
and his assets. 'So now any younger son may justify losing his
father's and elder brother's estate on precedent,' was Walpole's
acid comment.[52] Fox went on to lose still more, and one day
Walpole was walking down St James's Street when he saw Fox's
furniture being loaded into a cart; his creditors had come to
collect. Then he saw Fox himself, imperturbable and
philosophic. Walpole went home and wrote, 'The more
marvellous Fox's parts are, the more one is provok'd at his
follies, which comfort so many rascals and blockheads, and
make all that is admirable and amiable in him only matter of
regret to those who like him as I do.'[53]

As it became clear that Fox was past reforming, his friends

hoped that he would find a boundless heiress to marry him and cope with his debts to infinity. Lord Holland had welcomed the plan, for it would oblige his son to go to bed at least one night in his life. Poor Fox was the victim of a practical joke in this regard; having been promised the hand of a rich West Indian lady who only liked fair men, he prepared himself to meet her by smothering his swarthy complexion in white face-powder.

It is impossible to determine exactly how much Fox squandered. When his father died in 1774, he left him £20,000 cash, £900 a year, estates in Sheppey and Thanet, and the estate of Kingsgate, Lord Holland's favourite retreat. Charles used every penny of the inheritance, even selling the estates, to settle immediate liabilities. Later the same year, his brother Stephen died, leaving him a sinecure worth £2,300 a year, which Charles promptly sold to the government for an annuity. By the time Georgiana was telling her mother of his visit to Chatsworth in 1777, he was again a pauper, having by one estimate got through a quarter of a million pounds.[54] Worst of all, he was unrepentant, incorrigible, apparently indifferent to the catastrophe. The spectacle presented by this delightful, impressive, carefree rogue to the impressionable young Duchess could not have been more repugnant to poor Lady Spencer, who knew only too well how easily her daughter could be led astray by the wrong examples.

For all that, Fox was admired and cherished as few men have the good fortune to be in their lifetime. Gibbon said, 'Perhaps no human being was ever more exempt from the taint of malevolence, vanity, or falsehood.'[55] Georgiana herself spoke of his 'candour and benevolence that renders him as amiable as he is great'.[56] That Fox returned the affection, there is no doubt. 'To serve you, if I could do it, would always by the greatest pleasure to me,' he told her.[57] Small wonder, then, that she would later declare her longing to make common cause with him. She had not met anyone so luminously intelligent in her life. He inspired her, kindled her interest in politics, gave her cause selflessly to admire.

The qualities which most endeared Charles James Fox to Georgiana were those which she shared – a capacity for friendship which was deep and loyal rather than the fragile social bond of acquaintance, and a certain prankishness or delinquency. Talleyrand noticed the contradictions in a per-

sonality which contained simplicity, gaiety, childishness and
profundity all at once,[58] an assessment which Georgiana's
daughter would later echo when she said that 'with his superior
talents and abilities, he is with all the nature and simplicity of a
child'.[59] Like children, Fox and Georgiana would both skip and
bounce through life governed almost entirely by their feelings,
and would both be accused of lack of judgement. It was this surrender to the emotions which was to be the *leit-motif* of the select
band of merry folk who clustered round the new Duchess of
Devonshire.

✳   ✳   ✳

A recent recruit to the set was the ambitious and versatile Irish
dramatist Richard Brinsley Sheridan, whose elopement with
and subsequent marriage to the beautiful Miss Linley had
caused a spectacular fuss a few years before. His play *The Rivals*
had been first performed in 1775, and was already a standard
favourite, but now, in 1777, he had succeeded Garrick as
manager of the Drury Lane Theatre and gained the *entrée* into
Devonshire House, where he proceeded to gather material for
his masterpiece, *The School for Scandal*. When the best of society
gathered for the first performance of this play on 8 May 1777,
they saw before them a spirited parody of their own lives and
enjoyed the exquisite pleasure of being party to an 'in' joke.
Lady Sneerwell, Mrs Candour, and the archetypical Macaroni
Sir Benjamin Backbite with his long curls and spy-glasses, were
all drawn from the people Sheridan met in Georgiana's circle.
The play was fulsomely dedicated to one of them, Mrs Crewe,
with whom Sheridan was currently in love. While it is virtually
impossible to capture the *cachet* and style of Devonshire House
conversation from letters and diaries, Sheridan has made it
rather easier for us, as a reading of his play is the nearest we can
approach to the atmosphere of those drawing-room sallies.
Georgiana is not represented by any one character, but the
elegant phrases of the repartee which surrounded her are
present in many of the lines. When Lady Teazle says 'I know very
well that women of fashion in London are accountable to
nobody after they are married', it is the voice of Lady
Melbourne that we hear. Crabtree is talking about Charles

Surface, but Sheridan is evidently thinking of Fox, when he makes the character say 'Whenever he is sick, they have prayers for the recovery of his health in all the synagogues.' It could be James Hare who says, 'For my part, I own, madam, wit loses its respect with me, when I see it in company with malice'; and Johnson who replies, 'There's no possibility of being witty without a little ill nature.' A comment on the morals of the age is in the exchange between Lady Teazle and Joseph Surface: 'I admit you as a lover no farther than fashion requires.' 'True, a mere Platonic cicisbeo, what every wife is entitled to.' And it could very well be Georgiana herself who inspired the line, 'Oh lud, you are going to be moral, and forget that you are among friends.'

Sheridan would later identify himself still further with the Devonshire crowd by abandoning the theatre for politics, and devoting his amorous attentions to Georgiana's sister Harriet.

Georgiana and her friends evolved a particular way of talking which delighted in exclusive jargon and made the language adopt their personalities so that it became almost a dialect. They gushed and cooed, lingered over the syllables. Yellow was 'yaller', gold was 'goold' and Rome was 'Room'. Spoil was pronounced to rhyme with mile and London was called 'Lonnon' even by imitators. Stresses fell on unexpected syllables, as in contémplate and balcóny. Tea was never referred to as anything but 'tay', and you had to be 'much obleeged' if you were offered some. When John Kemble was engaged to teach the Prince of Wales elocution, he implored with exasperation, 'Sir, may I beseech your Royal Highness to open your royal jaws and say "oblige"?'

Examples may be multiplied. Cucumber was 'cowcumber', china was 'chayna' or 'chayney'. The very words chosen were excessive, in keeping with the habits of the speakers. If you got on well with someone you were *violent* friends, and if you enjoyed a book you would *die* over it. Baby talk was depressingly frequent, when 'you' would be contracted to 'oo' and hope was written and pronounced 'whop'. As the years passed, the Devonshire House pronunciation became more and more bizarre, affecting a nasal drawl which identified a member of the set immediately. Lisping was considered attractive, its greatest executant being

Lady Caroline Lamb, who baa'd like a sheep and was heard to say to William Harness, 'Gueth how many pairth of thilk thtockingth I have on? Thixth!'*

By the time *The School for Scandal* was produced, Georgiana was already the acknowledged queen of fashion, and references in the play to exaggerated hairstyles were made with her in mind. From Paris she had imported the idea of building up the hair to fantastic heights, and in her defiant whimsical way she overtook the Parisians by taking the fashion still higher, enveloping the monstrous construction in a fog of white powder, and crowning the whole with gigantic feathers. 'Nothing is talked of so much as the ladies' *enormous* dresses', wrote Mrs Delany. 'The three *most* elevated plumes of feathers are the Duchess of Devonshire, Lady Mary Somerset, and Lady Harriet Stanhope . . . it would be some consolation if their manner did *not* too much correspond with the lightness of their dress!' Georgiana's supremacy was not long threatened by the insolent Mary Somerset; Lady Clermont wrote to reassure her, 'Lady Mary Somerset's head is low in comparison to many I have seen. They give five and twenty guineas for a headdress.'[60] Mama seemed to enjoy Georgiana's antics in this regard at least, for she denigrated the unfortunate rival still further by telling her daughter, 'She is more marked with the smallpox than I thought she was and has either very bad or very dirty teeth.'[61]†

As Georgiana carried her feathers even higher, and every other lady followed suit, the whole world remarked upon the phenomenon. 'The Duchess of Devonshire had two plumes sixteen inches long, besides three small ones', wrote a certain Mrs Harris. 'This has so far outdone all other plumes, that Mrs Damer, Lady Harriet Stanhope, etc., looked nothing.' Mrs Moser invited a friend to 'come to London and admire our plumes; we sweep the sky!' When coiffeurs could not extend the hair beyond three feet above the head, and mere feathers were no longer astonishing appendages, ladies took to covering the hair with roses, acorns, even turnips and potatoes, and wearing

---

* Some vestiges of Whig pronunciation continue to the present day. Conversation with the late Bertrand Russell, whose godfather John Stuart Mill was born the year Georgiana died, was always enlivened by archaic vowel-sounds.

† Mary Somerset married the Duke of Richmond in 1775.

not one, or two, or six feathers, but eleven. Georgiana dispensed with this competition with sublime superiority; she sported one single ostrich feather, given her by Lord Stormont, which reached a height of four feet.

The fashion soared to such absurdity that it became difficult for ladies to enter a room without damage, and they had to sit on the floors of their carriages to avoid crushing the headdress against the roof. A print entitled *A Warning to Ladies to Take Care of Their Heads* showed a woman whose feathers caught light in the candles of the lofty chandeliers, but Georgiana remarked with *sang-froid* that a fashionably dressed head would burn for an hour at least before the scalp was reached. In a pantomime at Drury Lane Harlequin was shown scaling a ladder to reach a lady's hair.

The Queen scorned such extravagances, and forbade the ladies of her Court to wear any feathers at all. Mrs Delany, too, was scathing in her disapproval. 'Extravagance of fashion is vulgar', she wrote, 'and shows levity of mind.' She was probably correct. At a rout that year, where a good many of the *bon ton* were assembled, she noted the 'waving plumes, preposterous Babylonian heads towering to the sky, exciting both my wonder and my indignation at their immense folly'. In the prologue to his forgotten play *A Trip to Scarborough*, also produced in 1777, Sheridan made fun of the fashion:

No heads of old too high for feathered state
Hindered the fair to pass the lowest gate:
A church to enter now they must be bent,
If ever they should try th' experiment.

There, in the Royal Box of the theatre, Georgiana was sitting in splendid confidence, a tuft of pink ostrich feathers on her head.[62] Mrs Crewe thought the Duchess cut a very fine figure in the farce.[63]

Fox and Townshend left Chatsworth on 11 September 1777, followed soon afterwards by the Devonshires, who broke their journey to stay with Lord and Lady Melbourne at Brocket Hall. In October, Georgiana was in Brighton, sitting for portraits to Lady Di Beauclerk and Lady Anne Lindsay. As the year 1778 matured, Georgiana was back in Devonshire House. Her position was now unassailable. She was far more Queen in the

popular imagination than was George III's consort; she was the
one woman Londoners hoped would pass as they stood in the
street. However, after four years of marriage there was no sign of
an heir to the Devonshire title. Frivolity seemed to occupy all the
Duchess's time, and heads were shaking. As if in acknowledge-
ment of the gossip, she tried briefly to mend her ways, and could
at least boast that she was not so giddy as to take a lover before
she had done her duty. Lady Melbourne's advice was still
heeded. Lady Cowper felt relief that her grand-daughter had
not entirely gone overboard, and wrote to express her feelings to
Mrs Port. 'The Duchess of Devonshire is *much quieter* than she
was', she said, 'and is always at home *before* the Duke; and
whatever people may say, and tho *so much admired*, she has no
cicisbeo, which is now so much ye *ton*.'[64]

The sad truth was that Georgiana had not discovered in
marriage what her romantic soul had yearned for. Of course,
she knew, and Mama had carefully explained, what were her
duties towards her husband, how lucky she was to have been
chosen by such an important man, how she was the envy of the
town. Love was something which would grow in time, with a
little effort and a great deal of good fortune. This was all very
well, but a young woman who feels intensely cannot stop herself
by sheer willpower. Georgiana was still a passionate, romantic,
demonstrative girl who dreamt of a warm embrace and the
ecstatic pleasure which was the reward of overwhelming affection. She wanted, as we say now, to be swept off her feet. Jean-
Jacques Rousseau's abandoned descriptions of love were then
all the rage, though women of Lady Spencer's generation considered them unsuitable reading. *La Nouvelle Héloise* had been
published only a few years before. Georgiana's own copy of this
revolutionary book was recently discovered by chance at
Chatsworth, and a perusal of the passages which she underlined
with her own pen illustrate very vividly the state of her mind.
Those paragraphs which made the deepest impression upon her
were the most passionate. 'Sens-tu combien un coeur languis-
sant est tendre, et combien la tristesse sait fermenter l'amour?'
wrote Rousseau; Georgiana marked that for re-reading. And
here is another passage, in approximate translation, which has
her pen beside it:

O Julie, O Julie! shall we not be united? shall our days not be spent together? Could we be separated forever? No, may my mind never contemplate such a frightful idea; which transforms in a moment all my tenderness into wild anger. Fury makes me rush from cave to cave; I moan and I weep in spite of myself; I take colour like a lion who has been disturbed; I am capable of anything, anything save giving you up, and there is nothing, no nothing that I would not do to possess you, or I shall die.

Besides these transports one must set Georgiana's own situation. Years later she defended her subsequent follies in a note which has since disappeared, but the essence of which has passed down the generations. Lady Louisa Egerton (sister of the 8th Duke of Devonshire) found the note, told Lady Antrim about it, and Lady Antrim told the late Dowager Duchess, wife of the 9th Duke. In it, Georgiana said, 'Before you condemn me remember that at seventeen I was a toast, a beauty, and a Duchess, and wholly neglected by my husband.'[65]

Chapter Four

GOSSIP

Georgiana was coming home at night earlier than the Duke for a special, unexpected reason: she was busy writing a novel. It was not such an uncommon thing to do, as intelligent young ladies often tried their hand at a story in the eighteenth century, generally with tedious results. There was one, however, which rose above the ordinary and was a constant topic of conversation, *Evelina, or A Young Lady's Entrance into the World,* by Fanny Burney. In Devonshire House parlance, everyone was *dying* over it. Perhaps Georgiana simply thought she could do better, or perhaps she wanted to use her mind more than her hair-pins for a while. Perhaps even, she needed to write out her frustration. Whatever the case, a new novel called *The Sylph* appeared shortly afterwards, by an anonymous hand, and was advertised and sold in tandem with *Evelina.* This led many to suppose that Miss Burney had also written *The Sylph,* and to tease her upon it. Sir Joshua Reynolds thought so, as did Sheridan and Mrs Thrale, who wrote to Miss Burney and challenged her outright to admit authorship. Dr Burney was thereupon obliged to instruct the publisher, Mr Lowndes, to cease advertising both books together and to issue a public statement to the effect that they were by different authors. Sheridan might have laughed behind his hand, for surely he must have been privy to the secret, and was enjoined no doubt never to disclose his knowledge of the true authorship.

It is sad, almost incomprehensible, that in all the mountain of letters written by Georgiana to her mother and others, there is not so much as a whisper about *The Sylph.* Did she enjoy the mystery? Did she discuss it with anyone? Did she take weeks or months to write it? Is it a *roman à clef,* and who is intended to be who in the book? Lady Spencer was always warning Georgiana against reading novels. Did she know she was actually writing one? We cannot say. All that is certain is that after a time the Duchess was suspected of having written *The Sylph*, and that she never denied it. A close reading of the novel shows that it is Georgiana's voice one is hearing. The reviewer of the *Gentleman's Magazine* thought that the novel displayed 'too great a knowledge of the *ton*, and of the worst, though perhaps the highest, part of the world, to be the work of *a young lady*'. But there was one young lady who had accumulated over the past four years all the acquaintance with the *ton* a novelist could desire, and that was the Duchess of Devonshire herself.

The story concerns another young lady's introduction to the world. The heroine, Julia, is an innocent naïve country girl who, just before her seventeenth birthday, is married off to rich, sophisticated, dissipated Sir William Stanley and thrown into the terrifying whirlpool of London society. She gives an account of her life there in a series of letters to her younger sister which occupy the entire book. All the characters write to each other interminably. The new Lady Stanley is not happy, for her husband is cruel to her, but she finds solace in the advice of an older woman and a curious correspondent who signs himself 'The Sylph'. Eventually, Sir William commits suicide, releasing Julia, whereupon the Sylph turns up in person to reveal himself an eligible young man ready to marry her and make her happy at last.

The parallels with Georgiana's own life are obvious. She had married at the same age, she had a younger sister, she benefited from the wise counsel of Lady Melbourne. But she was hardly unsophisticated, as the Spencers were by no means country yokels, nor was the Duke of Devonshire a villain. Perhaps it was these discrepancies between fiction and reality which persuaded Georgiana to publish the book anonymously.

The Sylph is chiefly interesting for the small events which we know to be drawn from direct experience, and the views the author gives on the society in which she moves. There is the incident when Julia sits on her husband's knee and is brusquely reminded that she must be content with tenderness in private, and the exciting preparations for presentation at Court, when she is told by the hairdresser that it would be positively indecent to be seen without hair-powder. Julia confides in her sister how

tiresome it is to keep up with the fashions, 'so though I may
dance and sing in taste now, a few months hence I may have
another method to learn which will be the taste then'. The
comments on marriage echo the words of Lady Melbourne and
may well have expressed Georgiana's own feelings in sadder
moments. 'Marriage is now a necessary kind of barter', she says,
'and an alliance of families, but little else.' The husband is permitted by the rules to keep a mistress, while those same rules
dictate that it would be *mauvais ton* for husband and wife to be
seen too often together. Sir William states his opinion that his
wife is 'extremely docile' and is therefore unlikely to disgrace the
family, but the author does not see Julia at all in this light; she is
described as 'animated nature', in which phrase Georgiana
achieved a marvellously concise self-portrait. While the novel
cannot be regarded as pure autobiography, it cannot fail to
suggest a frame of mind in the author as she viewed her life so
far, in the spring of 1778.

Though Georgiana scarcely mentions international affairs in
her correspondence, the early years of her marriage coincided
with the American War of Independence. The Boston Tea Party
of 1773 had led eventually to the Declaration of Independence
in 1776. France had recognised the Colonists and negotiated an
alliance with them, and war had broken out in Europe between
England on the one hand and France and Spain on the other. As
an officer in the Derbyshire militia, the Duke of Devonshire was
called upon to go into camp at Cox Heath, near Maidstone in
Kent, and the Duchess accompanied him. The experience was
much less spartan than might be supposed, for even in camp
there were balls and social gatherings. One could uncharitably
suggest the ladies of London enjoyed playing at soldiers, for
Georgiana's letters to her mother are full of gossip about the
handsome captains, and her pride at seeing the Duke look
'vastly smart' and taking the salute 'vastly well'. She lived in
camp, with a bed in the Duke's tent, which also had room for her
maid, with another huge tent for a dining-room, at the ends of
which were recesses containing bedrooms, dining-room and
kitchens for the servants. After three months of this, Georgiana
went on 20 July to take the waters at Tunbridge Wells, where she
stayed another three months while military exercises continued
at Cox Heath.

'I think this is a vile place', she wrote to Mama, 'it is too like a town to be pleasant in summer and I liked the camp a thousand times better. It was then so much pleasanter to pass one's evenings as I did there, than as I do here in a nasty room.'[1]

The vileness of Tunbridge Wells was however alleviated by the company of Lady Clermont, Mrs Crewe, and the seven-months pregnant Lady Melbourne, and they managed to pass the time in games of whist and a frolic called 'laugh and lay down, which is great vogue amongst us'. At one of these parties, Mrs Greville, it seems, added to the fun by setting her head on fire.[2] It was the ladies' condition which attracted most attention, for they were either with child or doing their best to become so, the Tunbridge waters being expected to aid pregnancy once established, or to prevent it if threatened. Georgiana reported on 26 October that Lady Clermont had miscarried, adding the delicious gossip, 'To tell you the truth as it is pretty certain Mr Marsden the apothecary was the Father, I fear some wicked method was made use of to procure abortion, and this is more likely as Mr Marsden might bring the drogue from his own shop. You will allow that her toothache was very symptomatical, tho she carryd the affair off with her usual art.'[3] This letter confirms that Georgiana occasionally scratched out her own writing, for she defies her mother to decipher it, but she makes even more mysterious the moral standards which they all lived by, as this astonishing news about Lady Clermont did not outrage the pious Lady Spencer as much as one might expect; subsequent months and years show Lady Clermont staying as welcome guest with the Spencers at Althorp and Holywell.

Occasionally Georgiana was able to visit Camp at Cox Heath, where she found that the Duke was tanned to the colour of mahogany and had improved his saluting to such a degree that 'he is reckon'd to have saluted the best of anybody'.[4] One evening there was great confusion in the tent 'for I was to undress very near in publick, as my bed was brought in by some of the footmen'. The event, though trivial, is worth recording for the presence of Lady Clermont's apothecary lover, who clearly must have travelled around with them. 'I was very near laughing at the gravity with which Marsden brought a chamber pot into the tent,' says Georgiana.[5] She continues to reflect, in French, how nice it would be if Marsden could concoct a bottle

of 'moral spirit' which Georgiana might take whenever she felt
inclined to commit a folly.

   This was no idle chatter; Georgiana was carefully preparing
her mother for some worrying news. Back at Tunbridge Wells
she wrote to Mama, 'I had rather not see you than see you
because a certain thing has happen'd – I cannot help having
some faith in my presentiment.'[6] Georgiana was concerned
about the lateness of her period, which she referred to archly as
'the Prince'. That turned out to be a false alarm, but Lady
Spencer was still not free from anxiety, for Georgiana confided
that she received visits from a 'Green Man', presumably
referring to the jealous intrigues which amused the ladies of
Tunbridge. They did not amuse Lady Spencer. 'What is the
green man about that he stays so long?' she asks. 'I have more
than once found my dearest Georgiana that you make me quite
uncharitable and unchristian. I used to hate no human being
and now I hate almost everything that approaches you that can
hurt you.'[7]

   A circumstance which might 'hurt' Georgiana arose when
Lady Derby ran off with the Duke of Dorset and all the ladies of
society had to decide whether or not they should receive her.
Lady Derby was a popular and affectionate girl, the daughter of
the Duke of Hamilton and the luminous Irish beauty of a
previous era, Elizabeth Gunning. She had married the Earl of
Derby in 1774 at the age of nineteen, with a conspicuous lack of
enthusiasm, and had recently fallen in love with the wicked Duke
of Dorset, a notorious womaniser who had counted
'everybody's mistress' Nancy Parsons among his amours. That
would have been fair enough, had not the young lady committed the unforgivable sin of leaving the marital home to go and
live with her Duke. Georgiana, who was friendly with Dorset,
begged her mother's permission to visit Lady Derby, for whom
she felt sorry in view of the ostracism she suffered from everyone
else. Lady Spencer was quite adamant in her refusal, talking of
Lady Derby's 'crime' and her 'guilt', going so far as to say that
she 'insults the world with her Vice'. She took the cue to show
oblique disapproval for Georgiana's other friends:

   If you sacrifice so much for a person who never was on a
   footing of Friendship, what are you to do if Lady J[ersey] or

Lady M[elbourne] should proceed (and they are already far
on their way) to the same lengths?[8]

When Georgiana appeared slow to learn the lesson, her
mother was obliged to write in yet stronger language:

Consider if you were now to see Lady D[erby] again in even so
private a manner, you could not refuse doing it when she
became Duchess of D[orset], and from that moment your
Father and I should be oblig'd to forbid your Sister ever
coming into your house.[9]

In fact, the unfortunate woman never did become Duchess.
Lord Derby in righteous fury burnt her portrait and refused to
divorce her, being determined at all costs to prevent her re-
marriage. She was ruined for life by the sorry adventure. What is
most bewitching is the light it throws upon a moral system which
could destroy a woman for daring to find love outside marriage,
when marriage itself had failed to engender any such settlement,
while allowing Lady Clermont incongruously to submit to a
nasty abortion after a clandestine affair with the resident
chemist, without damage to her fame and reputation.

Wisely, Lady Spencer warned Georgiana that she might
expect to be pilloried for her imprudence. 'I cannot feel comfortable my dearest Georgiana while I know there is anything unpleasant in your situation which I think there is at present,' she
wrote. 'Your conduct from being irreproachable will possibly be
the subject of every ill natur'd lampoon or libel, for you must
expect to classed with the company you keep.'[10] The prog-
nostication proved accurate, for when the Devonshires
returned to London in November, they had to withstand an un-
precedented onslaught from the press, which was amazingly
free from inhibition in making frankly libellous and insulting
attacks on public figures. 'You know how exaggerated are the
English newspapers,' Comte d'Adhémar told his superiors in
Paris. 'To be obliged to drink this daily cup in this country is no
small ordeal.'[11] Georgiana was fair game because the satirists
believed she was not setting the example which should be
expected of her; she suffered the fate of all who attract public
attention without appearing to deserve it. Most of the scurrilous
lampoons put about in pamphlet form were anonymous, but

William Combe was known to be the author of some which charged the Duchess with irresponsibility, such as a silly poem entitled *The Duchess of Devonshire's Cow*. Her friends were loudly indignant. 'The scribblers weekly let fly their pop-guns at the Duchess of Devonshire's feathers,' said one. 'Her Grace is innocent, good-humoured and beautiful; but these adders are blind and deaf and cannot be charmed.'[12]

One pamphlet chastised Georgiana for being ready to have a good time: 'When you began to breathe from the hurry which must have accompanied your marriage with the Duke of Devonshire, and to turn your thoughts to the character you ought to support in the world; it was rather singular that among the many parts of importance and dignity which solicited your choice, you should fix upon one so trifling in its nature and so unworthy your rank and understanding as the Dispenser of Fashions and the Genius of Pleasure.' Another example, extending to more than a hundred pages and called *An Interesting Letter to the Duchess of Devonshire,* sought more firmly to upbraid her. 'I am fully persuaded', intoned Mr Combe, 'that your Grace might give Vice and Folly a very considerable check by becoming yourself an example of Christian Virtue.' Alas, Georgiana had given the pompous author little hope that she might heed his remonstrances. By being a Priestess of Pleasure and adorning herself in ridiculous fashions, she had given 'the same decoration to every unhappy Female who patrols the purlieus of Prostitution'. There might still be time for repentance, however. 'Instead of unfolding your charms to catch the gaze of a curious multitude, or as traps for the flattering and admiration of the idle and dissipated Men of Fashion which surround you, instead of resting your consequence on that Beauty whose duration will be so short, use the winning graces which are yours to give Virtue its most lovely appearance. . . . Extend your example to the applause and imitation of distant Times, when your fine form shall be mouldered into dust.'

Not the least disquieting reflection that beset Georgiana as she read these lines was that her mother, in less verbose and grandiloquent fashion, had been saying much the same thing for four years. Combe came close to insult when he lectured Georgiana with the remark that 'high rank does not sanctify

Folly', and compared her to an ostrich, that foolish bird and hopeless mother – 'She drops her eggs in the sand.'

Like everyone else, Georgiana simply had to learn to tolerate attacks of this kind. Fox, Sheridan, the Prince of Wales himself, were all regularly belittled and calumniated in print, and while it might be irritating to some and infuriating to others, it was for most a precious freedom which they did not wish to see compromised. Sheridan, who was made miserable by scandal, nevertheless maintained that the freedom of the press must remain unfettered. 'Even one hundred libels had better be ushered into the world', he thought, 'than one prosecution be instituted which might endanger the liberty of the press of this country.'

The following summer Georgiana went with her parents and sister to Spa, returning in September, when their packet was unsuccessfully attacked in the Channel by French privateers. Georgiana joined her husband on further military manoeuvres at Warley Camp, and was back in London for the first night of Sheridan's latest play *The Critic*, which she thought was 'vastly good . . . it occasion'ed peals of laughter ev'ry minute'. She went in company with Lady Melbourne, while the Duke and Charles James Fox were in Mrs Sheridan's box.[13] A sadder event was the death of David Garrick, at whose funeral both the Duke of Devonshire and Lord Spencer were pall-bearers.

Georgiana's customary merriment concealed from outsiders her real anxiety during this month, an anxiety which she confided only to her mother at the privacy of her writing-table. She wanted desperately to give the Duke children, yet the years passed and still she appeared to be barren. Now, in October, she again thought she might be pregnant, and once more she used the code of 'the Prince' to refer to her period. 'The Prince is not come yet but my pains are frequent. I continue the Spa water,' she wrote on 12 October. Two days later, 'I have no Prince yet but the strongest signs of him, pains both behind and before that are very clear.' Mama counselled that she should avoid eating fruit or walnuts, but whatever other thoughts she may have had have been denied us forever, as a whole page of her letter has been torn off. Obviously, the moment passed disappointingly, for a month later Georgiana is again in hopes that she might be carrying, and her correspondence is obsessed with the pregnancies of other women; Lady Jersey has just given birth to a daughter, why cannot she? Teasingly, but with an edge of unhappiness, she thought there was more likelihood of her mother conceiving again, to which Lady Spencer retorted that 'I have done entirely with the follies you hint at'. Then, on 14 November 1779, comes confirmation that hopes are frustrated: 'As for me', says Georgiana, 'the Prince came yesterday so that I am quite in despair.'[14]

For the next two years, the Duchess is increasingly crestfallen about her apparent infertility, as examples of life-giving force abound in her immediate circle to compound her sense of isolation. Unfortunately, she consoled herself more often than not in reckless gambling, but there are signs of a creeping sadness which threatens to repress her lively nature. In March 1780 her attention was momentarily distracted by the Duke's maiden speech in the House of Lords, in which she took considerable pride. Edmund Burke wrote to congratulate her on her husband's performance, claiming that 'it will become, by habit, more disagreeable to him to continue silent on an interesting occasion than hitherto it has been to him, to speak upon it'.[15] Alas, this was the most insubstantial wishful-thinking, for the Duke immediately reverted to his customary mute taciturnity and hardly ever uttered another word in public.

While her brother Lord Althorp was busy wooing Lord Lucan's daughter, Lavinia Bingham, and sister Harriet, now of marriageable age, was being courted by Lord Duncannon, Georgiana suffered another disappointment in April; she talked of being confined and her mother enquired eagerly about her motions, but an early miscarriage presumably followed, for the subject was quickly dropped.[16] Georgiana was beginning to think that she was in some way being punished for her way of life, that the children she wanted 'I am tempted to believe are denied me till I deserve them'.[17] Her response to this realisation was characteristically warm and unexpected; she determined to take charge of the Duke's illegitimate daughter Charlotte, to provide her with education, and, as discreetly as she could, with love. Georgiana's rich maternal impulses, so far thwarted, would generously be turned upon the product of her husband's *amour*, and in lavishing attention upon Charlotte, she would compensate for her failure to provide the Duke with a child from her body.

We do not know how long Georgiana had been aware that her husband had a daughter. In view of the fact that she is not mentioned in letters until 1780, it seems likely that the Duchess had just been told. She welcomed the news with total lack of resentment or displeasure, despite the fact that the girl's age indicated she had been born at about the time of the Duke's marriage. Arrangements were made for Charlotte to be housed with Mrs Garner, wife of the Captain Garner who had bravely defended Georgiana and her parents from attack on their cross-Channel voyage seven months before. The Duke's agent, Mr Heaton, should pay Mrs Garner's rent and her expenses in looking after the girl out of the estate purse, in order to disguise the personal aspect of the arrangement. Mrs Garner duly took residence in the London lodging rented for her on 6 May, and Charlotte arrived two days later.

An initial problem presented itself in deciding what the girl should be called. Until then, she had taken her father's christian name as a surname and had been known as 'Charlotte William'. Lady Spencer thought that the surname 'Ven', from the middle syllable of Cavendish, would be preferable, to avoid confusion with the illegitimate offspring of another peer who also bore the name William, but Georgiana said the girl was already so inquisitive and intelligent that her suspicions would be aroused by a change of name at that stage. Eventually she settled upon 'Williams'.

Georgiana first met her on 8 May. 'She is a very healthy good humour'd looking child', she told her mother, 'not very tall; she is amazingly like the Duke, I am sure you would have known her anywhere. She is the best humour'd little thing you ever saw, vastly active and vastly lively, she seems very affectionate and seems to like Mrs Garner very much. She has not good teeth and has often the toothache, but I suppose that does not signify as she has not changed them yet, and she is the most nervous little thing in the world, the agitation of coming made her hands shake so. . . .'[18] Sensing her daughter's excitement, Lady Spencer was careful to advise some circumspection. 'I hope you have not talk'd of her to people, as that is taking it out of the Duke's and your power to act as you shall hereafter choose about her.'[19] Mrs Garner was instructed to put it about that Charlotte's father was dead and her mother a distant relation of the Spencers. Lord Melbourne was so deceived that he professed to detect a distinct family likeness between Charlotte and Lord Althorp.[20] Charlotte was brought to see the Duke on 15 May, and he was 'vastly pleas'd with her'.

No sooner were Mrs Garner and Miss Williams established than they had to be uprooted to escape the dangers of the Gordon riots, their lodging being very close to some Catholics who were threatened with attack from the mob. Georgiana sent them to stay with the Melbournes at Brocket Hall, while she stayed in London to brave it out. The riots had been started by Lord George Gordon, a fanatical anti-Papist, in opposition to a Bill in Parliament which sought to rescind the oppressive laws against Roman Catholics. Since Charles II's time, Roman Catholics had lived in England as secondary citizens, deprived of an education at public school or university, banned from the House of Commons, prevented from open worship in their chapels. Sir George Savile introduced the Bill, which was a non-party measure, receiving the support of the whole House. Burke and Fox were particularly assiduous in advancing the cause, in which they were abetted by the great Whig families and by the extrovert enthusiasm of the Duchess of Devonshire and her friends.

Lord George Gordon, however, convinced no doubt that he was on the side of God, took the debate out of Parliament and inflamed the superstitious and illiterate in the streets of London with his forebodings of Papist ascendancy. In a very short time, he was followed by a thoughtless mob bent on insurrection and eager to vent their aroused energies in destruction. An angry crowd marched from the East End to Mayfair and Westminster, sacking the chapels of foreign Ambassadors, setting fire to houses which belonged to known Catholics, and finally turning their attacks to the mansions of Whig families. Georgiana had to escape from Devonshire House by a back door in the night, and take refuge with Lady Clermont, sleeping in a tent fixed up in the drawing-room. Eventually she was forced to move out to Chiswick, the Duke's small country estate to the West, declaring that if she could lay her hands on Gordon, she would happily kill him herself.[21]

The riots were subdued only by the intervention of the military and the firm courage of the King, but not before much of London had been set on fire and anything up to two hundred people had been killed. Gordon was incarcerated in the Tower of London, where he repented his role in unleashing the horror and even earned the pity of the Duchess. By July it was safe for her to move back to Devonshire House.*

One of the consequences of the upheaval was a General Election in the autumn of 1780, at which Fox was elected for Westminster, notwithstanding the King's having spent £8,000 in an attempt to prevent him, and a candidate new to politics came in to represent Stafford. It was in conversation at Devonshire House one evening that the idea was suggested to Richard Brinsley Sheridan that he should stand for Parliament. He needed little persuading. Georgiana was instrumental in securing a seat for him, as she prevailed upon her parents to use their considerable influence in Stafford in his support. Sheridan quite properly wrote to thank Georgiana; still under thirty, he had already scaled every rung of the ladder to wordly success. From being the son of an impoverished actor, he had risen to be the owner of the Drury Lane Theatre, London's best, to be the favourite dramatist of the day, a friend of the aristocracy, and now a politician allied to the most brilliant *côterie*. A month later, he was elected a member of Brooks's Club, on the sponsorship of Fitzpatrick (two earlier attempts by Fox to have him admitted had failed). He needed only the *cachet* of a forbidden love affair to become society's darling, and this was not to be denied him for long.

At the same time, Georgiana's sister Harriet became a fully-fledged member of the set by reason of her betrothal to Lord Duncannon, son and heir to the Earl of Bessborough, and a first cousin to the Duke of Devonshire. Duncannon's mother was a Cavendish, the daughter of the 3rd Duke of Devonshire, so was his uncle's wife. The Cavendishes, the Spencers and the Ponsonbys had known one another all their lives, and this ideal marriage would bind them ever more closely together. Duncannon was a serious, sober young man, totally uninterested in

---

* Lord George Gordon was arraigned before the House and escaped sentence on the evidence that he had attempted to stop the riots. He later became a Jew and died in Newgate Prison.

politics, much more inclined towards country avocations. He
was a collector of fine art and a relatively solitary man; grand
parties he abhorred. Indeed, he possessed all the qualities of admirable dullness that Lady Spencer could wish for her daughter.
It was a pity only that the Bessboroughs were poor and could
provide only £2,000 a year for the Duncannons to live on, plus
£400 pin-money for Harriet.

Harriet, on the other hand, now nineteen years old, was an
adorable, vivacious creature, widely admired, and clearly
destined to be as much an adornment in society as her sister. She
was more regularly beautiful than Georgiana, and probably
more clever, her intelligence not subject to such breathtakingly
erratic fancies as her sister's. Men would happily discuss politics
and literature with her without feeling they need condescend.
But she was deeply fond of Georgiana and could easily perceive
the attractions of self-indulgence in Georgiana's life; it was too
much to expect that Harriet should resist her sister's example,
even though her income was a mere fraction of the resources
available to the Duchess of Devonshire. Mama saw the dangers
and dreaded Georgiana's influence:

> Think of this most seriously my dearest Georgiana and let
> your affection for her prompt you to avoid with the utmost
> care leading her in the smallest degree into your way of life or
> set of company.[22]

Georgiana was of course quick to aver that nothing could be
farther from her mind, but mother and daughter both knew that
Georgiana was simply incapable of keeping a promise of this
sort. When Mama even suggested that it might be better for her
to stop seeing Lady Melbourne, she told her, 'I hope you will
not object to my continuing a friendship which it would be so
terrible for me to break off.'[23] Lady Spencer viewed the helter-
skelter of undesirable examples which threatened Harriet, with
impotent concern. She might also have noticed that the new
member of Brooks's Club and her own *protégé* as fresh Member
of Parliament, that attractive young Sheridan, was paying her a
little too much attention. The marriage took place in
November, the Duncannons spending their honeymoon at their
residence in Roehampton, not far from Mama in Wimbledon.

Shortly afterwards, Lord Althorp declared that he would

marry Lavinia Bingham, eldest daughter of Lord Lucan. This time there was no family connection to suggest the match, and moreover Lucan had only recently been ennobled, but these considerations were set aside in the light of Althorp's evident enthusiasm and Lavinia's modest, sensible character; it was a relief that she was not a wild sensualist given to larks. They married in March 1781, with blessings all round.

In the summer, Georgiana went with the Duke to camp with his militia at Plympton, where she learnt that on 31 August Harriet Duncannon had given birth to her first child, John William Ponsonby, exactly nine months after her marriage.* Georgiana was hugely excited, and not a little envious. She begged her mother to give her all details concerning the little boy, what colour were his eyes, is he pretty, does Harriet suckle him? At the same time, she received a childish note from Charlotte Williams, then being looked after by Lady Spencer while the Devonshires were at Plympton, saying 'Dear Dutchess, I have done my French lessons very well today. I love you dearly and long to see you. Your dutiful Charlotte.'[24] It was nice, certainly, to receive a fond note from the Duke's daughter, but how much nicer it would have been had she been her own! 'How much more than words can express should I be oblig'd to dear demure Dr Denman† would he enable me to give little Ponsonby a Playfellow or a wife', she told her mother.[25]

At the end of the year, Althorp made his maiden speech in the House of Lords, an occasion which excited general interest and such attention that, as Dr Moore reported to Georgiana, 'a pin would have been heard to fall on the floor'.[26] By another report she was told that her sister-in-law was expecting a baby. It was all too unfair. After seven years of marriage, Georgiana was beginning to have serious doubts about her fertility. In spite of repeated attempts, a successful pregnancy was denied her, and the sadness which had invaded her heart the previous year now assumed ghastly proportions. (The fact that neither she nor the Duke was moved by the impulse of love cannot have made their attempts at parenthood any easier). In vain did Mama beseech her not to be disappointed; the worry of her situation was affecting her health, she complained of listlessness, inertia, ner-

---

* He grew up to be the 4th Earl of Bessborough.
† Dr Thomas Denman, accoucheur.

vousness and tormenting headaches. Her eyes especially were giving her trouble. After a fearful application of a solution of water, brandy and vinegar to one inflamed eye proved to do more harm than good, the Duke's physician prescribed washing it in warm milk.

In May 1782 the Devonshires went to Bath. Georgiana wrote her mother a letter which so lacked the vivacity of earlier years that she had clearly reached the lowest point of her morale.

> Dearest Mama [she said], I am afraid that instead of rejoicing at my letters you will complain of the dullness and stupidity of them – the kind of life I have led lately has put me *hors de mon assiette*, and tho this sounds vain as it implies that I think if I was *quite myself* I should amuse you, yet it is not so as I only mean that I do not feel myself inclin'd or capable to give you those wild *sallies* of my imagination that you used to approve of. Tout cela reviendra.[27]

Then, just as her spirits were most in need of a lift, there came into her life a new friend who was to have the most profound effect upon the course of her destiny. As so often happens, the friend's first entry into the story was subdued. On 22 May, 'The Duke went with me to see Lady Erne and Lady E. Foster . . . by the appearance of things this is the dullest of all places.'[28] Three days later, Lady E. Foster accompanied the Duke and Duchess to a performance of *The Merchant of Venice* in which Mrs Siddons played Portia, and on 1 June Georgiana confirmed that the friendship was ripening: 'Lady Erne and Lady E. Foster are our chief support or else it would be shockingly dull for the D. indeed.'[29]

Before long, Lady E. Foster was the Devonshires' inseparable companion. It was the first time they had encountered someone who awakened the affection of them both and thereby brought them closer together. At last the Duke and Georgiana were sharing something, and far from being wounded that her husband's discontent with the dreariness of Bath could be relieved by another woman, Georgiana was overjoyed, for the lady in question was one of life's casualties, whose unhappiness excited all Georgiana's compassion. Within weeks the trio were on terms of the fondest intimacy.

In her first note to the Duchess, the new friend made an astonishingly prophetic remark. 'Adieu', she said, 'this is a cruel prologue to a very deep tragedy to your own poor little Bess.'[30]

'Bess' was the endearment preferred by Lady Elizabeth Foster.

Chapter Five

MY DEAREST LOVELIEST
DEAREST BESS

'We are delighted with Lady Erne and Lady E. Foster. You cannot conceive how agreeable and amiable they are, and I never knew people have more wit and good nature.'[1]

Georgiana was mistaken. Her mother certainly could conceive how agreeable the distressed sisters could be, for she suspected that they made a profession of making such appeals and she knew only too well what an easy prey they would find in her emotional daughter. From the moment of Lady Elizabeth's appearance on the scene, correspondence between Georgiana and her mother became suddenly more circumspect. Lady Spencer was uneasy about the relationship from the first, from a mixture of motives. She had for years been Georgiana's closest friend as well as her mother, the woman in whom she most readily confided; this position of trust was now threatened by the intervention of a woman whose character and ancestry she did not think suitable to exert disproportionate influence over the personality of her daughter. She was quick to detect an abrupt change in the mood of Georgiana's letters, a definite happiness, and, it must be admitted, she was churlishly jealous that she was not herself responsible for this improvement in her morale.

'Avoid with care all such confidential conversations on other people's matters or your own (and I have reason to believe you often meet with such) as indulge you in a train of idle or pernicious thoughts', wrote Lady Spencer on 26 June, about a month after Lady Elizabeth had insinuated herself into the Devonshire *ménage*. She went on unconsciously to reveal the roots of her disquiet:

Those were happy days my dearest child when every thought

of your innocent heart came rushing out without a wish to disguise it, when my eternal rummages were born with perfect composure without any previous precautions and no little drawers or portefeuille were reserved – have things been better or worse since this has been avoided? . . . I see you on the edge of a thousand precipices, in danger of losing the confidence of those who are dearest to you. . . . I see you running with eagerness to those – must I miscall them friends? – who tho' their intentions may not be wrong, are by constantly talking to you on subjects which are always better avoided become imperceptibly your most hurtful enemies, all these and more keep me on the rack.[2]

Georgiana's letters from this point are markedly more adult, the handwriting more sprawling and carefree, the content swiftly put down with a less deferential regard for her mother's opinion. Gone is the childlike desire to earn approval. Georgiana listens to her mother's admonitions, and as often as not ignores them. Her reply to the above, for example, cheerfully relates that she and Lady Elizabeth have been drawing a picture together. She tries obliquely to divert her mother's fears by showing how worthy of respect is her new friend, 'She delights me by her enthusiasm about you, she says very often that she is sure from what she has heard that the religion you practise is, whilst it diffuses happyness to those around you, what must secure it the most to yourself.' Not only that, but Lady Eliz. adores a country church above all things![3] What could be more admirable? Lady Spencer was not so easily deceived.

Why should she have taken so immediately against Elizabeth Foster? Lady Spencer knew her parents well enough, and knew something of her circumstances – that she had been unhappily married and was now separated from her husband, that she had two little boys who were about to be snatched from her by her husband's agency, that her father was immensely rich yet forced her to live in abject penury. Surely she deserved pity, surely it was not untoward that Georgiana should respond to her need? Georgiana was with her in Bath just at the time her 'poor little children are going from her', as she told her mother, and her personal tragedy had reached the point of maximum harm to her wistful, pathetic psyche. The friendship of the Devonshires might rescue her from the abyss of despair into which fate had plunged her. Lady Spencer thought differently, as she reflected that the woman's father, Lord Bristol, was perhaps England's most bizarre and improper man, in the sense that his behaviour lacked that essential control which befitted a man of quality, that he was the head of a family distinguished for generations by its extreme oddity, and that Lady Elizabeth could not fail to inherit, in some degree, the fatal flaw of personality which erupted from time to time in her family. Elizabeth Foster was a Hervey, and the Herveys were unlike anyone else.

Lady Mary Wortley Montagu, in a challenging and oft-quoted phrase, considered that mankind was divided into Men, Women and Herveys. By this she did not necessarily mean to imply that they were sexually ambiguous, though the excessively cultivated habits of some of them had certainly given rise to suspicions of the sort, but that while other families might stray from the norm in eccentricity and peculiarity, the Herveys were so outrageously unorthodox as to be a law unto themselves. They defied categorisation. With alarming regularity, their genes produced characters who scarcely fitted in with the rest of sane humanity.

The Herveys could boast a lineage dating back to the thirteenth century. They were gifted, intelligent, and brave, wrote poetry and history, liked music, were generously cultured. They resembled one another in feature, having thin, weightless faces and a bony, bird-like frame which seemed hardly substantial enough to fill a suit of clothes. Their freakishness had exploded upon the world comparatively recently.

The first Hervey of note had been elevated to the peerage in 1703 as Baron Hervey of Ickworth and in 1714 as Earl of Bristol. These were rewards for his staunch Whiggery and support of the Hanoverian succession in the House of Commons. Having received his ennoblement, he sensibly retired from public life. Bristol married twice, the first wife producing a son and heir, Carr Hervey, who died unmarried in 1723, but is generally supposed to have been the father of none other than Horace Walpole. Supposed, that is, by everyone but Horace himself, who never doubted that he was the son of the Prime Minister, Sir Robert Walpole, despite the singular lack of resemblance between them. Sir Robert was vast and unwieldy, Horace as fragile a bird as any Hervey.

Be that as it may, the first Lord Bristol's second wife gave him eleven sons and seven daughters, ensuring that within a generation there should be Herveys all over the place; she still found time to have two lovers at once, according to Mary Wortley Montagu. She it was who introduced the peculiar strain into Hervey blood. The eldest of her brood was styled Lord Hervey after the death of his step-brother Carr in 1723 and entered the pages of English literature as the original of Pope's masterfully bitchy satirisation – 'Sporus' –

> What! that thing of silk?
> Sporus! That mere white curd of ass's milk?
> Satire or sense, alas! Can Sporus feel?
> Who breaks a butterfly upon a wheel?
> Yet let me flap this bug of gilded wings,
> This painted child of dirt that stinks and stings!
> Whose buzz the witty and the fair annoys;
> Yet wit ne'er tastes and beauty ne'er enjoys;
> As well-bred spaniels civilly delight
> In mumbling of the game they dare not bite.
> Eternal smiles his emptiness betray,
> As shallow streams run dimpling all the way.
> Whether in florid impotence he speaks,
> And as the prompter breathes the puppet squeaks;
> Or at the ear of Eve, familiar toad!
> Half froth half venom spits himself abroad,
> In pun or politics, or tales or lies,
> Or spite, or smut, or rhymes, or blasphemies.
> His wit all see-saw between that and this,
> Now high, now low, now master up, now miss,
> And he himself one vile antithesis.
> Amphibious thing! that acting either part,
> The trifling head or the corrupted heart,
> Fop at the toilet, flatterer at the board,
> Now trips a lady and now struts a lord.

The portrait is exaggerated and unfair, which is why it is so good. Hervey fought a memorable duel with Pulteney, which ought to have smothered any rumours of effeminacy, but then it

was possible to be foppish without being womanly. He married
Molly Lepell, maid-of-honour to the Queen, admired another
maid-of-honour, Miss Vane, and was loved by the King's
daughter, Princess Caroline. He was quite the wittiest and most
lively person at the Court of George II, leaving us the most vivid
memoirs of the period. Some truth there is behind Pope's
wicked lines: Hervey did drink ass's milk, mainly because his
health was so frail that he had to keep to a rigid diet. Once a
week he ate an apple and took emetics every day. His father
ascribed Hervey's constant illness to an over-indulgence in tea,
but it was more likely to be congenital epilepsy which upset his
system. Sarah, Duchess of Marlborough said he had a painted
face, and not a tooth in his head; Sir Robert Walpole referred to
his 'coffin' face. But there was reason too for his cosmetics: he
wore rouge simply to soften his otherwise ghostly visage.

Lord Hervey predeceased his father, so never inherited the
earldom of Bristol. He had eight children, and his three eldest
sons were 2nd, 3rd and 4th Earls of Bristol in succession, the last
being the father of our Lady Elizabeth. Thus the brilliant,
acerbic and foppish Lord Hervey was uncle to Horace Walpole
and grandfather to Lady Elizabeth Foster.

Hervey's eldest son George became 2nd Earl of Bristol in
1751. He, too, was required to demonstrate that effeminate
manners, and the habit of walking on tip-toe as if stepping
through puddles of water, in no way denoted cowardice. A
brutish bully like Lord Cobham was too thick to understand
this, and once approached Hervey as he was leaning on a chair
talking to some ladies with his hat held loosely in his hand, and
promptly spat into it. Then he laughed aloud and told his companion Nugent that he had won his bet. Hervey quietly asked if
Cobham had any further use for his hat. 'Oh, I see you are
angry,' said Cobham. 'Not very well pleased,' replied Hervey,
whereupon Cobham took the hat and wiped it clean,
apologising profusely. He thought the matter would end there
as a silly joke, but Hervey the next day with greatest dignity
asked to whom he should address himself for satisfaction,
having been insulted in public, to Nugent or to Cobham?
Cobham was required eventually to write submissive letters of
apology in order to avoid loud humiliation, and Hervey was
triumphant. This was Lady Elizabeth's uncle.

Her next uncle was Augustus Hervey, an Admiral in the Navy, who on a foolish impulse one day in 1744 married the foul-mouthed, ambitious and beautiful Elizabeth Chudleigh only to separate from her soon afterwards. The marriage was secret, but rumours were sufficiently widespread to cause embarrassment to them both, until with the connivance of Augustus, Miss Chudleigh brought a suit of jactitation against him accusing him of having falsely boasted of being married to her. The verdict was carried in her favour, and Hervey was sworn to silence. Four weeks later, she achieved her greatest ambition by marrying her lover the Duke of Kingston. When the Duke died, his family arraigned her before the House of Lords on a charge of bigamy, bringing witnesses to prove that she was already married to Augustus Hervey and had borne him a child. The case was justly celebrated, causing a furore of epic proportions in 1776, only two years after Georgiana had married the Duke of Devonshire, so that the affair was still prominently in the memory of all pro-tagonists in 1782. The farce was further compounded when Augustus succeeded as 3rd Earl of Bristol in the same year, thus making Miss Chudleigh a genuine Countess as well as a bogus Duchess. She was found guilty and banished, though she con-tinued to be known by her spurious ducal title.

Augustus died in 1779, making his brother, the Bishop of Derry, Elizabeth Foster's father, 4th Earl. Before we consider his character and career, there are two more Herveys worthy of note. Thomas Hervey, younger brother of Pope's Sporus, was a friend of Dr Johnson and wrote the famous postscript to a letter, 'P.S. I am going to part with my wife.' Another member of the family wore padded waistcoats to fight his duels and kept his father tied to a bear. Lord Lonsdale was fond of relating an incident when a man tried to insult this Hervey. He walked up to him in a coffee-house and said, 'I smell an Irishman', to which Hervey retorted, 'You shall never smell another', and cut off his nose with a knife.

No wonder, then, that Lady Spencer had misgivings that one of this strange brood should be on terms of intimacy with her beloved daughter. The 4th Earl of Bristol was a notoriously un-predictable character, who had wanted to make a career in law, but opted for the church in the hope that it might be more lucrative. With the help of his elder brother, he was made

Bishop of Cloyne, and later advanced to the Bishopric of Derry. He was an extremely good Bishop, careful and attentive to the interests of the parishes, by no means a distant or an absent figure. There were manifestations of oddness, however. Whimsy, for one. He instructed neighbouring parishes to build spires on their churches, that he might enjoy a better view. Grandeur, for another: he built a pretentious palace at Downhill which he furnished with the most exquisite examples of modern Italian secular taste. And even his religion was in question; those who met him could never be sure whether or not he believed in a Christian God, and there were many who suspected he was supremely indifferent to such matters. Certainly his conversation, well informed and wise, was equally blasphemous and disrespectful.

The Bishop of Derry had married Elizabeth Davers, daughter of a Suffolk baronet, who gave him two sons and three daughters. The second daughter, Elizabeth Christiana, was born at Horringer in Suffolk in 1757, which made her an exact contemporary of Georgiana. The children grew up happily near Ickworth, the seat of their uncle the Earl of Bristol, and were much beloved by their parents, who themselves doted on each other. The idyll was, however, short-lived. The Bishop conceived a ridiculous passion for being at the scene of every event in Europe, which meant that he was constantly travelling, dragging his young family with him, from hotel to hotel. He was present at riots, rushed to the arena of the latest scandal, made his poor family climb the Alps, and was seriously injured by wishing to watch an eruption of Vesuvius from too close quarters. All the time, of course, he was buying up *objets d'art* and furniture and having them shipped over to England. The one benefit which devolved upon the children from these peregrinations was a mastery of French and Italian; otherwise they were denied a normal home life, educated in a variety of places before settling with a Mademoiselle Chomel in Geneva, and forever packing trunks.

In 1779 Frederick Hervey succeeded to the earldom of Bristol on the death of his brother, and would henceforth be known as the 'Earl-Bishop'. A number of hotels throughout Europe renamed themselves 'Hotel Bristol' in honour of his esteemed patronage over the years, and some of these still receive charabancs of American tourists. Shortly after the Comte d'Adhémar was appointed Ambassador to the Court of St James, Lord Bristol wrote a letter of congratulations, which shows at least that he had a sense of humour and did not take himself seriously all the time. 'Est-il bien possible?' he said. 'Le Comte d'Adhémar se trouve depuis quelques mois à Londres et l'Evêque de Derri n'en a rien su, et le Comte de Bristol n'en a point été informé! Voilà ce qui arrive à des Rustiques!'*[4] The house and estate at Ickworth were now his, together with a vast inheritance. Domestic quietude did not, alas, follow; instead, the Earl-Bishop turned his grandiose schemes to the pleasant house and set about 'improving' it. Elizabeth was now twenty-two, and had been married for three years to a man called John Thomas Foster; husband and wife moved into Ickworth.

Elizabeth always protested that she had married very much against her will. 'I really did on my knees ask not to marry Mr F. and said his character terrified me, and they both have since said it was their doing my being married to him,' she told Georgiana.[5] John Thomas Foster was the son of one of the Earl-Bishop's Irish friends, the Reverend Dr John Foster of Dunleer; he was also a member of the Irish House of Commons. Very little else is known about him. The marriage took place in Brussels in 1776 and the couple settled down in Dunleer, a place too dreary for Elizabeth, who brooded in isolation. She bore him two sons, Frederick in 1777, and Augustus, born at Ickworth in 1780 when the Fosters had moved to the ancestral home. Shortly after this, the marriage collapsed beyond repair, owing to Mr Foster's intractable character; he was 'parsimonious, exacting, irascible, intemperate, and unfaithful'.[6] A terrible row occurred one day in London, after which Lady Bristol refused ever to have dealings with her son-in-law again, though Elizabeth, by her own account, vowed to suppress her misery and do her duty. 'I really told him at that crisis in London that his conduct had lost my affections but that I should fulfill all my duties towards him, and he should never know that I was un-happy,' she wrote. 'And more, that if there was any éclat about my maid, which he dreaded, I would go with him wherever he

---

* Could it be? The Comte d'Adhémar has been in London for several months, and the Bishop of Derry knew nothing about it, nor was the Earl of Bristol informed! You see what happens to country-folk!

chose, to any part of the world, as I never would quit him in any misfortune. It was after all that, that he went down to Ickworth and my mother would not see him.'[7] The implication is that Mr Foster showed rather too much attention to his wife's maid-servant.

Everything went wrong for Elizabeth Foster. Her husband was not interested in her loyalty; he demanded separation, and successfully claimed custody of the two children. Her father, moreover, turned viciously against her, refusing to offer any financial aid now that she was living without support and forcing her instead to subsist on charity in cheap lodgings. Thus, in 1782, she was at the lowest ebb. She had gone to Bath with her sister, Lady Erne (whose marriage had also disintegrated), presumably to settle her nerves, for the two little boys were due to be removed from her care that summer to be brought up in Ireland; she would wait fourteen years before she saw them again. She described herself at this point in her life, 'without a guide; a wife, and no husband, a mother, and no children . . . by myself alone to steer through every peril that surrounds a young woman so situated'.[8] A pitiful creature, indeed. All she had were her natural charms, 'manners that pleased' (in her own words), a desire to be loved and approved, and a wish for friendship.

To make matters worse, later that year her parents had an almighty squabble from which they never recovered. The story is that they went out for a drive together one afternoon and returned in dead silence, never to speak to each other again. Nobody has revealed what happened or what was said during what should have been a normal, pleasant ride. The Earl-Bishop seems to have considered the release from conjugal ties as a cue to unleash all the latent lunacy in his blood. Without telling his wife, he let their London home in St James's Square for a rent of £700 a year and disappeared again to the Continent, where he spent lavishly; all this while expecting his disconsolate daughter to live on £300 a year. Walpole spoke scathingly of him, notwithstanding that he was probably his uncle. 'In truth, his extravagant indecency has been as serviceable to the Government, as overwhelming to himself. His immorality, martial pretences, and profaneness, covered him with odium and derision. Blasphemy was the puddle in which he washed away his episcopal Protestantism,' he told Sir Horace Mann, calling Hervey the 'mitred Proteus' and claiming he was such a hypocrite as now to be seeking favour with the Church of Rome. 'Do you know that this champion of liberty was so violent an anti-American, that when last at Paris, he was so abusive on Dr Franklin and the Colonies, that he was ordered to depart on pain of the Bastile?' Walpole did not mince his words – the Earl was nothing short of 'detestable'; he wore diamond buckles on his shoes, courted publicity, lived grandly on £25,000 a year, and suffered his daughters to be paupers;[9] even the meagre £300 promised to Elizabeth was not forthcoming.

Such was the position of Lady Elizabeth Foster when Georgiana and the Duke made her acquaintance at Bath that summer, and Lady Spencer would reflect with discomfort that it was she who had first brought the woman to her daughter's notice. The pathos of her story, weighted no doubt in her favour as she herself makes quite clear in begging Georgiana not to believe rumours which circulate to her discredit ('the stories you hear of me pray communicate to me that at least I may be justified to you, and that you may know truth from falsehood'),[10] was rendered irresistible by the frailty of her health and her constant racking cough. Georgiana took her part without hesitation. 'If you see Lady Bristol', she told her mother on 8 June, 'I wish you would say as from yourself that the D and I are very happy in seeing a great deal of Lady Erne and Lady Eliz, for that strange man Lord Bristol is, I have a notion, acting the strangest of parts by Lady Eliz and we thought perhaps if it was known we saw something of them it might make him ashamed of not doing something for her.'[11]

The Devonshires decided that they would do something for her. In Georgiana's case, the 'something' meant bestowal of her deepest affection, an emotion she possessed in abundant measure and which had throughout the years of her marriage been frustrated by the coldness of the Duke. As for the Duke, his response to Lady Elizabeth was identical in appearance but fundamentally different in essence. Yes, he felt sorry for her, in a way he had never been required to feel sorry for Georgiana, but there was something about Elizabeth which excited emotion of a different order. She was undeniably prettier than Georgiana, and while everybody loved Georgiana's personality, it was easier

for men to be infatuated with Elizabeth's looks, with her frail
femininity. The Duke was a changed man in her company, more
ready to mix in frivolous society, more given to laughter,
altogether more at ease. Georgiana was delighted to see her
husband relax at last.

On 29 June, all three moved to Plympton, where they spent
the most delightful summer of their lives, a summer all three
were to look back upon in years to come as a period of un-
relieved happiness. The Duke was constantly in the company of
both his ladies, and the three of them adopted private
nicknames for each other which they would retain forever.
Devonshire was called 'Canis' because of his devotion to dogs, a
devotion which Elizabeth fortunately shared, though there were
some who thought her ostentatious fondling of the animals was
a trifle affected; there was, indeed, much about her manner that
seemed contrived, including that awful 'Hervey whine' in her
voice, but the Duke was unobservant, being happy only that his
beloved pets were so pampered. Elizabeth herself was called
'Racky', probably owing to her cough, and Georgiana was
known as 'Mrs Rat' for reasons which have disappeared.

At Plympton they were a jolly crowd that summer. There were
Lady Erne, and Georgiana's aunt Mrs Poyntz, poor Lady
Lincoln who had not long to live, talented Mrs Siddons, Lady
Conyngham and Lady Drogheda. Georgiana's letters home
were genuinely happy; she did not need any longer to invent
news to please her mother, and the melancholy she had felt in
June had gone without trace. 'We all go on deliciously here', she
said, 'and are so comfortable that we look upon it as a misfortune when we are obliged to go out.'[12] The trio were joined by
sister Harriet and her husband Lord Duncannon. Still the idyll
continued. There were odd sentences in Georgiana's letters
which caused Lady Spencer to wonder. 'We stayed at home all
the evening', she wrote on 29 August; 'we drew and the Duke
and Lady Eliz read.'[13] Could it not be that the Duke and Lady
Elizabeth were spending too much time in joint amusements?
And what were they reading? *Les Liaisons Dangereuses* and
Rousseau's recently published *Confessions* are two books
shamelessly mentioned by the Duchess as being avidly devoured
by the little company.

The Duke, Georgiana, Harriet and Lady Elizabeth were

united in one paramount purpose at Plympton that summer, namely how best to ensure that the Duchess should become pregnant. It was now a matter of urgency that the Duke should have a direct heir, for his sister-in-law, Lady George Cavendish, was expecting a baby in January who, if it was a boy, would be heir presumptive to the Devonshire titles and estates after the Duke and his brother George. Mama, too, was anxious from a distance to promote the longed-for event. 'I thank you from the very bottom of my heart for your goodness in wishing me to have children,' Georgiana told her in August. Now another ally was enlisted to help the cause. Dr John Moore, a man of letters as well as a physician, was a trusted friend of the Devonshire clan and happened to be in Plympton. Moreover, he was one of the many who admired Georgiana above all other women, and once charmingly told her, 'The particular disposition of mind and those qualities which form the special parts of your character, would have attached me, had I only heard that such a woman existed at Constantinople.'[14] Dr Moore's counsel was sought. The precise nature of his advice is not clear. All we know is that he recommended the Duchess should drink lots of milk and ride often, but it is difficult to believe anyone could have expected the strictest obedience to those rules alone would produce pregnancy. Whatever the case, in September Georgiana conceived, and Dr Moore was inordinately proud of the part he had played in the great event. Months later, he confessed:

> I shall carry through life the pleasing reflection that what I again and again assured you (as soon as I was fully made acquainted with your situation at Plympton) would happen, has happened, and I shall likewise die in the Faith that it happened through my advice. It was the most earnest wish of my soul to contribute to your happiness – I have obtained my wish – and there is every reason to believe you will have repetitions of the same source of happiness for many years to come.[15]

As soon as Georgiana knew she was carrying, her health relapsed and she weakened alarmingly, giving rise to fears that she might suffer yet another miscarriage. At this point, Lady Elizabeth's presence proved crucial, and the foundations for the rock-solid friendship between the two women which would

endure every assault in the years ahead was laid during those
weeks of October and early November 1782. Quite simply, Bess
looked after Georgiana with uncommon devotion and nursed
her through the difficult period. Between them, she and Dr
Moore ensured that the baby should survive the mother's feeble
condition. For that, Georgiana was to be eternally grateful. This
is why there are so many teasing references made by both
women to the fact that the baby is as much Elizabeth's as
Georgiana's.

At the time, something more murky was suspected, in view of
the Duke's evident attachment to Bess. The suspicions have
endured for two hundred years. True, Elizabeth did become the
Duke's mistress before long, but to suggest, as one recent
account has, that all three went to bed together at Plympton, is
unwarranted speculation.* Georgiana made the record quite
plain in a letter the following year: 'You have saved your brother
Canis and dear Canis' child,' she told Bess,

> What could be more interesting than our journey last year, a
> man and a woman endowed with every amiable quality and
> loving one another as brother and sister, nursing and taking
> care of a woman who was doatingly fond of them and who
> bore within her the child that was to fulfill the vows and wishes
> of all three.[16]

Perhaps Georgiana was a trifle naïve in seeing the relationship
between her husband and her friend as purely fraternal, though
it may well have been at that stage. But there is nothing more
mysterious. The vows they all three made were to see that the
Duchess bore children by keeping her quiet and at home during
the early stages of pregnancy instead of allowing her to indulge
in the usual 'dissipation'. They also vowed to remain loyal to
one another despite gossip. If Dr Moore's role in the conception
is enigmatic, Elizabeth's certainly is not.

---

* Arthur Calder-Marshall, in *The Two Duchesses* (1978), advances the theory
that the Duke was excited by Elizabeth in order to effect penetration with
Georgiana. There is no evidence that the Duke and Duchess had a 'sexual
problem'; indeed, she had been pregnant before without difficulty on his part.
Any man who has attempted coition by this means may well think it unlikely to
produce results.

Meanwhile, news arrived that Lord Spencer was seriously ill. His wife had taken him to Hotwells in Bristol and asked the Duke and Georgiana to visit them there. She did not, however, extend the invitation to Lady Elizabeth, as she did not wish to encourage whispers that the *ménage à trois* was decidedly odd. She put it in a tactful way: 'Your father is too ill to see a stranger with any comfort,' she said. But Georgiana was adamant. 'Lady Eliz comes with us, my dearest Mama', she wrote, 'and, poor little soul, it is impossible it should be otherwise, but my father need not mind her in the least, she is the quietest little thing in the world, and will sit and draw in a corner of the room, or be sent out of the room, or do whatever you please.'[17]

Alas, we cannot know how the sojourn passed, well or ill, for naturally there were no letters between any of the principal actors, all of them being gathered together under one roof for the first, and indeed the last time.

After two weeks in Bristol, the Devonshires and Bess went first to Bath and then on to London, and Bess was given a room at Devonshire House, in preparation for her departure to Nice. It had been decided that the best way financial support could be offered to Bess without causing tongues to wag more than was necessary would be to appoint her governess to Charlotte Williams, send them both to Europe for a while, and provide for their upkeep. The money would ostensibly be used for Charlotte's education, but in reality would also give Bess an income and a purpose. Besides which, with the Duchess confined, it would be better that both the Duke's child and his 'sister' should be absent for a while. Thus several birds would very neatly be despatched with one stone.

Not only that, but there was much exciting work going on at Chatsworth, to which Georgiana had also to give her attention. It was both in accordance with prevailing fashion, and with Georgiana's own natural inclination, that the private apartments of the house be restored and refurbished rather than demolished and rebuilt. The private rooms today are to a significant degree as Georgiana left them. Her dressing-room was fitted with a chimney piece by Henry Watson (descended from Samuel Watson, a carver at Chatsworth under the 1st Duke), and a ceiling by Joseph Palfreyman, both still there. She and the Duke were the first to employ Anglo-French craftsmen, with the result that they assembled the largest collection of furniture by François Hervé, much of which is, again, still in use.*

Bess, Charlotte and Mrs Garner left England on 29 December 1782 for an indefinite period. In fact, they would be away for eighteen months, an absence which Georgiana would find almost unendurable. Already in January she was missing Bess, whose mother wrote from Ickworth, 'I saw your Duchess several times before I left Town. She behaved like an angel in everything, supported her loss with fortitude and felt it with the utmost tenderness, was warm and interested about you to the smallest trifle, and infinitely kind to me on your account.'[18] Elsewhere Lady Bristol referred to Georgiana as 'your heavenly friend'. The Duchess then began a series of extraordinary letters to Lady Elizabeth, full of overflowing endearments such as she had never expressed to anyone else. The first came from Devonshire House, and began, 'I judge of you by myself, my dearest, dearest, dearest Bess, my lovely friend, nothing would give me so much pleasure as an unexpected letter from you.'[19] Another typical example begins, 'my dearest loveliest dearest Bess, my angelic dearest dear love', and ends pathetically, 'but why don't I hear from you? God bless you, do write, I beg it on my knees.'[20] Emotion at this pitch passed between the two women for months on end. Bess's letters were equally as 'gulchy' (to use one of their favourite words), but there is undeniably something studied about them. When Georgiana poured forth her unrestrained ardour, her heart wrote directly on to the page, without pause for grammatical attention or even punctuation. Bess's replies are more correct, as if the apparently spontaneous emotion has been tutored. The endearments are usually a preamble or a postscript to a request for more money. In June 1783, for instance, came this note:

Dearest ever ever dearest Love, why have I no letters from you? I cannot express nor describe the anxiety I feel from it, nor how my peace depends on everything that concerns you . . . how necessary you are to my heart.

* Further details may be obtained from the *Burlington Magazine*, June 1980, 'A Neo-classical episode at Chatsworth', by Ivan Hall.

And so on for some lines. Then to the finance:

> You will allow me to *borrow* it of you, let it my love be a debt, and do not with your usual liberality supply the wants my weakness creates to me.[21]

Not that Bess was not sincere. Merely she had to think and reflect how to keep the friendship alive when she was so far distant and naturally felt isolated. Georgiana did not reflect for two seconds. Her response to the appeal for money was touchingly ingenuous; she felt entirely responsible:

> I am in an agony of despair, my angelic heavenly love . . . you are kept at Turin for want of money. Good God – Good God – and all from my fault. . . . Oh God, what will you do? . . . I send an express to town to stop the 50£ and send it to Turin or if it is gone from London to Parma to send it from thence to Turin. I send 50 tonight, that's a hundred. Canis will give me the day after tomorrow 200 which I shall send, and then I will send 200 or 300 more in three weeks where you will direct me. . . . Do not talk of expence, you would break my heart and neither use Canis or I like Brother and Sister, if you did not spend. . . . God bless you, my angel love, I adore and love you beyond description, but I am miserable till I know you have received this. Canis sends a thousand loves.[22]

With almost every letter, Bess would make some reference to the awful life she had led and the torment of a marriage into which her parents had forced her. She was much given to self-pity, a characteristic many found unattractive but which tied the compassionate Georgiana to her even more tightly. There were long lamentations on 'the too deep impression of the wrongs I have endured and the misfortunes I experience. My heart like a bruised Plant cannot regain its vigour, but droops even in the blest sunshine of your affection.'

The manufactured gush of these sentiments, so ponderously poetic, came close to irritating the Duke, who reproached Bess frequently for dwelling too complacently on her misery and indulging her pessimistic streak. In privacy with his Duchess, he would imitate Bess's voice and mock her whining. 'I am glad dearest Canis still loves his little Bess, and mimicks her', she wrote, 'though it makes you gulchy still it makes me more present to you.' Still she was unable to learn restraint and wrote more and more pages of plangent self-regard:

> Oh my dear dear children, had I them with me I think I should find a resting-place, and maternal fondness should prove a sufficient channel to turn the tide of my tenderness. But even all intercourse is denied me with them, and their cruel father has never even answered my letter: is it not hard upon me? and are not these my early years sadly stamped with griefs and trials? My love, my lovely friends, I have I see been discharging a full heart to you – do not be alarmed, I shall be better after it, but I must write to you as I feel and think, you are my dear object in life, your child shall be my child, and perhaps I may yet see happy days.[23]

There was a moment when Bess saw the devotion of her benefactors perceptibly shift a degree as a result of her own behaviour, and she was terrified. While she had been busy telling them how miserable she was, they received intelligence from other sources which painted quite a different picture. Bess was flirting wildly, received admirers, had even been so festive as to be crowned with flowers at the fountain in Nice. All this accorded ill with the image of a forlorn 'little soul' bemoaning her fate and weeping into her ink-bottle. There was never the remotest danger that she would lose the affection of Georgiana and Canis, but she may not have been so sure of this when she realised that she could be suspected of portraying her life abroad with less than total honesty. Georgiana wrote imploring her to be careful and telling her that the innocence of her conduct blinded her to the wicked interpretations which unpleasant people would place upon it. The stories about the incident in Nice were 'ridiculous', she said.

Bess immediately dashed off a long, abject letter full of excuses and apologies, in which flattery predominated and anxiety intruded at every line. It is not difficult to recognise that Bess was scared. How awful it would be if Georgiana were to turn against her! On her friendship depended the comfort and well-being of her present situation, and on the Duke's good opinion depended the future of their 'brother and sister' relationship. She must tread with the utmost caution. Choosing her words as if her life rested on each one, Bess decided to be submissive. Her letter is unique in their correspondence in making clear the efforts she exerted to ingratiate herself. 'Do not suppose that the flattery that surrounds me deadens me to the sense of imprudence I have been guilty of,' she said. 'The idea of having made you uneasy counterbalances all. I am wretched till I know you again tranquil on my account, and assured that I cannot err against your will again.' She promised she would never again be so silly, 'my ruling sentiment being to please you', and protested that Georgiana could have no sense of obligation 'to such a bankrupt as me. I owe you everything and can repay you nothing.'[24]

The crisis passed and Bess breathed again.

The big event of the year was, of course, the birth of Georgiana's first child, which affected the whole of Whig society, if only because Devonshire House was no longer a rendezvous for everyone while the Duchess was confined. The French Ambassador, busy with the Treaty which was to end the war between France and England, was much put out by it, for he was accustomed to meet the elusive Fox on a daily and casual basis at Devonshire House, where he had himself become enchanted by the constant friendly activity. 'Je passe ma vie avec ses amis,' he injudiciously admitted; d'Adhémar would always 'call in' at the house some time during the day. 'Mr Fox is careful to avoid every possible opportunity to talk politics with me', he said, 'the house of the Duchess of Devonshire, where I usually meet him informally, has been closed to us all for three weeks, owing to the lady's confinement. The painful consequences of this event will doubtless make her invisible for even longer, until she is obliged to leave for the country and I shall be deprived entirely of this daily means of seeing Mr Fox.'[25] This evidence alone, incidentally, makes quite clear the degree of importance attached to the role played by Devonshire House in the political life of London.

In May, Georgiana had written Bess a joint letter with her husband and sister, in which she had said that she was being blooded 'as they are afraid my cough shall hurt your child', and the Duke had said he was 'in whops' that he would soon receive a letter from his 'dearest sweetest Bess'.[26] Harriet Duncannon gave birth to her second child on 6 July, and Georgiana's was born on 12 July. It was not the heir for which they had all so prayed, but a good healthy girl, and the sheer joy of the event deflected any disappointment. The Duke wrote immediately to Bess to inform her, and as soon as Georgiana was strong enough to sit up in bed she gave her friend a detailed and vivid account:

> Canis watches her at my breast . . . how gulchy you would have been at her birth. I was laid on a couch in the middle of my room, my mother and Davis* supported me, Canis was at the door, and the Duchess of Portland† sometimes bending on me and screaming with me and sometimes running to the end of the room and to him. I thought the pain I suffered was so great from being unusual to me . . . some symptoms made me think the child was dead, I said so and Dr Denman only said there is no reason to think so but we must submit to Providence. I had then no doubt and by watching my mother's fine eyes (and this strained mine), I saw she thought it dead, which they all did except Denman . . . when it came into the world I said 'only let it be alive'. The little child seemed to move as it lay beside me but I was not sure, when all at once it cried. Oh God I cried and was quite hysterical – the Duchess and my mother were overcome and cried and all kissed me . . . I fainted. I would not change her for ten sons nor Canis either, nor you either I hope, my Bess.[27]

Upon receipt of the news, Bess declared 'my fondest wish is thus accomplished'. Even at Georgiana's happiest hour, however, she could not resist turning the attention to herself, and measuring the event by the degree of happiness it caused *her*. Because she had had such a hard life, she said, she was not accustomed to such good news, and should be pitied on that account. Georgiana will remember, won't she, Bess's contribution! 'You will know how anxiously my heart watched over you in the first moments of your being with child', and so on, ingratiating herself, wanting to claim an important place for herself in the affair, insisting that no one could be more concerned or happier than she, desperate not to be left out. The personal pronoun 'I' is present throughout. It is a most un-

---

* Probably an assistant accoucheur.
† Sister to the Duke of Devonshire.

attractive response from a woman who feels unfairly treated and is intent on grasping anything which can compensate for past deprivation. She concludes, 'Kiss *our* child for me. How happy are those who have a right to be its godmother, but I am to be its little Mama – Canis said so.'[28] Canis also said that the child was very like Bess 'only she is not so naughty nor so apt to be *vexed*'.[29] Georgiana reported that she was much better now and Bess should not worry; 'if the Gods had made pleasure without pain they would have kept it for themselves'.[30]

Georgiana's daughter and Harriet's son were christened in a double ceremony at Wimbledon in August, with Lord and Lady Spencer and the Duchess of Portland standing godparents to the girl. She was called Georgiana Dorothy. The Duchess continued to feed her at the breast, much to the dismay of her husband, who thought that the longer she did so the longer he would have to wait before he could beget another child. The Duchess of Portland advised Georgiana to drink port in order to fatten up the little girl, but most of the port seems to have been diverted to the maid who was specially employed to take care of the baby, and whom they called 'the Rocker'. The Rocker drank so much that she stank of wine and strong drink whenever she came near the cot, and Georgiana finally got rid of her when she fell down and vomited all over the floor.

Georgiana ceased to feed her daughter after six months, as her milk turned sour in the baby's stomach. This caused the mother inordinate anguish. 'May my dear little child be ever the better for having suck'd me, and oh may she love me or I could not exist,' she cried. She later apologised for an unworthy selfish thought, telling her mother that it was the child's happiness which mattered of course, not her own.

She posed for the famous portrait by Reynolds,* said by many to be among his best, though not a good likeness of Georgiana.

One result of her daughter's birth was the increased fondness Georgiana felt for her husband, whom she now frequently referred to as her 'angel'. He was already a victim of the gout at the age of thirty-five, receiving a stern warning from Erasmus Darwin who told him that wine and spirits, being the product of art, should not be classed among natural food and ought properly to be found in the apothecary's.[31] On his advice, the

* See plate 2.

Duke went to Bath, where he could get drunk only on water, and
from there he wrote Bess a tender, nostalgic note:

> This place has been very unpleasant to me compared with
> what it was a year and a half ago. For then I had the Rat and
> Bess and good health and fine weather, and now I have had
> none of them until a day or two ago the Rat and her young
> one came down here. There are many places in Bath that put
> me so much in mind of you that when I walk about the town I
> cannot help expecting upon turning the corner of a street to
> see you walking along it, holding your cane at each end and
> bending it over your knee, but I have never met you yet and
> what surprises me likewise very much is that somebody or
> other has the impudence to live in your house in Bennet
> Street.[32]

Meanwhile, in Europe, nasty rumours were being spread concerning the nature of the relationship between Bess and the
Duchess. Georgiana had warned Bess to be tactful in her
dealings with Mme de Polignac in Paris, a woman who fancied
herself a close friend of Georgiana's and on that account
resented Lady Elizabeth. Mme de Polignac's closeness to Marie-
Antoinette had itself given rise to evil whispers, and something
of the sort was now being put about in connection with Bess and
Georgiana. Curiously, though she pretends to be indignant, the
tone of Bess's reaction is rather more confident than when she
thought she had annoyed her friend; better that people should
talk about their being united than being divided:

> Who has any right to know how long or how tenderly we love
> one another! Why are excuses to be made for its sharpness
> and its fervency? Why am I to pay court to anybody but your
> mother? Why is our union to be profaned by having a lie told
> about it? Can I ever forget the note that contained – 'the first
> instant I saw you, my heart flew to your service'. No my
> dearest love, let spite and envy and jealousy do its full, I am
> proof against its sharpest arrows, it has done its worst, for I do
> not reckon among possible things its *now* hurting me with
> you. Does the warm impulse then of two full hearts want an
> excuse to be accounted for, and must your partiality to me be
> ushered in by another connection?[33]

It would be foolish to deduce anything more from this ambiguous note than that Mme de Polignac was jealous, but it is
again significant that Bess constructed her prose with care and
with an oratorical flourish, in stark contrast to Georgiana's impulsive outpourings. 'Why won't they let me, poor me, alone?'
she bewailed. She went on to say more, but the remainder of her
letter has been carefully scissored away.[34]

Lord Spencer succumbed at last to gout and general ill-health
on 31 October. He died at Bath, with his dear wife and dutiful
son at his bedside. Lady Elizabeth, now at Naples, rather
pointedly adopted mourning clothes.

Georgiana thanked her profusely, and reminisced on the
happy days they had spent together. Writing from Bath, she
said, 'I am gulchy, gulchy when I reflect at the length of time that
is elapsed since we first knew one another here, at the length of
time since I have lost you and at the distance to our meeting, but
I comfort myself by thinking what a sacredness all this gives to
our friendship.'[35] Bess had now been away for a year. 'I hope we
shall renew our Plympton days,' she mused from her exile in
Naples.

As if to clarify the nature of their *ménage à trois*, which looked
more and more peculiar to outsiders and which distance had
manifestly failed to render more orthodox in the eyes of the
world, Georgiana wrote Bess a note establishing once and for all
the essence of their bond:

> What a happiness it is to me that my dearest loveliest friend
> and the man whom I love so much and to whom I owe
> everything, are united like brother and sister, that they will
> ensure one another's happiness till I hope a very great old
> age, that I am equally loved by both and that we three may
> pass our lives in making one another happy.[36]

This turned out to be an accurate prediction.

It was time to plan for Bess's return. Georgiana hoped that
she would occasionally stay at Devonshire House, in the red
room, but she accepted that conventional wisdom would
prevent her living there constantly, much though she would
welcome it herself. The world might scoff and look askance. In
the meantime, there were other considerations to claim the
Duchess's attention. First, there was the question of little

Charlotte Williams' future. She was now ten years old and plans must be laid to secure her a proper place in the world once Bess had relinquished her position as 'governess'. There was also a General Election pending, and with Fox standing for Westminster it promised to be more exciting than ever.

Chapter Six

CANVASSING IN WESTMINSTER

The Westminster election campaign of 1784 is justly famous for a variety of reasons. Probably no election in England's history attracted so much attention from the Press or provoked such a vitriolic use of propaganda. It marked a turn in the fortunes of the Whigs, who had been in control of England for most of the eighteenth century, and was especially significant in the career of Charles James Fox. It was also the first time that a woman had played an important role in electioneering, and given that the woman in question was the most glamorous lady in the country, it was hardly surprising that the newspapers should be excited to a degree which exceeded anything that had gone before. The better to appreciate the turmoil of events in April and May of that year, a few words need to be said about the political inheritance of the participants, and an attempt made to define exactly what was meant by a Whig.

The Glorious Revolution of 1688 had established a new way of thinking towards the monarchy. The principle of Divine Right, according to which a King governed in accordance with the rules of God, and was not answerable to the vagaries of man's opinion, was defied, and in its place rose a new principle, according to which a King was the servant of his people and sat on his throne only by their consent. The authors of this principle were called Whigs, and though they might differ in detail as to their motives for wishing to make the King subservient, they were agreed that severe limits should be set upon the powers of the monarch in order to protect something which they regarded as more important than monarchy itself. This 'something' they normally called Liberty, but they did not mean by this freedom for the masses, whom they despised whenever they deigned to notice them, so much as freedom for the great governing families to govern as they thought best, for the economic good of the country and their own continued well-being, without having their plans thwarted by the whim of a single man who might make important decisions without reference to any authority save his own conscience. These governing families it was who had displaced James II and invited William of Orange to assume the throne; they included the Cavendishes (Dukes of Devonshire), Russells (Dukes of Bedford), Manners (Dukes of Rutland), and they united with Dutch families who came over with William, notably the Bentincks and the Keppels, to consolidate their power and emasculate that of the monarchy. This handful of families became the effective rulers of the land, never ceasing to remind the King that the throne was his and the kingdom theirs, that he occupied his place at their request and would continue to do so only as long as his conduct met with their approval.

In opposition to this view the Tories maintained that a King was King by legitimate right of inheritance, ordained by God, and that it was nonsense to suggest that he could be made or unmade by lesser mortals, however well organised. To them the Whigs were at best illogical, at worst anarchical. They threatened the basis of law and the orderly arrangement of affairs and they promised by their actions a tyranny far more horrific than any a king might impose. The Tories were composed mostly of squires and local gentry, far inferior to the Whigs both in the number of their acres and the extent of their influence. Yet they, in their small way, were also privileged, and were at one with the Whigs in wishing to protect the privilege of the ruling classes. Never was there any suggestion of introducing into the debate the rights of the people as a whole; the argument concerned how best to secure the continuance of the privilege which enabled men of property to govern, by upholding the legitimate right of succession to the Crown, as the Tories wanted, or by subordinating the Crown to the right of Parliament to enact, as the Whigs desired. 'Parliament' meant of course the heads of the great families in the House of Lords, their brothers, cousins and dependants in the House of Commons.

Hence the Declaration of Rights, being the crucial achievement of the revolutionary settlement of 1689, had been concerned above all with the liberties of Parliament, with ensuring that an Act of Parliament should be the supreme arm of government, and that the King could only rule through Parliament.

In the course of the eighteenth century, the Whigs were to look back upon the 'glorious revolution' with blinkered and absolute veneration. Woe betide any King who dared to tamper with its precepts. King William was naturally acquiescent, as he was placed on the throne to demonstrate the Whig theory of kingship, and they in their turn were glad to owe allegiance to him despite their traditional distrust of kings. With the Hanoverian Georges it was a different matter. They grew to hate the limitation on their powers repeatedly imposed by Whig governments, and to seethe with a frustrated fury which grew to the point of explosion by the time of George III. But they were at a disadvantage from the start, in that English was not their language and English ways not their ways. Unable to be articulate in defence of their own views, the Georges sought to assert their authority by insidious, though perfectly legal, means. They could be sure of majority support in the House of Lords by creating more peers, and they still had the power to appoint their own creatures in the House of Commons to positions of responsibility under the Crown and make these positions lucrative. Men who accepted these jobs were called 'placemen', and the House of Commons was full of them. Indeed, there was usually an undignified scramble to secure such a post, a scramble in which Whigs and Tories alike joined, their consciences unafflicted. The system naturally gave rise to corruption and bribery, which reached huge proportions under George III at the time material to this narrative.

The real achievement of the revolutionary settlement was not suspected by contemporaries and not recognised until generations later. This was the establishment of the party system, by which one group governed while another group waited in the wings to take over if the policies of the first should prove unpopular. The idea of His Majesty's Opposition, which we now take so much for granted, was born of the alternation between Whig and Tory and the acceptance of the proposition that when a government was overthrown it was not because it was irremediably bad, but because the time was opportune for a different set of ideas to be tried. This agreement to disagree as to means was the basis of parliamentary democracy as it evolved in England by slow imperceptible stages, and the monarch, by accepting advice from men not perhaps of his choosing, contributed as much to this evolution as did the Whigs. They, however, would have none of this; the Whigs regarded themselves as almost sacred guardians of the Constitution.

With the exception of Lord Bute and Lord North, the Whigs had provided every Prime Minister since Sir Robert Walpole, including the 4th Duke of Devonshire in 1756. Yet their apparent cohesiveness concealed a progressive division which had broken them into fragments each with the support of a few dozen members. These splits became even more pronounced during the long term of office of the Tory Lord North, who was Prime Minster from 1770 to 1782. There were three main Whig parties: the Bedford faction, territorial and unscrupulous, bent on maintaining their huge revenues and profits at all costs; the Rockingham faction, led by the Marquis of Rockingham and including the Dukes of Portland and Richmond, who stood for traditional Whiggism and the maintenance of the principles of 1688; and the Whigs who discerned the need for reform and fresh approaches, with the veteran Chatham as a figurehead and the immensely clever Lord Shelburne as their active leader. Together with the Court party, supporting the King and composed mostly of Tories, these were the four main political parties which could claim noticeable support.

In 1782 the Whigs were returned with Lord Rockingham as Prime Minister and Charles James Fox as Foreign Secretary. It helps to explain the disintegration of Whig power to observe that they held such an exaggerated respect for the landed families that they were prepared to be led by a man who was a marquis and very rich, but without talent. The far more able Edmund Burke they welcomed as a spokesman but distrusted on account of his low birth.

When Rockingham died a few months after taking office, the King asked Lord Shelburne to form a new administration. Fox, who was the *de facto* leader of the Whigs by this time, would not serve under Shelburne, whom he despised by hereditary habit (his father had thought little of Shelburne). Fox first approached the Duke of Richmond and asked him to assume the leadership, on condition that he did not serve in Shelburne's government.

Richmond protested that Shelburne had done nothing dreadful yet. So Fox offered the leadership to the Duke of Portland (Devonshire's brother-in-law), a man devoid of understanding or brain-power ('beneath mediocrity' was the French Ambassador's estimate). This proved to be a fatal mistake. His next was to form a Coalition government with Lord North, under the Premiership of Portland; it looked like an unprincipled abnegation of cherished beliefs.

Portland went to George III armed with a list of seven cabinet ministers (including Fox as Foreign Secretary and North at the Home Office) and asked the King to appoint him. George III was beside himself with anger. Not only did he have to accept Whigs in the Coalition government, but he was expected to take them without any prior consultation. Even the pretence that he could choose his own ministers was being denied him. He refused even to look at Portland's list. The King asked the young Pitt, who had been Chancellor of the Exchequer under Shelburne, to form a ministry, but Pitt declined. He tried to prise Lord North away from the Whigs. This too failed. He thought of abdicating, or of appealing to the House to rid him of the Whig conspiracy, but eventually relented, giving Portland blank warrants of appointment for him to fill in as he and Fox saw fit. Thus the Coalition government took office in April 1783. It was the fall of this government which brought about the famous election of 1784.

The roots of the King's fury were many. In the first place, the Cabinet had formed the habit of considering matters without reference to the Crown, and of informing him afterwards. This he considered an impertinence. It is nowadays common procedure, but the custom dates only from George III's reign. The King suspected Fox's hand had been responsible for the innovation. He already hated Fox for his lamentable influence upon his son, the Prince of Wales, who was being dragged into habits of dissipation and vice by his association with the Whig magnates and with Fox and the Devonshire House crowd in particular, habits which caused the puritanical King to shudder with distaste. The third cause of his hatred of Fox was his conviction that Fox was behind all the encroachments on royal prerogatives. The House of Commons was increasingly revered as the essential principle of the constitution, the essential check upon royal tyranny. So deeply did Fox hold this belief that he openly proclaimed the rights of Parliament superior to the rights of the people, notwithstanding his being championed by his supporters as the 'man of the people'. It was not Fox who had introduced the famous resolution of 1780, 'That the influence of the Crown has increased, is increasing, and ought to be diminished', but it was he who gave frequent and loud voice to dangerous republican sympathies of the sort. The cartoonist Gillray depicted the King packing his bags for Hanover and the politicians making off with the Crown Jewels in their pockets. George III had more than once threatened to abdicate, and even prepared a message to Parliament (which he did not send) to the effect that 'His Majesty with much sorrow finds that he can be of no further Utility to His Native Country which drives Him to the painful step of quitting it for ever'. The new Coalition government, by denying the King any say in the selection of his ministers, was trying to push him out of politics altogether. Fox said that the King's powers could be exercised only through his ministers, and that it was entirely irrelevant whether or not he personally had confidence in those ministers. The Crown, he said, 'was endowed with no faculty whatever of a private nature', did not exist except as a figurehead, and had no opinion other than that expressed on its behalf by the House of Commons. King George could not begin to understand such views.

The King was simply not equipped to speak the same language as Charles James Fox. There was no area in which they could meet and compromise, for every aspect of Fox's life and career was like a stone which stuck in the King's throat. George was pious, moral, austere, shy, with a sacred sense of duty which made him force himself to overcome a natural diffidence. He was abstemious where Fox was epicurean, religious where Fox was not even a Christian, took improving exercise when Fox was slouching about in Brooks's. He had a certain intellectual curiosity, but compared with Fox's wide culture he was a philistine. The two men were opposite to each other on every conceivable count. The contest of 1784 would turn to a very marked degree upon the antipathy between the King and Fox. 'Ce ministre est absolument en guerre ouverte avec son maître', said d'Adhémar, who found the situation simply 'incredible'.*

* This minister is in absolutely open warfare with his master.

Of course, Fox was very much part of the aristocratic clique which regarded itself as superior to the King. It was an age when aristocracy was all. Political patronage wielded by the lords was so advanced that only four of the men in a list drawn up in 1783 who controlled more than three seats in the Commons were themselves commoners. The elder Pitt was not exaggerating when he described the Commons as 'a parcel of younger brothers' – the younger Pitt was at first the only commoner in the cabinet of 1783. Most M.P.s were either related to the lords in the upper house or were dependent upon them. This meant that the idea of representation of the people, as we now understand it, would have been nonsense to a Whig. 'The House of Commons is a second-rate aristocracy instead of a popular representation,' said Flood in 1790. To a Whig, the idea of representation was so foreign that he did not reject it – it did not even enter into the scope of subjects worthy of his consideration. Even parliamentary reformers ignored the principle that the members of the House should represent the population outside, and Fox's contempt for the loudest huzza of the multitude, quoted in an earlier chapter, was perfectly in accord with the feeling of the age. Hence the number of insurrections in the streets, being the only means for the voice of the people to be heard; one historian described the political system then in operation as 'aristocracy tempered by rioting'.

With sublime arrogance, the Whigs behaved as if George III alone obstructed the good of the country, whereas it was arguable that he more closely echoed the will of his subjects than they did. (Even today, the British know by intuition that the monarch in some obscure way represents not so much their point of view as their 'feelings' rather better than do the politicians.) Certainly, George III had the support of the country in not granting dominion status to the American colonies earlier than was necessary. The Whigs would not have understood this. To them, the future of civilisation depended upon the maintenance of aristocratic supremacy. They went magisterially about their business in the knowledge that they were right by predetermined fate. A Whig was not defined by any policy he might recommend or any political shopping-bag of coherent ideas. These were irrelevant. He was a Whig simply by virtue of his belonging to or adhering to one of the natural governing families. The real seats of power were behind the stark impregnable walls of the great country palaces. Fox came from within those walls; the Prince of Wales was being enticed behind them; George III was firmly excluded.

The King could still exercise some influence by the astute granting of his 'places'. No matter how vehement their objections to royal favour, very few men would actually go so far as to refuse it when offered. The number of places, pensions and sinecures available made it clear that one of the benefits of a parliamentary career was the opportunity to line one's pocket. Fox's own father had amassed a vast fortune filched from the Treasury. George Selwyn was clerk of the irons and surveyor of the meetings of the mint, with the single duty of dining once a week at public expense. Lord Buckingham held sinecures worth £25,000 a year. The traffic in honours was lamentable, avarice and rapacity so rife as to be taken for granted and regarded as the norm.

Inevitably, corruption was practised on a large scale, colossal bribes were offered in return for favour. It is much to the credit of people like Fox, Sheridan, Pitt and Grey (but not, alas, Burke) that they were conspicuous for being quite above bribery. They cherished their 'amateur' status and despised the chaotic thrusting of greedy hands into the public purse. They were in politics essentially because they enjoyed it, and because it was a family affair.

William Pitt was to change all this. The country, which meant the middle classes, was mightily sick of endless quarrels and regroupings, of government by clubs and disdainful families, of nepotism and sinecures and dynasties, above all of an unprincipled Coalition. Pitt took over in December 1783. Fox was invited to join his government in the following January. He rejected it, clinging instead to the old system of privilege. It was to be his last chance. 'Tory' and 'Whig' degenerated into abusive epithets much as 'reactionary', 'fascist', 'red' and 'liberal' are now. 'Mama, are Tories born wicked, or do they grow wicked afterwards?' asked the daughter of a Whig family. 'They are born wicked, and grow worse,' came the reply. Fox's mistake was not to discern the mood which was nauseated by these petty attitudes. Georgiana said that he would never yield what he thought was right to the bias of public opinion. More to the

Georgiana Poyntz,
Countess Spencer, mother
of Georgiana, Duchess of
Devonshire by
Thomas Gainsborough
Chatsworth

Georgiana, Duchess of
Devonshire, 1780,
by Sir Joshua Reynolds
Chatsworth

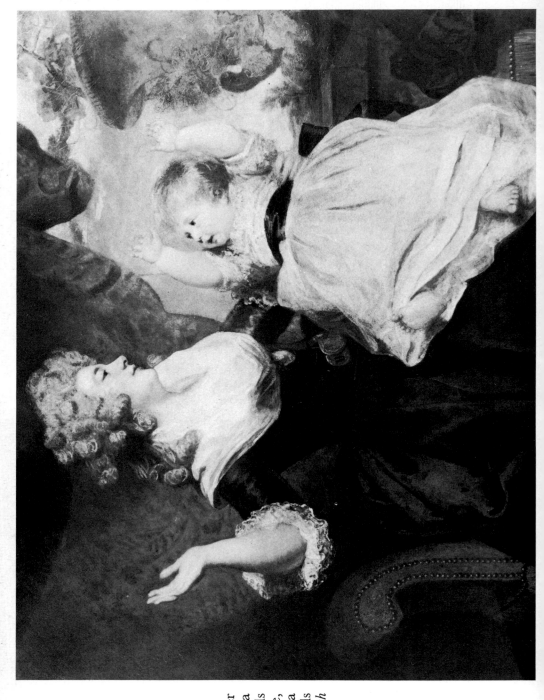

Georgiana with her daughter, Georgiana Dorothy, afterwards Countess of Carlisle, by Sir Joshua Reynolds
Chatsworth

William Cavendish, 5th Duke of Devonshire, 1768, by Pompeo Batoni
Chatsworth

Lady Elizabeth Foster, later Duchess of Devonshire,
by Sir Joshua Reynolds
Chatsworth

Georgiana, after Thomas Gainsborough
National Gallery of Art, Washington

Lord Hartington,
aged 15, 1805,
by Sir Martin Arthur Shee
Brooks's

Lady Georgiana Cavendish (left) and Lady Harriet Cavendish (Hary O),
both paintings, c. 1790, by Mrs Surtees (Elizabeth Royall)
Chatsworth

Georgiana as Diana.
Described by her son as
'the only likeness of her
that reminds me of her
countenance'.
Detail from the portrait
by Maria Cosway
Chatsworth

Lady on horseback
(believed to be Lady
Elizabeth Foster),
by Richard Cosway.
Recently acquired by the
11th Duke of Devonshire
Chatsworth

Eliza, Georgiana's daughter by
Charles Grey
(reproduced by courtesy of
Viscount Hampden)

Pendant given to Georgian
by Charles Grey
inscribed with thei
initials, the word
'Il m'est fidèle
and containing lock
of their hai
(reproduced by courtesy c
Viscount Hampden

Charles Grey,
2nd Earl Grey,
c. 1800,
by Sir Thomas Lawrence
Private Collection

point, he could not conceive that public opinion might have more title to being right than he.

Another aspect of the political scene must be considered as it prepares us for Georgiana's role. The House of Commons was the theatre of England. There one heard the best oratory, the finest talk, one witnessed dramatic moments when opinion was swayed by a perfect address, one discussed the speeches for days afterwards. The great Whig ladies sat in the lobbies for hours listening to reports on the performance within, anxious for news, tensely waiting for the result of a division. It was common enough, therefore, to see ladies enjoying the fun of politics, even supporting their menfolk at the hustings. Gossip about the latest political shift was a main course in the desultory chatter which went on around the watering-holes of Tunbridge Wells and Bath. Georgiana's innovation was not to bring women into politics, but to bring them out of the discreet half-light and thrust them into a leading role. She herself, not Fox, would be the star of Fox's campaign.

And so we come to the election contest of 1784, fought on the unspoken but brilliantly clear antipathy between George III and Charles James Fox. The King had provoked the election by persuading the House of Lords to throw out a Bill from the Commons and give him the excuse to dismiss his hated Ministry. No one cared particularly about the ostensible cause for dissolution. It mattered only that the King could rid himself of a government forced upon him by insufferable Whigs; the clash was head-on between the prerogative of the Crown and the rights of Parliament.

Fox fought the battle on high-sounding but nebulous issues. He would reform abuses and oppose Court influence. He would also do something to abolish the shabby trade in sinecures and places. He kept to himself, however, that he would support a huge undeserved income for his friend the Prince of Wales. Fox stood for the maintenance of established order, according to which the accumulated wisdom of the great families made honour an aristocratic monopoly, and government by benevolent condescension was the traditional way in which natural hierarchy should be maintained. The man of the people, as he was called, was, as the people well knew, nothing of the sort. The odds were very much against him before the campaign

began, his popularity had seriously diminished, his attachment
to truth placed very much in doubt by his expedient alliance
with North in the Coalition. He would have a hard struggle.

His opponents were Admiral Lord Hood, an estimable but
ordinary Tory, who hardly stood for anything but would be
elected anyway for being such a good chap, and Sir Cecil Wray,
formerly a Whig but now standing for the Court party. Of these,
two would be elected for Westminster, and as Hood's success
was beyond doubt, the contest turned upon who should get the
second seat, Fox or Wray. Wray's policies included the abolition
of the Chelsea Hospital for old soldiers (though he claimed he
only wanted to reorganise it), and a Tax on Maidservants, which
Fox said would drive the poor girls into prostitution. On such
momentous issues was the electorate approached.

Fox launched his campaign even before the dissolution of
Parliament with a mass meeting in Westminster Hall on 14
February, at which an address to the King was drawn up and circulated for signatures. The address was a typically high-handed
remonstrance full of phrases about the glorious revolution and
the inalienable rights derived therefrom. Only a Whig could
expect the King to be frightened by such language. The assembly
in the Hall certainly wasn't. Amid much booing and cat-calls,
Fox and his friends (including Fitzpatrick, Burke and Sheridan)
were pelted with a bag of what purported to be donkey excre-
ment, but which turned out upon examination to be a
dangerous mixture of capsicum (cayenne pepper) and euphor-
bium (a purgative). Fox was cast to the ground in the ensuing
scuffle, then made his way through a hostile crowd tugging and
annoying the horses of his carriage, to Devonshire House. On
arrival, he harangued the crowd from the balcony.

The night before the Dissolution, the Great Seal of England
was stolen from its unlikely home in a drawer of a spare room in
the Lord Chancellor's house in Great Ormond Street. Without
the Seal there could be no dissolution and no Lord Chancellor,
whose comment on the thieves was 'be damned to them'. The
King had a new seal made by the next day, and all was well again,
but not before whispers had spread that Fox was behind the
dreadful deed.

As the campaign got under way, great feasts took place nightly
at Devonshire House, where all the 'matadors' of the party

assembled (the expression is d'Adhémar's). Loud toasts were drunk to 'the Prince of Wales and may the Princes of the House of Brunswick ever countenance those principles that seated their family on the throne of England', or to 'the Duke of Devonshire and the whole House of Cavendish'. Contrary toasts were drunk in Hood's camp to 'the Royal Family' or to 'Constitution and prerogative'. This was well mannered enough, but soon gave way to more robust cries. Fox was accused of being a vice-ridden drunkard, was called the Regicide or Oliver Cromwell II, and suffered the nastiest insult when a fox was caught and roasted alive in Dover, which Walpole called 'a savage meanness that an Iroquois would not have committed'. He went on, 'Base, cowardly wretches! How much nobler to have hurried to London and torn Mr Fox himself piecemeal! I detest a country inhabited by such stupid barbarians. I will write no more tonight; I am in a passion!'[1]

There followed a torrent of lampoons, cartoons, libels, pamphlets and poems openly circulated which, had anyone the stamina to collect them, would fill a volume of some hundreds of pages. Many were boldly indecent in the best tradition of British iconoclasm, but the worst were yet to come, when the ladies joined the fray.

After a build-up of forty days, the hustings opened on 1 April, in Covent Garden. Large crowds milled around the narrow streets waiting for the arrival of candidates, as it was then the custom that voting should take place amid the loudest possible noise, as part of a wild lawless carnival. Voting did not occur on one day, but was spread over several days, with the result that the fortunes of candidates could be followed with all the excitement of a horse-race. Each candidate approached the hustings with a motley procession of hangers-on, waving banners and shouting slogans, while the people leaned out of windows or hung from lamp-posts cheering or jeering. Fox's procession was the most impressive, being graced by the carriage of the Duchess of Devonshire. When they all converged, the High Bailiff introduced them to the crowd, and they each bellowed a speech soliciting support, at the same time and above the din of an excited mob. Nobody could hear a thing, of course. Then the bailiff asked for votes to be cast by a show of hands, and since this was inevitably inconclusive and moreover threatened to produce a riot, voting by poll was resorted to. At the Westminster election, nearly 19,000 votes were cast, but on the first day only 900 were registered, Fox gaining a majority with 302 votes against 264 for Hood and 238 for Wray. The proceedings over, candidates withdrew to their respective mansions, leaving the mob to tear down the scaffolding and make as much mess as they could with the platforms erected in Covent Garden. Normally a good-natured street-battle might ensue.

Thereafter the performance was repeated daily, with Hood and Wray gaining ground at the expense of Fox, whose share of the vote dropped to third position. Fox grew disconsolate at the way events were turning out. To his mistress Mrs Armistead he confessed that he thought of withdrawing from the fight. 'I must not give up yet, tho' I wish it,' he told her. 'I have serious thoughts, if I am beat here, of not coming into Parliament at all, but of all this I will talk with you more as soon as this business will let me go to you.'[2]

There was one card which Fox had not played to its proper advantage. The Duchess of Devonshire was present with him every day, and his committee made sure everyone knew he had her support. What if the Duchess were actually to canvass on his behalf? Surely nobody could resist persuasion from such a quarter!

And so an army of grand ladies assembled to ride into the grubby streets of London and dazzle the electorate with their favour. Not only Georgiana, but her sister Lady Duncannon, her sister-in-law the Duchess of Portland, Mrs Bouverie and Mrs Crewe, all put on their finest clothes and made themselves look as glamorous as possible to solicit votes for Mr Fox, knowing full well that the Cockney crowd was easy prey to a spot of beauty from on high.

Wraxall recalled the excitement which this generated. 'These ladies, being previously furnished with lists of outlying voters, drove to their respective dwellings. Neither entreaties nor promises were spared. In some instances even personal caresses were said to have been permitted, in order to prevail upon the surly or inflexible, and there can be no doubt of common mechanics having been conveyed to the hustings on more than one occasion by the Duchess in her own coach.'[3] Georgiana had such success that the opposition was obliged to counter with ladies of their own, notably the Countess of Salisbury who was so condescending that she required everyone to pay due respect to her rank, whereas Georgiana seemed not even to be aware of it.

Wray's committee, understandably worried, was driven to hurl personal abuse at the Duchess. 'There will always be some *influence* and certain *stairs* which honest men do not scruple to mount on certain occasions,' they said. On Georgiana's frequent forays into streets inhabited by prostitutes, Wray's men had this to say: 'Considering the frequent visits they pay to Covent Garden it is no wonder that the Ladies catch the *contagion* of party spirit and are so *warm* in support of their favourite *member*.' Of the 62 satiric prints published between 29 March and 29 April, 36 depicted the Duchess, which alone may illustrate the impact she achieved. Lord Temple wrote to the

The MATTER REVERSED, or one good turn deserves Another.

One of many caricatures published during the 1784 election

Duke of Rutland, 'Their exertions have been incredible, particularly on the part of Her Grace of Devon, who in the course of
her canvass has heard more plain English of the grossest sort
than ever fell to the share of any lady of her rank.'

Georgiana was deeply dispirited by the vile attacks she was
made to endure. 'I would give the world to be with you', she told
her mother, 'for I am unhappy beyond measure here and abus'd
for nothing, yet as it is begun I must go on with it. They will not
give up and they insist upon our all continuing to canvass. . . . It
is very hard they should single me out when all the women of my
side do as much.'⁴ Lady Spencer could not for the life of her see
why they had to continue. 'Is this detestable thing to go on for
ever?' she wrote.⁵ At last she persuaded her daughter to
abandon the fight and join her for peace and rest in the country.

After only a few days at St Albans, Georgiana received entreaties from the Portlands who feared her sudden withdrawal
would be harmful to Fox's chances. 'I am worn out almost and
must beg of you to come tomorrow,' wrote the Duchess of
Portland. 'There are a great many votes that you can command
and No One else.'⁶ Georgiana protested that she could not be all
that significant, that they could manage without her, and besides
she was tired of being referred to as Doll Common by the Press.
A couple of days later the Duke of Portland himself wrote to
beseech her. 'Every one is convinced that your exertions have
produced the very material alteration which has happened in
Fox's favour,' he said. 'Be assured that if it could be imagined
that your absence was imputable to any other Cause than Your
affection to Lady Spencer . . . a general Languor would prevail,
Despondency would suceed, and Triumph of the Court would
be the inevitable Consequence.'⁷

Georgiana was incapable of resisting an appeal to her loyalty.
Typically, having once decided to return to London and see the
battle through to the end, she threw herself into it with even
greater abandon than before. She determined that she would
not only take her carriage into the worst slums, but would alight
and walk into people's houses, if such be needed to secure a
majority for Charles. She dressed in the buff and blue colours
which had been his trade-mark for so long (and which, it will be
recalled, were the colours of Washington's uniform, which Fox
had defiantly worn in the House of Commons during the

American war). She also wore a hat festooned with fox's tails. Nobody could doubt the strength of her allegiance. From eight in the morning, throughout the long day, Georgiana covered the ground from Temple Bar to Hounslow, winning hearts wherever she went.

The French Ambassador's breathless reports to Paris were despatched every day instead of every two weeks. D'Adhémar simply could not believe what he saw. The Duchess of Devonshire and other grand Whig ladies carrying banners which proclaimed FOX AND LIBERTY, while ladies allied to the opposing party carried banners saying PITT AND CONSTITUTION. That was unorthodox, but harmless enough. It was the licence and passion of the hustings which shocked d'Adhémar. 'Crowds smash the windows of houses belonging to the opposing side,' he said; even the Prince of Wales had his windows broken, and did not seem to think it untoward. Pitt's supporters tried to storm Brooks's Club, but found that they were expected; the porters and servants charged out into the street and a pitched battle took place in St James's. 'Il y a une animosité et une fermentation générale qui pourraient conduire à des événements tragiques si le peuple anglais n'étaient essentiellement bons et flegmatiques,' commented the Ambassador perceptively.* If such things were permitted on the continent, a bloody insurrection would follow. D'Adhémar also noticed that loyalty to party was far stronger in England than patriotism, a fact he deplored, and he was astonished and disgusted by the degradation and jocular atmosphere of electioneering. Seeing Lord North's son dressed as a lackey on Fox's carriage, his response was to castigate 'ces scènes dégoûtants pour les honnêtes gens'.†[8]

Once more, Georgiana's efforts brought a deluge of calumny upon her. The Press explained its attitude thus: 'When people of rank descend below themselves and mingle with the vulgar for mean and dirty purposes, they give up their claim to respect, forfeit their privileges and become fair game for censors.'[9]

Georgiana's and Harriet's technique was to enter inexpensive little shops and pay exorbitant prices for simple goods, then

---

* There is a mutual enmity and general commotion which could lead to tragic consequences, were the English not essentially good and phlegmatic.

† These scenes disgusting to a gentleman.

entice the delighted tradesman to vote for Fox, offering to take
him to the hustings in their impressive carriage. It hardly failed.
They were said to have paid 5 guineas for broccoli, 8 guineas for
a leg of mutton, and £20 for a French loaf. Not surprisingly,
methods such as these were thought by her opponents to be little
short of bribery. 'Some say she has pushed matters too far',
wrote Daniel Pulteney, 'and may be brought before a committee
for bribery.'[10]

Not so. Georgiana pushed matters even farther by giving a
butcher a kiss in exchange for his vote, the most famous kiss, no
doubt, in the history of electioneering. It worked so well that she
did it again, and again, and before long the Duchess's caresses
were the talk of all London. One of the lucky Cockney electors
recalled the occasion with obvious relish. 'Lord, sir, it was a fine
sight to see a grand lady come right smack to us hardworking
mortals, with a hand held out, and a "Master, how-dye-do",
and a laugh so loud, and talk so kind, and shake us by the hand,
and say, "Give us your vote, worthy sir, a plumper for the
people's friend, our friend, everybody's friend", and then, sir,
we hummed and hawed, they would ask after our wives and
families, and, if that didn't do, they'd think nothing of a kiss,
aye, a dozen of them. Lord, sir, kissing was nothing to them, and
it came all natural.'[11] A chimney-sweep, likewise beguiled, said
that if he were God he would make Georgiana the Queen of
Heaven. Her success was total and irreversible.

In retaliation, Wray's party printed placards saying
'WESTMINSTER, To be hired for the day. SEVERAL PAIR OF RUBY
POUTING LIPS OF THE FINEST QUALITY. To be kissed by rum Dukes,
queer Dukes, Butchers, Draymen, Dustmen and Chimney
sweepers. Please to enquire at Devon and Cos Crimson
Warehouse, Piccadilly.' Hood's sailors concocted a bawdy song
which they shouted through the streets;

> I had rather kiss my Moll than she,
> With all her paint and finery;
> What's a Duchess more than a Woman?
> We've sounder flesh on Portsmouth Common;
> Then fill our Nectar in a glass,
> As for kissing – kiss my arse.

A trifle disingenuously, Georgiana sought to allay Mama's

anxiety by pointing out that it was her sister and another lady who bestowed the kisses, not she, 'so it's very hard I who was not should have the reputation for it'.[12]

Far more damaging was the insinuation that Fox was Georgiana's *cicisbeo* and that infatuation was the motive for her involvement. There was absolutely no hint of a justification for this, and Georgiana only alluded to it once, in a letter to Philip Francis many years later: 'As I am very sure you do not think that I, as a woman, ever was, could be, or am in love with Charles Fox, you will allow that, in fervour, enthusiasm, and devotion, I am a good friend.' At the same time, she averred her belief that Fox was 'the greatest of men . . . who had sacrificed even his darling popularity to his principles. . . . Would I were a man, to unite my talents, my hopes, my fortune with Charles', to make common cause and fall or rule with him.'[13]

Not once did Georgiana depart from her faith in Fox. 'I will not enter into any discussion of right or wrong', she would much later tell her children, 'and I carry it so far that if anything ever appears wrong or inexplicable in Fox's conduct . . . I feel sure that he might be right and that when I see him he will explain it.'[14]

In the election of 1784, she had boldly made 'common cause' with Fox. At length her tireless work brought its reward. When the poll closed on 17 May, the final figures were Hood, 6694, Fox 6233, Wray, 5998. Fox had beaten Wray by a margin of 235 votes and was assured his seat in Parliament.* Everyone knew that Georgiana and her friends had made the victory. Had there been anyone in England who did not know of the Duchess of Devonshire before, he certainly knew now. The madness of the past six weeks had turned a dazzling spotlight upon her. The Whig party as a whole suffered a most humiliating defeat, losing support even in counties which they more or less owned to themselves, but at least their champion, their heavy-browed, sweaty giant with the charming manners and the greatest intellect of them all, was saved.

The celebrations were ecstatic. A huge procession formed to take Fox in triumph from the hustings at St Paul's, Covent Garden, down King Street and Bedford Street into the Strand,

* Uncertain of victory, Fox had taken the precaution of standing for Kirkwall in Scotland, where the contest was safer.

and up to Piccadilly and Devonshire House. There were twelve
carriages, twenty-four horsemen, and bands playing victory
tunes. The whole proceeded through a tumult of noise, crowds
drinking and cheering. Everyone wore buff and blue, the horses
were bedecked with ribbons of these colours, servants wore buff
and blue livery, ladies buff and blue dresses. At the rear of the
procession were the state carriages of the Duchesses of Portland
and Devonshire each drawn by six horses. The party atmosphere
was heightened by the footmen on Fox's carriage, who were
friends and cronies passing for servants on this special occasion.
Behind him came twenty-four gentlemen of the Prince of Wales'
household, while the Prince himself, together with Devonshire,
went ahead through the back streets to be present at Devonshire
House when Fox arrived. There Fox addressed the crowd from a
platform specially erected in the courtyard, beneath a banner
proclaiming SACRED TO FEMALE PATRIOTISM. Never before had
such a triumphal procession been so adorned, said the French
Ambassador, and never had there been such prostitution with so
little glory.[15] The great cavalcade was followed by a celebration
dinner at Willis's Rooms, and a gigantic ball at Mrs Crewe's, at
which Georgiana was partnered by the Prince.

Nor was this all. The next day the Prince of Wales held his own
celebrations with a garden fête at Carlton House, at precisely the
same time as the King's procession passed on its way to open the
new Parliament. Apart from anything else, it was a gesture of
supreme impertinence from son to father, for the rival factions
were separated only by a brick wall. The toast was TRUE BLUE AND
MRS CREWE. The day finished with a firework display and much
good-humoured rioting. Had anyone suspected that Fox's
effective political career was at an end, that he would spend the
rest of his active life in frustrating opposition, he certainly dared
not voice it.

A little while later there was a great ball to celebrate the King's
birthday. D'Adhémar reported that a 'monde prodigieux' was
at Court, although the glaring absence of the Duchess of
Devonshire and 'toutes les belles dames du parti Fox' was the
subject of much comment. In the House of Commons, debates
were still being conducted in uproar, Fox frequently being
called to order. D'Adhémar was irritated above all by the
election having so claimed everyone's attention that inter-

national affairs were completely forgotten for weeks on end. There might just as well have been no French Ambassador at all.[16]

Meanwhile, Georgiana's frantic involvement with Fox had not closed her mind to her dear friend in Europe. Even as she slumped at home after a day's canvassing, she had found time to write to Bess and implore her to come home. She should spend a week at Devonshire House, then take the whole summer at Chatsworth. Canis was dying to see her, too.

*   *   *

If Georgiana thought that Bess was bored to tears in Naples, Turin, Paris, Lausanne, and the other social capitals of Europe, she had a false impression. The pretended point of the journey, to educate Charlotte Williams, had been forgotten, or at least submerged beneath other interests. There were such charming and interesting people to meet, for a start. And odd it was that there were always plenty of admirers to hover near Lady Elizabeth, waiting for encouragement to approach closer. One such was Count Fersen, the Swedish statesman who had already been suspected of having a clandestine affair with Marie-Antoinette.

Fersen was nearly thirty, good-looking, slim, with sleepy eyes. He spent a considerable amount of time with Bess in Italy, driving her to Pompeii on one occasion, and generally arriving rather earlier than other gentlemen to pay his respects. She confessed she found him 'very, very amiable', and was much gratified by his bursting into tears when she told him she was not allowed to write to her sons. Men could not easily resist a pretty face furrowed with self-pity; sighs and lamentations brought the gallant to Bess's feet. To her credit, she did not keep Fersen's courtship secret, but told Georgiana how well she thought of the noble Swede. She painted a scene which vividly depicted the tender emotion upon which their fragile relationship was based:

The other evening he was a little while alone with me, and I was very low, and leaning on a chair with both my hands on the frame and my head resting on them. He stooped down and kissed my hands, and at last – oh, dearest G – my cheek. Pray, pray, don't be angry. I neither started nor was angry,

but took his hand and said, 'this must never be again.' He said
'no' – he was very melancholy – so was I.[17]

Fersen was not the only man to be charmed by Bess's
melancholy. There is a portrait of her painted by Angelica
Kauffman in Naples and Rome during this long exile, which
shows to perfection the demure, utterly feminine pathos of her
frailty. One admirer, known only as H, had been so taken that
he had given expression to the wildest passion. This was not
what was meant by 'falling in love' in the Devonshire House
circle – it passed the bounds of well-behaved flirtation, and had
to be discouraged. No less a man than Edward Gibbon was also
known to have a soft spot for Bess. Gibbon had known the
Hervey family for twenty years or more, and presumably
remembered Elizabeth as a little girl. He called her the Goddess
Eliza.

At Lausanne that year Gibbon was visited by Bess, whom he
found 'poorly in health, but still adorable (nay, do not frown!),
and I enjoyed some delightful hours by her bedside'.[18] It was
even reported that the ungainly, ugly, middle-aged historian
had fallen on his knees to profess devotion to his goddess, and
had to be helped up again. Nobody can be sure whether or not
the story is true, but that Gibbon and Bess maintained a gentle,
friendly, bantering relationship for many years afterward there
can be no doubt. She felt at ease with him, could tease him and
tick him off, with no fear of retaliation. 'If I do not find a letter
from you at Florence', begins a typical note, 'I do swear that this
shall be the last letter you will receive in a long, long time. – You
may hear from others of Rome being pillag'd, Italy conquered,
and us made prisoners, but not a syllable from me.'

It is interesting that Bess never wrote to Georgiana in such
vein. Despite protestations of undying devotion, Bess never felt
free to tease Georgiana, because she was never quite sure that
the relationship would survive good-humoured mockery.
Hence, on her part, there was not a letter but started or finished
with a restatement of love and dependence. Georgiana's similar
endearments were utterly different at source, springing not from
thought but from unreflected emotion.

Bess began her homeward journey on 5 June, her mother
Lady Bristol conferring with Georgiana as to when it would be

best for her to arrive. The situation in her family at the moment would be death to her, said Lady Bristol (she and her husband were still not on speaking terms), so she was perfectly content that her daughter should resume her strange equivocal position in the Devonshire household.[19] The next few months would make it even stranger.

* * *

Georgiana found herself right in the centre of yet another event of great importance in that extraordinary year, although at least it was allowed to run its course in close privacy in spite of its potential effects being of a public order. This was the occasion which nearly robbed England of its heir, as the Prince of Wales, maddened by love, appeared ready to kill himself rather than face the future without his chosen lady.

The Prince had been fully adopted into the Devonshire House set since he had reached his majority three years before. The King watched with righteous fury the descent of his son into a sybaritic daydream, squandering his time with gambling, with drink, with women. He ought not in truth to have been all that surprised, for the Prince's upbringing had made it virtually inevitable that he should plunge headlong into pleasure as soon as he had the opportunity. His childhood had been drab, austere, gruesome. At the age of eight, he had been delivered into the hands of tutors who were instructed to treat him exactly as they would any other boy, and to flog him hard whenever they thought fit. This they did for several years, until the Prince and his brothers, in their early adolescence, tore the weapon from a teacher's hand and flogged him with it themselves.

One of the Prince's brothers had been whipped for having asthma, another was pinned down by the arms in order to be flogged, in the approving presence of his father. George III was presumably doing his best, and thought himself democratic in these proceedings, but the effect was disastrous as far as the Prince was concerned. Repressed and bullied throughout his youth, he nursed an abiding hatred for his parents, which they returned in full measure, so that society was carefully scissored down the middle, and those who were friends of the heir to the throne were sworn enemies of the King who sat on it. Naturally, they mostly numbered Whigs.

Prominent among them was Charles James Fox, whom the King blamed for everything that was wrong with his son; he saw Fox as an evil corrupter. Certainly, Fox introduced the Prince to a way of life and to habits which were entirely new to him. The King had tried to prevent his son from enjoying anything at all. The son then chose to ally himself with the one man among his father's subjects who was notorious for enjoying everything. From a life of restraint he catapulted into a life of abandon. Together with Fox and Sheridan, the Prince would dress in shabby rags and spend jolly hours in a loud, smelly tavern of the lowest sort, the trio disguising themselves as Slimstock, Blackstock, and Greystock. Not only was the King bitterly resentful against Fox, but so in some degree were the middle-classes, who did not think it congruous that Fox should be hob-nobbing with the heir. As for the Prince himself, it was a pro-tracted awakening.

Being naturally soft and affectionate, and having been denied the expression of these qualities, the Prince responded to friendship with abundant warmth. It was also nice for a young man who had been taught the perils of vanity to find that he was admired, flattered, even liked. It was all too intoxicating.

His official debut into Society had taken place on New Year's Day of 1781, when he had been virtually mobbed by the huge crowd which jostled for the privilege of acquaintance. But he spent most of the time talking to Fox, and chose as his partner in the dancing the lovely Duchess of Devonshire. After that, his parents tried to chaperone him, with little success, for the attrac-tion of Brooks's Club with its talk and its wine was too potent a drug. Georgiana and the Prince became firm friends in no time, calling each other 'Brother' and 'Sister' and enjoying each other's company on terms of the closest confidence.

'The Prince of Wales looks too much like a woman in men's clothes,' wrote Georgiana in a private note which she did not intend to be seen. 'He certainly does not want for understanding and his jokes sometimes have an appearance of Wit . . . he loves being of consequence and whether it is intrigues of state or of gallantry he often thinks more is intended than really is.'

This lack of discernment was to land him in hideous trouble with women. At the age of sixteen, he had taken the actress Mrs Robinson as his mistress, and called her 'Perdita' after the character in *The Winter's Tale* which she played to perfection. Three years later he had grown tired of her, and passed her on to Charles Fox. Mrs Armistead followed in the Prince's affections, and she too had moved over to Fox, with whom she was to remain for the rest of his life. (Mrs Armistead had also been loved by Lord George Cavendish, the Duke of Devonshire's brother, until Cavendish, finding it difficult to get into her room and she strangely unwilling that he should, discovered His Royal Highness behind a door. Poor Cavendish was very drunk. He burst out laughing, made a deep bow, and withdrew).[20] It was probable that Lady Melbourne had gratified the Prince, for she had already given Lord Melbourne his son, and it was firmly in accordance with her principles of ambition to accommodate the heir to the throne in any way he might desire. She was constantly entertaining him.

There was the time when the Prince was dining at Melbourne House when news came that an attempt had been made on the King's life while he was watching a play at Drury Lane. The Prince was all for nonchalantly continuing with his meal, until Lady Melbourne prevailed upon him and made him see that he really ought to go and enquire. Ambitious she may have been, but she was not silly.

Rumour suggested that Georgiana was another royal mistress, but this is to say the least unlikely in view of her need to produce a Devonshire heir without any risk of confused paternity. Wraxall records that the general impression was of there being a special relationship, 'but of what nature was that attachment, and what limits were affixed to it by the Duchess, must remain matter of conjecture'. When Georgiana was pregnant in 1785, the Prince 'manifested so much anxiety, and made such frequent morning visits on horseback to Wimbledon, where she repaired for a short time, as to give umbrage to her brother Lord Spencer, and even it was supposed to excite some emotion in the phlegmatic bosom of the Duke her husband'.[21]

But we advance. The crisis of 1784 was caused by the Prince's most overpowering love, of such magnitude that he was almost robbed of his sanity, if, that is, we are to believe his own account of himself. Outsiders thought him a little given to dramatic effect and hysterical scenes. The object of this passion was Mrs Fitzherbert.

Maria Fitzherbert, twice widowed and a few years older than the Prince, had recently been introduced into Devonshire House. She was beautiful and she was free, but two circumstances made her the least appropriate choice for the Prince to fall upon. She was a devout Catholic and a lady of iron virtue. The Prince fell in love with her, and for once 'madly' would be the adverb of accuracy. Passion was doubled by her refusals. Not that she did not return the affection – she was decidedly in love with him – but her strict principles would never allow her to entertain an illicit affair, no matter how illustrious the catch. His importunity became an embarrassment to her. He raged and wept, drank himself into paralysis, begged her to marry him, promised that he would give up the throne for her and emigrate to America, anything, anything she asked if only she would take him.

'The Prince of Wales has been like a madman,' reported Georgiana. 'He was ill last Wednesday and took three pints of Brandy which killed him. He was confined three days to his bed – I fancy he has made himself worse than he was in hopes to prevent the departure for Spa of a certain lady who goes in spite of all on Wednesday.'[22]

When all his entreaties proved ineffective, the Prince resorted to the last hope of the disappointed lover, to make himself so pitiful that the loved one should feel such guilt for the condition to which she had brought him that she would give in. It worked in a certain measure.

The night before Mrs Fitzherbert's departure for Spa, Georgiana was entertaining at Devonshire House when she was suddenly called from the room, and found Bouverie and Onslow 'pale as death'. In her own words, 'They told me P had run himself through the body and missed his heart by the breadth of a nail and that to prevent his tearing off his bandages Mrs F was to send him some flattering message such as a kind of promise of marriage . . . I saw Keate the surgeon who swore that he had barely missed his heart and they said Lord Southampton was sent for as there was an idea of informing the King for if P had died they might all have been tried for their lives. I was frightened and I wrote to Lord S an account of all I knew – marriage and all – he wrote me word that he should not tell the King and that he looked upon it as a boyish act.'[23]

Mrs Fitzherbert agreed to see the Prince at Carlton House before her departure for Spa, and besought Georgiana to accompany her as chaperone. What the two women discovered there was far worse than either had anticipated. The Prince had worked himself into such a violent state that his hysteria was now genuine; he foamed at the mouth, beat his head against the wall, rolled about in agony with blood on his shirt. Time and again he said he would kill himself if Maria did not marry him. The doctor who was present looked significantly at Mrs Fitzherbert to indicate that he really did fear for the Prince's life, whereupon she asked Georgiana if she could borrow a ring. The Prince took the ring and presented it to Mrs Fitzherbert with solemn promises of his intention of devoting his life to her. With that, he seemed to recover some semblance of rationality, and the ladies drove away, confident that a scandal had been averted and no real harm done by the acceptance of the ring. The Prince was behaving like a delinquent child, and must be treated accordingly.

Immediately afterwards, she and Georgiana both signed a note declaring that they regarded promises extracted in such circumstances as null and void. Georgiana was horrified to discover the following day that they had been duped, that the Prince had staged an elaborate pantomime suicide in order to trap Mrs Fitzherbert, who forthwith left for Spa, while Georgiana stayed at home to absorb the blame and try to make amends.

It had been a nasty, worrying episode, and for once the giddy Duchess trembled at the thought of possible consequences. She wrote a stern rebuke to her 'Brother' advising him that he should not think of coming to Chatsworth unless asked, to which he wrote a laborious contrite reply. In private he was as distracted as ever, begging Maria, 'Save me, save me, save me on my knees I conjure you from myself.'[24]

For the moment, with Mrs Fitzherbert safely out of the country, Devonshire House could afford to relax a little.

* * *

The summer at Chatsworth was perfect. Dr Johnson was there, and Edmund Burke's son Richard, as well as regulars like 'Fish' Crauford and Jack Townshend. The weeks passed in carefree enjoyment, with much talk, fun and games, and spirited harmless gallantry. When Elizabeth Foster joined them after so long an absence abroad, she immediately became the centre of attention. Lord Jersey and Sir William Jones both fell in love with her, said Georgiana, who likened her friend to Susannah among the Elders. Her stay in warmer climates had done little to improve her health; if anything, her cough was rather worse than before, which gave Lady Spencer the excuse she needed to recommend getting rid of her almost as soon as she arrived. 'When does Lady Eliz go?' she asked, 'she should not delay for she will not bear a winter in England with that cough.'[25] The reasons for Lady Spencer's eagerness to see the back of Bess were all too apparent from the naïvety of Georgiana's letters, in which again and again she told her mother how they had all enjoyed themselves out riding or walking, except 'poor Lady Eliz' who was too ill and had to stay at home. With the Duke.

Bess did everything she could to ingratiate herself with Lady Spencer, which, as she must have felt the Dowager's displeasure, required no small amount of cheek. It was all right for Georgiana to tell her mother that her child had grown six teeth, but when Bess appended a postscript to one of her letters giving news of Lady Spencer's grand-daughter with proprietorial pride, the impertinence was evidently lost on her. 'Our dear little Lady Georgiana', she wrote, 'now distinguishes letters, aims at words and comprehends things that really seem beyond her age . . . I wish I had a Plympton piece of news to communicate to you [i.e. that Georgiana was again with child] my dear Madam, but tho I never saw my beloved friend look better than she does now, I fear another season at Bath will be necessary for our wishes to succeed. I wish I could attend her there, for far beyond any circumstances in this world, much as I have to wish for, do I most anxiously wish she had a son . . . I own that I am irresistibly attached to you with all a daughter's respect and affection.'[26]

Lady Spencer did not directly reply to this cunning approach, but made a gloriously frigid reference to it in her next word to Chatsworth. 'Pray thank Lady Eliz for her postscript,' she said, pointedly ignoring the mention of 'our dear little' grand-daughter. 'From the account your brother gave me of her cough I cannot help wishing she was safe in a warmer climate. Loving her as well as you do you ought to insist on her not risking the effect of November fogs in England.' Then, with controlled malice, she sought to remind everyone that Lady Elizabeth's purpose in the household was as governess to Charlotte Williams. 'Lady Eliz will I dare say with her excellent understanding try to instill as much solidity and humility into her as she can.'[27]

The Duke and his two ladies were at Devonshire House in November, preparatory to Bess's departure to the Continent for the winter. It was a month of momentous importance for the trio and their shared fate, a month of furtive confidences and circumspect rendezvous. Georgiana had innocently thrown her beloved friend at her husband's feet, wanting to make Bess welcome and cherished, wanting to see everyone happy around her. As Bess herself put it, in her secret Journal, 'she had been my comfort and happiness, tho' her unthinking kindness has hurried me down the precipice'. The result was that Bess and the Duke were now irrevocably in love, yet somehow had to conceal their passion for each other from Georgiana. Georgiana's guileless sunny nature made it even harder, instilling at least in Bess's heart feelings of horrid guilt. She was in the most unenviable position, trusted and loved by both, outwardly bent on securing their happiness with each other, secretly wishing that circumstances would allow her to be the sole source of the Duke's happiness. If the Duke was irritated with his wife, Bess did everything she could to reconcile them, and when she saw the success of her efforts, she inwardly wept with jealousy. 'Depositary of both their thoughts', she told her diary, 'I have sought, when her imprudences have alienated him, to restore him to her, and when my full heart has mourned over her avowal of his returning caresses, I have checked and corrected the sensation.' It was hard to smile and look pleased when Georgiana reported how tender had been the Duke in his embraces.[28]

There was no longer any need for Bess to insinuate herself into the Devonshire family. She was there. Matters had gone too far, and the fears which Lady Spencer only partially managed to disguise had proven justified. When Bess left for Europe in December, Georgiana was two weeks advanced in pregnancy, though she could not have known it at the time. Bess was likewise about four weeks with child, and the father of her baby was also the Duke of Devonshire.

*   *   *

The lascivious Duke of Dorset, who had made Lady Derby's life such a misery, was Ambassador in Paris when Bess arrived there in January 1785, once again lonely, forlorn, and with good cause this time desperately anxious about her bleak future. As soon as she realised she was expecting a child, she knew that custom would require the greatest secrecy and her exile would have to be long. She suffered an intolerable emptiness at her enforced separation from Devonshire, for whom she now felt a very real love, and with all prospect of normal happiness denied her, she accepted the attentions of the Duke of Dorset with the relief of a woman who has been shipwrecked. She told him that she could only regard him as a friend, but admitted that from vanity she allowed him to cherish a warmer sentiment for her. Georgiana, still innocent of her friend's condition, was alarmed. Dorset, she said, was 'the most dangerous of men, for with that beauty of his he is so unaffected and has a simplicity and persuasion in his manner that makes one account very easily for the number of women he has had in love with him'.[29]

A few days later, Georgiana burst into her husband's room 'in a great fidget', because Bess had misunderstood her letter and the Duchess was afraid she might be 'vexed'. She prevailed upon Canis to tell Bess not to take her words too seriously, for they were meant well, and 'proceeded only from her love for you being as great as ever, and from an apprehension that yours for her might be diminished, by your new acquaintance at Paris'.[30]

Bess left Paris in March, and journeyed south to Lyons, sinking further and further into despair as the weeks passed. The journal she kept betrays the pitiful depth of her misery, the cause for which she could share with no one. If only she could have unburdened herself! She even considered submitting herself to the ordeal of an abortion, 'I tremble to think it came through my mind to try by exercise to destroy the cause of my fears. I weighed the criminality of the act with the great object of saving my mother, family and friends from the sorrow I should bring on them', but she had not the courage. And by the time the baby within her began to move, tenderness overcame all other emotion.[31]

From Lyons, Bess went to Chambéry, crossed the Alps, and settled for a while in Turin. Still she kept her dreadful secret from everyone, resigning herself to the inevitable and looking upon 'all suffering as trivial compared to the horror of ignominy'. In Turin she was so weak from the journey that she was forced to consult a doctor, who bled her profusely, not knowing that she was four months pregnant. Bess half hoped that his ministrations would cause a miscarriage, but 'Nature as if to torture me more, spoke all a Mother's language within me', and she prayed her baby would be saved. She reflected with the most poignant heartache what kind of life she could promise to the child she was bringing into the world, 'not daring to own thee, yet anxious for thy safety – oh till this hour I knew not what misfortune was'.

There were many people in Turin only too glad to entertain Lady Elizabeth, yet she had lost all heart for social gaiety and wanted only to be left alone in a quiet obscure corner. She had nevertheless to feign enjoyment for fear that her lack of spirit might give rise to suspicions, and went through agonies of discomfort to disguise her shape and maintain a cheerful air. She determined that she would make her way as far as Naples before the baby was due. There she could withstand the ordeal that awaited her in remote secrecy. 'I am wretched – oh God, great God – what shall I do?'

It is impossible not to sympathise with Lady Elizabeth in her predicament. The confessions of her diary tear the heart with the deep distress they reveal. In Florence she wrote, 'I dread a confinement I may not be able to conceal – yet my soul yearns to cherish the dear Babe I bear. Oh I could bear all but giving my mother pain. She has had sorrows enough. I know not what to do. Oh, God pity me.'

Pisa, Rome, and finally Naples on 4 May. If her condition were discovered, she would lose friends, family, reputation, everything, and would never again see England. She longed to hear from the Duke, but his letters were necessarily circumspect and uncommitted, while the Duchess continued to write friendly notes. It was all too much to bear. She was never tempted to blame the Duke, – 'oh no – his nature is noble, kind, tender, honourable, and affectionate. Passion has led us both away – his heart suffers for me I know.'[32]

At dinner with the Countess of Upper Ossory, to whom Horace Walpole addressed so many of his letters, Bess had to endure a conversation about the difficulties of women concealing pregnancy and the torment of clandestine confinement when all the joy normally attendant upon birth is denied the unhappy mother; this with a smile on her face and no more than ordinary theoretic interest. If only the man she loved could have been with her, she could have endured all.

At last, with one month left her, Bess made her way over to the island of Ischia, where she thought she could give birth in the utmost obscurity. Even there, however, there were acquaintances of her connections in Naples, and the risk of discovery was too great. Weak with fatigue and anxiety, not even sure that she would live, she eventually sent for her brother to come to her, and told him the truth of her condition, without however revealing the identity of the father. Fortunately, he was able to give her comfort and understanding enough to make the final journey across rough seas to the gulf of Salerno and to the little town of Vietri.

From the normally uncommunicative Duke, Bess received in July and August some soothing letters which he entrusted to Lord Keppel and which he could be reasonably sure would not be opened. He was alone at Chatsworth, having left Georgiana in London to await the birth of *her* child, and there the solitude of the great house gave him time to reflect on how much he was missing Bess. 'I am terribly in want of you here, Mrs Bess', he wrote, 'and am every minute reminded of the misfortune of your not being here by things that I see, such as the couch you us'd to sit on in the drawing-room, amidst all your sighing lovers. The blue bed you slept in, and little Mr Phaon* who is at grass in the park.'[33] He warned her that her letters should contain nothing but generalities. Through Georgiana she sent her love to Canis and a kiss to the little girl; 'I wonder if ever I shall see her again.'[34]

Georgiana was clearly still in utter ignorance of the danger which threatened her friend. She told Bess that Canis was made a

* Bess's pony.

'very happy dog' by her keeping so regularly in touch, and thanked her for 'the dear secret letter'. Whatever this contained has been lost to us, so we cannot guess what Georgiana meant by saying 'I have not a fear about the pride'. She finished, 'Oh my dearest Bess how I do love you. I cannot live without you. You and Canis and G are the only comforts I have.'

There was a new comfort in the shape of a fresh companion, Charles Grey, whom Georgiana said she admired but was not in love with. She did however recognise that he was dangerous, because very amiable.[35] Time would tell how dangerous he would prove.

Just as Bess was preparing herself to undergo labour in a squalid anonymous backstreet at the hands of a grim stranger, she received a cheerful letter from Canis telling her that Georgiana was so big she could only waddle and may well be carrying twins, in which case they would make a present of one of them to Bess. Her feelings at this time need not be conjectured. She has left a graphic description in her Journal:

Imagine a little staircase, dark and dirty, leading to the apartments of these people. The family consisted of the *Archi-Prêtre des Amoureux*; his woman-servant, a coarse, ugly, and filthy creature; the doctor (his brother) and his wife – the doctor an honest man, the wife everything that one can imagine of wicked, vulgar, and horrible; two young girls pretty enough but weeping all day; a married elder sister – who was the best of the lot; the nurse who was to take charge of my child; and some babies which cried from morning till night – there you have the family of the respectable *Archi-Prêtre*, who had a sort of seraglio around him.

We entered. They clustered about me, and, seeing how weak I was, they installed me on a sofa, but could not refrain from making a thousand comments upon myself and my supposed husband. . . .

I heard everything but pretended to understand nothing. I wished to escape from their comments and went to bed – but not to sleep. My faithful servant wept for me and wept that he was compelled to forget that he was my servant in the familiar terms upon which we had to live. How many things increased my unhappiness! I had to dine with him, and endure the odious company of these people; I had to live in a house which was little better than a house of ill fame.

She gave letters to her brother to be posted a hundred and fifty miles away to give everyone the impression they were enjoying themselves on holiday. Then he left, and Bess was abandoned with her servant, passing as her husband. 'I waited patiently for death, regretting only my child, and its father, and my friend.'

> Fifteen days were passed in waiting – and at last, just as I was thinking of looking for another refuge, on August 16, at 9 o'clock in the morning, after strong but short pains, I gave birth to a daughter.[36]

In stark contrast two weeks later, and in the comfort and security of Devonshire House with good Dr Denman in attendance, Georgiana gave birth to her second daughter. Canis wrote to inform Bess, 'I have the pleasure of acquainting you that the Duchess is safely brought to bed of a girl, and she and the child are both as well as can be.'[37]

*   *   *

Georgiana's second daughter was given the name Harriet, after her aunt Lady Duncannon, later shortened to the form by which she was always known in the family – 'Hary-O' (the freakish Whig pronunciation insisted on turning 'Harriet' into 'Harriot'). Lady Elizabeth Foster's daughter was called Caroline, and Lady Duncannon's daughter, born three months afterwards, was also called Caroline. By a peculiar coincidence, both Carolines would eventually grow up to marry sons of Lady Melbourne, and would both thereby share the same name – Caroline Lamb.

For the moment, no such bright future appeared possible for the little girl born in the nondescript abode of a noisy grubby Italian family. So appalled was Bess at the ignorance of the women folk in that house, that she determined to nurse the child herself for as long as she could do so without arousing comment. 'The moment I took her in my arms I felt only a mother's tenderness.' When on August 22 she left Vietri to return to Naples, she had perforce to hand the child to the care of her servant, the pretended father, and a maid, visiting her only as a disinterested benefactress. She would sometimes arrange to take the baby out for a walk, and when she was sure no one was looking, pick her up and cuddle her.

The servant provided Bess with flannels to cover her breasts and hide the evidence of her motherhood while she reassumed her place in the society of Naples. Visitors at Naples then included Georgiana's brother, Lord Spencer, and his unpopular wife Lavinia, who 'seemed to raise herself three feet in order to look down with contempt on me', as Bess told Georgiana. 'I was as civil as I could but I could gain nothing, she tossed her head and seemed determined to despise me.'[38] Nevertheless, the Spencers suspected nothing.

Bess reproached Canis for his apparent indifference to her wretched ordeal, in a letter since destroyed, to which he replied that his ease was entirely counterfeited 'for it was impossible for anyone to be more uneasy than I was about you for many months'.[39] He had naturally to be careful what he wrote, and was not predisposed in any case to be effusive.

Before the end of the year, another amorous intrigue in Georgiana's circle reached its culmination. Mrs Fitzherbert returned to England, once again giving rise to hints and suppositions that she was to become the wife of the Prince of Wales. Fox wrote to his friend warning him against any rash action. A marriage of the sort, he said, would be a mockery; it would be neither honourable nor safe; he would recommend that Mrs Fitzherbert be the Prince's mistress and leave it at that. Marriage with a Catholic was anyway prohibited by the Act of Settlement, and would in law deprive the Prince of his right to the succession. It was further rendered impossible by the Royal Marriage Act of 1772, according to which it would be legally non-existent. The prince told others that he intended to repeal this Act when he was King, but to Fox he wrote a letter full of re-assurance and dissemblance. 'Make yourself easy, my dear friend', he said. 'Believe me the world will now soon be convinced that there not only is not, but never was, any ground for these reports which have of late been so malevolently circulated.'[40]

A few days later, on 15 December 1785, the Prince of Wales was married to Mrs Fitzherbert in a secret ceremony at her house, with her uncle and younger brother as witnesses. Fox took the Prince's part in the House of Commons, denying in the most vehement and certain language that any such marriage had taken place. When he was proven wrong, the Prince's betrayal of his trust added a further nail into the coffin of his once glorious reputation. The Dowager Lady Spencer's main concern in all this was to protect Georgiana's reputation, which would suffer irremediably if she were observed to be friendly with Mrs Fitzherbert. 'When, my dear Georgiana, shall I see you out of scrapes that injure your character?' she sighed.[41]

Meanwhile, Bess had found a surname for her love child. The Comte St Jules for an unexplained reason was content to be regarded as the grandfather, though not, of course, with Lady Elizabeth as the mother. She was 'taking an interest' in Caroline St Jules and purposed eventually to bring her to England, where she trusted the true paternity could no longer be suspected. Still she wrote to Canis painting a glum picture of her endless peregrinations around Italy. 'I make allowances for your disposition', he told her, 'which is always so apt to magnify all your distresses, and to despond about everything.' This was true enough, but tactless of him to remind her in the circumstances. He promised her that they were all three as much attached as they would always be 'at all times and in all situations', and further put her mind at rest as to the Duchess's ignorance. She had no idea why Bess was so unhappy, 'and I, of course, shall never mention it to her, unless you desire me, but I am certain that if she did, she would not think you had been to blame about it, particularly after I had explain'd to her how the thing happen'd'.[42]

Bess responded with an agitated letter to Georgiana which showed that she now thought it safe to reclaim her friend without risk of hurting her. 'If you could forsake me I would not bear to live', she said, 'I am miserable without you – our hearts are formed for each other', and much more in the same vein.[43] Bess began her journey home via Spain, and was due to arrive in London at the end of July 1786. Georgiana rose to a fever of excitement at the promised reunion. Lady Spencer was considerably more controlled. Would nothing dislodge the ever-recurring embarrassment of Lady Elizabeth?

Chapter Seven

MÉNAGE À TROIS AND GAMBLING

'The private (for *secret* it never was) history of Devonshire House would be curious and amusing as a scandalous chronicle – an exhibition of vice in its most refined and attractive form, full of grace, dignity, and splendour, but I fancy full of misery and sorrow also.'[1]

Greville wrote these words forty years after Georgiana's death, and twenty-two after Lady Elizabeth's. The conviction that a hidden tragedy was played out within those walls has persisted. Another hundred years, and Lord David Cecil was able to write that 'life at Devonshire House was a continual strain on the spirit; beneath its shining surface seethed always a turmoil of yearning and jealousy, crisis and intrigue, gnawing hope and unavailing despair'.[2] Lord David quoted his hero Melbourne's aphorism 'To those who think, life is a comedy, to those who feel, a tragedy', which might be especially apposite to the inmates of Devonshire House. The Duke was one who thought, and could have been amused by the *ménage à trois* of which he was the pivot. Georgiana and Bess were indisputably creatures who felt, and of the two, Georgiana had the edge, being a woman for whom the emotions were everything. Her descendants have inherited the tradition that she was a tragic figure.

Although the pretence of propriety was maintained, there were few who did not guess what was really going on, and they assumed that Georgiana consented to the arrangement because it relieved her from irksome conjugal duties towards a husband whom she did not love. The situation as it appeared to contemporaries was summarised by a French author, whose account is here given in translation:

Lady Elizabeth Hervey was at one and the same time the

mistress of the Duke of Devonshire and the most faithful
friend of her lover's wife, without this equivocal situation in
any way damaging their mutual affection. The two women
lived side by side, in the same house, inseparable companions. The famous and beautiful Duchess of Devonshire,
far from being jealous of her rival, was grateful to her for thus
releasing her from her marital obligations . . . the aristocratic
world grew accustomed to tolerate the abnormal position of
Lady [Elizabeth] Foster and her illicit relationship with the
Duke of Devonshire, pursued with the full knowledge of the
Duchess, who seemed to give it her approval and authority.[3]

So, was Georgiana jealous or not? To all outward
appearances, she was not, yet the conviction remains that she
must have suffered greatly. This, I think, is to impose upon her
reactions which we suppose we should have felt but of which she
gave no evidence. Her mother's conventional attitudes were
outraged by the assault on cherished moral standards, but
Georgiana time and again implored her to accept the fact that
Elizabeth would never be abandoned by either herself or the
Duke. 'You are wrong, grossly wrong, Dst M,' she told her with
unaccustomed defiance. 'The Duke added just now that he
could not help thinking it a most extraordinary circumstance
that when a man and his wife both agree in living with a person,
that you should be persuaded to imagine that there was a cause
of complaint.'[4]

Perhaps it was arch of Georgiana constantly to avoid men-
tioning the real 'cause for complaint' – that Bess was the Duke's
mistress – of which she was certainly by this time aware, but we
must be careful not to regard this omission as proof of naïvety.
We simply do not know if she gave voice to any heartache, for
her huge collection of letters at Chatsworth has been
scrutinised by so many who were intimately involved in her
story, and so many of them have been tampered with, that it is
reasonable to assume that embarrassing confessions have been
removed. When Georgiana died, her mother went through all
the correspondence, 'but it is sometimes almost too much for
me', she admitted.[5] Bess also reread them, as did the 6th Duke.
Some of the letters have whole paragraphs crossed out by a later
hand in darker ink, others bear the marks of pages removed by

cutting. The great majority of letters Georgiana wrote to her sister Harriet, in whom she confided deeply, were purposefully burnt in 1821, much to the annoyance of the 6th Duke, who thought they should have been returned to Chatsworth.[6] It is therefore fair to presume, though not to conclude, that any record of Georgiana's unhappiness could have been excised for posterity.

There is still the evidence of her behaviour and her appearance. She said often enough that she loved the Duke, but in muted, dutiful tones which were blazingly at variance with her unrestrained attachment to Bess. She gambled like a mad woman, as one who sought to suppress sorrows in amusement. She took medicines to help her get through the day, others to send her to sleep, causing her health to deteriorate rapidly. She was a constant victim of debilitating headache. Her poor health could not be ascribed to a specific illness, but rather to the insidious weakening of a burdened mind. Walpole commented that the empress of fashion 'verges fast to a coarseness',[7] and the astute eye of Fanny Burney discerned a coruscating sadness beneath the ebullience. 'She seems by nature to possess the highest animal spirits', wrote Miss Burney, 'but she appeared to me not happy. I thought she looked oppressed within, though there is a native cheerfulness about her which I fancy scarce ever deserts her. There is in her face, especially when she speaks, a sweetness of good humour and obligingness, that seem to be the natural and instinctive qualities of her disposition; joined to an openness of countenance that announces her endowed, by nature, with a character intended wholly for honesty, fairness, and good purposes.'[8]

In one of her strongest letters of reproof, Lady Spencer implored Georgiana to take more care of her health, discreetly blaming the accumulation of her debts as the root of her anxiety, when it was possibly, as they both knew, only the symptom. 'For God's sake try to compose yourself,' she said. 'I am terrified lest the perpetual hurry of your spirits, and the medicines you take to obtain a false tranquility, should injure you . . . nothing is so bad for you as continual fretting. Why will you not say fairly: – I have led a wild and scrambling life that disagrees with me. I have lost more money than I can afford. I will turn over a new leaf and lead a quiet sober life from this moment, as I am sure if I do not I shall hurt myself or my child. . .?'[9]

Did she 'fret' over the deepening attachment between her friend and her husband? All the indications are that she did not. It was not part of her nature to be resentful or bitter. She would blame no one for her unhappiness, which derived not from jealousy but from an obscure discontent that while others appeared to enjoy the warm glow of romantic connections, she was obliged to endure a staid, dull, ordinary marriage which blunted the flow of her generous affections. The Duke would sometimes scribble a P.S. on the back of one of Georgiana's letters to Bess, such as 'I hope you are not out of humour with, or forgetful of C[anis], who loves you as much if not more than ever'. A jealous woman would have collapsed within; Georgiana gaily referred to her husband as 'your' Ca when addressing her friend: 'Your Ca is as drunk as a piper and as imprudent as you ever saw him.'[10]

She went further. She told Bess, 'Always write to him if you have not time for both . . . you must write to him as you have done for it makes him proud and happy.' This was saintly generosity indeed. Is it too harsh to set against it Elizabeth Foster's laughingly pious reflections in a letter to her son Augustus? She said she was pleased to hear 'William Lamb say with earnestness that if he felt a growing passion for his friend's wife he would fly to the further end of the earth to resist the danger'.[11]

If there was a tragedy, it lay in the fact that Georgiana possessed a capacity for love far in excess of any of her circle, a love which she had to deflect into trivial distractions when her exemplary devotion to her children or to unfortunate Bess was unable to absorb it all. She needed a man to kindle her passion as her husband had never done; that man had already appeared in the person of young, handsome Charles Grey, but Georgiana was yet to learn how deeply he had moved her.

For the moment she was content to boast about Grey's achievements in the House of Commons. He made the finest of speeches today, some thought it was the equal of anything of Charles Fox or Burke. 'Burke in his transport took his hand and squeezed it.' As for flirtation, no, she would be sensible. 'When he was by me Lord Henry Fitzgerald told me it was right that the

handsomest man and woman in England should be together,
but I will not be childish enough to let anything so foolish as my
liking to talk to so young a man be thought of.'[12]

*   *   *

In July 1786, Lady Elizabeth Foster disembarked at Southampton after an absence of eighteen months. There to meet her, even
if not precisely at the dockside, was the Duke.

> I arrived – he had dined out but left a note; he came; Oh,
> heavens, such moments do indeed efface past sorrows! – yet it
> was happiness mixed with fear and agitation.[13]

Fear and agitation? How much did Georgiana know? How had
she taken it? Would London be hostile to her? Could she
continue to mask her feelings for her Duke?

London society welcomed Bess back into the fold and she got
on well with Lady Melbourne, which was an asset. But Lady
Spencer remained fiercely distant. Once more Bess was foolish
enough to append a postscript to one of Georgiana's letters to
her mother, saying that she was bouncing little Georgiana up
and down on her lap, laughing and chortling as usual, which
was not the piece of news most calculated to delight the
Dowager. Bess also made a remark to Lady Spencer which was
heavily significant. In her usual convoluted prose she regretted
'the uneasiness and apprehension I had the misfortune to be the
occasion of your suffering'.[14] As Bess had done nothing else to
cause Lady Spencer any 'apprehension', this can only refer to
her position in the Devonshire household and more specifically
to her relations with the Duke. It is one of the few references in
the correspondence which has escaped the censor's scissors and
throws some tiny light on the degree of honesty displayed by all
the protagonists in the drama. If Lady Spencer knew something
which gave her apprehension, then presumably Georgiana
knew it too, for this sentence was written on the back of one of
her own letters.

It is extremely difficult to disentangle who knew what. Lady
Spencer certainly did not know that Bess had borne a child by her
son-in-law, for three years later Georgiana described Caroline
St Jules to her mother as 'a young lady from the provinces', with
the air of one who had mentioned her for the first time. But it is

very probable that Georgiana herself was informed about Caroline during this happy re-union summer of 1786. There is no trace in the documents which survive of any conversation between the two women on this subject; Georgiana's devotion to Bess did not diminish, nor did she display any reluctance to welcome Caroline when the time came. One explanation could be that she was still kept in ignorance, but this would stretch our credulity too far. More in keeping with the woman as we know thus far is that she understood and sympathised. Well might Bess declare that her heart could never alter towards dear Georgiana. 'No, never, never, never.'

That summer at Chatsworth a similar farce was played below stairs which subtly mocked the sedate sexual minuet pursued above. Lord Barrington wrote to the Earl of Huntingdon the following intelligence: 'A man at Chatsworth suspected the Duke of Devonshire's French cook to have got an infant that his wife had lately brought into the world. He consulted the chaplain, who advised him to stay till the child could talk; then, said the doctor, if it speaks French you may conclude that you are injured, but if it speaks English you may be quite easy.'[15]

Canis, Bess and Georgiana were as much together as possible for the rest of that year and all the following year, darting about from London, to Chatsworth, Bolton Abbey, Hardwick and Bath. Georgiana was obliged to juggle very carefully with dates to avoid an unseemly clash between her mother and her friend, as Mama made it perfectly clear that she would not deem it proper to be under the same roof as the 'friend'. When Lady Spencer came to stay at Chatsworth, Bess was packed off to see her mother at Ickworth. They never coincided. Apart from that, there was no longer any question where Bess belonged; her home was with the Devonshires, her life was spent in their company, her clothes hung in their wardrobes. Sheridan made the saucy remark that Lady Elizabeth was in love with the Duke, at which we may only presume everyone laughed. In the privacy of her journal, she reflected that 'every day my tenderness for him increased and so, I think, did his confidence and affection for me'.

By the autumn of 1787, there was visible proof that Bess was right. The family (Duke, Duchess, mistress, and Duchess's two little girls) spent Christmas in Bath, returning to London at the end of January 1788. Plans were now being laid for Bess to make yet another trip to Europe, the intention being that Georgiana and the Duke should accompany her part of the way. The Duke had to withdraw from this arrangement in order to be present in London for the trial of Warren Hastings, but Georgiana still entertained the idea of going with Bess for a month. Lady Spencer was horrified. She put her foot down. Unable to summon any solid excuse for persisting, Georgiana relented. She and the Duke went with Bess as far as Dover, stayed two days with her in idle simplicity, then saw her off. After some nostalgic sentimental walks along the beach, the actual leave-taking was hard for Bess.

> Oh it was bitterness of grief to lose her [she wrote] but him – his last embrace – his last look drew my soul after him – I remained motionless – even now, it is present to me. I see him – he is fixed in my heart – this guilty heart – Oh, why could I not love him without crime? Why cannot I be his without sin?[16]

The truth was, Bess *had* to disappear again, because she was already six months' pregnant with the second child the Duke had given her. This time there was no need for furtiveness, at least within their own happy circle. Whatever discussion had taken place between the three, Georgiana was now privy to the bond which united her husband and her friend, and seemed perfectly happy to regard conception as one of its inherent risks. When she had proposed going with Bess to Europe, she was well aware of the purpose of the journey; it had been a joint decision, made by all three of them.

Bess's travels took her to Toulon, where she saw her daughter Caroline St Jules for the first time in two years and pledged that she would henceforth watch over her with a mother's fondness 'and compensate for the error which gave thee birth'. She intended to bring Caroline to London to be brought up with her half-sisters Georgiana and Harriet. For the moment, however, she must first contend with the imminent birth of her new love-child.

Having confided her secret to her maid Lucille, Lady Elizabeth went with her to Rouen for the lying-in. The Duke sent over a 'Dr G' from England to attend her (though he was obliged to return before the birth), and she was housed in a 'tolerable' apartment with a respectable doctor to care for her; it was a great improvement upon the sordid circumstances surrounding the birth of Caroline. On 26 May, after a short but severe labour, the Duke's first son was born. In accordance with the curious customs of the day, his paternity was tacitly acknowledged by the names he was given – Augustus William James Clifford. 'Augustus' was a frequently recurring name in the Hervey family, 'William' was the Duke of Devonshire's christian name, 'James' was a tribute to her friend James Hare, and the surname 'Clifford' derived from a subsidiary title of the Duke's, the barony of Clifford which he had inherited from his mother. In the midst of her joy at suckling the child, Bess found time to tell her diary that she wished Georgiana could have a son, too.

Little Augustus Clifford (who would one day be the celebrated Admiral Sir Augustus Clifford, Gentleman Usher of the Black Rod), was placed with a foster-mother in Normandy when his mother reurned to England, only a month after his birth. After a couple of weeks with Lady Bristol at Ickworth, Bess was once more re-united with her beloved friends at Devonshire House. This time her absence had extended to barely five months.

Caroline St Jules was despatched with her *other* half-sister Charlotte Williams to Paris, to be housed and educated by a certain Monsieur and Madame Nagel. This was to be only an interim solution to her fate. The decision had already been reached, as we know, that Caroline should assume her place in the nursery at Devonshire House. It was simply a matter of choosing the right moment. Lady Spencer must be kept in ignorance of her paternity (why? when she would certainly guess the reason for Augustus's surname!), but intimates already knew. One such was James Hare, who visited Normandy a year later and reported to Bess that her little boy was perfectly well, and 'promises to be a giant'. On the subject of Caroline, Hare thought that the Nagels' apartment was so scruffy and their attentions so inadequate that she ought to be brought to London where she could be properly looked after:

It would be dealing insincerely with you if I were to say that I think her introduction at D. House will occasion no surmises or scandal, but this consideration is in my mind infinitely over ballanced by your having her under your own care, whether one thinks of her advantage or your amusement. As to the difficulties which seem to terrify the Dss so much, I guess that they must be, and I wish that they did not exist, but they cannot last long, and when once the little woman has gained a footing, I am not afraid of her being disturbed. As to any scruples that you may entertain about imposing upon people whom you ought to love, and do, I confess it would be pleasanter if no deceit were necessary, but when things have gone so far as they have, there is no choice left, and it becomes a duty to consult the interest of poor little helpless wretches, even at the expence of feelings, which may be sometimes distressing.[17]

* * *

The tangled mess of Georgiana's financial affairs, of her debts incurred at the gaming-tables, was now threatening to engulf her. It is true that gambling was the curse of the aristocracy for the last thirty years of the eighteenth century, affecting every noble family in some measure; Georgiana was not by any means uniquely sinful in this respect. 'Play is a detestable occupation,' wrote Greville some years later. 'It absorbs all our thoughts and renders us unfit for everything else in life. It is hurtful to the mind and destroys the better feelings; it incapacitates us for study and application of every sort; it makes us thoughtful and nervous; and our cheerfulness depends upon the uncertain event of our nightly occupation.'[18] There were some alive in Georgiana's time who held similar stringent views. Lady Stafford wrote to her son Granville Leveson-Gower (who would be Harriet Duncannon's lover and subsequently Hary-O's husband) that gaming 'leads to ruin, not only by hurting the Fortune, but it erases every good Affectation, it destroys Health, it brings into the worst Company, and destroys all good Principles . . . when once the Inclination takes Place, it is with difficulty restrain'd.'[19] And Lady Holland had this to say: 'There is no one poison in the human breast that operates so powerfully to the exclusion of every good feeling, as that of gambling. It produces misanthropy, meanness, and avarice, and I do not know a real amateur and practitioner of the vice in favour of

whom an exception can be made . . . the scandalous expedients
a certain Duchess has, to my knowledge, been able to bring
herself to resort to, have inspired me with horror and contempt
for the class.'[20]

The 'certain Duchess' was of course Georgiana, and the
damage to her health and peace of mind which gambling caused
her, dragging her into the net of deceit and false promises,
cannot be denied. We have already seen how her friend Fox
squandered his patrimony with sublime nonchalance. Scores of
other examples may be cited to fill out the picture. The Duke of
Northumberland lost £20,000 at the quinze table. Green
young men would habitually lose up to the same amount every
night at Almack's. Bets were placed on everything under the
sun; which raindrop would reach the bottom of the window-
pane first, or which of two flies would reach the top; which of two
men would outlive the other; whether it was possible to find a
person fatter than the Duke of Cumberland. On one occasion, a
man collapsed outside Brooks's Club (some say it was White's).
The body was brought in, and bets immediately placed upon
whether he was dead or not. It was proposed to bleed him to find
out, but those who had placed money on his being alive objected
that the knife would unfairly affect the outcome of the bet. When
Mr Flood and Mr Grattan started a fight in the House of
Commons and engaged to settle the matter by duel, d'Adhémar
commented how odd it was to observe statesmen placing bets
upon which one would die, as if they were gambling on horses.[21]

Thomas Whaley bet he would jump from his drawing-room
window into the first carriage that passed beneath, and kiss the
occupant, whoever it was. A man at White's bet £1,500 that it
was possible to live for twelve hours under water, hired a poor
fool to submit to the experiment, and drowned him. Sometimes
it was considered manly to back one's opinion with cash rather
than waste hours in fruitless debate; if you were not prepared to
lay money to support your view, then your confidence was
questionable.

Yet more whimsical examples are preserved in the 'Betts
Book' at Brooks's Club. Mr Stewart wagered with Mr Coke on
the average weight of sheep sold at Smithfield. Mr Fitzpatrick bet
Lord Cholmondeley that no Minister would be beheaded before
6 February 1778. General Tarleton bet Mr Sheridan that the

shortest way from Debrett's shop in Piccadilly to No 4, Old Burlington Street, was through Bond Street and not through Sackville Street.

Not everyone lost. An Irish adventurer called O'Byrne amassed a fortune at the tables and became an intimate of the Prince of Wales. He won £100,000 one evening from a Mr Harvey, who had just inherited an estate. 'You can never pay me,' said O'Byrne. Harvey proposed to sell his estate for the debt. 'No', said O'Byrne, 'I shall accept £10,000, and you shall throw for the odd ninety.' They did, and Harvey won. The most successful player was General John Scott, of Balcombie, who unlike his opponents stayed sober and understood the game of whist. He won a total of £200,000 at White's and was able to retire, the wealthiest commoner in Scotland, to a beautiful house in Edinburgh which he won from Sir Laurence Dundas. He emerged from retirement to win a fortune for his daughter. Scott kept an even temper, iron control, and held to a rigid diet of boiled chicken, toast and water before sitting down to play.

Pitt and his supporters in the Court faction lost their money at White's, while Fox and his Whigs kept exclusively to Brooks's, into which they inveigled the Prince of Wales. When George III went mad, it was *de rigueur* to say at cards, instead of 'I play the King' — 'I play the lunatic'.

At Almack's, Brooks's, White's, the Cocoa-Tree, Graham's, gamblers prepared themselves for a night's play with serious aspect. At Almack's, for instance, they took off their heavily embroidered clothes and donned coats made of green felt, or turned their coats inside out for luck. They wore pieces of leather on their wrists to protect their lace, and broad-brimmed hats to deflect the glare of the light. To conceal their emotions they sometimes even wore masks.

Were it only the men who dribbled their fortunes away, it would have been bad enough, but in addition their wives frittered what was left and presented them with the bills. The favourite game with the ladies, the game which caught Lady Spencer and both her daughters, was faro. 'The trade or amusement which engrosses everybody who lives in what is called the pleasurable world is Pharo,' wrote George Selwyn to Lord Carlisle in 1781. 'Poor Mr Grady is worn out in being kept up at one lady's house or another till six in the morning. Among these, Lady Spencer and her daughter the Duchess of Devonshire, and Lady Harcourt are his chief punters . . . there is generally two or three thousand lying on the table in rouleaus till about noon, but who they belong to, or will belong to, the Lord knows.'[22] Harriet Duncannon tells how a man once came to her parents with a fool-proof scheme for winning at faro and persuaded them to part with some stakes for him to place on their behalf with his infallible method; no more was heard of him.[23]

Faro (originally Pharaoh, then Pharo) came to England from France, where it was very much in vogue at the Court of Louis XIV. It was quiet, extremely easy to learn, and rested entirely upon chance. It was played with a pack of fifty-two cards, the banker on one side of the table, and any number of punters opposite him. The pack would be exposed, and from another pack the banker would draw two cards, one for himself on the right, the other, called the Carte Anglaise, for the punters on the left. Players then had to guess this card, and won double the stakes if they were right; they lost everything to the banker from cards which were of the same suit as the one on the right. Faro was described as the most 'bewitching' game of the day (an appropriate adjective), 'for when a man begins to play he knows not when to leave off; and having once accustomed himself to it he hardly ever plays anything else'.[24]

Nobody seemed to be deterred by the knowledge that games of chance, including the two most popular – faro and hazard – were strictly against the law and players subject to penalty. The Act of 1738 specified that these games were forbidden, at all times and in all places, whether public or private, with the sole exception made that they were permitted within the precincts of a royal palace when the sovereign was in residence. Devonshire House, despite appearances, did not qualify. Nor did Lady Buckingham's residence, wherein several fine ladies were arrested one night in 1797, including Georgiana's sister Harriet, and actually convicted at Bow Street Court. The women were fined £750 for playing faro, and Henry Martindale, with whom Georgiana had many dealings, was fined £200 for keeping the faro bank. Apart from isolated embarrassments such as this, gambling proceeded in London with blatant abandon, under bridges, at street corners, in grand mansions. It was a veritable social disease which contaminated more or less everyone. As is usual with gamblers, few of them had the funds to meet the debts they incurred, which were always unfailingly in excess of their resources. Georgiana was typical in this respect. Her allowance from the Devonshire estate was £2,000 *per annum*; she regularly spent thirty times that amount.

The Duchess did not gradually learn to be a gambler. Hereditary inclination made it impossible for her to avoid it. Her parents both played without secrecy, rendering rather empty their pious exhortations to their daughters to steer wide of the perils. Lady Spencer was painfully conscious of 'the bad example I have set you, and which you have but too faithfully imitated'. She thought to keep a careful watch on the dangers which loomed above her daughter, asking her to play only with what she had and not to borrow, and 'I shall be very glad if you will tell me *honestly* in each letter what you have won or lost and at what games every day'.[25]

Nevertheless, she had only been married one year when her first troubles began. The losses were more than she expected, she owed money to several people, she was afraid to tell the Duke, what could she do? On this first occasion, Mama intervened to explain the circumstances to the Duke and the debts were forthwith settled without further comment. That was a pity, as it turned out, for Georgiana needed to be taught a lesson. Her debts immediately mounted again. Moneylenders, such as Howard & Gibbs, advanced funds to be repaid at extortionate interest, with the additional threat of revealing all to the Duke of Devonshire if their terms were not met. Sheridan was seen helping the weeping Duchess into her carriage after a spectacularly bad evening at the tables, and matters reached the point where she had sometimes to hitch up her clothes and make a quick dash across the courtyard of Devonshire House to get into her carriage before waiting bailiffs might seize her.

'The Duchess of Devonshire is in debt to all the banks she has ever been connected with,' wrote Daniel Pulteney in 1787.[26] As soon as she managed to get hold of some money to *reduce* a liability, she considered herself rich again, though the amount still owing might be several thousands of pounds. The fact that she borrowed in order to lavish her generosity upon others did not, of course, exonerate her, but it did make it impossible to face such good nature with anger. One of the beneficiaries was naturally Lady Elizabeth Foster, who told Georgiana in 1786, 'I am rich now you heap wealth upon me. You are too good to me.'[27]

A new craze took hold of the smart set around 1780, when lottery offices were opened behind the opera. After the performance, ladies went to place bets on numbers. If the number you chose came up the next day, you could receive forty guineas; if it did not, you paid five. In one day Georgiana improved her finances by winning £900 at the lottery.[28] Emboldened by this, Georgiana and Harriet ventured to trading on street corners and in back alleys. Walpole tells the story:

> Two of our first ladies, sisters, have descended into the *basse cour* of the [Exchange] Alley with Jews and brokers, and waddled out with a large loss of feathers, though not so inconsiderable as was said – yet twenty-three thousand makes a great gap in pin-money.[29]

This was a dangerous rumour. Harriet felt obliged to issue a firm denial, published in the *Gazeteer* and the *New Daily Advertiser*, to the effect that 'I have not the most faint idea what could give rise to so shocking an insinuation'. It convinced nobody.

The first crisis erupted during the rough and tumble of the Westminster election in 1784. Georgiana confided to Bess that she had incurred 'a very, very large debt. I never had courage to own it, and try'd to win it at play, by which means it became immense and was grown (I have not the courage to write the sum, but will tell you when I see you), many, many, many thousands.'[30] Having assured Bess that all the money sent to her 'flowed from Canis' and was anyway a mere drop in the ocean compared to her gigantic losses, she begged her friend not to hate her for this confession. 'Oh, love, love, love me ever.'

To her mother, Georgiana's confessions were more specific. She owed £700 to Lord Trentham, £400 to Lady Archer, £300 to Charles Greville, and £200 to Lord Duncannon. There was a further bill of £700 which she had not told the Duke about, and all this was trivial compared to the gaming debts, which had soared to sums beyond her ability to understand. If she did not comprehend mathematics of this heavenly order, the Duke for his part could not be bothered to try. His affairs were managed entirely by his agent, Mr Heaton, whom Georgiana distrusted because she suspected him of having spread rumours about her relationship with the Prince of Wales. Poor Georgiana fancied that the Devonshire estates were close to ruin as the result of her extravagance, so she had to be nice to Heaton if he was to dip into the ducal purse to rescue her. She trembled to imagine the Duke's response when he found out, her stomach turned over, she took medicine for her nerves, but in the end Heaton found the money to settle all her debts and she breathed again, thankful that the Duke would not have to sell one of his estates. If only she had realised, the Devonshire fortune was so vast that it could absorb a hundred follies of the Duchess and not be visibly hurt; it was so huge that the Duke had no idea how much money he had and cared less; it would simply always be there. Everything was left to Heaton. Georgiana suffered agonies of anxiety for nothing.

Lady Spencer hoped that Georgiana had been sufficiently shocked to give up gambling for ever, but it was not to be. Another two years and she had once more plunged her husband into catastrophe, or so she thought. This time it was so serious that it was suggested Georgiana must leave London (and temptation) to live in the country, if necessary apart from the Duke. At Althorp with her brother? At Londesborough? At Newmarket? Anywhere as long as she could spend at least a year away from London and be forced into the retrenchment which she had not the personality to undertake voluntarily. Heaton was again apprised of the full extent of Georgiana's calamitous deals, and the shock appears to have affected his nerves. The Duke merely said it was 'distressing'. Lady Spencer begged her daughter to wake the Duke up to the seriousness of the situation and form some determined plan with her. 'This is the first real difficulty you ever have met with', she wrote, 'do not allow yourself to sink under it.'[31]

It was Lady Elizabeth Foster who casually pointed out that if the Duke and Duchess were to live apart for a year, in order to prevent Georgiana from contracting new debts, then of course she, Bess, could no longer visit the Duke. It would not be proper. Nobody had thought of this aspect before, and they all immediately agreed that the idea of *this* separation was preposterous. So the plan was quietly forgotten, retrenchment being limited to the dismissal of four servants at Chatsworth and promises from the Duchess that she would behave herself in future. 'I wish I had a good managing head,' she told her mother.

Alas, no amount of disturbing shocks could rid Georgiana of her habit. She was becoming devious in an attempt to conceal her faults even from herself. In 1788 Louis XVI's former Finance Minister, Monsieur de Calonne, settled with his wife in England and quickly became a frequent visitor to Devonshire House. Georgiana confided her losses to him, implored his advice, asked for a loan. While she told Calonne that she owed £9,000, Mr Heaton was given a different amount, the Duke still another one. They were not confusing estimates of a single debt, but entirely different debts, which meant that no one person was ever fully informed of the Duchess's troubles. In fact, though she never had the courage to add it all up herself, and merely kept borrowing from one person to pay off another, her total liabilities were close to £60,000 by 1789.

Perhaps it was Calonne who introduced Georgiana to the French banker Comte Perregaux, with whom she now began a correspondence which does her little credit. She owed thousands to Perregaux, and sought to pay him in bits and pieces, with a thousand here and a thousand there, constantly playing with dates to make sure that Perregaux did not make his claims before she had funds to meet them. An extra forty-eight hours was all she needed to honour her obligations, she said, would he please be patient? She sent drafts over to Paris with the Pall Mall banker Hammersley, or with her step-daughter Charlotte Williams. She was even once reduced to sending money via Elizabeth Foster's servant Louis Rossi (the same who had pretended to be her husband when she gave birth to Caroline St Jules), always without the knowledge of her husband or Mr Heaton. 'Je vous prie de ne rien dire au Duc comme je ne lui en parlerai qu'en cas de retard et qu'il soit nécessaire qu'il avance l'argent,'* she said. On another occasion she sent a watch over to Paris hoping that her creditors would accept it in lieu of payment. When this failed, she asked the dealer from whom she had bought it, Deschamps, to buy it back from her, at

* I beseech you to say nothing to the Duke as I shall only speak to him about it in case of delay or should it be necessary for him to advance funds.

a price higher than he had originally sold it! Either she was scatter-brained or distracted with worry, or, perhaps, she was attempting a little mild dishonesty. Deschamps irritably told her that the cursed watch had caused him no end of inconvenience, and reminded her that she had bought it for only £19,000. She retorted, 'Mes affaires m'obligent à mettre tout ce que je puis en argent pour payer mes dettes.'*

She had indeed reached rock bottom. Her drafts were being refused, her trust was placed in question, she was selling objects to raise money, and still the amount seemed endless. One letter mentions a total of £42,000 owing in Paris alone. Desperate ('j'en suis au désespoir'), Georgiana instructed Perregaux to continue paying the Nagels their allowance six months after Charlotte Williams had left their house, 'comme si Mlle Williams y était'. This might have been kindness towards the Nagels, but since they were not held in high esteem by now, it is more likely that Georgiana wished to have the money secretly deflected to alleviate the distress on her own account.[32]

The degree to which Georgiana suffered as a result of her weakness, was in fact drawn into a kind of self-loathing which drained all her strength, is shown by one particular letter, un-catalogued and undated, written to Bess after a day of reckless gambling. Having confessed some of her debts to her husband, she immediately rushed off to increase them. No single document is so pathetically self-revealing or so poignantly dis-tressing as this unpublished fragment, recently discovered tucked into a little blue note-book containing her poems and scattered thoughts in Georgiana's hand, with 'carissima' written on the cover in Lady Elizabeth's script. 'My dearest dr Bess', she writes,

This is the last time perhaps you will ever speak to or love me – I really am unworthy of you and Canis and you must be shocked at my levity all today but there was no medium. When I first told all my debts to Ca at C [Chiswick or Chatsworth?] I had reserved 500 £ which I agreed to insure in this Lottery as a hope of regaining him some money – My good genius often prompted me to stop this but as I had agreed to do it and paid the money into Baker's hands for the

* My affairs are such that I must convert all I have into cash to pay my debts.

First and last pages of Georgiana's letter to Bess

purpose I resolved unwillingly to do it. I went to Newmarket
and left an insurance meaning to stop – but I had some money
distress about Mr Cater [?] which I will explain to you. Oh
God Bess, I have gone on and I have lost an immense sum – I
dare not tell you that it is 6000 – It is madness and I ought not
to live on with Canis – but what am I to do? You must not tell
him this – and you shall advise me when I return what I am to
do – whether to tell him or not – it could be settled without
and so that it never should come to him – you know he *could*
not forgive me. My Bess, I am desperate. If the Eyebrow* had
been here I should have thrown myself into his arms, to have
completed myself – you see that doating on Ca how I have
used him. I scarcely have pleasure in looking at my Babes. Say
nothing to him until I return – Oh Bess!

In similar vein, Georgiana wrote to her old friend the Prince of
Wales. 'I cannot conceive why anybody should interest

---

* Charles James Fox.

themselves about a being as little valuable as myself,' she said. 'I do not think anybody would lose by my ceasing to exist. I am only a burden and plague to all my friends.'[33]

Salvation came to Georgiana from an unexpected source. Of all the bankers with whom she dealt in London, there was one who was disposed by inclination and ambition to help her more than strict professionalism would have allowed. When Thomas Coutts was approached by the penniless Duchess, he was completely knocked off balance by her charm and flattered by her confidence in him. She called him her 'second father', encouraging the avuncular smile and tender respect with which he treated her. Georgiana's irresistible vitality was, she finally realised, her greatest asset. With it, she could induce Mr Coutts the banker to behave less like a banker where she was concerned, and more like a friend. Besides, Coutts was a snob. To be counted a friend by Her Grace of Devonshire was like the sound of tinkling bells to this canny cautious Scotsman who was now sole partner in the firm of Coutts & Co. and was steadily building up a clientele almost exclusively noble. Coutts was naturally a kind man, likely always to help a lady in distress independently of her ability to return any favour, but in Georgiana's case, she was not only in terrible danger, as he could see at a glance, but she could use influence on his behalf.

Gradually Thomas Coutts was drawn into a pernicious spiral, advancing money on virtually no security to Georgiana, in return for which she bestowed on him the glory of her friendship (no mean gift), introduced his daughters at the French court, and spoke on his behalf with the Prince of Wales to procure for him the Royal account. Only when it was too late did Coutts realise that he had been seduced; Georgiana realised it quite plainly, and would say in her last years that Coutts had been her best friend.

The Duchess's initial appeal as a helpless woman ('I am so ignorant of business of any kind') was quickly followed by a hint that she might do something silly if Coutts did not come to her rescue. 'The despair that the Duke or even Crauford's knowing of my distress would put me to, would, I am afraid, drive me to ev'ry ruinous expedient.'[34] The Duke had paid some of her debts, but unfortunately not enough to lift her out of trouble.

What she did not say was that the moneys advanced by the Duke were lamentably insufficient for the simple reason that she had not dared tell him the truth. Everything now depended upon Mr Coutts. 'In this situation I entreat and conjure you to give me this chance, this trial of my conduct. Lend me £3,300.'

Coutts responded gallantly, and Georgiana was reprieved. Ecstatically she wrote, 'You, oh, God bless you, restore me to peace, health, happyness and prudence. It does indeed take me out of ev'ry hand but yours.'[35] This was not true, but never mind, it gave Mr Coutts the feeling of close and special responsibility which would keep the pounds flowing. It also gave the gentleman a superb excuse to offer advice, expressed in elegant language half-way between business accuracy and friendly concern, covering many pages in a precise careful hand. Coutts was undoubtedly right in all he said, lightly reproving the Duchess for her stupidity, but she had never yet been able to act upon advice.

> It shocks me to think what your Grace puts into hazard by indulging a passion for play [he wrote]. There is nothing your Grace can acquire; you have already titles, character, friends, fortune, power, beauty, *everything* superior to the rest of the world . . . all these you risk to gratify this destructive passion. . . . I should be happy beyond expression if I could think that I had even the smallest share in saving your Grace from the dreadful consequences I foresee . . . pecuniary obligations even among the best friends should be avoided. I hope your Grace will confine them to me, and I should wish you to order the Duke's agents to pay in your Grace's annual allowance of pin-money etc etc to my House to be drawn for by your Grace as you have occasion.[36]

This suited Georgiana perfectly. She would hand all her affairs over to Coutts (apart from those she had given to Hammersley, and those Monsieur Calonne was looking after, and the other debts which were too embarrassing even to remember); she would keep a little book into which she would record all her transactions, if she knew how. 'If you please you shall give me my book then and teach me how to use it,' she wrote, with a feminine subtlety which now makes one smile. Poor Coutts had filigrees of tender guile wrapped remorselessly around him. As

for the Misses Coutts in Paris, they would have nothing to worry
about. She would speak to the Duchesse de Polignac and the
Duchesse de Luynes, who would be happy to take them to the
theatre and present them in the best society. Then there was the
Duchesse de la Vallière and Mme de Matignon. Of course, the
Duke of Dorset, our Ambassador, would be useful too. Thomas
Coutts reeled at the list.[37]

When George III suffered a mental breakdown in 1788 giving
rise to fears that he might die, Coutts, who was already banker to
the King, asked Georgiana to put in a word for him that he
might retain the royal account if the Prince of Wales succeeded
in the near future. 'If the King dies I lose a good friend', he said,
'but I am in hopes I may still be employ'd by his successor, for I
was his *first* banker and he has always approved my conduct. I
should wish much your Grace would speak to the Prince in case
the melancholy event proves true. My honour is so much interested in being continued banker to the King's Privy Purse at
least, if not to the other branches of his employ.'[38]

There it was, naked and to the point. In the circumstances, it
would be wise to help the Duchess further with a loan of £6,000.
As his biographer has pointed out, it was in fact very unwise of
Mr Coutts to allow himself to be sucked into furtive intrigues
with a delightful unreliable lady. 'He was not her banker, and he
ought not to have lent her a single sixpence except on
marketable security, and with the knowledge and assent of her
husband.'[39] He was lured by fascination for a beauty in distress,
whose tears and importunities he could not resist. 'It was not the
Duchess but the woman who silenced his scruples and overcame
his prudences.' Not quite. It was the woman who silenced his
scruples, but the Duchess who promised influence.

By the beginning of 1789, Georgiana was beseeching her
friend to advance another £6,000 which, she assured him, would
save her once and for all. Coutts now began to be apprehensive.
The new request drew from him a long letter, with two
postscripts, in which for the first time he voiced doubts. Coutts's
letters so vividly reflect his thoughts that they are worth quoting
in some detail:

It is really *romance* what I have done with money already, and
how to reconcile to any bounds of discretion (with my little

means) to do more, I know not. Besides, tho' you say it will *save you*, how does it appear that the second £6,000 will succeed (in this charming purpose) better than the first? . . . While I am essentially hurting the fortune of my family beyond what I can answer to them or to myself, how do I know that I am saving you from anything but a mere temporary inconveniency? Indeed, indeed, I fear, I should be doing no more. . . . I really think the best thing is to lay before the Duke the very worst of your situation at once, and at the same time take an absolute determination to reform your system. If *his* excusing the *past*, together with *your viewing* the precipice you are standing on the verge of, does not cure you I can only say you have gone beyond the point of recovery (I have mentioned) and are ruined and undone. Your Grace will excuse me, I write with the tear in my eye, and the utmost horror at the danger I see you have exposed yourself to.

Coutts was reluctant to provide another £6,000, but before he posted the letter, his wife prevailed upon him to relent, with the result that he enclosed instructions to his bank to make the money available after all:

At the same time I flatter myself you may settle matters without wanting it, or at least that the Duke will give me his bond for the whole £12,000; *for he alone should save you — nobody else*. I beg you, if possible, not to use my credit till I see you in London, and even then, and at all events, I *more than* entreat, I *conjure* you . . . that you will not distress me by drawing the money, for it is really more than I can in justice spare.[40]

Georgiana did not yet lay all before the Duke. She was afraid that the colossal amount might prove disastrous. She did however sign an oath pledging her 'wishes for the Salvation of her Children, of the Duke and Lady Eliz., not to sign any paper to raise money *upon interest*.' One event, and one event only, would make such difference as to give her the courage to confess. If she could at last give her husband an heir, thus securing to his progeny the succession of the Devonshire line which still looked as if it would pass to his brother's heirs, then he would tolerate anything. Besides, the entails on the estate would be released, and vast quantities of money would be available at a stroke. As she told Calonne, 'Si je suis grosse je n'hésiterais pas à tout dire au Duc, puis que la naissance d'un fils serait probablement la fin de tous nos embarras.'[41]* To this purpose she and Bess would bend all their efforts.

* * *

In the midst of financial worries, there was also the excitement generated by the Regency Crisis of 1788, when many thought, and some shamelessly hoped, that the King might die. The illness which first manifested itself in the summer had grown steadily worse and progressively more mysterious. Recent research has indicated that George III's illness was probably physical in origin, not emotional, and has diagnosed it as porphyria.[42] To his contemporaries, however, there was little question that the King was simply mad. Even if he did not begin so, the treatment he suffered at the hands of doctors was sufficient to turn his mind. Hot poultices were applied to his shaven head in order to draw out the evil humours, forcing such agonies upon him that he lost control over his behaviour. Dr Warren told Pitt that there was 'every reason to believe that the disorder was no other than direct lunacy', from which he probably would not recover.[43] The Whigs rejoiced at the King's discomfort; here at last was a chance to rid the country of a 'tyrant' and place the acquiescent Prince of Wales in authority. Opposition press was cruelly indifferent to the man's fate:

> If blisters to the head applied
> Some little sense bestow
> What pity 'tis they were not tried
> Some twenty years ago.

Georgiana was naturally at the centre of developments during the hurried weeks of that autumn. The Prince of Wales confided in her, and she learnt the views of the Court party from the Duke of Richmond, thus placing her in a position to record events at first hand. She kept a diary during this period, of little interest to us but useful to successive historians, which Mr Sichel published in an appendix to his biography of Sheridan. 'We are all in the greatest anxiety and ferment about the King's illness,' she told

* If I were pregnant I should not shrink from revealing all to the Duke, for the birth of a son would probably signal the end of all our difficulties.

her mother, which was putting it mildly.[44] She also recorded an intelligence from Richmond, that the King almost set the Queen on fire, by pushing a candle into her face to identify her.

The Prince of Wales did not stop to think that his father might recover. Nor did it cross his mind that anyone other than himself should be Regent. He immediately began to make arrangements for his regency, displaying quite callous indifference to his father's condition or his mother's feelings, laying down the law, stamping his foot and spewing out resentments accumulated over the years. He refused to kiss his mother's hand on leaving her presence. Although it was supposed to be a secret, Brooks's Club was alive with the news that the Prince had sent a message to Fox, on holiday in Italy, announcing his intentions. Obviously, when the Prince was Regent, Fox would form a government, and Utopia would begin the following morning. In the excitement, Fox and his Whig friends managed to turn all their cherished principles on their heads, and proclaim that the Prince should be permitted to assume power immediately, without waiting for the authorisation of Parliament. This was quite rightly seen as a Whig plot to by-pass the irksome necessity of election and take over by decree; astonishingly, it would have been a step backwards which ignored all the precious gains of the 'Glorious Revolution' of 1688, of which even now they were celebrating the centenary.

The King was taken by force to Kew, where he was refused the company of his wife and daughters and became more violent than ever, attacking his pages by pulling their hair or kicking them. He hardly ate anything, turned away from all medicine and threw out what he could. At night he had to be tied to his bed, whence he begged his pages to put an end to his miseries by killing him, and when they refused, uttered the most uncharacteristic obscenities. Matters became worse when on the orders of Dr Willis, who had much experience with lunatics and firmly predicted that the King would respond to the right treatment, he was confined to a straitjacket whenever he refused to eat; his compliance was demanded in everything. The humiliation he suffered was far worse than any of the medicines, which included camphor, digitalis, quinine, and one horror which upset him so much he again begged that he might be allowed to die rather than submit.

The Queen clung to the opinion of Dr Willis, that the King would recover in time, while the Prince of Wales and his brother the Duke of York accepted Dr Warren's contrary view that he was irretrievably mad. The Prince gave out his orders as if he was already the Regent. Pitt recognised that he would have to introduce a Bill to establish a Regency, and prepared one so arranged as to limit the Prince's powers severely. As it happened, the King did recover in the early weeks of 1789, snatching victory from the very fists of the Whigs, who thereupon hated him with even fiercer passion. The crisis had done the Whigs no good at all, and the people were grateful to Pitt for having been slow enough to hold them at bay. Georgiana and her hero Fox, who could do no wrong in her eyes, were disgraced by their unseemly eagerness to have the King dead or shut away. So, at least, was how it appeared. Lady Spencer was more than ever relieved that her incorrigible daughter had avoided another 'scrape'.

After their behaviour in the Regency Crisis, Foxite Whigs were extremely unpopular, and association with them was a liability. Whig doctors found it difficult to have patients, Whig lawyers were not offered briefs.

On the domestic scene, there were excitements of a different order. The assistant confectioner at Chatsworth called William Mason was caught stealing gold medals, six gold watches, and bank notes. Upon investigation it was discovered that he had made off with a variety of objects during the whole time that he had been employed there. The young man's father petitioned for a total acquittal, which hurt the Duke who had decided to be lenient and not have the boy hung for what was a capital offence punishable by death. In a trial lasting two hours on 13 September, Mason was found guilty and sentenced to seven years' transportation. The Duke had only charged a felony. Georgiana told her mother that Canis thought advantage had been taken of his docile nature and that the boy ought to have pleaded guilty.[45]

Then there was the engagement of a governess for the growing girls. Mrs Sarah Trimmer was the author of the most revered and popular nursery classic of the day, *History of the Robins*, and her eldest daughter Selina was recommended to the Duchess by Lady Spencer. Selina Trimmer took up her duties in the Devonshire household towards the end of 1788, when Lady Georgiana was five and Lady Harriet but two years old. The appointment was to prove of momentous importance to the assorted inhabitants of that schoolroom in years to come, for Selina would gradually assume a place as part of the family and remain with them all until the children were grown up. Though she did not know it, she would before long have a disparate clutch of high-spirited children in her charge, upon all of whom her strong personality would leave some mark.

In many ways, Selina was an ideal governess. She was fond of children and anxious to do her duty by them. Most importantly, she had none of that bright clear intellect which might interfere with moral precepts. Teaching girls what was right and wrong was the essential part of her function, and if that meant preventing their reading undesirable books, such as the detestable Rousseau's awful treatise on education, *Emile*, so be it. Miss Trimmer knew that she knew best. The more intelligent of the children would in later years think differently, but always retain for her the devotion deserved of a friend.

Because she was highly moral, Miss Trimmer tended to teach by denial; whatever was forbidden was done so for the good of the soul. 'Miss Trimmer does not know where to shelter her morality', wrote Hary-O years later, 'and her comments are for the most part groans.' The same pupil also remarked that Selina 'always likes administering a little bitter into one's cup'.[46] Elizabeth Foster noticed the same harsh streak, though she would have special personal reasons for regretting Miss Trimmer's inclination towards disapproval of everything. She said she was like 'the North East wind which in the brightest sunshine still has some chill in it'.[47] It was typical of her immediately to amend the indulgent habits which the Duchess had allowed to take root, of staying up till all hours, for example; under Miss Trimmer, it was unthinkable that they should be awake one minute later than she decreed.

For the moment, the one person who was to feel the effect of Miss Trimmer's arrival more than the children was Bess. Since Lady Spencer and the new governess shared the same gloomy uncompromising outlook on life, it was inevitable that they should be allies in some measure, notwithstanding the difference in rank. After all, Lady Spencer had wanted Miss Trimmer at Devonshire House precisely because she hoped the young lady would exert the influence which distance prevented her from exerting herself. It was also hardly surprising that a stern moralist should look askance at a mistress living with a husband and wife. She took her disapproval of Bess to the length of pointedly remaining seated when she entered the room. Almost coincidental with Selina's appointment came the first overt reference by the Dowager Lady Spencer to her unhappiness at Bess's continued leech-like presence. On 8 August she wrote to her daughter,

> I always avoid naming Lady E.F., and if anybody is injudicious enough to mention her to me, I endeavour to give such answers as will shew them I am determined not to enter into the subject. My behaviour was not premeditated, it arose at Chatsworth from my own feelings at scenes I was unfortunate enough to be witness to, and finding I have so little power to command myself when I am deeply affected, I thought it better to avoid all opportunities of acting in a manner that might distress us all. I certainly mean to behave civilly to Lady E.F. whenever I meet her, and I hope of late especially I have done so. I never wished to avoid speaking to the Duke on any subject and if ever he should mention this I shall, as on others, listen candidly to him and tell him truly, if he chooses I should, what my sentiments are.[48]

It is doubtful whether the Duke needed to be told what the Dowager's sentiments were, and very unlike him to invite a lecture upon the 'scenes' she had witnessed; so we may assume the threatened colloquy never took place. Georgiana certainly would do nothing to encourage such an encounter. With debts piling up around her, the last kind of discussion she wanted was one examining the role of her husband's mistress. He must not be upset on any account.

As if in cheeky confirmation of Lady Spencer's fears, there arrived almost by the same post as the above letter one from Bess, who was living at Devonshire House while Georgiana was at Chatsworth, telling of her flirtatious exploits during her friend's absence. It is a letter written with the confidence of one now firmly established, one who no longer has to protect her position with tact or nurture her friendship with flattery. Clearly, Devonshire House was now home. She wrote,

> Here has been Lord Frederick* and I as thick as possible — hand in glove — in vulgarer terms hail fellow well met — in more refined language the inseparable inimitables. . . . Lord Macartney came in for a smile — Crauford had a squeeze of the hand at coming away, but Dutan, — poor hideous Dutan — no nothing could make me leer, smile or attend to him — well dear Rat, you think I am still a wild little thing . . . let nothing surprise you that I say do or write — I am not myself, and have but one fixed constant and consolatory sentiment, the inexpressible love I bear to you and Canis.[49]

The following year, Canis took both his ladies to France and Belgium for a period of fourteen months.

---

* Lord Frederick Cavendish, the Duke of Devonshire's uncle, then aged fifty-nine.

Chapter Eight

BIRTH OF AN HEIR
AND BANISHMENT

On 20 June 1789, the entire Devonshire cavalcade set out from Dover for what was to be a protracted and eventful sojourn abroad. Georgiana's two daughters were left in the care of their grandmother, but the rest of the household, including the Duke, his wife, his mistress, his daughter Charlotte Williams, and assorted servants, were of the party, which would swell with additions in the coming months to a travelling company of almost one hundred persons. The initial purpose of this extraordinary exodus was to take a season at Spa, both to relieve the Duke's gout, and to encourage the Duchess's fertility. Another pregnancy must somehow be achieved, and this time it would simply have to be a boy. All Georgiana's troubles would magically evaporate if she could at last produce an heir to the Devonshire estates. First, however, they would pass by Paris in order to visit old friends and absorb the four-year-old Caroline St Jules into their number as if by accident. This latter intention was of course premeditated, though it would have to be presented to Lady Spencer as an act of impulsive kindness.

The impending avalanche of popular insurrection in France, of which ominous and unmistakable rumbles were already heard, weighed little in the Devonshires' plans. As good and honourable Whigs, they were historically and by inclination on the side of revolution anyway, and could not have predicted that the French experience would turn out to be so bloody. They no doubt assumed that it would not touch them. How they reconciled their friendship with Marie-Antoinette on the one hand, and their sympathy with revolution on the other, is not the first mystery of subtle Whig tergiversation.

Despite distance which rendered their meetings infrequent, Georgiana and Marie-Antoinette had been friends even before

their respective marriages in 1774, when Georgiana had become
Duchess of Devonshire a few weeks after Marie-Antoinette
became Queen of France. Lady Spencer had been a lifelong
intimate of the French Court, and before her, her mother Mrs
Poyntz had known Louis XV. Whenever an Englishwoman was
presented at the French Court, the Queen invariably asked after
Georgiana and sent messages and presents for her. It must have
been a tremendous bore for everyone to discover that the
Duchess of Devonshire was the one woman in England esteemed
above all others by the French Queen. The English Ambassador,
the Duke of Dorset, scarce ever omitted a reference to the Queen
(whom he called 'Mrs Brown') in his frequent chatty letters to
Georgiana. Added to which the two women shared the same interests in fashion and were virtual contemporaries; there was a
sense in which Georgiana was, in the vulgar mind, 'Queen' of
England, George III's wife being for the most part ignored by
the arbiters of popularity. It was perfectly natural, then, that the
Devonshire procession should pause to be received at Versailles.
Reported unrest among the populace promised to be a wretched
nuisance, but not much more.

James Hare, who was already in Paris, wrote mischievously to
Georgiana that he thought Marie-Antoinette one of the most
disagreeable looking women in the world, but 'I confess I
should be rather diverted with seeing her, you and Lady
Elizabeth all trying who should be most gracious'.[1]

On 27 June, Georgiana and Bess went to Versailles and dined
there, in spite of increasing tumult. The Duke stayed in Paris to
dine with the Duke of Dorset. Two days later, all three of them
were at Versailles and witnessed a scene when the populace
broke into the palace and saw the King, Queen and Dauphin.
Riotous behaviour of this order was not unknown in London.
Nevertheless it was sufficiently disquieting for Georgiana to
deem it unwise to take Mr Coutts's daughters to court; 'Versailles is in such consternation that it would be a very bad
moment to carry them there', she said, well aware that she must
nourish Coutts's snobbery if he was to keep quiet about the
financial mess she was in. She did manage to take the Coutts
ladies to the theatre, protesting that 'no hurry or dissipation can
make me neglect your daughters'.[2]

Devonshire submitted to the ritual splendour of formal

presentation at Versailles on 1 July, when all the elaborate machinery of etiquette and protocol was set in motion as if the clamour from the streets outside were a trivial disturbance of no consequence. The King spoke to Georgiana and Bess at length. There followed the majestic ceremony of the *Messe du Roi*, and a private meeting with the Queen at five in the afternoon. Georgiana told her mother that Marie-Antoinette was 'sadly altered, her belly quite big, and no hair at all, but she still has great *éclat*'.[3]

As for the mobs who were screaming and shouting at the Palais Royal because the guards had been released from prison, Georgiana admitted that she had been frightened, but went on a couple of sentences later to say that 'I confess I amuse myself at Paris and have been well the whole time I have been here'. Only two weeks after this amazingly nonchalant remark, on 14 July, the Bastille fell and France was plunged into the most momentous months of its history.

To Georgiana and Bess it seemed more awful that the Queen's friend, the Duchesse de Polignac, who was personally known to them both, had to flee the country and seek refuge in Switzerland. The National Assembly was after her blood, possibly because she was suspected of being the Queen's lover, and her removal rendered Marie-Antoinette's position slightly safer, at least for the time being.*

Charles James Fox was in no doubt that the taking of the Bastille was no mere temporary rebellion, but a revolution of the first magnitude. 'How much the greatest event that ever happened in the world!' he exclaimed, 'and how much the best!'[4] Dorset sent a rapturous report to the Duke of Leeds: 'Thus, my lord, the greatest revolution that we know anything of has been effected with, comparatively speaking – if the magnitude of the event is considered – the loss of very few lives. From this moment we may consider France as a free country, the king a very limited monarch, and the nobility as reduced to a level with the rest of the nation.'[5] Burke was much less complacent. He hated the tyranny of the masses above all others, and could see little cause for rejoicing in the fact that the Governor of the Bastille had been decapitated, his dripping head stuck on

* When the Duchesse de Polignac learnt that the Queen had been murdered four years later, she placed her hands on her heart and died.

a stick and carried through the streets of Paris. Bess recorded in her diary that the jailers had been killed and the prisoners condemned to die of starvation because their liberators did not know how to open the doors of their cells.[6]

Politically, Georgiana followed Fox in everything, so she was bound to think it a good thing that the monarchy should be made to behave itself as it did in England; could she have foreseen the horrifying events to which 14 July was only a preamble, she would have shuddered. While applauding the rightness of the rebellion, she and Bess had somehow to think with another part of their minds when it came to commiserating with the fate of their friends, people they had dined with, to whom they had shown miniatures of their children, with whom they had gossiped in the drawing-room. Those now humiliated and soon to be slaughtered were, as they well knew, people like themselves, noblemen and noblewomen who enjoyed a delightfully privileged life. Bess thought it 'really affecting and distressing' when noble families were ordered to paint over the arms emblazoned on their carriages and efface the visible illustrations of pride in rank.[7] She further recorded that the Duchesse de Fitzjames had been stopped by a working-class mob on her way from St Cloud to Paris and cheerily told that the labourers were on their way to dig the aristocrats' graves. The atmosphere was fraught with danger. A noble cortège of such importance and size as the Duke of Devonshire's could not count on its safety. The Duke of Dorset warned as much when he wrote to England that 'I really think it necessary that some public caution be given to put those upon their guard who may propose to visit this part of the continent'.[8] Yet no word from Georgiana or Bess gave any indication that they considered themselves to be in peril. In retrospect, they ought to have been terrified. Why were they not?

At first, they simply did not believe it was a cause for anxiety. It appeared to be a movement for the kind of constitutional reform which they would welcome, hence Fox's rhapsodic cry and Dorset's joyful announcement. The French Royal Family would surely recognise the justice of their enemies and consent to fundamental limits on their powers. That they would be cruelly butchered was not yet a possibility which occurred to people like the Cavendishes and the Spencers, who took for granted the orderly conduct of political affairs and assumed that transition, progress, change, were effected in debate by persuasion. The street riots were an irritant. 'Tout cela fait frémir en vérité,'* wrote Georgiana, but that did not prevent her staying on the continent for more than a year just when the French Revolution was on the boil.

The trouble was, they expected the French to be English. Let them have their political upheaval, but they would not be so mean as to trouble the path of an English nobleman. The clue to their insular blindness is given in a letter which Harriet wrote to her children back in England a few months later, in which she showed her detestation for the 'horrid French':

> How grateful we ought all to feel at being born under a government whose wisdom protects and preserves the laws, while it allows such a degree of liberty to the people & is so calculated for their happiness as to prevent their even forming a wish for a change. A revolution (even the best) must always be dreadful at the moment of its happening, but when it is the entire overthrow of every Law divine and human, & attended with every circumstance of cruelty and violence, how odious it becomes, but I believe the national character of the English, the generosity and real courage of their nature, would alone preserve them from ever acting as the French have done.[9]

Had the French allowed the English Whigs to conduct their revolution for them, it would have been a much more civilised affair!

In July, the party made its way by easy stages via Mons and Liège to Spa. Charlotte Williams was left behind in Paris with Monsieur and Madame Nagel, together with Caroline St Jules. Georgiana wrote to her mother as if she had barely heard of the girl: 'Luckily there is only one other pensioner, Mlle de St Jules, a young lady from the provinces.'

By the time they reached Liège, word had come through that Paris was in turmoil. Georgiana hurriedly penned a note to her mother. God! What a situation! And we have left poor Charlotte there! The Duke was so worried he even wept for the first time in his life. What Georgiana did not admit to Mama was

* All this really makes one shudder.

that the Duke was weeping for little Caroline, whom he had seen for the first time only a few days before and who might now be abandoned to the mob. He was genuinely fond of the girl, and as we shall see, so in time was everyone else.

James Hare stayed in Paris throughout the disturbances. He advised that Caroline and Charlotte were quite safe with the Nagels for the time being, and the Devonshires should not worry unduly. As for the long term, well, it would soon be time for them to return to England and take Caroline with them. Bess had already decided that her daughter would take her place in the Devonshire House nursery. Georgiana was willing, but anxious to avoid gossip. Lady Spencer would have to be handled very gently indeed. Caroline was advertised as a useful playmate for little G. and Hary-O, who would benefit so much from having to converse in French! 'I have got you a charming little companion in Mlle de St Jules', Georgiana told her eldest daughter, 'she is like Caro Ponsonby, but as she don't speak English, she will soon teach you and Haryo French in play.'[10] Hare made clear his own view that both girls should be taken from the Nagels as soon as circumstances permitted. To Georgiana he wrote:

I do not see how Charlotte is to improve by being there, except by learning French, and to say the truth, I think she wants other sorts of improvement, which she is not likely to get under Madame Nagel, I mean in point of manners. It is a pity that there should be any obstacle to your taking little Caroline more immediately under your own care, for she is the prettiest child I ever saw. I shall be very glad to be acquainted with your children, and, I dare say, I shall like them, tho' I think it is a great disadvantage to children to have five nurses and footmen to attend them, and to see their parents but seldom, and under a sort of constraint, which prevents their behaving naturally and being as entertaining as they would be otherwise. It also gives them an early habit of dissimulation, which they would have soon enough without help. You see that I was intended for an old nurse by nature.[11]

The more one reads of James Hare's witty and affectionate letters, the more one realises that he was in a quiet unspectacular way perhaps the best friend to all three of them, to Georgiana,

Bess and the Duke. He was never dishonest, never pompous, never sanctimonious. The moral intricacies of Devonshire House were not his concern; he wanted only to offer sage words which might afford the surest road towards easy happiness for all.

By the end of July they were in Spa, where they remained throughout August and most of September. Some time in the last week of August one of their primary purposes was achieved and all worries about the events in Paris became suddenly subordinate. The Duchess, now thirty-two years old, conceived. After four weeks she was fairly certain she was pregnant, as she told Mr Coutts, 'The aim of my journey, I hope, is answer'd (this, Dear Sir, must be a secret) I am in hopes I am with child.'[12] She also told Hare, who teasingly replied that she must not let everyone down. 'I think I have been talking of what was meant to be a secret', he wrote, 'but as you did not enjoin secrecy, I told several people that you had promised us a boy, so that you cannot now be let off, but must keep your engagement with the publick.' By the same post, Bess told Lady Melbourne that she hoped to send *very* good news soon, and confessed that if it turned out to be a girl she would cry.

Georgiana was quick to realise that a boy would be not only a joyful addition to the household, but a much-needed benefit to her chaotic finances; it is significant that Mr Coutts, who continued to hold her up whenever she showed signs of sinking, was almost the first to be informed. The Duke was still in ignorance of the extent of his wife's indebtedness, largely due to his unassailable taciturnity, for he could easily have discovered all had he bothered. Georgiana was frightened to tell him because she still imagined that her mistakes would ruin the Devonshire estate, but a son and heir would change all that and render a confession opportune. James Hare urged her to reveal everything; if she could not bring herself to it, then he or Bess would willingly take on the task for her. 'The sooner he knows of it the better', he said, 'but, for God's sake, if you tell him anything, tell him all, or let Lady Elizabeth or let me tell him. There is no situation so desperate where there is not something to be done, and if you were in debt more than his whole estate would sell for, it would be equally advisable to acquaint him with it, as if you owed but £5000. My advice is exactly the same as your nurse would give you, and I do not think it the worse on that account. What I dread most is that you should be sanguine enough to trust to some future good fortune to extricate you out of your difficulties, and so get more deeply involved.'[13]

With Georgiana still dithering, Hare and Bess took it upon themselves to break the news to the Duke. Bess extracted some sort of statement from Georgiana and passed on the intelligence to Hare, who showed her letter to the Duke. Canis went alone in December to London, whence he wrote to Bess in the most undisturbed fashion, 'I wish you would let me know by the next post what the new debt of 2000£ is, and who the people are that it is owing to. I think the best thing that can happen is that she should not be able to pay the interest of her debts regularly at present, as that will make her creditors more willing to settle their accounts with her upon fair terms.'[14] He appended an affectionate word for his little daughter Caroline.

Through Hare, he eventually forced his wife to face facts and admit her liabilities, bringing from her a letter so cleverly phrased, so feminine in its appeal to her fragility and the precious burden she bore within her, so cunning in its apparent precision while it withheld far more than it confessed, that she probably had help in drafting it. 'Why do you force me, my dear Ca, to an avowal to you which agitates me beyond measure', she begins, 'and which is not necessary now? Could I tell you, pay this for me, I owe no more, I should not hesitate to expose myself to all your reproof. But as I am still further involved I dread the opening of an explanation I should not dare encounter in my present situation. . . . I shall think it my duty to inform you of all before my lying in.' There follows a list of figures, excuses, circumstances: then, 'I humbly and earnestly entreat you not to mention this subject either to Denne* or Calonne till my return to England. This is a request made from the bottom of my heart, and I trust you will not refuse it me indeed after my various agitations. Your granting it is of more importance than I can express to me and my child.'[15]

With Mr Coutts, she employed similar tactics, promising social advancement for his daughters, and even signing herself, with underlinings, 'Your ever affectionate *eldest daughter*.' 'You are my second father', she said, 'and I must tire you out as such.'

* The Duke of Devonshire's banker.

The fact was, she could not pay any interest on loans, because she had promised the Duke and Lady Elizabeth that she would not borrow any money on interest. This she perversely interpreted as meaning not that she should not borrow, but that she should not pay interest on what she borrowed, so the person who was to pay for her undertaking was not herself, but poor Coutts. 'My not having infring'd the Duke's promise depends on your goodness in not charging me interest this once. I hope it will be no loss to you.'[16]

Coutts saw the matter rather differently. Georgiana pleaded with him: 'With regard to the overdrawing, my Dearest Sir, I only entreat you to have a little patience. . . . If you are angry with me there is no help, so, Dear Sir, do as you will, I expect nothing but sorrow and misery.'[17] As for the Misses Coutts, no she did not abandon them to a doubtful fate in Paris. Had she anticipated any danger, would she have left Charlotte Williams there?

The banker replied with a laborious and irritating letter enumerating what debts he was aware of, which amounted to £1,429, though there might be others which had not yet come to his notice. This was the last kind of letter she wanted to read in Spa, though it was alleviated by Coutts's continued desire to remain in favour. 'I wish to do whatever is best for you', he said, 'and most conducive to your happiness and future comfort. You *are* not, you *cannot* be more interested in your own honour and character than I am, which is the reason I have always wished you to tell me frankly everything.'[18]

It was then that Georgiana told Mr Coutts she hoped soon to produce a son, at which time she would tell the Duke everything. Meanwhile, it was important that she should not be agitated. 'I must take great care of myself, for I have always been subject to miscarry.'[19] One way and another, she succeeded in assuring a further reprieve.

At the same time, she prevailed upon the Prince of Wales, her 'brother', to lend her £3,000, assuring him that all her liabilities would soon be settled, except for debts to Calonne, this one to the Prince, and 'a trifling one to Mr Coutts'. This trifling matter was the £1,429 which Coutts had just analysed for her with such painstaking care. It was important, moreover, that the Prince should not breathe a word to the Duke of Devonshire; their transaction must remain private and secret. Georgiana emphasised that it was necessary to deceive the Duke, for he would never forgive her for having turned to the heir to the throne for help in rescuing her from her lamentable indiscretion. Explaining to the Prince that she intended to borrow £10,000 from the banker Hammersley, repay the Prince from it and use the rest to settle her affairs once and for all, she did not wonder for a moment how she was to repay Hammersley. The Prince would use his influence so that the bond would not mention interest, she having promised never to borrow on interest again; her sister would see to the interest covertly. 'How ashamed I am to tease you at a moment like this,' she wrote.[20]

Throughout 1790 there was a constant to-ing and fro-ing across the English Channel, especially in the months preceding the birth of the child whom everyone knew to be the heir; at least, there is no trace of doubt on anyone's countenance that Georgiana would have a boy. First, the Duke went to England on the last day of the old year, to be back in May on the Continent. The expected heir caused him to be in better spirits than at any time his wife could recall. On 17 March, Georgiana's two daughters, little G. and Hary-O, came over to Brussels with Miss Trimmer (*plus* nurses, maids, footmen, and so on; James Hare's hint that it was bad for children to be so attended was obviously ignored), and ten days later Lord and Lady Duncannon came too, with their own less spectacular procession of servants. It seemed that Brussels could hold no more Spencers, Cavendishes or Ponsonbys. In May, the Duncannons went to England, to be replaced by none other than the Dowager Countess Spencer herself, who made the crossing to be with her daughter for the lying-in. For the first time, she was to find herself in daily close proximity with the detested Lady Elizabeth. The Dowager resigned herself for the time being to Bess's immovability, besides which it was clear even to her that the mistress adored the wife, however odd it may appear. Lady Spencer's iron morality had perforce to allow a mild adjustment to ensure the even flow of relations as the Duchess approached her term.

Gossip had pursued the Devonshires continuously since their marriage sixteen years before. Now that the Duchess was said to be on the brink of presenting her husband with an heir, there were whispers which quickly grew into the loudest rumours ascribing perfidious intentions to the threesome. Why was the baby not to be born at Devonshire House, or at Chatsworth? The birth of such a child, heir to a dynasty of such importance, was no ordinary occasion. It should be attended with all the pomp and significance of a royal birth. To have the child born away from Chatsworth was almost an insult to the dependants who lived there and considered him theirs. And why abroad? Why had the entire cast disappeared across the Channel to make a temporary home in a foreign place? Why was that Lady Elizabeth with them? And why, in God's name, did they decide at the last minute to go to, of all places, Paris?

Wanting sensible answers, extravagant ones were supplied. Perhaps the Duchess was not pregnant at all, the trip was all part of a treacherous deceit? Georgiana was now getting plump all year round, and it was by no means easy to detect any significant change in her shape. She did not agree. When she heard of the rumours, indignantly she responded, 'If those who say I am not with child were to see me, they would, I believe, have an *evident* answer to that, as well as to many other infamous lies.'[21]

Bess implored Lady Melbourne to come to Europe and visit them. 'You will be another witness of the reality of her being pregnant, my not being so, and of the sex of the child when born,' she said, indicating that the suspicion of trickery was heard even before the lying-in. At the same time, Bess revealed that 'a fine piece of work' was being made of the presence of Caroline St Jules, yet nothing would ever persuade her to change her manner towards the unfortunate little girl, and 'when you know her you will say we are right'. It was going to be a delicate problem to keep these rumours of Caroline's identity from Lady Spencer, due to arrive in a few weeks, yet Bess still longed for her arrival. 'I can't express to you how my courage fails me as the time [for Georgiana's lying-in] draws near.'[22]

Another question arose when it was learnt that the Duchess was not to be attended by the eminent *accoucheur* Dr Denman, who had delivered her two daughters, but by his young unknown son-in-law Dr Richard Croft. Why? Denman was said to be too busy. Too busy to answer the summons of the Duke of Devonshire? It did not ring true. Something or other was being concealed.

Georgiana did not return to England for the birth because it was thought the ordeal of a Channel crossing would be a hazard to her frail condition; she was, as she said herself, prone to miscarry, and (who knows?) this might be the last chance of producing an heir. No risks must be taken. As for the removal from Belgium to Paris at the eleventh hour, Dr Warren was responsible for that. He told Lady Spencer that the Devonshires must on no account remain in Brussels, where they were no longer welcome. He did not disclose the source of his information, nor why Georgiana had offended her host country. But the intelligence was taken seriously enough for the whole company to pack bags and remove to Paris, which, paradoxically, was supposed to be safer than Brussels at the time, revolutionary fervour having spread to Belgium and temporarily spent itself in France.

Dr Croft arrived on 20 April. Lady Spencer followed on 6 May. On 10 May they all left Brussels, Georgiana saying that she was unwell and very low and dreading lying in on the road. Four days later they arrived safely in Paris. For the first five nights, they squeezed into the Hôtel de l'Université, but more spacious accommodation was made available by the Marquis de Boulainvilliers, who offered his *hôtel* at Passy. Thus on 19 May, they made their way to Passy, just as the Duchess was beginning her labour.

Georgiana was not installed until 11.00 a.m. the next morning. She was the first to arrive, with her mother and dear Bess. The Duke followed later in the day, accompanied by all four daughters. Speed was now essential. The birth could not be more than hours away, yet there were no impartial witnesses to testify that the Duke was not being cheated by a fraudulent heir, a substitute baby imposed at the last minute. Rumours that the Duchess was not pregnant at all had been so widespread and loud that it was important to establish legitimacy beyond doubt. With this in mind, Bess drove back to Paris, where she attended the Opera in full display in Lord St Helens's box. Everyone could see that she was there, and what was more, everyone could see that she was thin and definitely unburdened. (Of course, some said, she might have had a baby some days before, and her present show might be part of an elaborate act; gossip is not easily assuaged, least of all by the truth.) Lady Spencer sent for the Dowager Duchesse d'Ahremberg and Lord Robert Fitzgerald, secretary to the British Ambassador, requesting their presence in Georgiana's chamber. Lord Robert had already gone to bed and his servant did not think it worthwhile to wake him. But the Duchesse did receive the message, and hastened to Passy, arriving there after Bess had returned from the opera. Georgiana was in the final stages of a difficult birth. Canis was waiting in another room.

Late that night, just after 1.00 a.m. on 21 May 1790, the infant Marquis of Hartington was born. As arranged, the Dowager Duchesse d'Ahremberg was the first to enter the room and see the new-born. The Duke, Lady Elizabeth, Lady Spencer followed. Georgiana was saved. The Devonshire line would continue from her body. Thus finally the Duchess 'redeemed the reproach that had shadowed her life'.[23]

Unfortunately, the precautions taken to guarantee belief in the heir's legitimacy were insufficient. Gossip remained unsated. It was said that two babies had been born, one to Georgiana and one to Bess. Georgiana's was a girl, Bess's a boy, and the amenable Dr Croft had swapped them before witnesses came into the room. That the timing should be so accurate was not considered impossible. Had not the two women given birth to children by the Duke within two weeks of each other some years before? That at least was true. A just mingling of fact and fancy could develop into a wonderful tale too beautifully romantic to be disbelieved. And so the rumour endured for years. The little boy grew up and heard it repeated. He was said to have been told the truth and to have promised his uncle, Lord George Cavendish, who would have inherited the title and estates had Hartington been illegitimate, that he would never marry, thus ensuring the inheritance should pass to George's children in time. Well, he never did marry, and the inheritance did pass as it would have done had he never been born. This was regarded by some as proof positive.

In 1818, long after Georgiana's death but in the lifetime of Bess, Caroline St Jules asked her mother whether there as any truth in the story. Bess had turned Catholic, and the gossip of the day proclaimed that she had confessed all to her priest, had written to the Prince Regent to admit that Georgiana had never had a son. She had implicated Dr Croft in the deception, who had thereupon shot himself. 'Strange and absurd as this story is', said Caroline, 'nothing else is talked of in London.'[24]

Once more, fantasy was bending the fact. It was true that Richard Croft committed suicide in 1818, but the delivery of Georgiana's baby twenty-eight years earlier had nothing whatever to do with it. Croft had attended the Princess Charlotte in her confinement in 1817, when she died in childbirth. Croft was blamed.* Public rage against him was vociferous, causing him to withdraw into the deepest despair from which he could not emerge. He shot himself on 13 February 1818.

All his life, Georgiana's son was dogged by variations on this rumour. Even beyond, the suspicion persisted. At his death in 1858, Greville's diary faithfully reflected the general impression:

> There was for a long time a vague notion that some mystery attached to his birth, and that he was not really the Son, or at all events the legitimate Son, of his father. The idea was that Lady Elizabeth Foster . . . and the Duchess had been confined at the same time at Paris, and that the latter having a girl and the former a boy, the children had been changed, the Duke being the Father of both children. I always treated this story as a myth, but Fullerton† told me the other night that *he knew* that Lord George Cavendish so much believed it that he had intended to try the question of the Duke's legitimacy after the death of his Brother, and was only deterred from doing so by receiving the deposition of the woman who had received him in her arms upon his birth,‡ which he considered conclusive evidence to prove his legitimacy.[25]

Canis, the Rat, and Racky had only themselves to blame for the conjectures their extraordinary relationship engendered. With babies arriving in and out of wedlock, journeys to and from the Continent for surreptitious purposes, colossal debts

---

* Recent enquiries make it quite clear that Dr Croft's ministrations were not neglectful and in no way contributed to the Princess's death.

† Alexander George Fullerton (1808–1907), son-in-law of Georgiana's daughter.

‡ Ann Scafe, maid to the Dowager Countess Spencer in 1790. She wrote, on Hartington's birth, 'There never was a more welcome child.'

threatening the very basis of the Devonshire estate if a direct heir was not forthcoming, it is no wonder that the birth of Lord Hartington miles away from the ancestral home, close to revolutionary Paris, and occurring in the most hurried unsuitable circumstances, should give rise to speculation.

Fortunately, evidence has now come to light which must leave no room for any further doubt. The man who delivered the baby, Richard Croft, wrote chatty letters home to his mother throughout the period from April to August 1790, letters which have been preserved by the family and now belong to his descendant, Richard Page Croft. They reveal that as late as 25 April, discussions were still under way as to where exactly the Duchess should lie in; the decision to move to Paris was not taken until the early days of May, news having reached the party that Paris promised to be quiet for three months. Georgiana told Croft that she counted from 24 August 1789 as the day of conception. On 21 May, the doctor scribbled a very quick note to his mother. 'About an hour after I sealed my letter of last night', he said, 'Her Grace's labour came on pretty violent, and after one of the best times I ever attended, she was delivered at one o'clock this morning of a remarkable fine boy.' There is no reason at all to pretend the doctor was lying.

The correspondence is interesting on other counts. It shows that the poor man had a very difficult time finding out when or what he would be paid, although he was expected to be available at all times of the day or night for weeks on end. 'Most heartily do I wish his Grace would either give me something or let me know what I am to expect, as til then I am determined not to buy one single thing but what I find indispensable.' Not only did he have Georgiana to attend to, but the rest of the family and servants as well, with the result that he confessed in late May he had to walk up and down the stairs about eighty times a day. A minor duty, which he described in proud detail, was the removal of a polypus from a servant's nose. Dr Croft told his mother that he would never allow any of his patients to read medical books.

Though Georgiana and her baby continued to make satisfactory progress, their return to England was delayed by a serious and mysterious illness contracted by little G. Throughout June and July Croft devoted all his attention to saving her life. She was hysterical, her lips were black, her pulse raced at 150, she complained that she felt her inside was coming out. Croft spent three hours a day compounding new medicines with which to treat her, taking them himself to encourage her not to be afraid. Still the delirium continued, until the doctor himself feared that she might be lost, and confessed his distress to his mother. It was, he said, a very extraordinary case, possibly hydrophobia. He was up night after night, reporting at the end of June that he had not undressed for five nights in a row. He could not have gone through the ordeal without the support of his wife, to whom Lady Spencer sent a sermon every day. Georgiana and Bess watched helplessly by her bedside as the little girl's life seemed to slide away, resisting all attempts to retain it. 'I am vex'd and perplex'd to death,' Georgiana told her mother. Bess was a tremendous comfort, a circumstance which bound her even closer to Georgiana and distanced her once again from Lady Spencer, who returned to England in advance of them.

At last, the illness passed as strangely as it had come, and little G. was out of danger by the beginning of August. For his services, and for his successful delivery of her baby boy, Georgiana gave Dr Croft a little cup and saucer; they are still in the possession of his descendant.

*　　*　　*

On 19 August, Georgiana, Bess and company arrived in Dover, where they walked about for a while, proudly displaying the baby Lord Hartington to an admiring crowd. 'The common people seemed quite delighted to see an heir to the Duke of Devonshire,' Bess noted in her journal.[26]

The immediate problem·was where to take little G. for her convalescence. Dr Warren advised a spell with grandmother Spencer at St Albans, whereas Dr Croft told the Duchess she should take all three children to Compton Place at Eastbourne. Georgiana inclined towards the latter suggestion. Bess would naturally be with her. Would Mama come to Eastbourne to join them? Georgiana, who longed to see her mother again and to please her (for there was still much of the girl in her), but would never abandon Lady Elizabeth, tentatively, hesitatingly asked if Mama would come to her. She knew the reply in advance, for Miss Trimmer had been pert enough to indicate that she thought the Dowager Countess would stay away, and Georgiana was irritated by this evidence of collusion between her mother and her servant. 'I am sure you will come to me', she said, 'but I look upon you as one of the most *bias'd* persons I know. I am sure I don't know by whom, but whenever I lose sight I lose ground with you.'

Mama's response was decidedly colder than Georgiana anticipated. No, I am not biased, she said, I follow only the counsel of my own heart, and it is anyway a subject too humiliating to talk about. 'I thought you would have gone with your children only to the sea, and I should have been happy to have been with you. As it is otherwise you would not, I am sure, wish me to go if you could know what torture it is to me to endure all I have so long done.'[27]

'Torture' and 'endure' were far stronger words than the normally controlled Countess was accustomed to employ. They show that she was finally exasperated by the eternal presence of Lady Elizabeth Foster. The reason, as Lady Elizabeth had after all been a welcome part of the company during those anxious days in Belgium and France, can only have been the discovery by Lady Spencer of Caroline St Jules's true identity. No one mentioned it, yet the supposition underlies all the renewed antipathy towards the mistress.

There followed the long, anxious, firm letter from the Duchess which at long last made perfectly clear that Bess would forever remain a part of the family, and neither she nor the Duke would even think of throwing her out. This is how it must be, and if Mama did not like it, Georgiana was prepared for the unhappy consequences. As for Miss Trimmer, 'Now I must be quite sincere with you . . . I have a great opinion of Miss T's principles and talents for education, but I see her so alter'd, thinking herself so independent of me, that it is really impossible for me not to suspect her, especially by the hints she is forever dropping about your intentions and notions. Now, Dearest M., it was my consolation to think I had such a person about my children, and it is my anxious desire to retain her, but if I ever can discover that she interferes in anything but the care of their education, or that she stands between you and me in any way whatsoever, I could not submit to have a person whom I look'd upon in that light another moment in the house with me . . . I cannot suffer the additional uneasiness of seeing that a young person whom you have known but 2 years has more of your confidence and knows more of your intentions than I do.'

It was uncommon for Georgiana to write in such assured terms to her mother; there is a scolding note in her letter which is entirely new, after the usual pleas and excuses, the whimpering and self-admonishment. At last Georgiana is in charge of her own destiny, she thinks, and Mama must understand this. Now for Lady Elizabeth:

> Dearest M., you must feel how impossible, how cruel it would be to expose her to the malignant ill nature of the world and to expose ourselves to all the misery of parting with her for what we know to be unjust and false.

This was indeed a naïve view of the situation, and Georgiana was quite aware that Mama did not object so much to Lady Elizabeth's friendship as to her role. Boldly avoiding the issue, she stated in the fairest terms she could the picture of their triangular relationship which she wished to present to inquisitive outsiders:

> I am born to a most complicated misery. I had run into errors, that would have made any other man discard me; he forgave me; my friend, who had likewise stood between him and my ruin, was likewise his friend; her society was delightful to us, and her gentleness and affection sooth'd the bitterness of the many misfortunes I had brought on us.[28]

Yes, but what was Lady Elizabeth doing in the Duke's bed? This was a question Lady Spencer never put, and one would not expect her to. The matter was once more dropped, unresolved. Georgiana begged Mama to conquer prejudice, Mama declared the subject 'hateful', and the reunion at Eastbourne never took place.

Poor Georgiana! Troubles were again multiplying and squeezing the spirit out of her. Her daughter's illness, her mother's quarrel with Bess, and then money too. Just as she thought that she had accounted for everything, there was another demand on her, which she had quite forgotten, for £1500. Mama was understandably at the end of her patience and could show no more sympathy. 'I grieve at your distresses, but that alas! is all I can do, for it is so long since I have had the smallest share of your confidence on these subjects, or since my advice about them has been in the least regarded, that I must feel how useless it is for me to attempt to interfere in them.'[29] Quite so. Wise advice had achieved nothing for nearly twenty years. In desperation on Christmas Day, Georgiana sat down and tried to work out exactly what she owed where and to whom. There were £16,000 due to Mr Coutts, £15,000 to her husband's banker Denne, £8,000 to Calonne, even £2,500 borrowed from the brother of Ann Scafe, her mother's maid! The total amounted to £62,000 which she could account for, not including the sums she had forgotten either by accident or design. She wrote to Coutts. Please do not force me to press the matter with the Duke now, she implored. It will all be all right in time. If only you will be patient, 'the best thing to be done is to leave him to himself, and to let the kindness and generosity of his nature operate'. This was the opinion of Lady Elizabeth, and she by now was more intimate with the Duke on a personal private level than the Duchess herself.

To make matters worse, the whole might of the Cavendish family was turning against her and her seemingly endless extravagances. One must allow that they were right to be alarmed. In the presence of her husband, Georgiana had a furious argument with her sister-in-law the Duchess of Portland, in which they were both excited (the current word for it was 'warm') and said more than they should have done, after which she felt obliged to write an abject letter begging forgiveness for any offence caused. Before the year was out, there would be offence of a far graver kind, for which no apology would be adequate. Decidedly, 1791 was to prove a disastrous year.

It began with the death on 23 January of her nephew Richard Spencer, second son of her brother Lord Spencer, at the age of eighteen months. Then her sister, Harriet Duncannon, fell critically ill in February. The fact that she had a racking debilitating cough and was spitting blood leads one to suppose that Lady Duncannon suffered from tuberculosis, but she was in addition afflicted with a mysterious disability which paralysed her left arm and leg and might have been attributed to a stroke. Whatever it was, Harriet, still in her early thirties, gave every sign of approaching a slow, early death, and Georgiana, who had only a year before watched the pathetic struggles of her eldest daughter against severe illness, now had the unhappy contemplation of her beloved sister's fierce spirit subdued by a powerful unknown infirmity. She told Coutts that Harriet had suffered a miscarriage followed by inflammation of the womb.

Immediately following the christening of Hartington at St George's, Hanover Square, on 21 May (his first birthday), Georgiana and Harriet left for Bath, where it was hoped the waters would expedite Lady Duncannon's recovery. She could now only move with the help of crutches. They intended to stay a few weeks, but the sojourn was extended to almost six months, for reasons which had nothing to do with Harriet's illness, though this was a fortuitous excuse for the Duchess's prolonged absence from London and from the society of her husband. Bess was in Bath as well (she and Harriet Duncannon were now united by a friendship almost as firm as and certainly much simpler than the bond between Lady Elizabeth and Georgiana). The worldly Elizabeth Melbourne would now be more useful than ever before, because the dreadful secret which Georgiana must at all costs hide, and which cast her other worries into the deepest shadow, was the knowledge that she was again pregnant, and that the father of her child was Charles Grey.

Ever since the youthful Grey had been enchanted by Georgiana six years before, he had remained a faithful but frustrated lover. She had at first found him merely 'amiable', but now that the heir to the dukedom had been born, according to Melbourne principles she was free to indulge in an affair of the heart and succumb to Grey's persistent attentions. Though she revered and honoured her husband, she had never loved him with passion, and if it is true that a woman gives herself wholly to a man but once in her life, then that man in Georgiana's was Charles Grey. In seventeen years of marriage she had not betrayed the Duke once. For the rest of her life she would not betray him again. He, on the other hand, had fathered two bastards on her closest friend. It is nothing less than tragic that Georgiana's one abandoned love affair, her one fulfilment of desire, should carry such miserable consequences when she, of all her contemporaries, was the most lovable and endearing.

Grey would eventually be the Prime Minister in 1830–4 who

immediately preceded Lord Melbourne, Elizabeth's son and Caroline Ponsonby's (i.e. Lady Caroline Lamb's) husband in that office, and whom history associates most closely with the Reform Bill. In 1791, however, he was still the young member for Northumberland, a disciple of Fox and one of the finest orators in the House of Commons. Addington said of his maiden speech in 1787 that 'he went through his first performance with an éclat which has not been equalled in my recollection'.[30] Being the representative of an impressive Northumbrian family which traced its ancestry in that county to the thirteenth century, Grey was a proud, austere man, shy in private but of a forbidding, imposing countenance and bearing which afforded him an aristocratic air of the utmost distinction. He was not popular. A supercilious manner and quick temper kept his friends to a small number, but they at least were devoted to him. As a lover he was fiery, jealous, demanding. From Georgiana's point of view he had the advantage of formidable good looks and a fervid constant attachment to her. Eventually she ceased to resist. It was far better that she should fall into his arms than into those of an apothecary, as Lady Clermont had done at Tunbridge Wells, but in Georgian morality it was far worse, for the result of the liaison could not be decently concealed. Georgiana was in serious trouble.

There is a story, traditionally believed, that the Prince of Wales called one day at Devonshire House and was refused admittance. As he was driving away he saw Charles Grey looking out of the window, and from that day found it difficult to disguise his dislike of Grey.

This must have been in the early months of 1791, when Grey was a frequent visitor at Devonshire House during the Duke's absence. Clandestine meetings multiplied as Georgiana found herself falling irrevocably in love, watched anxiously by the only three people who were privy to her secret – Bess, Harriet, and Lady Melbourne. The latter, wise adorable Themis, advised the utmost caution, finally admonishing Georgiana when she thought the *affaire* threatened to engulf her; she knew that it was foolish to go beyond a certain point and that it was necessary Georgiana should be stopped.

There was a long, terrible weekend in early May when the Duchess, careless and chuckling with happiness in Grey's company, was set upon by Bess. You must make him go, said Bess, you cannot rely upon Lady Spencer's remaining blind to what is going on, her ignorance simply will not last. Listen to Lady Melbourne, do as she advises. 'The storm however now broke', she said, reporting the events of the weekend to Lady Melbourne, 'and your letters and my entreaties would have been as a drop in the ocean – for Lady Spencer had received an anonymous letter and her commands are you know absolute and her vigilance extreme.' The anonymous letter, informing Mama of Georgiana's intrigue, collapsed her fragile defences. She had perforce to agree not to see Charles Grey again, at least for the time being. 'He is gone,' wrote Bess, continuing her account for the benefit of Lady Melbourne. 'From Friday to this morning that he went away we have lived in fear and misery, but I have the happiness of telling you that she gave him no secret meeting, and there was no taking leave, which was what I dreaded. Her dear mind has not gone through any such trial as at D.H., and though she distracts me by working herself up to think she is more attach'd to him than I know she can be, yet at least she has not entangled herself further, and his present absence must set all things right . . . all I beg of you is to write to her as of your own accord and say you hear he is gone, and to beg she would be guarded in her letters to him.'[31]

Alas, it was too late for all things to be set right. Georgiana was already carrying Grey's child when she left for Bath at the end of May. She was, moreover, still deeply in love with him.

The crisis erupted in the autumn, when she was nearly six months advanced in her pregnancy. Still the Duke and Lady Spencer were unaware of the truth, though it was during this visit to Bath that the acute Fanny Burney noticed the Duchess seemed to be 'oppressed within'. Bess and Harriet protected Georgiana as best they could, and the three women prayed that somehow they would withstand the ordeal together without bringing catastrophe upon their heads. Secrecy was crucial. What they would do when Georgiana's term arrived they had not the foresight to predict. As it happened, their minds were made for them, and their uneasy calm shattered, when one day in October the Duke of Devonshire wrote to announce that he was coming to Bath to confront them. Somebody had given him

certain information. The ladies' frantic alarm was given no time
to subside, for the very next day, he arrived.

For once in his life the Duke was shaken from his lethargy. He
was indignant, angry, and in no frame of mind to compromise.
A long, heavy discussion took place, as a result of which
Georgiana had to retire to bed with one of her fierce headaches.
Nothing had yet been resolved. Harriet was in an adjoining
room, but dared not interrupt. At length Bess emerged, looking
grave. The Duke came to Harriet's room, stern, furious, but
saying nothing. He walked up and down in silence while Harriet
wondered what on earth was to happen. She had not the courage
to ask any questions. 'My heart sinks within me at everything I
see and at the cruel uncertainty we are in,' she told Lady
Melbourne. 'I know not what to think but I fear it is very bad.'

After the Duke left, Harriet lay awake all night in a state of
intense anxiety. She heard her sister moving about next door,
and sent a maid to find out what was happening. The note she
received in reply 'only confirms my fears as to what he intends'
and also confirmed that the Duke knew everything. The only
question now was what exactly he would propose, and a Cavendish needed time to deliberate. Georgiana cannot have known a
worse night in her life than 10 October 1791.

The most likely result would be a separation. If that happens,
said Harriet, she would beg to be sent abroad so that Georgiana
could use her as a pretext and suffer her humiliation a long way
from home. The Duke might miss the society of his wife so much
that he would soften during their absence and not insist upon a
total separation. The sisters promised each other that wherever
one went the other would go too. It was determined Harriet
should go to Bordeaux, and embark post haste from Southampton.[32] On 11 October, Harriet told Lady Melbourne, 'We must
go abroad – immediately – nothing else will do, neither prayers
nor entreaties will alter him. He says there is no choice between
this, or public entire separation at home. Bess has very
generously promised to go with us . . . write to me, come if you
can, give us some comfort but do not betray me.'[33]

Throughout the days of prolonged crisis, all three women
wrote in utter candour to Lady Melbourne, and there is no disguising their distress. Just when they thought a solution had

been found, another trial was thrown at them. Before a final decision was taken, the Duke insisted that Lady Spencer be brought to Bath and fully informed of her daughter's disgrace. 'There will be much to fight against,' said Harriet. 'Lord Bessborough, my mother, Lord D[uncannon] perhaps', but still there was a breathing space of a few days, and they might all be allowed to remain on in Bath after all.

But it was not to be. Lady Spencer, as they might have guessed, complicated matters. 'My mother is come and our difficulties encrease,' wrote Harriet. 'Vexation and unhappiness surround me. I almost wish myself at the bottom of the sea.'[34] Lady Spencer agreed that Georgiana should go somewhere distant, and that Harriet's illness should be the excuse, but she was not at all happy that Bess should accompany them. Bess, far more fearful of Lady Spencer's attitude than she was of the Duke's, was restrained in her company and made overt compliance with her every wish. Secretly she confided in Lady Melbourne, 'Lady S has begun as bad as possible about me, even so as to say I should not travel with them – but on your life say not a word of it to anybody. If the Dss goes, I will.' Harriet thought this would be the very gesture most likely to reconcile her mother to Bess, should she see to what lengths of loyalty her friendship should take her.[35]

After yet more days of painful discussion, an agreement was reached that Georgiana and Harriet should go to Penzance in Cornwall. Lady Spencer appeared satisfied with this. Then the Duke changed his mind again and battered their frail resources of strength. 'If the Duke had purposely intended to perplex and torment us, he could not have done it better', said Harriet, adding the only word of sympathy for the man who was the injured party, in the whole correspondence: 'his only excuse is being himself excessively unhappy, which indeed poor fellow I am afraid he is.'

Shortly after Penzance had been fixed as the scene for the last act in the drama, the Duke came to see Harriet alone, paced up and down the room in great agitation, and finally burst out, 'If you wish to save your sister and me from the most unpleasant disclosure, break off your going to Penzance and go abroad directly.' Harriet confessed she was terrified to hear him speak in so forthright a manner, being used to his cold and reserved nature. So, 'it is determined as far as the Duke can determine anything'.

Could Bess perhaps dissuade him? She was the only person who might have some influence. But she resisted, pointing out that she could not press him on a subject in which she herself had been so deeply concerned, as party to the conspiracy to deceive him, otherwise he might never trust her again, and attribute everything she says to interested motives.[36] Nevertheless she would go wherever Georgiana went.

The Duke was in effect placing his wife in the hands of his sister-in-law. 'His soliciting an open publick separation or not depends upon my entire acquiescence in everything he wishes,' wrote Harriet. Lord Duncannon and Lady Spencer still thought the ladies were going to Penzance, and it was Dr Warren's task to announce the new plan and bring them to consent. Harriet continued, 'Dr Warren is inform'd of everything, the Duke spoke to him, and at his return he is to order me abroad and undertake to persuade Lord D and my mother. The D wish'd me to pretend to have a cough, which would make [Dr] Fraser join the wish of my going, but it is impossible to act illness with any hope of being believ'd, and there is a duplicity in it I cannot bear. I have done better and taken every means to get a real one, and have succeeded . . . but my health is now so good a trifling cold cannot hurt me . . . it will smooth a thousand difficulties.'[37]

So Harriet was not as ill as everyone supposed. She had certainly improved since the collapse in February, and it was highly politic now that her health should still be thought to be poor. 'My illness is not feigned,' she insisted, adding mysteriously that she did not know whether she gave it herself or it came 'otherwise'. The notion that she was pretending illness must not be allowed to gain credence, or all would be lost. Dr Warren was prepared to join in the deception.

There remained the Ponsonbys and the Cavendishes to convince. Lady Melbourne thought it had been pressure from the Cavendish family which had precipitated the Duke's change of heart. Harriet confirmed this was true; they had extracted 'some promise' from him and probably insisted on exile. As for the Ponsonbys, Lord Bessborough and Lord Duncannon were absurdly obstinate (in Georgiana's words) and it must therefore be left entirely to Dr Warren to persuade them Harriet must go immediately to France, and Georgiana must accompany her as devoted sister and nurse. At least it was a good sign that the Duke wanted the purpose of the journey kept secret, for if he never intended to live with Georgiana again, he would not care what was said. Such was Harriet's reading of his mind.

As for Bess, her pretext for going was to return Charlotte Williams and Caroline St Jules to school in Paris (her official *raison d'être* was still as some kind of governess). She could later change her mind and travel southwards in order to take Caroline to visit her St Jules 'relations' at Aigues Mortes.

The departure in November was rapid. Georgiana had one further matter to attend to. The cause of the drama, Charles Grey, was forgotten by all save Georgiana herself. She would maintain contact with him through Lady Melbourne, sending him letters at her address and using the name 'Black' when referring to him. 'I shall make every possible use of you about having Black's letters sent you when I am gone,' she told her friend.[38] This done, she proceeded into banishment directly from Bath to Southampton, without even a few hours in London to bid farewell to her three children, whom she would not see for two years.

No sooner was she across the Channel than her first thought was to write to 'Black'. By a Mr Stewart she sent a parcel to Lady Melbourne containing a secret letter for Black 'which I am very *very* anxious he should get safe . . . oh my love, I find by a letter from him all your kindness – Bless bless you for it – he was very cruel, but very deserving of pity too – and I have in leaving him for ever left my heart and soul; but it is over now – Heaven bless him . . . he has one consolation, that I have given him up [for] my children only.'[39]

* * *

For the second time in two years, a Cavendish-Spencer-Ponsonby caravan was wandering through the capitals of Europe. Having joined up in Paris in late November, they travelled together through Lyon as far as Hyères in the south of France (near Nice) – that is Georgiana, Harriet, Lady Spencer, Lord Duncannon, Bess, Caroline Ponsonby, and Caroline St Jules. There they separated, but they had first to endure three months on the road in tense proximity. Charlotte Williams went

only as far as Paris; she was now a young woman and a trifle embarrassing to have around. She 'is much grown and improv'd',
said Georgiana, 'but she still stoops' and her 'Prince' was
irregular. It was time she was off their hands, settled somewhere
with an establishment of her own. The ideal solution presented
itself as if guided by destiny. Charlotte returned to England to
live with the Duke of Devonshire's agent, Mr Heaton, on the
Chatsworth estate. Not long after, she married Mr Heaton's
nephew, bore him a child, and lived perfectly contented.

The journey southwards was little short of a nightmare. The
Duke ignored his wife as totally as if she were dead. 'Would you
think it', Harriet told Lady Melbourne, 'he has not sent her one
farthing. I always depended his sending her some by Bess.'[40]
Harriet had to hide Georgiana's jewels lest she be tempted to sell
them in order to survive. The Duke let it be known to everyone
his wife might approach that in no circumstances was money to
be advanced to her. To make matters worse, they had constantly
to separate, for except in the large towns there were not hotels
or houses large enough to accommodate them all. They felt like
refugees, living as cheaply as possible.

Most acute of their burdens was the loneliness of exile. The
Duke did nothing to alleviate this (and who can blame him?)
while Charles Grey did everything to exacerbate it. By Christmas
the Duke had written twice to Elizabeth Foster, but not a line to
Georgiana. Bess would not say what the letters contained, only
revealing that Canis was very much out of spirits. Perhaps he
suggested she should return? 'She is our only security,' said
Harriet. 'I do not think she will go back without us.' As long as
Bess remained with them, they were safe from total neglect. For
it was neglect rather than wickedness that lay behind the Duke's
silence. Apart from the dreadful weeks of crisis in October, he
had not been one to demonstrate thoughts, feelings, or intentions. As Harriet put it, 'It is more from want of consideration
and wrong judgement than from real intention that he has
aggravated every unpleasant circumstance of her situation in the
terrible manner he has done.'[41]

By the last day of the year Harriet was beside herself.
'Sometimes we think everybody is afraid of writing,' she told
Lady Melbourne from Marseille. They all wrote constantly, but
their letters disappeared as if into the sea. Only one note came,

from the Duke of Devonshire's banker, Denne, begging for God's sake that Georgiana keep up her spirits and arm herself with as much courage as she can, as if in readiness to face a yet worse catastrophe. This was hardly the kind of message calculated to cheer them all up. 'If it was possible for anything to encrease my love my adoration of *her*, it would be the persecution she is going through,' said Harriet.[42]

Isolation, separation from her children, forlorn tramping across France with the burden of her secret, all might have been alleviated had Charles Grey been kind. Georgiana might have been sustained by the knowledge that she at least had the love of the man for whom she was suffering. She begged Lady Melbourne to be circumspect in talking about her in London, not to give the impression that she was anything but happy, but she may talk of her more freely to 'Black'. 'Pray except to Black be very careful not to let it be thought that I am low,' she said. And again, 'Tell me all the news, all you do, all you hear either of me or of others, but only talk to Black much of me.'[43] She yearned for a word of solace or affection, but she waited in vain. When he did write it was either with an indifferent tone or a voice of reprimand. None of his letters to Georgiana, or hers to him, have survived, but we know from Harriet that he scolded her for everything she did and for everything she did not do, and we have the plaintive admission of Georgiana, writing to Lady Melbourne, that 'Black has been again very cruel, and my letters from him yesterday have given me a headache [which] is not yet gone – why will people be harsh at such a distance?' Typically, she added a word of understanding even *in extremis*: 'However, he is quite in the right, de ne pas se gêner.' Only two months were left before she would bring forth Grey's child.[44]

Bess was quite outspoken in her anger. 'He is a brute, a beast, and I have no patience with him,' she wrote. 'There is a want of feeling and consideration that makes me quite mad with him . . . we shall not probably return until April, and then I hope she will have acquir'd strength enough to mind him less.'[45]

There is evidence that Lady Melbourne was virtually the only person who really knew just how much Georgiana was in love. Georgiana sent far more letters to Charles Grey than she owned to Harriet and Bess, and tried to have them think that her depressions were due to the Duke's neglect of her financial needs and her own worries about debts. She succeeded at least in part in giving the impression that her attachment to Grey was fading, which in turn made Harriet and Bess more hopeful of her recovery. To Lady Melbourne alone she confessed the truth: 'Remember dearest love that my dearest sister does not think I am out of spirits except about affairs . . . I send you a letter for Black.'[46]

Amidst all this, there was the additional strain of keeping Lady Spencer free from worry, which involved keeping her as much as possible in the dark. This was by no means an easy task, for she was constantly anxious, always watching every move, and permanently suspicious, which Harriet said was almost unbearable. The atmosphere of deceit, calculated admission, and heavy silence was claustrophobic. At least Lady Spencer was more civil to Bess than she had ever been before, touched by the demonstration of wicked Elizabeth Foster's loyalty. But her suspicions were aroused again when, in February 1792, Bess, Georgiana and Caroline St Jules left the main party to travel west to Nîmes and Aigues Mortes. The mystery which still surrounded Caroline St Jules's identity gave rise to persistent conjectures which had to be parried. Bess maintained she was taking Caroline to see the St Jules family, as the old count was seriously ill. (He did in fact die a couple of months later.) 'Now I am convinc'd my mother thinks there is some very particular reason why Bess wishes to be away from here [Nice] and instead of proving anything to her about Caroline, she always says if I meant to deceive anybody I should do it less clumsily', Harriet told Lady Melbourne, adding a trifle impatiently, enough to suggest the innuendoes which passed between the women, 'I know she thinks Bess has a hundred and fifty children, and is now lying in of twins.'[47]

Unaccountably, Harriet also seemed to want Charles Grey to be in ignorance of the purpose of this detour. Cannot he believe that this long journey is to settle Caroline's affairs and see her friends? she asked. What other reason could there be? 'Another child of Bess's?'

The truth was that Georgiana's pregnancy was about to reach its term. They did not stay long at Aigues Mortes, but moved on to Montpellier, where they arrived, Bess and the Duchess, on 10 February. There were advantages in Montpellier at this time.

Georgiana was to some extent familiar with the town, having accompanied her parents there twenty years before; she was certainly known and welcomed there. Moreover, it was the centre of the most famous medical school in Eurŏpe, where Rabelais himself had been a doctor, and where now there were plenty of first-rate *accoucheurs* to assist Georgiana in her hour of need. If Bess reflected how different were the circumstances from the furtive back-street squalor which accompanied her own deliveries, she said nothing.

On 20 February 1792, Georgiana gave birth to Charles Grey's daughter, who was called Eliza Courtney (Courtney had been a family name on the Poyntz side – remote enough not to be shocking).*

Only two weeks after Eliza's arrival, Georgiana and Bess left Montpellier to travel eastwards and join the main party at Nice. Passing through difficult roads and riots at Aix and Toulon, they eventually came to Nice on March 10. Harriet reported that Georgiana looked extremely beautiful, though very much thinner.

And so the exile continued. Georgiana suffered deeply at being separated from her children. She wrote to her eldest daughter almost every day, charming notes which combined tenderness and instruction, giving her lessons in the history and geography of all the places she visited and never failing to mention how much she missed her company.

As the months dragged by, she grew more and more afraid that her beloved children would forget her. 'Oh my dear child', she wrote, 'I can only assure you that your love and the hopes that you will not forget me are the comfort of my life now that I am absent from you. When I am to return is now very uncertain – I hope it will be soon as I do not feel that I have strength enough to bear so long an absence.' And a little later, 'Hartington must forget me I fear.' In return, she received endearing little pictures of the home life of which she was no longer a part. 'We employed ourselves one day in sweeping the snow in a heap till Selina's back was so stiff she felt it for two or three days after.'

* It looks likely that Lady Spencer told Miss Trimmer why the Duchess went to Montpellier, but the relevant page of her letter has (once again) been torn off.

Occasionally, the Duke himself would feature in the news. 'Papa came to see us yesterday', wrote little G. 'My sister and I played to him. He thought we were improved. I like to have his approbation more than anybody's because I know he means what he says.' Little G. assured Mama that she was not forgotten. 'I shall enjoy your company more than ever now I know how to value it and profit by it,' she said. Selina Trimmer would often append footnotes to tell the Duchess how Hartington says 'Mama gone' twenty times a day, which cannot have made her banishment any more bearable. One sympathises with Selina, who had the task of trying to explain why Mama and Grandmama were away for so long, and was not helped in this by the Duke.

Lady Elizabeth Foster also wrote regularly to little G. but with a different purpose. It was to her just as important that little G. should miss Caroline St Jules as well as her mother, if Caroline's place within the family should be secured beyond doubt, so she never failed to mention her. 'She loves you with more tenderness than belongs to so young a child, thinks and talks a great deal about you,' wrote Bess. 'Consider my love what it is at her age to be witness to all the anxiety which she sees, no other child with her . . . I fret all day long about her and her pale looks, and that she should pass this miserable time here. Poor little soul, I found a scrap of paper on which she wrote, "I only thought that my friend would partake of my sorrow".' Lady Elizabeth assured little G. that the happiest day of her life would be the day that reunites 'us all'.

For her part, Georgiana wrote sentences that she knew would be read by her husband, and might soften his harsh resistance: 'I am grown a very different creature I believe', and 'I beg of you dearest love to make oo Papa come and fetch me soon'. From him, however, she heard nothing.[48] To Mr Coutts she confessed, 'Oh, my dear, dear Sir, my heart is sick for my children and for England. But when I do return, I hope it will not be to leave them again.'[49]

The doubt in her voice was understandable, for the Duke's neglect was so total, his anger so unabated, that all the womenfolk turned against him. His behaviour was typical of the man whose response to personal humiliation needed a period of

cathartic retribution before a more conciliatory attitude could
be nurtured. The legendary Cavendish honour could brook no
insult.

Inevitably, word was spread that the Devonshire marriage was
at an end and the Duke and Duchess would separate. 'It seems to
be very certain that the D. and Dss of Devonshire are never to
meet again,' wrote Mary Noel. James Hare saw the Duke
frequently in London and attempted to gather some idea of his
intentions which he could relay to the Duchess, but Devonshire
was not the confiding sort and Hare not intrusive. Hare was apparently questioned on all sides by people who thought he must
be in the know. To Georgiana he wrote,

> I have probably passed this winter for a greater liar, or rather
> for a more trusty person than I am, for in answer to all the
> questions that have been asked me about your staying so long
> abroad without any of your children, and about the time of
> your return, and the footing upon which you are with the D., I
> have always said what was literally true, but believed by no
> one person, viz: that I know nothing of any disagreement or
> separation, and that I concluded your stay would depend on
> your sister's health. I have seen a great deal of him this year,
> and frequently dined with him *tête à tête*. As he never entered
> upon the subject of your situation I never suggested it. He
> must be very sure that I am not indifferent about anything
> that concerns him and his family, and I believe too that he has
> no doubt of my secrecy, so that his silence must have pro-
> ceeded from an unwillingness to start a subject on which I
> could only partake of his uneasiness without relieving it.[50]

That rumours of an impending separation were rife in
London was made clear to Georgiana in Europe; she tried
bravely to deny them from a distance. Mr Coutts, above all,
must be placed in no doubt. 'All I can assure you is the reports of
separation are groundless', she told him, 'at least I have no
reason in the world to imagine that the Duke has the least intention of the kind.' Coutts's reply merely confirmed what the
Duchess most feared. 'I am happy to hear from you there is no
truth in the separation, for it has been too much talk'd of
here.'[51]

At one point, Georgiana contemplated returning to England

uninvited, but Harriet, who longed to go home as much as anyone, knew this would be a disastrous move, resulting in the very separation predicted by the gossips. As usual, the Duke of Devonshire's temper must be allowed to subside at the most leisurely pace and his natural goodness to reassume dominance in time. If Georgiana could hold on for a year, thought Harriet, all might be well.

Evidently forgiving the slight he suffered when he found himself excluded from Devonshire House while Grey was inside, the Prince of Wales wrote Georgiana a long, affectionate letter, full of endearments underlined, calling her his 'best beloved friend' and assuring her that 'no circumstances in life *can ever cause any change in ye sentiments of yt heart with wh you have long been acquainted*'. He went on to reflect that Georgiana was so near perfection that everyone else he knew suffered in comparison with her, and to reiterate that 'no human event' (presumably the birth of Eliza was a human event) could ever alter his feelings towards her. As an afterthought, the Prince gave his opinion that the French had behaved so badly that the world would be better if it were rid of the entire race.

Georgiana was grateful for any kind word from home. 'I would give the world to be with my poor little children', she told the Prince, 'but I dare not take upon myself the determination, and I have left entirely to the D to decide for me. With naïve impudence, she told her 'dearest brother' to be cautious about getting into debt: 'my own irregularity and extravagance about money gives me a right to *preach* to you.'[52]

Meanwhile, Canis was sunk in his own loneliness, spending his time mostly at Brooks's and neglecting both himself and his home. The sparkle of Devonshire House disappeared in Georgiana's absence, to be replaced by unaccustomed gloom ('dismal and dirty' Hare called it). The Duke's drinking increased, his gout grew worse. Eventually, after eight months, he wrote, only to say that he did not think it wise yet for Georgiana to come home, but he might come to meet her 'somewhere' the following April, after yet another eight months, and go with her to Spa for the summer.[53]

Georgiana could do nothing but make the most of her unhappy situation, imploring her husband, through letters to little G., to relent. On her son's birthday, she wrote from Turin,

'This is dear Hartington's birthday, my own Georgiana – I write him a letter but give him a kiss from me – when shall I see you all?' Crossing the Alps, she said, 'I shall feel myself much nearer you and getting nearer home at Geneva, and I hope your Papa will come for me very soon; I am sure he will as soon as he can for he knows how much I long to see you.'[54] It was a man bereft of emotional resource who could read such heartache with indifference. Was not Georgiana punished enough by having to declare to her nine-year-old daughter, 'This year has been the most painful of my life'?[55]

With time on her hands, Georgiana gave way to self-analysis, introspection, regret. After parting from her mother, she wrote from Belgium, 'I have had incessant and serious thought lately, dearest M. Alas, the result of *thought* in me is always remorse and condemnation of myself. But I think I condemn myself as much almost for the misuse of time in my *banishment*, as anything else. . . . My mind and my heart always wish'd to do well, but despair at myself and my situation often depriv'd me of all energy, and drew me into errors. . . . What I hope I return impress'd with is very deep humility, and the wish of atonement, by doing more for another, and by perfect acquiescence in all *his* intentions and wishes. I hope likewise to make use of the very great good fortune that has attended me by increas'd prudence and care. I fear and tremble, but my only dependence is on my penitence and gratitude to God and on my adoration to my children, for I am not bold enough to depend on strength of character which I feel I have not.'[56] Even allowing for the ruse which no doubt hoped these words would be read by the Duke, it is a genuinely sad woman who penned them. 'Ten times a day I am oblig'd to hide myself not to show what I suffer,' she said.

Even more desolate is the letter Georgiana wrote to her infant son in her own blood, to be handed to him when he was eight years old in the event of her death. This was before the birth of Eliza Courtney, when the possibility of an ignoble death a long way from home had to be taken seriously; it was not intended for the eyes of the Duke while she was alive. The letter is now locked up safely at Chatsworth, separate from the rest of the collection.*

---

* There is a similar letter to little G., in blood, now at Castle Howard.

My dear little boy [she says], As soon as you are old enough to understand this letter it will be given to you; it contains the only present I can make you – my blessing, written in my blood. The book that will be also given you is a memorandum of me you must ever keep. Alas, I am gone before you could know me, but I lov'd you, I nurs'd you nine months at my breast. I love you dearly. For my sake observe my last wishes. Be obedient to your dear Papa and Grand-mama; consult them and obey them in all things. Be very kind to your sisters. Join with your dear Papa, when you can, in increasing their fortunes, and if you have the misfortune to lose your dear Papa, double your dear sisters fortunes at least. Love always dear Lady Elizabeth and Caroline [St Jules]. Be kind to all your cousins, especially the Ponsonbys. Make piety your chief study, never despise religion, never break your word, never betray a secret, never tell a lie. God bless you, my dear child, oh, how dearly would I wish again to see your beloved face, and to press you to my wretched bosom. God bless you, my dear little boy,

> Your poor Mother, G. Devonshire.

To this there was a repetitive, anguished postscript – 'May God Almighty bless and preserve you, my dear Hartington, and make you good and happy. God bless you my child. Your poor Mother, G. Devonshire.'[57]

The letter was accompanied by a draft will, asking the Duke to give small remembrances to each of her children, and to take for himself one gift which more than any conjecture of motive or interpretation of letters testifies to the unique bond which brought Canis, Mrs Rat and Racky together. 'Everything I have is yours', she wrote, 'therefore I can leave you nothing as a remembrance but a green antique ring which was given me by Bess, and which I beg you to keep as a mourning ring.' Hartington's life, she wrote obliquely, was *trebly* precious.

* * *

Distance did not offer release from Georgiana's money troubles. On the contrary, the Duke seemed determined that she should suffer the humiliation of bankruptcy as well as banishment. His own bankers, Messrs. Denne, refused to pay her draft for £138 in February. 'What a pity Your Grace should suffer such an affront from the Duke of Devonshire's banker', commiserated Mr Coutts, 'it hurts me tenderly!'[58] Tenderly was an odd adverb to use in the circumstances, as the money was due to be paid to *him*. Georgiana put on the usual brave face; she wished the Duke knew 'how cruelly I have been treated by Mr Denne, who has regularly refus'd my drafts, tho' I know he has orders to the contrary'.[59] The fact was, as she well knew, Denne would only refuse to honour her financial obligations if he were so instructed by the Duke. She had somehow to placate Coutts, who was beginning to wonder if he would ever see his money again. The Duke, she told him, was 'naturally shy and reserv'd, and has not settled in his mind the manner of payment'. Coutts should, yet again, learn to be patient. As for herself, he should be pleased that she has taken her affairs very seriously to heart – 'I am grown very exact'. She only left England without settling her debts on the understanding that the Duke would look after outstanding matters on her behalf.[60]

Not satisfied with this constant temporizing, Coutts acted on his own initiative. He left his card with the porter at Devonshire House. It was completely ignored. Four weeks later, he bumped into the Duke by chance, and was cut dead. 'I think myself deserving of more civility,' he complained, and boldly went on to tell the Duchess that her husband discredited himself by ignoring the bond he had signed promising to pay with interest.[61] In May, Coutts dined at Fish Crauford's house. There was the Duke. 'Whether he knew I was in the room was more than could be discover'd by his looks or manner. I make every allowance for his habits and usual silence, yet, everything consider'd, surely he might have somehow noticed me, as one he had seen before.'[62]

Coutts then rehearsed the familiar strain of remorse that he had ever allowed himself to be seduced into this trap. 'I now see that I judg'd ill and have done you no manner of good, nay perhaps I have aided you to pay debts you ought not to have paid, and which never could have been made legally or honestly clear against you. . . . I have never yet refused a draft of yours, perhaps it would have been quite as well for you, and much better for me, I had never *paid one*.'[63]

Eventually, the exasperated banker wrote to the Duke directly, invoking the honour of the House of Cavendish and pleading his obligations to support his family. The total amount owed by the Duchess, he said, was £20,200, including the bond for £4,400 which bore the Duke's endorsement and promise to consider it his own debt. This elicited a cold and proper response, paying Coutts the sum of £4,400 with five and a half year's interest (i.e. £5,610), for which Coutts thanked the Duke, adding a P.S., 'The sum now remaining due to me by the Duchess is £15,800.'[64]

Still, the saga dragged on. Georgiana wrote telling Coutts that he had been receiving £500 a quarter, and really should have a little patience for the rest. 'I absolutely know nothing of this regular 500£ a quarter', spluttered poor Coutts, 'any more than I do of my want of patience, for I think I have shown patience beyond example. But in money matters 99 favours granted are annihilated by the hundredth when refused. In fact, however, I have never refused anything . . . I will pay no more for the future and hope nothing will be expected from me, which will at least save me the mortification of receiving angry letters. Mrs Coutts and my three daughters are at present all ill in their beds, and myself in a very weak state of health, not much the better for being ill treated where I least expected to be so.'[65]

The Dowager Lady Spencer watched all this bickering over money with growing chagrin and despair. What on earth had gone wrong with the education she had devoted to her daughters that they both should prove so lastingly amoral, in every respect? Harriet, too, was constantly wrestling with debts, and with far less hope of a timely rescue. To Harriet she said, 'May I have the unspeakable joy, before I die, of seeing you and your sister leading useful, exemplary and blameless lives, and enjoying that calm and solid happiness that can be procured by no other means.'[66]

In March 1793, Lord Bessborough died at the age of eighty-nine, which meant that Duncannon, who succeeded to the title, had immediately to leave the party and return to England. He found his wife's finances in a sorry state, and joined his mother-in-law in imploring her henceforth to try to be more careful.

The protracted exile was not, however, characterised by un-relieved gloom. There were happy times as the assembled ladies travelled from country to country, covering hundreds of miles in their peregrinations, meeting people, watching the two little

Carolines grow into charming, effervescent girls. Not the least
pleasure was to see the austere Lady Spencer melt in the
presence of Caroline St Jules; she might despise the mother, but
she undoubtedly loved the child. On one occasion, she spent a
whole day alone with Caroline visiting Tivoli on horseback,[67]
evidently delighting in her company. Georgiana was quick to
notice, and informed her daughter G. by letter that Caroline was
'mended with your dear Grandmama – your grandmama is the
only person she minds at all . . . living so much with her in this
journey I have learnt to know her better than ever; she has great
good sence; attention like yours; and sweetness of disposition
and manner like you'.[68]

In Naples, the two Carolines dined with the King and Queen
and behaved admirably well. Caroline Ponsonby could not
always be relied upon to conduct herself with the requisite
decorum. She was already mischievous, mercurial, unpredictable, showing signs of the wild uncontrollable delinquency
which would one day make her, as Lady Caroline Lamb, the
most discussed woman in England. 'She is very haughty and says
anything which comes into her head, which is very distressing,'
mused Georgiana.[69] When Harriet, now Lady Bessborough,
had a birthday on 14 July, both Carolines sang a song to cheer
her up, so sweetly that Harriet was reduced to tears and the girls
faltered into silence.[70] Lady Bessborough was quite genuinely ill
– the spitting of blood continued to weaken her for nearly two
years.

In August 1792, they were all in Switzerland. The party now
included Mr Pelham (later Earl of Chichester), Mr Ellis, and Mr
Poyntz (Georgiana's uncle), and they passed a merry time
enough in Switzerland with Elizabeth Foster's great friend
Gibbon. Caro Ponsonby, precociously teasing the huge ugly
Gibbon, suggested that the footman who had been giving her a
piggy-back should perform the same service for him, which
might well have broken the man's neck had he tried. Gibbon
was forever playing with the two Carolines, presenting the
curious and highly entertaining spectacle of a bulky philosopher
rejuvenated by the society of two ebullient little girls. 'Caroline
Ponsonby does what she will with him,' said Georgiana, and
once told him that his face was so big that it frightened the little
puppy she was playing with.[71]

After leaving Switzerland to cross the Alps into Italy, Lady Elizabeth Foster kept up a correspondence with Gibbon in a relaxed friendly vein which revealed an aspect of her character quite absent from the effusive emotional letters at Chatsworth. It says much for her charm and intelligence that she could maintain a genuinely affectionate relationship with this massive intellectual, who teased her without malice. He reported that he had been visited by the beautiful Duchess of Devonshire and the wicked Lady Elizabeth Foster, but everyone knew the adjective was used in a jesting spirit. For her part, Bess was cheerful, bright, witty. Before crossing the Alps, for example, she told him, 'I would fain have written from the top of St Bernard, but we are still in all humility at the bottom.' Having crossed the Pass, she wrote from Milan, 'As to us, the courage which we showed in climbing the grand St Bernard is nothing in comparison to that which we show in traversing the once peaceful country of Italy – troops dispos'd everywhere, anxious and fearfull countenances, sudden alarms, and bold attempts & strange successes are what characterize each days experience.' With this letter Caro Ponsonby sent '*mille amitiés*' to her admirer, and Georgiana appended a note to assure Gibbon that Bess was well, '*belle comme un Ange*', and that he should come to visit them in Tuscany.

Bess's letters to Gibbon give the impression of a happy band of travellers, visiting palaces and churches from eleven in the morning until 4 in the afternoon, combining study with social life. They all shared a passion for mineralogy and botany, which, however, took second place to Raphael in Florence. 'We could make ourselves very independent of bad inns and tiresome roads,' she said, so much were they enjoying themselves. Gibbon's replies were flirtatious; he would like to be her Cicerone amidst the magnificence of Chatsworth, the melancholy beauties of Hardwick, or the elegance of Chiswick.

From Florence they continued westwards to Pisa and down the coast to Rome. 'We think of hastening to Rome before these Goths and vandals destroy everything that is worth seeing there, the merits of which they will be perfectly insensible to', Bess told Gibbon, 'and then returning to Pisa or Florence which is to be the asylum of all wanderers like us.' They were in Pisa when the terrible news arrived in February 1793 that the King of France had been murdered. Exiled from the security of England, they began to fear for their lives and wonder if they would survive many more months on a continent in turmoil. 'If you ever pray'd, I should ask you to pray for us,' Bess wrote again to Gibbon. 'What our motions will or can be this summer I have no guess.'[72] When the French revolutionaries declared war upon England and the Netherlands, their situation became even more dangerous.

A new friend was adopted into the circle as a result of the prolonged absence abroad, a woman who would later leave a very definite mark on London society and share the confidence of both Georgiana and Bess. She was then Lady Webster, but it is as Lady Holland that history is familiar with her. Born Elizabeth Vassall, the daughter of Richard Vassall of Jamaica, she was one of the first transatlantic heiresses to enter London society. Indeed, she would eventually almost dominate it. Married at the age of fifteen to Sir Godfrey Webster of Battle Abbey, Elizabeth was an energetic, intelligent woman who would not easily settle for a tedious married life to a man she did not even like and who was twenty-three years older than she. Sir Godfrey was content with the sedate English country life, demanding little movement and no thought; his young wife longed for fun and stimulation. Having persuaded her boring husband to take her to Europe for the winter of 1792, after six years of marriage, there she fell in with the Devonshire *ménage* and formed a friendship which was to last. Later, she eloped with Lord Holland, Charles Fox's nephew, and subsequently married him, to preside over the idiosyncratic parties at Holland House which would compete with those of Devonshire House for intellectual sparkle. Capricious and selfish, Lady Holland would receive visitors with her page kneeling at her feet, his hands beneath her dress rubbing her aching legs. Stricter society would never entirely accept her for her unconventional ways, and we can only surmise that old Lady Spencer viewed her arrival on the scene with yet more misgivings.

By May 1793, word reached the nomads that at last the Duke desired them to come home. 'Oh my G. how can I express my happiness to you', wrote Georgiana, 'God of heaven bless him for his kindness to me – in 3 months at latest I shall be with you my Dearest Children and this cruel absence will be amply made up by the delight of seeing you – oh my dearest love what joy it will be and how very very good your dear Papa is to me.'[73] Leaving Lady Bessborough behind in Bagni, to benefit from the sun, and Lady Spencer with her, Georgiana, Bess and company began their slow journey home.

They crossed from Ostend to Dover on 18 September. Meanwhile, Miss Trimmer and the nurse Mrs Brown had dressed the three children, Georgiana, Hary-O and Hartington, and taken them in the coach to meet their mother. The reunion at Dover was rapturous. 'I have seen them, I have seen them,' Georgiana wrote to her mother the same day. Little G. and Hary-O knew her well enough, but Hartington, now three-and-a-half years old, did not recognise her and would not look at her. He kissed the strange lady dutifuly, without enthusiasm. Arriving at Devonshire House, all the servants, who had been given wine to celebrate, were lined up to welcome her. 'I never knew anything so touching as the reception of the servants, they were all mad with joy.' The Duke, too, appeared pleased to see her. The nightmare was over. From now on, the Duchess would determine to lead a quiet, maternal life. But after nearly two years, she was in an agony of apprehension whether she would manage it. 'I am so agitated, so happy and so anxious.'[74]

Chapter Nine

ILLNESS

Georgiana's homecoming was nothing less than triumphant. The Duke, apparently all forgiveness, gave a servants' ball in her honour, which turned out to be the happiest party ever held at Devonshire House. All three children were present. A woman so essentially nice as Georgiana enjoyed more than ordinary loyalty from those in her service, and they manifested their pleasure at her return with heartwarming sincerity. After two years of dreary sepulchral silence, the house was again alive with feminine chatter and the gay exhilarating spirit which Georgiana breathed into every room. A year later she injected the same transfusion of life into Chatsworth, where the villagers overwhelmed her with a joyful welcome at a large but intimate garden fête. The local people, who never forgot Georgiana's good heart, made it a family affair, an occasion for personal celebration; the Duchess belonged not to the world, but to Derbyshire. Little Hartington was precociously grand and witty. Someone asked him if his legs ached. No, he replied. Did his heart ache? 'Oh no' the four-year-old said, 'I'm not come to that yet.'[1]

Anxiety cleared within days of Georgiana's return, for not only was the Duke good to her, dining with her *tête à tête* like a devoted married couple who had never known dark days, but the whole might of the Cavendish relations softened in her favour. They treated her with kindness and affection. The Duke of Portland even wrote to say how happy he was that she was back home. As for the awkward subject of money, Canis would look after that; 'I feel no doubt of his clearing my bills,' Georgiana confided to her mother.[2]

Mr Coutts had not learned any lessons. In the same year, 1793, he lent £60,000 to the Prince of Wales in the expectation of royal beneficence,[3] and was soon seeking the Duchess's influence to get him a box in Sheridan's playhouse, and complaining of neglect when she did not reply immediately. Years of dealing with Coutts had taught her how to use feminine winsomeness to keep him tame. Asking for just a little money, not for herself, but to help her poor sister out of trouble, she said, 'God bless you. Don't say anything to make me afraid of opening your next letter.'[4] It worked.

From now on, Georgiana's life enters a more placid period. Youthful frivolity gives way to more mature concerns – with the growing family, with her husband's health, and finally with her own. The Duke's gout had reached serious proportions. Georgiana was certain that his heart and lungs were affected, for he occasionally spat blood, and passed uncomfortable nights. 'I am quite low about him,' she said. 'All my hope is that this may get him into a regular way and change of life, that might make quite a new person of him.'[5] 'This' was the peaceful country existence to which Georgiana, Bess and Canis were increasingly devoted. In November 1793 they all three took a house in Bath for some months, then continued the secluded life at the Duke of Bedford's house, Oakley, and in the summer of 1794 at Chatsworth. The Duke no longer boasted a wife and a mistress, but in effect two wives. No longer was there any question of separation; no longer did the ladies pine for the glitter of London. 'I have long left off dancing but I allow it myself on my dear childrens' birthdays,' Georgiana said. Georgiana and Bess were in their late thirties, the Duke was over forty – a little early to settle for domestic peace perhaps, but the 'dissipation' which had been so central to their youth was beginning to claim its price.

Flirtations, too, were a dim echo of the past. There was talk that Lady Elizabeth Foster was being wooed by the widowed Duke of Richmond. This virtuous and estimable man, whose political views were so radical that he introduced a Bill for universal suffrage above the age of eighteen two centuries before it was finally adopted, was now nearly sixty. He would have been a fond and dutiful husband, but Bess would not allow the friendship to pass the bounds of *amitié*; she much preferred the Duke that she had, even if she was not his Duchess.

As for Charles Grey and Georgiana, they henceforth met

socially and publicly, with no more intimacy than was proper. Grey was a guest at dinner in October 1794, along with Sheridan, Fitzpatrick and Townshend, but only a few weeks later he was married, to a Ponsonby no less – Mary Elizabeth Ponsonby, daughter of Lord Ponsonby and a cousin of the Bessboroughs.* For the rest of their lives, Georgiana and Charles Grey had to be circumspect to avoid the tattle of gossips, as is indicated by a starchy letter Grey wrote her in 1803, saying that if they are to meet at a social gathering, 'I beg there may be no particular conversation between us . . . the subject is immaterial if we are seen in a long whisper together.'[6] The romance, at any rate, was well and truly over, leaving no real cause for long whispers. It had taken Georgiana a considerable time to kill all feeling in her heart for Grey. She had maintained contact with him through Lady Melbourne, and confessed she heard constantly from him, 'but not comfortably'. Gradually she learnt not to be hurt by his austerity and even not to expect anything else. It was a much calmer Duchess who told Lady Melbourne, 'I had one kind letter from him and that is all, and I have wrote to him twice such letters as the universe might see – and I think our correspondence is likely to end there.'[7]

The issue of the romance, Eliza Courtney, was brought up at Howick as Grey's sister, the only one of the various children born to Georgiana and Bess who did not eventually take her place among the inmates of Devonshire House.

It has been traditionally believed that Georgiana was never permitted to see her love-child. This is not strictly true. Meetings were extremely rare, and were made to appear simply social. In 1797, for instance, Georgiana informs Lady Melbourne that she has been 'chiefly taken up lately with Eliza, who goes next week with Mrs O for ages to Northumberland to Lady Grey'. As for Grey himself, he 'is now very good-natured to me, but I do not see him often and I do not believe anybody knows I ever do see him'.[8]

When she was with Eliza, the Duchess had to act under the constraint of betraying no more than polite affection. This much

---

* Mary knew nothing of Grey's liaison with the Duchess, and would not, so her family maintained, have married him if she had known. It is difficult to believe the other family tradition, according to which the Duke of Devonshire presented Eliza to the unfortunate Mrs Grey on the day of her marriage.

is attested by a poem which she wrote, containing the only reference to Eliza which has escaped the family censors. It is hidden in the little blue note-book, mysteriously separate from the main collection of her letters, which was presumably left to Elizabeth Foster, for it bears in the latter's handwriting on the cover the word 'carissima', as well as Georgiana's initials in her own hand. All the contents are in Georgiana's script. (The despairing letter to Bess about her debts, quoted on p. 160 is also in this booklet.) The poem, though flawed in more ways than one, opens a window on to the goodness of this extraordinary lady:

> For there is one, whose looks display
> Of hope the sweet but transient ray,
> As often he afraid has prest
> The poor Eliza to his breast.
>
> And there is one I've sometimes seen
> With friendly eye and anxious mien,
> Who timid, trembling, yet benign,
> Has bent her glowing cheek to mine.
>
> I know their fear, I hear their voice,
> Midst thousands they would be my choice.
> Yet sooner I'd unknown remain
> Than give to others heart a pain.

* * *

Georgiana turned her attention to the dry rot and redecoration of Chiswick House, the beautiful Palladian villa in a village ten miles from London, which had been erected by the architect Earl of Burlington and had passed by inheritance to the Duke of Devonshire. It has now been absorbed into Greater London, but was then a distant abode of quiet charm, some of which can still be felt by ambling through its small, cosy rooms. Georgiana aptly called it 'very comfy' and was soon to treasure it as one of her favourite places. Her daughter Hary-O complained that the days at Chiswick 'had not one inch of difference', and that her father was wont to snore there in ignorance of all around him, but it was precisely this lack of bustle which Georgiana found increasingly enchanting. Lord Hervey had said that the house was 'not large enough to live in, but too big to hang on one's watch-chain'. To Georgiana it appeared an adorable cottage after the grandeur of Chatsworth and the formality of Devonshire House. The aesthetic Lord Ronald Leveson-Gower, one of Georgiana's descendants, said that Chiswick had an in-describable charm that no other place possessed, which is the kind of hyperbolic remark uttered by those who cherish the memories of happy childhood days; for children especially, Chiswick was a huge delight, a wonderful toy house with its wild garden in which they could play for hours without fear of treading where they ought not. Restrictions were lifted, for-malities forbidden.

In time, so many would come to feel the warmth of the place that it risked being over-praised and over-inhabited. For nearly half a century already members of the public could visit Chiswick House upon application for a ticket, but at least Georgiana was used to the public days at Chatsworth and could tolerate a certain amount of intrusion with style. After her death, two Tsars of Russia and Queen Victoria were all entertained there. Two famous politicians, Fox and Canning, died there. In 1794, however, it was still a relatively private retreat.

Great events touched Georgiana now only obliquely. She wept to hear of the execution of Marie-Antoinette, heard that the Prince of Wales had broken with Mrs Fitzherbert, then married the awful Princess Caroline, then turned to Maria Fitzherbert again, but she was no more placed in the centre of these upheavals, and, such was the change in her, she was relieved not to be.

Georgiana did not think the Prince should marry Princess Caroline, having given Mrs Fitzherbert to the world as he did, but her opinion was not sought, and she did not proffer it directly. To an unnamed person, close to the Prince, she was 'more frank than prudent' in her conversation, by her own account, and suffered abuse for her pains. 'He [the Prince of Wales] has so good a heart *au fond* that some day or other he will value me more for my sincerity,' she thought. Time would prove her right.[9]

In April 1794, Harriet Bessborough and her mother, who had been several months in Naples, began their journey home. For Harriet, it had been an absence from home of three years, made necessary by fragile health, yet it produced one highly attractive and ultimately dangerous consolation. In Naples Lady Bessborough had made the acquaintance of Lady Stafford's handsome son, Granville Leveson-Gower, and had entered upon a friendship which was to last for the rest of her life. At this stage, everyone was alarmed except Harriet. Vivid and intelligent (Lady Hester Stanhope said she had ten times more cleverness than her sister the Duchess),[10] Harriet was used to admirers. Charles Beauclerk, son of Topham and Lady Diana, was openly in love with her, Sheridan himself would a few years later pay court. That this handsome young man, twelve years her junior, should be devoted to her was, in her view, an uncomplicated delight. Encouraged by Lady Webster, they indulged in frequent meetings and held intellectual conversations. Harriet convinced herself she merely liked him, but others could see that the friendship threatened to develop in the same way as Georgiana's had with Charles Grey. When Harriet came home, she was besieged on all sides with advice and dire warnings. She must not make a fool of herself, she must be wary of the powerful Lady Stafford, who distrusted Devonshire House and could make a terrible fuss if she chose. Harriet was quick to reassure everyone that there was nothing to worry about. (Lord Byron unkindly called her, much later, the 'hack whore of the last century').

* * *

While Georgiana spent the summer of 1794 reconquering Chatsworth, Bess stayed behind at Devonshire House enjoying the social life of London. There was the enormous excitement of Admiral Howe's naval victory at the beginning of June. Bess told Georgiana that Lady Howe had received the news at two in the morning. She 'heard the sound of horses, the messenger called out "glorious news my lady" – she quite out of breath with agitation called to the servant to open the door and bring her the letter. "I can't, my lady, I am naked." Well, says Lady Howe, I will get into bed again, don't stay to dress, but lay the letter on the table and get away.'[11]

A few days later, and Bess is at the opera. 'Banti sang like an angel from heaven – after the opera they called for her to sing God Save the King. She was gone home – in vain did the people tell the house so, no ballet would be heard of, and she was obliged to come on in her nightgown and to sing it twice.'[12]

Life at Chatsworth was placid in comparison. Georgiana devoted herself to arranging her books, building her grotto, and collecting her fossils. She could often be found, at this period, climbing the library steps to catalogue the contents of each shelf, then pin a little list in her own writing to the side of the bookcase. She was happy to spend hours at this quiet avocation. The grotto she built in the garden at Chatsworth still stands as a monument to the patience she could muster when she was in the mood. Finally, the fossils she collected amounted to over 1,000 separate specimens, none of them British, and the Derbyshire mineral collection was (and is) justly famous.* A visitor a couple of years later, when Bess had joined the Duke and his wife, was Sir Philip Francis.† He gave an account of his stay there to his wife and children which in its gentle wit serves to illuminate the lugubrious temper of existence in the big house during the last years of the century.

> Events never happen at Chatsworth, except a public dinner every Monday [he wrote]. It must be my own fault if I don't make reflections enough while I am here, to last me for a year or two . . . as for Silence, the Abbaye de la Trappe is a mere Babel to this house. I asked the gardener, how long he had lived here, and who he conversed with. He said, 40 years, and seldom spoke to anybody. Talking, it seems, had been left off ever since the marriage of the present Duke's great grand-father . . . the Dutchess tried to bring conversation into fashion, but to no purpose; and even poor Lady Elizabeth is not allowed to talk, except upon her fingers.[13]

Sir Philip ought to have been sensitive enough to realise that poor health was largely responsible for the apparent gloom which enveloped Chatsworth. James Hare also noted that conversation 'never goes beyond a whisper'. Not only was the Duke's gout a constant worry, but Georgiana's headaches had assumed sinister proportions. She had always been prone to colds, which affected her more seriously than they did other

* Georgiana's descendants have consistently added to the collection, and continue to do so.
† Generally thought to be the author of the Junius letters.

people. Back in 1788 there were signs of the trouble to come when she complained of a 'thumping cold – I had it in my eyes, and a cough that tore my breast to pieces'. She consulted Dr Denman, who thought that her constant inclination to headaches, the lowness of her pulse and 'something that seems to hinder my breeding' (this was before the birth of Hartington and Eliza Courtney) indicated 'something wrong', which was not uncommonly perceptive of him. He recommended regularity of diet to strengthen her nerves and promote circulation, but was not especially alarmed by the pain in her eyes. There was also some trouble with her gums. On Denman's advice, Georgiana began to eat only boiled or roast meat, no puddings or cakes, and to drink one glass of Madeira with dinner and one glass of port after. She was encouraged by the cure Monsieur Calonne had effected for a very bad stomach, which was to eat three hundred and sixty-five roast chicken, one a day for a whole year.[14] (It is astonishing that there was almost a complete lack of vegetables in the diets and menus of the day, which led rich and poor alike to suffer frequently from scurvy.)

The ignorance of the medical profession in the eighteenth century is scarcely conceivable. Guesswork and superstition played a greater role in diagnosis than knowledge. The universal cure for everything was to bleed the patient, which was not much advance upon the notion that evil spirits could be banished by witchcraft. Within Georgiana's own circle there had been ample evidence of these barbaric practices. Her mother had once reported that Mrs Bouverie 'gave me a sad fright by an uncommonly violent bleeding at the nose which lasted near five hours without intermission'.[15] The doctor was sent for, and the remedy he prescribed, in spite of her being heavily pregnant, was that she should lose yet more blood. The Duke's younger brother, Lord Richard Cavendish, had died in 1781 after prolonged and useless attentions from the doctors. 'The Duchess is vastly miserable at Lord Richard's death,' Fawkner wrote to Lord Carlisle. The Duke and his other brother, Lord George, were 'very unhappy about it; they fancy he died from taking improper medicines; his sufferings were horrible'.[16] When Lord William Russell's seven-year-old son was bitten by a dog as he was playing with snowballs, the doctors took three hours to cut out the flesh that was bitten (without, of course, anything like anaesthetic); the boy asked that his eyes should not be covered, so that he could see how it was done.[17]

There being no palliatives available, operations were undergone in full consciousness, or, at the most, with the patient in a state of inebriation. Sometimes it was necessary to hit the sufferer over the head with a mallet in order to stun him. Dr Johnson was known to have seized the surgeon's knife and make a deeper incision into his own flesh because he thought the poor man had been too timid. Casualties at sea were hauled screaming on to chests, where surgeons hacked off limbs without a moment's preparation and dipped the stump in hot tar. Severed arteries were tied with silk. Not many of the wounded survived such treatment.

The medicines commonly taken sound to us now like a joke. Chilblains were cured with turnip water. Poultices were made from fantastic ingredients, such as the crust of a toasted loaf of bread, spread with soft soap. Lady Caroline, Georgiana's niece, was told by a doctor to eat chickens fed on frogs, while Lord Fermanagh drank posset made from horse manure and another victim drank snail tea. A negro servant found drowning in a tub of water was revived by sticking a pipe of tobacco in his anus and blowing. Dr James's Powder, the most widely used proprietary medicine, was based on antimony; it was followed closely in popularity by laudanum and calomel. There were even a few quacks who believed that the breath of young women might prolong life, and one who rented a room in a girls' boarding-school to be close to the invigorating vapours. Doctors advised Lord Stafford that he could only avoid creeping blindness by abstaining from conjugal intercourse for a year; this counsel he dutifully followed, only to discover that his wife was none the less pregnant after a few months.

It was against such a background of haphazard medical inventiveness that Georgiana's headaches assumed disquieting proportions in 1795. The cause of the pain was now evidently located in one of the eyes, which was swollen and ugly. 'I am mortified and extremely sorry that anything should be the matter with your eyes', wrote Mr Coutts, 'but I hope the complaint will soon be removed.'[18] In the summer of 1796 Georgiana came down to London to undergo an operation. Her sister and her mother both moved into Devonshire House to be near to her, and Lady Elizabeth Foster naturally did not want to leave her side. Dr Warren was so worried by the extent of the inflammation that he called in various specialists for an opinion, including John Gunning, Senior Surgeon-Extraordinary to the King, and Jonathan Phipps, who treated the King for cataract and was to write a dissertation upon the subject. All the eminent men agreed that the Duchess would probably lose the sight of her eye, but offered consolation that their ministrations should not affect the health of the other eye. They thereupon took some blood from the eyeball and professed themselves pleased with what they saw.

Lady Spencer reported progress to Selina Trimmer. 'The inflammation has been so great that the eye, the eyelids and the adjacent parts were swelled to the size of your hand doubled, and projecting forward from the face . . . a small ulcer has formed on the top of the cornea and has burst . . . if the inflammation should increase, the ulcer form again, and again burst, it would destroy the whole substance of the eye, which would then sink.'[19] Selina's response to this intelligence was typically pious. 'I doubt not but she will resign herself to the loss', she said, 'and should it be so we must comfort ourselves with reflecting on the spiritual advantage it will most probably be to her.'[20]

Meanwhile, Georgiana was comforted by Bess, whom Lady Spencer described as 'a most tender nurse', and her sister Lady Harriet. All three women stayed by Georgiana's bedside for four nights, although Lady Spencer could not bring herself to look at the grossly enlarged eyeball. The lids were only slightly parted, and between them was a thick white pus. The room in which Georgiana lay was kept mostly in darkness, and when lights were allowed they had to be shaded. Mama reported to Selina that her daughter had 'little sight with the right eye and cannot yet lift up the eyelid except a very little way without assistance – it is still horrible to look at'.[21] The children (who were at Worthing with Miss Trimmer) were not allowed to visit their mother, and had to promise that when they did eventually see her they would restrain themselves and not seem shocked by her appearance. Little Caroline Ponsonby sent a rhyming message:

Angels, guard her while she sleeps:
She who blesses should be blest.

The treatment which Georgiana had had to endure was un-
believably nasty. The doctors had almost strangled her with a
tourniquet around her neck to force the blood into her head,
and had then applied leeches to the eyeball.* The wounds made
by the leeches added to her pain. Not surprisingly, Dr Warren
was sure that the eye would never recover.[22]

Harriet Bessborough communicated her distress to her new
friend Granville Leveson-Gower. 'I have no thought, no hope,
no wish, but seeing my Dear, Dear Sister get well again', she
wrote, 'and I can know no peace or happiness till then. The
anxiety of my mind has been so near distraction that you will not
wonder at my not writing or my writing strangely. I scarcely ever
quit her room for a moment. While I am with her I use every
effort to keep up her Spirits and mine to be of use to her, and
appear calm and cheerful while my heart is breaking. My whole
soul is fix'd on that one object, and when I quit her, body and
mind sink at once, overcome with fatigue and anguish. . . . If
you could but see how well she bears the greatest tortures, tho'
hopeless, you would admire and love her more than ever. . . . I
have passed three hours in dreadful spasms; but Laudanum has
still'd them and made me feel drunk enough to write.'[23]

Such was the fame of the Duchess of Devonshire that her
sufferings were almost daily reported in the newspapers, though
with that want of accuracy which was then, as now, a *forte* of the
gossip column. On 10 August, the *Sun* said Georgiana had five
medical attendants, and on 18 August it informed its readers
that she had lost one eye and risked losing the other. By 27
August the same journal reported that eight physicians were
now in attendance. At the beginning of September, *The Times*
told the world that Georgiana was on the way to recovery and
had been for a walk in Hyde Park, adding 'she goes to Bognor
as soon as she can get out of the hands of the Faculty'.

The Doctors allowed her neither to read nor to write. She was
condemned to sit doing nothing all day, submitting to all instruction with 'the most unconquerable good humour and

* Dr Sinclair Evans, the incumbent at Chatsworth who retired in 1979,
remembers the use of leeches in his youth.

readiness,' according to her mother, and finding a smile for everyone. The apparent recovery in the autumn was quickly demolished by further interference from the doctors. No sooner had the eye healed, than it was opened and blooded yet again and another horrible operation was inflicted upon the suffering woman by applying caustics behind her ears and a blister to the back of her neck. 'I never saw anything like the agony she suffered', Harriet told Granville, 'and the exertions I made to hold and soothe her brought my old complaint of spasms with great violence.'[24] Dr Erasmus Darwin then came into the picture. He recommended a certain Mr Hadley to apply a galvanic apparatus, invented by Mr Strutt, to the Duchess's eye. 'The galvanic shocks appear to consist of a large quantity of electric ether', wrote Darwin, who clearly knew little about it and did not shrink from using Georgiana as a guinea-pig; 'they give no pain in passing from one temple to the other, tho' much light is seen in the eyes.'[25] Darwin politely tried to explain the contraption to Georgiana, with much talk of oxides and zinc, finishing with the assurance that Mr Hadley would explain more clearly, 'if you direct him to come over to galvanise your Grace's eye'.

Mr Hadley rode over from Derby to Chatsworth, and was spied in Chatsworth park, putting on a clean shirt, under a tree. He duly showed Georgiana what awaited her with the galvanic apparatus. Thirty half-crown pieces were placed on top of one another, to make a pile, with as many pieces of zinc, similarly shaped, between them, and as many circular pieces of cloth, soaked in salt and water. One thick brass wire, two feet long, was attached to the bottom of the pile and its other extremity to the patient's temple; another brass wire went from the top of the pile to the other temple. Both temples were previously dabbed in brine. Every time one of the wires was lifted from the pillar and replaced, it caused a tremendous shock, felt through both the temples, and seen as a flash in the eyes. This could happen one hundred times in a minute. The galvanic apparatus was made, said Darwin proudly, by one of Mr Strutt's own workmen, and was not for sale.

We do not know how many times Georgiana submitted to this gruesome ordeal, but in December Horace Walpole was writing that 'she finds herself benefited by being electrified'.[26]

Walpole also noted that Georgiana was 'much altered', which was putting it kindly. Her friend Elizabeth Vassall (Lady Webster, now Lady Holland) was more blunt. 'Her figure is corpulent, her complexion coarse, one eye gone, and her neck immense. How frail is the tenure of beauty!'[27]

From now on, Georgiana ventured out less and less, regarding herself as a monster to the view, unfit to be seen by anyone. As she could hardly make out the paper on which she was writing, her letters also became virtually illegible, and she sometimes had to dictate her words to an amanuensis. The eye operation finally achieved what no amount of sage advice had been able to effect for twenty years: Georgiana withdrew from the world, her exuberance flattened by too many discouragements.

* * *

At least there were the children to occupy her attention. Georgiana had always been a model mother in many ways, breast-feeding her babies for months after birth at a time when most aristocratic ladies employed others to undertake such unseemly tasks. It was clear from the first-born that Georgiana's frustrated affections, her abundant source of love which had to be kept in check while her frigid husband was near and had found expression only in the fulsome friendship with Lady Elizabeth and the affair with Charles Grey, would be lavished on her children. Georgiana was naïvely honest in her admissions to her mother that she longed for her children to love her and could not bear it if ever they turned against her. There was little danger in that, as she was indulgent to a fault, and they could never have doubted the depths and sincerity of her devotion to them. If ever beings were blessed with a happy childhood, it was the various and varied brood at Devonshire House. Never could they have thought they were not wanted.

In other ways, their upbringing was disastrous. They lacked the essential boon of consistent discipline, without which children feel rudderless at sea. The estimable Selina Trimmer (who on being told that her name was Greek for 'moon' adopted the spelling Selena) did her best to enforce regular habits, and to her must belong the credit for making her charges aware of such concepts as duty and propriety. But the Duke could not be bothered to take a personal interest, and the Duchess, in her desire to earn their favour, allowed them too much leniency. Lady Elizabeth's interference was resented by the three legitimate offspring who did not learn until adulthood what her role in the household had really been.

There had been little if any sense of reality in the nurseries at Devonshire House. Hartington had his own retinue of servants from the age of eighteen months. Caroline Ponsonby said she grew up thinking bread and butter came from trees and that the world was divided between dukes and beggars. The children ate only off silver plates, but sometimes had to carry the plates into the kitchen themselves. Life was haphazard, glittering, lavish, unrestrained, and quite out of touch with the rest of humanity. Caroline, again, drank damnation to the Tories in glasses of milk. They all ran about the house in wild, vertiginous abandon, enjoyment their purpose, indulgence their creed.

The 'children' were now (1796–7) growing up. Charlotte, the eldest, was in her early twenties and had departed to join the Heaton household, where she married and had a baby in 1794. She stooped, was rather ungainly, 'but behaves very well and seems very happy' as Georgiana told her mother.[28] She invited her half-sisters to her wedding breakfast. Georgiana ('little G') was now thirteen, a quiet, gentle girl, the most obedient of the lot, and emotional to a degree. Having no cunning to disguise her feelings, G.'s moods were evident to all. 'The least cloud takes from the vivacity of her eyes – she is all soul and heart and I adore her,' said her mother,[29] who also thought she was 'too languid'. She once said her father must be a very common man, because he could not command a procession as large as a king's.[30]

Hary-O, Caroline Ponsonby and Caroline St Jules were roughly of an age, now in their twelfth year. Hary-O was at once the cleverest and the most unpredictable. Like her sister, she too was emotional, but rather than sulk unobtrusively, she would fly into a temper. Strong-willed, Hary-O could be quite infuriating in her relentless determination to have her own way. Between her and Selina Trimmer there was always a contest for dominance, which in no way soured the fondness they felt for one another. It was part of the delicious game. 'She knows I have the upper hand and never struggles for it now', Selina told the

Duchess, 'and the most provoking thing she dares do is to walk across the room with a very stately air when I bid her do anything she don't like, and say "I shall do it very slow tho', for I won't hurt myself in a hurry for anybody" '.[31] On another occasion, Hary-O was in disgrace with Selina for being insolent to the maids. 'I wish you could have seen the grand disparata air with which she march'd out of the room just now,' said her mother with more than a hint of pride.[32] Hary-O's dramas vexed Selina, annoyed Lady Elizabeth, but amused her mother, who gaily called her old lazyboots.[33] She was also precociously witty. At the age of eight she had told her father that she was melancholy, for her eyes were too big; when he asked why this should follow, she replied that she saw too much of the world.[34] She tended to bully Caroline St Jules, whose gentleness was easily oppressed by her, according to her fretful mother Bess. Lady Elizabeth asked little G. to keep an eye on her and try to stop Hary-O's overbearance.[35]

Hartington was an affectionate little boy, though he also could be grand and ungovernable at times, for quite different reasons. One moment he would be quiet and uncommunicative, the next passionate and argumentative. He might disappear for hours at a time, refusing explanations when he was found. It was not wilfulness which made him difficult, but frustration, for what nobody yet realised was that partial deafness afflicted him. A scene typical of many was related by Georgiana to her mother when Hart was three years old. 'H for a week past is grown ungovernable, my face and hands and legs are all in pieces with his scratching biting and kicking – I never saw him so furious a little creature . . . poor Mrs Brown with the best intentions is mastered by him . . . I really have the marks of his poor little nails in my cheeks and hands, and bruises on my legs.'[36] Whenever he was chastised for being naughty, Hart was wont to blame it all on the Bath air. Selina noticed 'twenty little peculiarities of manner' which reminded her of the Duke his father. 'If anything puzzles him', she said, 'or is not quite what he likes, he is silent, looks serious, and winks his eyes until it is perfectly explained to him.'[37]

Then there were two Carolines, St Jules and Ponsonby, and Corisande de Gramont, the three known collectively to Hary-O as the 'pussies'. (They in their turn nick-named Hary-O

'Tybald'.) Caroline St Jules, eleven years old, was the perfect child – modest, pious and sensitive to others; she was almost the favourite of austere Lady Spencer. Corisande de Gramont was a genuine refugee from revolutionary France, adopted into the Devonshire family in 1793, aged 11, and treated as one of them. She was the daughter of the Duc de Gramont and grand-daughter of the Duchesse de Polignac, Georgiana's friend and Marie-Antoinette's favourite. Little is known of her, save that she was dutiful and fitted in well, causing no disturbance. Caroline Ponsonby, however, caused disturbance whenever she appeared. She was not of course permanently housed with the others, as her proper home was with her parents the Bessboroughs at Roehampton. But her childhood was somewhat nomadic, spending months on end with her grand-mother Lady Spencer at St Albans, occasionally joining the crowd at Devonshire House, and even more often at Chiswick. She found herself therefore frequently in the care of Miss Trimmer, whom she exasperated. Caroline was unquestionably the most original character to emerge from that family. Not as clever or as witty as Hary-O, she nevertheless possessed a freakish wit all her own, displayed in remorseless fearless teasing of her elders. Nothing would intimidate her. She was impulsive beyond correction, impertinent when it suited her, cosy and endearing when she sought favours (as when she was seen toasting muffins for the Duke), with those savage untamable manners which would later make her notorious as the lover of Lord Byron. Selina Trimmer's letters are full of references to her efforts to 'calm' Caroline, and Lady Elizabeth Foster called her 'the same wild, delicate, odd, delightful person, unlike anything'.[38]

Then there was Augustus Clifford, eight years old, solemnly overshadowed by these disparate characters and clinging to his quiet half-brother Hart for the only male support in a society dominated by extrovert females.

Over the whole presided Miss Trimmer, fighting a constant battle to maintain order, with little assistance from the Duchess. Her ally in this was the Dowager Lady Spencer, to whom she wrote in 1796 announcing her intention of speaking her mind freely to the Duchess in an attempt to remedy the damage done by lenience (and assert her own authority, in which she had full confidence). 'It is her great affection which makes her lean too much to indulgence', she wrote, 'but it is therefore the more necessary for me to exert myself and even with an impertinence unbecoming my situation.' A few days later she expatiated: 'I have taken upon me a very bold and a very arduous task which is to point out to Her Grace every instance in which she errs with respect to her children. . . . I have written to her with a freedom and severity to which she is little used.'[39]

Far from being appalled by the governess's impudence, Lady Spencer encouraged her. 'Had I been possessed of your strength of mind in opposing growing evils', she said, 'my daughters would have been the better and the happier for it.'[40] This astonishing conspiracy between the Dowager and the employee appears to have done no harm whatever to Selina's position, for she was now a very welcome member of the family. Georgiana, who knew her own shortcomings and was never able to do anything about them, was grateful to Selina for her civilising influence. 'Dearest Selina, from my heart I love you dearly', she said, 'I am sure you cannot misunderstand the sincere and grateful affection that dictates this, and the tears that run down my cheeks whilst I write would prove it to you.'[41] The Duchess had long since forgotten the irritation she felt at Selina's confidential relationship with her mother, and now took every opportunity to express her gratitude for the strictness she was herself unable to summon.

As for the children, they adored Miss Trimmer and remained faithful to her throughout their lives. Well might they deplore her severity and her insistence on their going to bed when they were enjoying themselves, but never once did they mention her with anything less than affection. They teased her as much as they teased their mother and Lady Liz. The Duchess was called, for some reason, 'Emmy', and Selina was always referred to as 'Selina Trimmer Adair', since the children insisted she was in love with and would eventually marry Sir Robert Adair, one of the Devonshire House set, and they would not listen to her indignant denials.

Lady Elizabeth Foster was also teased, but with an edge of sarcasm. Hart called her 'Lizzie', and the girls mimicked her affected manners and speech, especially her nauseating baby talk, and showed that they would rather take instruction from

Selina than from one whom they thought an outsider. '*My dear 'ady iz may chance* to give us a *spinkum spankum over her knee*,' wrote Hary-O to her sister Georgiana, with obvious malice.

The one member of the generation who is never mentioned is the child of Georgiana's disgrace – Eliza Courtney. There is no evidence that she even met her half-sisters and brother, though she evidently was brought up at Howick to believe that Georgiana was some kind of auntie.

At the end of 1796 the population was expanded by the addition of Lady Elizabeth's two legitimate sons, Frederick and Augustus Foster, whom she had not seen since the tearful separation in 1782, when she first made the acquaintance of the Devonshires. The Bishop of Kilmore now wrote to inform her that the unfortunate John Thomas Foster was dead. There appears to have been no hesitation at all before the decision to bring the two boys back home from Ireland and for them to join the throng in the Devonshire nest. They arrived in December. 'Bess is ill with happiness,' Georgiana wrote to her mother. 'I never saw a more touching sight. They clung to poor Bess, who cried terribly. Mr Foster is plain but a very interesting and sensible young man. Augustus a very fine boy of 16.' Bess herself confessed, 'I know Fred is not handsome.'[42]

As 'Mr Foster' was now nineteen years old, the pair were considerably more mature in years than the assorted children of Georgiana and Bess, but their lack of sophistication placed them at a disadvantage. In terms of real maturity, little G., Hary-O and Caroline Ponsonby in particular left them standing. Their provincial manners and tactlessness at first made them appear *gauche* in these splendid surroundings, to which of course they were by no means accustomed, and offered delightful new objects for teasing by the girls. Georgiana made excuses for them. They were 'remarkably well disposed and behaved young men, yet there is an awkwardness in the kind of crowding a houseful makes . . . they always prefer sitting quietly at home with her and me to going out, as we cannot'.[43] Where exactly they would go, knowing no one, Georgiana did not pause to consider.

Frederick Foster especially proved irksome by his laborious jokes, which the subtle Devonshire House girls did not find at all funny. Hary-O's caustic remark was that Lady E 'must lament

this extreme naïveté in everybody belonging to her'.[44] She also
expressed her certainty that Fred could always be relied upon to
say exactly that which one would prefer him not to say. Even
later, he remained shy of walking arm in arm with a Cavendish
girl, tending to linger behind to avoid the embarrassment of
being seen. 'To be sure, he is a strange man, so very unlike
anything else in the world,' said Hary-O.[45]

As 1797 began, the Duke of Devonshire was supporting his
three children by Georgiana, his two children by Lady
Elizabeth, Lady Elizabeth's two children by Foster, Corisande de
Gramont, and occasionally the mercurial Caroline Ponsonby,
his niece. The only absentees were Charlotte Williams and Eliza
Courtney. Another mathematical computation would show that
Georgiana and Bess were mother to four children each; of these
all four of Bess's were with the family, while only the three
legitimately borne by Georgiana had this honour. Bess had
inched her way towards a precarious supremacy.

Chapter Ten

MORE DEBTS

In the adult rooms at Devonshire House, the *ménage à trois* continued its happy course, though with a subtle shift in emphasis as the protagonists entered middle-age. We find that the Duke and Bess are more or less living as a married couple, with Georgiana a valued friend of them both and the mother of three of the Duke's six children. There are letters from Georgiana to her husband and Bess, which indicate that Duke and mistress were often away together while the Duchess remained in London. Rather touchingly, Georgiana tells Bess that she thinks the Duke is in a bad mood, and it is Bess who writes to reassure her that she has misunderstood; the Duke is out of sorts merely because he has not been feeling well, and Georgiana must not worry![1] The mistress enjoyed a more confidential relationship with the Duke than did the wife.

There was still no evidence of strain when the two women were together. Sheridan pictured them 'giddy, gay, and chirriping like Linnets and yellow Hammers, or sitting at home soberly like pretty Bantams and Peafowl on [their] perches.'[2] They were more than likely to be sitting at home these days, as Georgiana's fearful appearance made her reluctant to be seen in public. 'I grow more shy ev'ry day', she said, 'and hate going anywhere except to my own boxes at the play and opera.'[3] In cruel contrast, Lady Elizabeth Foster maintained her delicate beauty even when she was forty.

This is not to say that Georgiana lacked admirers. The politician and book-collector Thomas Grenville, for example, had been desperately in love with her from youth, to such an extent that 'he never married because her image remained enthroned in his breast, and he could never find any other woman to be compared with her'.[4] Georgiana was well aware of Grenville's

attachment, and certainly felt a fondness for him. Just how close
he had come to her was not revealed (and indeed never was,
except to Georgiana herself) until Grenville almost lost his life
in a catastrophe at sea, and Georgiana found herself prostrate
with nervous exhaustion at the news. Thomas Grenville had
accepted the post of Ambassador in Berlin, and set sail with his
despatches, ready to negotiate an alliance against France. The
ship which bore him was driven back by ice, and Grenville
transferred to the *Proserpine*, which was thereupon shipwrecked.
Many of the crew perished, Grenville himself only escaping by
the skin of his teeth, clutching his papers and abandoning all
else. Between the news of the shipwreck and the knowledge that
Grenville had survived, a whole week elapsed, during which
Georgiana had to assume, like everyone else, that he might be
dead. For all those days that Georgiana was tormented by uncertainty, she had to conceal her concern, confessing it only in a
scratchy and muddled diary account, on a scrap of paper which
has now turned up in the little blue note-book which also
contains the poem about her daughter Eliza.

Word of the disaster first reached her on a Friday. After a
nightmarish weekend, the following Tuesday was, she said, 'the
climax of everything disagreeable. Teazings of all kinds and my
own mind almost worn out – I did what I could, but by an
omission I miss'd the only favourable opportunity of improving
my situation.' On Wednesday she went to church alone, 'and
humbled myself in the most lowly manner and prayed devoutly
for poor Grenville'. Then on Sunday, 'the joy of Mr Grenville's
safety – great happiness all day'. The entry for Monday refers to
her 'relief', which may well mean relief at Grenville's safety, or
perhaps relief from further money troubles. It would be
dangerous to read too much into what must remain an
enigmatic entry, but it does indicate the depth of despair to
which Georgiana could at times descend. 'One of the wretched
days of my life,' she scribbled. 'I have too much perhaps
presumed on my relief, and am again plunged deep. Whole
series of black and ungrateful perfidy has come to my
knowledge. . . . I have not done ill, but I have suffered some evil
to creep over me. Oh misera, quanto sará da me.'

Nor could she resist the temptation to encourage a love-
match. Captivated by the good looks and impressive manner of

Francis Hare-Naylor, she introduced him to the daughter of the Bishop of St Asaph and then watched as interest matured into passion. Both families were furious, but Georgiana mischievously connived at secret meetings and eventually helped them to elope to Italy, where she sent them an allowance of £200 a year.[5] Making other people happy was still the prime motive of her heart.

There was plenty of opportunity. The appetite for sentimental flirtation seemed insatiable. The Duchess of Gordon had created a riot at the opera by kissing the Duc de Chartres. The French Ambassador, d'Adhémar (who had long since returned to France, when it was thought he accepted rather more invitations to Chiswick than was good for him), had placed his leg on Lady Parker's lap and then suffered the tortured embarrassment of being unable to remove it. Frivolity and emotional adventure were still the order of the day, Sheridan having calculated that he waded through as many *billets-doux* in a day as he did bills. How to deal with these affairs of the heart, if they brushed close enough to you, was still more a matter of tactics than morality. When the Prince of Wales, having married the deplorable Princess Caroline, began to be seen again with Mrs Fitzherbert, 'Society' was thrown into disarray. 'The opinion of the world is so whimsical,' wrote Lady Holland in her Journal. 'Every prude, dowager, and maiden visited Mrs F. before, and the decline of her favour scarcely reduced her visitors; but now they all cry out shame for doing that which she did notoriously five years ago. There is a sort of morality I can never comprehend.'[6]

Georgiana gradually withdrew from this glittering world. With her dreadful headaches, her worries about money, and her growing distance from the Duke, she entered a period of introspection, pouring out her heart to people she hardly knew in a kind of cathartic comfort. To Philip Francis she wrote in November 1798:

Oh! my dear Mr Francis, you must have spoilt me, since I feel a pleasure in telling you how worry'd I have been, tho I cannot tell you the cause, tho' you can do me no good, and tho my poor heart has been torn to pieces. You know not what you have done in taking some interest in such a being as I am!

You must often listen to lamentation, because tho in reality an old woman, my heart and mind are still childish – nor can I encounter without pain a world that is too wise for me – I must feel unkindness when I meet with it and anxiety when it presses around me. Don't be angry at my boring you with all this stuff. Indeed, if you knew me such as I am, you would know that I pay you a compliment in writing thus.[7]

Even more surprising are the letters Georgiana began to write about this time to a reverend gentleman who was little more than a stranger. Francis Randolph was an eminent theologian and scholar, sometime vicar in Buckinghamshire and in Wiltshire, and later to have the living of St Paul's Covent Garden from the then Duke of Bedford. His place in history is earned by his having sent some very important letters of the Princess of Wales by coach from London to Brighton, and their having been lost en route. His connection with the Duchess of Devonshire was minimal, which made it easier for her to treat him as a father confessor. Looking back over the sequence of errors in her life, she told him she had

an ardent mind that makes me too often act without thinking and sometimes an eagerness in the service of others which finally terminates in my own distress without doing them a jot of good. . . . I have done so many things at the press of the moment which I now regret. . . .

About her financial troubles, she said 'my heart is so little apt to bear the humiliation [of exposure] that I shrink from investigation, which however forces itself upon me. . . . I have a sad propensity to dream peaceful reflections and enjoy the intervals of calm. . . . I write fully, openly, confidentially to you.'[8]

Francis Randolph must be the only correspondent to whom Georgiana mentioned her 'pecuniary embarrassment' without actually asking for money. It certainly weighed upon her to the end of her life. The Dowager Lady Spencer continued her irritating habit of confiding her concern in this regard to Miss Trimmer. 'If she [the Duchess] would be open upon the single subject of money matters', she told the governess, 'I would live upon bread and water to relieve her, if I saw a possibility of doing it, but extreme difficulties have so long inured her to deceive herself and others that I am persuaded she knows not how she stands with regard to debts or engagements.'[9] This much was true; Georgiana was in a complete and hopeless muddle, though she would not have thanked her mother for telling Miss Trimmer so. She sought money from her mother, and received the predictable response: 'It is now five years and a half since you promised the Duke you would borrow no money, nor buy any article till you had the money in hand to pay for it. If you had kept that resolution, how comfortable comparatively speaking you would have been.'[10]

As a last resort, Georgiana turned to the Duke of Bedford, and to Lord Holland, first preparing the way with some painful entreaties via Lady Holland. 'In bed with a violent headache I can only beg you to give the enclosed to Lord H,' she said. 'I will write again tomorrow but am half distracted with my head and the anxiety the enclosed will explain.'[11] The enclosed was a request that Lord Holland should bail her out. 'I write to you as the best natured person in the world and besides the only person I know of in town to entreat you to send £200 for me to Drummonds to my name Saturday. It is of the most material importance to me . . . the event is of such consequence that I am in bed with a violent headache . . . you shall be repaid Monday – if not, by a week from today. I need not I am sure ask secrecy of you and Lady H.'

Lord Holland thanked her for the compliment, trusting she would regard him as less good-natured if he withheld from her the truth. 'I cannot without encroaching a great deal on my regular system of expense add anything to the extraordinary expenses of this year, as even on account of those already incurred Lady H and myself have been obliged to retrench much more than is pleasant.'[12]

Sister Harriet was in an equal mess. Lord Bessborough's affairs reached such a deplorable state, with income of £12,000 and debts nearly £50,000, that he was obliged to surrender all his property to Mr Coutts, on condition that Roehampton and the town house be not sold until his son Lord Duncannon should come of age, and that they should continue to live in them meanwhile. A Deed of Trust had to be set up, with the Duke of Bedford and Lord Holland as trustees of Lord Bessborough's affairs.[13] It is easier perhaps to understand why the Dowager Lady Spencer, who had wanted the perfect happy life for her two daughters, should now sigh and lament in the ear of Miss Trimmer as she watched both daughters bring misery upon themselves by the most reckless incompetence.

Horace Walpole's comment that Lady Spencer was 'the goddess of Wisdom' can be seen with hindsight to have been intended sarcastically, for her wisdom suffered from being too readily offered to those who did not ask for it. Fanny Burney said 'she would be one of the most exemplary women of rank of the age, had she less of show in her exertions, and more of forbearance in publishing them'. It is not too fanciful to imagine that Georgiana and Harriet were simply sick and tired of being told by Mama how naughty they were, though they loved her far too much to say so. At least Selina Trimmer would listen, and would more than likely agree with everything she said.

The children looked to their grandmother for lessons in life, without promising to heed them. They recognised her considerable learning and her useful experience of an earlier world, and they wondered admiringly at her knack of always knowing how to behave and what to say. As they developed characters of their own and established attitudes and ethics which were foreign to her, the Dowager gradually found herself being treated with almost patronising amiability. 'Very early hours, very good books, and most unwearied chess-playing are just what suit her,' said Hary-O.

Nor were they very keen on their uncle, the 2nd Lord Spencer, Grandmama's son. Amazingly handsome though he was, (and that gave much to his favour in the eyes of the Carolines), George Spencer was a hopelessly dull man, conventional to the point of tedium and quite humourless. It was difficult to realise he sprang from the same stock as Georgiana and Harriet. The reputation of Lord Spencer must not be allowed to rest on the biased view of some high-spirited children, however. He was First Lord of the Admiralty for six glorious years, from 1794 to 1800, was considered by many to have been the architect of victory, and was personally responsible for having picked out Nelson and promoted him to eminence. His lasting fame is due not so much to his achievements in office, but to his thirty years of retirement, during which he collected the finest library in

Europe. In a nation of bibliophiles and book-collectors, probably no one has exceeded the magnificent collection of the 2nd Earl Spencer. It includes more than three thousand volumes printed before 1501, and the earliest known example of European printing to which a date can be assigned – 1423. It also had the Mainz Psalter (1457), the first edition of Boccaccio's *Decameron* (1471), the Mamberg and Mazarin Bibles, no less than sixty Caxtons, of which thirty-six were perfect, and four were unique, being the only known copies to exist.*

Spencer's wife Lavinia, daughter of the 1st Lord Lucan, was a shrewish, interfering busybody who took great pleasure in showing disapproval of her errant sisters-in-law the Duchess Georgiana and the Countess Harriet, on the grounds that orthodoxy was innately superior to originality. The children knew better, and did not hesitate to make it clear that they had a pretty low opinion of boring Lavinia.

As for their son, Lord Althorp, cousin to Georgiana's and to Harriet's children, he appeared to combine all the faults of his parents and to have grabbed none of the virtues of more interesting relations. Hary-O in particular was quite scathing in her dismissal of a man who she thought had contrived to make himself 'so compleat a zero'. Althorp's only interest was in hunting; he wasted no effort in conversing about anything else, appeared to be dead most of the time, and was the despair of his family. Even the Dowager Lady Spencer gave up trying with him. Hary-O was entirely disgusted with him when she went to stay at Althorp and found this young man, her contemporary, surrounded by the vulgarest set, and worthy of less respect, she said, than a groom, for he at least is paid to rub down the horses and feed the dogs, whereas Althorp does so from obsession.

Althorp as he might have been, no *reasonable* woman could refuse or help loving or respecting [wrote Hary-O to her sister]. Althorp as he is, no reasonable woman can for a moment think of but as an eager huntsman. He has no more importance in society *now* (as he is, remember) than the chairs and tables. He neither improves, heeds or values it. It is all

* This collection stayed at Althorp until 1892, when it was sold to the John Rylands Library in Manchester, now belonging to the University of Manchester.

one to him if he is amused or bored with pleasant or unpleasant people, listening to musick, playing at cards. He does it all, but as a way of passing through that portion of his time which is a dead weight upon his hands. Evenings and Sundays are to him visible penance . . . when he appears at breakfast in his red jacket and jockey cap, it is a sort of intoxication of delight that must be seen to seem credible, and one feels the same good-natured pleasure as at seeing a Newfoundland dog splash into the water.[14]

Two things were becoming clear: the Devonshire House up-bringing had produced a crop of children, now growing into adulthood, who were so unlike their contemporaries, even unlike their relations educated in more conventional surroundings, that they appeared peculiar, extrovert, alarming. The other was that Hary-O already possessed a cruel wit which could devastate an adversary in one blow. Without being harsh, there was nevertheless something forbidding about a young lady who went her own way, said what was on her mind, and did not trouble to enquire if she injured anyone in the process. She had been imperious since infancy, overbearing to Caroline St Jules. Now she was wildly funny, sharp, headstrong; later she would be a severe and witty woman. Hary-O inherited her grandmother's strength of character more than any of the children, a strength which had squashed into marshmallow all Miss Trimmer's would-be influence.

Prickly as a porcupine, Hary-O was not one to waste time in suffering fools. Lady Cahir was, for instance, the 'most odious little woman in the world' for her sickening flattery, which Hary-O received with such cold scorn that the poor woman was silenced in a second. But this is not to say she was without heart, or warmth. Wisely she said she was convinced that 'a person who can never believe in disinterested friendship in others, is incapable of feeling it in himself'.[15]

Many years later, the diarist Greville would report that Hary-O had 'a great deal of genius, humour, strong feelings, enthusiasm, delicacy, refinement, good taste, naïveté which just misses being affectation, and a bonhomie which extends to all around her'.[16]

Her sister Georgiana was a different animal, reserved, even

stand-offish. Nevertheless, she was the oldest, and she would have soon to think of being married. This was not a matter of choice, but of custom, and of course, of finance. In May 1800 the Lady Georgiana Cavendish, aged seventeen, was presented at Court, which was the first step in announcing her availability to eligible bachelors. It was a great success, to be followed by balls and dinners and suppers in the coming weeks and months, to which all said young men would be invited and their interest in Georgiana solicited. The Duke was bored to distraction with all the fuss; he did what was expected of him, and no more. The Duchess, weak and sad in her premature middle-age, had to cope with all the arrangements in this heady atmosphere as best she could.

It was not long before it was noticed that Lord Morpeth, son and heir to the Earl of Carlisle, was aroused by young Georgiana's quiet attractions. This had to be encouraged. The Duke did his part by offering her a house if she would hurry up and get married, and £30,000 a year as well. Morpeth was invited to Chatsworth. He and Georgiana were carefully watched. Alas, it seemed that Georgiana could hardly be less interested; while no one had any doubt of the young man's intentions, the young lady's were difficult to discern. Lord Morpeth was kept waiting for some sign that a declaration from him would not be rejected, but she was indifferent and would give no such indication. Everyone talked about it except the young couple to each other. The Duchess was worried that her daughter 'certainly *retards* the declaration' and used some pressure upon her, which was harsh in view of her own marriage and its far from happy consequences. Georgiana must have known that her daughter's reticence was simply due to the total lack of any spark; she did not *love* Lord Morpeth, and was still young enough to want to love. As for the young man, he told the Duchess that he 'loves her the more for her hesitation', which was a preposterous misreading of the truth.[17] When the other house-guests left, Morpeth was asked to remain.

Whether she found further resistance to pressure impossible, or felt sorry for the swain, we do not know, but Georgiana relented before the end of the year and assented to Morpeth's embrace. She also assented to years of crushing boredom with a family no member of which was known to laugh, but this she would not mind too much. Lady Bessborough wrote to Lady Holland, 'a line to tell you a *secret* which I know will give you pleasure, but you must not betray me because I doubt Lord Morpeth will write Lord H himself and you know how he dislikes having anything told of him – but what you always foretold has happened – he has offered himself to dear G. and it is all settled. I am giving you pretty early notice for it was only this morning.'[18]

As soon as the news of little G.'s betrothal was known, letters of congratulation poured in on Chatsworth, to be opened jointly by Georgiana and Bess in a giddy fever of excitement. Had not Bess insisted, seventeen years before, that this first-born of her dearest friend was as much her baby as her mother's, that she had been born somehow as the result of joint effort by all three inseparable friends? Now they were to share maternal pride in little G.'s success.

Lady Spencer quite properly embraced her new relation. 'Tell Lord Morpeth', she said, 'from the moment he belongs to you he must allow me to love him as a grandchild.' Rather less proper, perhaps, was the response from Lady Elizabeth. Having replied on behalf of the Duke to an invitation to visit Castle Howard, which she looked forward to 'our going there' as a certainty (who? she, the Duke and Georgiana?), Bess took it upon herself to extend an invitation in the terms of a hostess; 'how delightful to have you and dear Lord Morpeth at Chatsworth'. Still she lacked the sensitivity to see her position as others saw it.[19]

But Fate had a nasty shock in store for Lady Elizabeth. As she and the Duchess read the mail in the sitting-room, a letter was brought for Bess from her sister Louisa. She opened it and read the words 'our sad loss', turned the page and read 'our Mother', and realised that her mother Lady Bristol was dead. She had not even known that she had been ill. The shock was so brutal that, as usually happened in that demonstratively emotional age, she immediately collapsed and had to be sent to bed. The next few days, over Christmas, were acutely worrying. Georgiana told what happened in several letters to the faithful Duke of Richmond, who still cherished a hope that he might make Bess his Duchess and in the meantime was content to remain a good friend. 'I am happy to be able to inform you of dearest Bess being better,' she told him on 30 December:

The dreadful shock of Lady Bristol's death being announced to her without any preparation . . . very nearly deprived me of my dearest friend – her convulsions were dreadful – we were in all the joy of having received Lord Carlisle's very pleasing letters with his consent to Georgiana's marriage with Lord M, when Bess unexpectedly and unsuspecting her mother's being even ill, opened this dreadful letter.[20]

Bess's own account was dramatic. 'I lost my reason – almost my life,' she said.[21] While not wishing to detract from her obvious grief, or suggest that it was not genuine, none the less it was ever Bess's response to bad news or emotional assault to sink into self-pity and magnify her distress. Canis had recognised this long ago. Now she fell into a listless state, full of dismay and despair, convinced that life was scarcely worth living or at least that it would progress more equably with her out of the way. She confided this mood to Richmond, who, incidentally, was one of the very few outside the threesome who clearly knew the truth about Bess's children.* 'I shall probably leave this dear country forever,' she told him on 11 January 1801. 'Caroline will find abler protection from the Duke and Georgiana than I can give her.'[22] The Duke of Richmond wrote several times to commiserate, knowing that Bess needed attention to lift her from this temporary depression. Everyone at Chatsworth turned from private affairs to devote love and care to Lady Elizabeth, whose condition caused, in Lady Spencer's cryptic words, a 'confusion of sensations' in the house.[23]

One who did not share the concern for Bess's health was Hary-O. The antipathy between Georgiana's clever, percipient second daughter and her friend grew more uncomfortable year by year. Hary-O considered Bess to have usurped her mother's position in the household; Bess thought the young lady too forward and undisciplined for her age. By their natures they were scarcely designed to get on well even in different circumstances, Hary-O blunt and honest, Bess devious and oblique. While Hary-O wisely and properly kept her opinions to herself, Bess made herself more unpopular by interference.

* Unfortunately, almost all the Duke of Richmond's correspondence has disappeared or perished; there is nothing relevant to his friendship with Lady Elizabeth Foster among the Richmond Papers at Chichester.

She went so far as to tell Georgiana that she ought to regulate
Hary-O's hours rather more severely. (Hary-O was by now a
mature and self-willed sixteen-year-old.)

> It is the extreme liberty she is allowed in everything [wrote
> Lady Elizabeth] that also tends to the negligence of her person
> . . . nor can it be quite right for a young person so totally to
> neglect the person who has educated them [*sic*] as she does
> little G.[24]

There was much more of this in similar vein. Hary-O certainly knew the advice that was being proffered for her better-
ment, for she wrote resentful letters of complaint on the subject
to, ironically, Caroline St Jules, who thereupon showed them to
Bess. (Neither Hary-O nor Caroline yet knew that Bess was the
latter's mother.)

It was eventually resolved that, while the Duchess and Lady
Georgiana should go to London to see about the trousseau, the
Duke and Lady Elizabeth were to remain together at Chatsworth
where they could look after each other. Not only was Bess still
recovering from the shock of her mother's death, but Canis, too,
was laid low with a more than usually severe attack of gout. Dr
Denman was too afraid of his august patient to recommend unpopular curative measures, which excited the irritable comment
from James Hare, 'It is his business to open his patient's eyes,
whatever he may do with his own.' Bess defended her decision to
stay at Chatsworth in a letter to the Duke of Richmond,
explaining that her movements depended upon Canis. 'I am
aware how much it may renew old stories', she said, 'and he has
been uneasy about it, but I have told him how little I mind if it
does so, and have made him consent to my staying.'[25] No longer
did she talk of leaving the country; the bad mood had been
repaired.

Georgiana, also alive to the possibility of gossip, sought to
justify the decision to James Hare, but of course she was
speaking to one already converted. Hare agreed with every word
she said about Lady Elizabeth; he wrote, 'there cannot be a
warmer, steadier, more disinterested friend'. In illustration of
the fact that even her most steadfast supporters were aware of
the impression of falseness which she gave, he added, 'I never
will be brought to say that she is not affected, tho' I allow it is the

most pardonable sort of affectation I ever met with and is become quite natural.'[26] As for the Duchess, she could demand anything and the gallant Mr Hare would answer. 'I am ready to enter into any articles of servitude.'

The *Farington Diary* makes it apparent that life at Chatsworth had temporarily resumed its erstwhile bustle after a period of quiet. 'The Duke lives in great style, having sometimes in his house 180 persons, including visitors and their servants. He kills on an average 5 bullocks in a fortnight and 15 or 16 sheep a week . . . he is a very quiet man, who gives no trouble to anyone.' Farington also records that Georgiana and her daughters attended service in the church at Edensor every week, in addition to the private chapel service at Chatsworth. Setting an example (at least in this respect) was part of her job.

The spring of 1801 was spent in preparation for the Morpeth wedding, which took place on 21 March. The bride's trousseau cost £3,368 and the bill from Nunn and Barber covered eleven pages.[27] The young couple went to live at the grandiose and stultifying Castle Howard, where the formality almost drove effervescent Hary-O mad when she visited her sister there a little later. She found that she was always having to stifle a laugh, and that conversation was too organised and contrived to be agreeable. One spoke to order, on a given subject. But it suited placid little G. well enough. The years to come would prove the marriage a greater success than anyone could have predicted.

Georgiana, tired and melancholy, doubtless sighed with relief that it was all over. Throughout the excitement of courtship, betrothal, and wedding, she had weighty matters on her mind, which kept her in such a state of almost continual tension that as the nineteenth century began, she was a crumbling wreck of a woman, with the spirit of her former self kept palely glowing by mere will-power. Her zest was gone, never to return. Moreover, in the course of 1800, it had become clear that her sister Harriet Bessborough had allowed herself to slide into real trouble.

Lady Bessborough did not want trouble. She had done her very best to avoid it. Being an enchanting, intelligent, amusing woman, it was only to be expected that she would have admirers, and a flirtation here and there was by no means reprehensible. Charles Beauclerk, son of Topham Beauclerk and great-grandson of Charles II and Nell Gwynn, had pined for her uselessly.[28] Walter Sichel wrote of the intrigues of that period, 'Lovers are rife, but love dwindles, and any gust of real passion soon dashes all the porcelain swains and shepherdesses to fragments.'[29] This is a harsh judgement, true only in the superficialities. Lady Bessborough was the exception. Her friendship for the beautiful young Granville Leveson-Gower, son of Lord Stafford, had slowly ripened in spite of her care into a deep love, such as she had not felt for her husband. Her eldest son was now eighteen; there were three other children of the marriage. That a woman of her maturity should flirt with Granville was perfectly all right, as long as it did not become serious. That she should fall in love with him was absurd, and in her case tragic. By the time she noticed that her involvement had touched the deepest springs of her heart, it was irreversible. She was to devote her life to him, feigning disinterested affection, long after his fascination for her had evaporated. The realisation that it was too late to prevent catastrophe came in 1800, when she found she was pregnant.

Georgiana and Bess were both taken into her confidence. Their deliberations have not come down to us, nor have Harriet's and Granville's thoughts on the crisis. Their abundant correspondence was carefully edited before being deposited in the Public Record Office, and all mention of the child of their union expunged from published selections. So successful was their concealment that even today embarrassment quivers at any attempt to dispel it, and the letters which refer to 'private affairs' in 1800 are still not available for public scrutiny.

Surprisingly, Lady Bessborough was not packed off to Europe for her confinement. The baby was born on 23 August at Roehampton, doctors having been summoned to attend her ladyship after a nasty fall. We do not know who delivered the child. Neither do we know how Harriet contrived to make her shape appear normal or to disguise the symptoms of imminent childbirth. The child, a girl, was called Harriet Arundel Stewart. Nearby there was a hostel for unmarried mothers operated under the patronage of Lady Bessborough.*

In the autumn, both Lord and Lady Bessborough joined the

* In 1824 she married George Osborne, ultimately 8th Duke of Leeds, but she died in 1852, seven years before he inherited the title. Her descendant, Lady Camilla, daughter of the 11th Duke of Leeds, is the wife of Nigel Dempster, journalist.

huge house party at Chatsworth when Lord Morpeth was busily courting Lady Georgiana Cavendish. Granville Leveson-Gower was also there, and even travelled' down to London with Bessborough afterwards. It is safe to assume that Lord Bessborough was in ignorance of his wife's surreptitious motherhood. Probably the Dowager Lady Spencer was also kept in the dark; this latest evidence of delinquence on the part of one of her daughters would have driven her swiftly to the confidence of Selina Trimmer.

When Granville left Chatsworth, Harriet was besieged by Lord John Townshend, who had married her cousin Georgiana Poyntz in 1787 and now declared that he really had loved her all the time, since she was fourteen in fact, and had been discouraged by her scorn for him. Looking at the situation now, it seems all too ridiculous. Lord John admitted his jealousy of Granville, upon whom he launched a violent attack [said Lady Bessborough reporting the event to her lover], 'chiefly, I think, for being handsome. I told him he must not abuse people for natural infirmities which they could not help, as you did not make yourself, you must bear the misfortune of beauty with Christian patience.' (Her veiled confession of admiration, disguised as the mere telling of someone else's words, is touching; the family censors missed that.) Lord John flew into such a rage of despair, beating his head and moaning, that Lady Bessborough had to escape to another room.[30]

Sheridan was yet another wooer whom Lady Bessborough had to fight off. For two years now he had pursued her, all unaware of the low opinion she entertained of him. One day he had turned up unexpectedly at her house in the morning, and, finding her alone, declared his intention of staying to dinner with her. She thought he was joking, but not a bit – he stayed the whole evening. 'He was very pleasant', she told Granville, 'but – it was not you, and the seeing anybody only increas'd my regrets, which I suppose were pretty visible. . . . At length, as I thought he was preparing to pass the night as well as the evening with me, and as he began some fine speeches I did not quite approve of, I order'd my Chair, to get rid of him.' He followed her out, and she could not shake him off. Eventually, she arrived back home, rushed in giving orders that no one was to be admitted, and heard him protesting with the porter at the door.[31]

Discouragement did not deflect Sheridan's attentions. In

1802 Lady Bessborough was again writing, 'I wonder how long Sheridan, Lord John, and Fitzpatrick will think it necessary to make love to me every time we chance to meet, cela ne sied ni à leur âge ni au mien; and if they mean it for flattery it has quite the contrary effect, and troubles me more than the worse abuse could.' She gave him cold looks and colder words, but still he persisted. Granville told her that she should be more angry if she really intended to rid herself of this bother, to which she quite logically replied, 'I am provok'd, vex'd, and asham'd. To feel more deeply I must care for the person who offends me.' None of them cared for her in truth, she said. With Fitzpatrick it was antiquated gallantry, with Townshend madness, and with Sheridan obstinacy; they think they stand a better chance because she is older now and must succumb to any admiration, which was the most offensive thing of all. Lady Bessborough wanted to make it quite clear to Granville that no one else could so much as hope to claim any part of her heart.[32]

Sheridan's ardour did not subside until it found another object. Had he known what Harriet really thought of him, he might have cooled sooner. 'If Sheridan did not tarnish all his talents by duplicity and inordinate vanity, I should approve of a great deal in his language and conduct, but then a great deal also is quite disgusting, and it is impossible to trust him for a moment.'[33] This she told Granville in 1803. So much for the darling of the theatre, the *parvenu* who had electrified the House of Commons with his speeches, gained admission to Brooks's Club and to the innermost circles which eddied around the Duke of Devonshire. It is possible to see from which sprig of the family tree issued young Hary-O's tartness.

When Sheridan lay on his deathbed in 1816, he sent a last terrible message to Lady Bessborough to say that his eyes, always noted for their brilliance, would 'look up to the coffin-lid as brightly as ever'.[34]

In 1802, the political hero of the Devonshire House set, Charles James Fox, sprang a surprise upon them all. For the last few years he had become unusually domestic, retreating as often as he could to the peace of St Anne's Hill with his mistress Mrs Armistead, walking, idling, chatting to the locals, even lying on the grass so still as to convince the birds he was dead. Mrs Armistead had shown herself a loyal and loving consort for nearly twenty years, and there was no question that Fox was happy. In the British Museum there are letters which he wrote her in the days when he was kept busy in London, as tender as any Romeo to a Juliet. 'It may sound ridiculous, but it is true that every day I feel how much more I love you than even *I* knew,' he wrote. 'You are *all* to me . . . indeed my dearest angel the whole happiness of my life depends upon you. Pray do not abuse your power.'[35] Far from abusing her power, Mrs Armistead had used it to great advantage, finally persuading Fox to do the impossible and give up gambling. His friends had subscribed to a fund to pay his debts, and he was now solvent. He spent as much time as possible with his son by Mrs Armistead, a sadly afflicted deaf mute; Talleyrand visited him and complained that he had dined with the most eloquent man alive, and only seen him talk with his fingers.

The relationship of Fox with Mrs Armistead had caused knowing whispers of the kind which Georgian England delighted in. Now he was able to shock the gossips with the announcement that Mrs Armistead was not his concubine, but his wife. They had been married secretly seven years before, in 1795, and no one, not even Lord Holland, had known. Alas, the gossips were not placated by the news; on the contrary, such was the contradictory nature of accepted moral behaviour, that while it was allowable to accept Mrs Armistead's position as long as it could be privately condemned, it was monstrous to deceive the world by revealing that there had been no moral grounds for condemnation at all. One likes to think that Fox relished the confusion he caused and watched with amusement the fussy realignment of moral attitudes.

Georgiana Devonshire was neither shocked nor surprised. She had long cherished her friend's utter freedom from concern about *qu'en-dira-t-on* and admired what she saw as his unshakeable integrity. She said that his greatest fear was 'seeming to yield what he thinks right to the bias of public opinion'.[36] It was right for Fox to love Mrs Armistead, right for him to marry her in 1795, right for him not to satisfy the world's curiosity; if it was right in his eyes, he cared not a sou for what others might interpret.

Besides, Georgiana was more and more involved in the various fates of her family. The two Foster boys had gone up to

Oxford in 1797 and were now fully grown men, Augustus a
diplomat and Frederick an M.P. Frederick continued his
reputation as an irrepressible joker, professing undying love for
Selina, who he said could resist him no better than all the other
women he beguiled. Augustus for a while nursed a serious
affection for another member of the 'family', the adopted
Corisande de Gramont. 'If you knew how happy it made me
when I saw her handwriting!' he told his mother in a letter from
Paris. 'Don't let Corise forget me, and tell her that she is never
absent from my thoughts in the middle of all this bustle.'[37]
However, Augustus Foster had perforce to learn to live with disappointment, for Corisande eventually married Lord
Ossulston, later Earl of Tankerville.

His half-brother, Augustus Clifford, was educated with *his*
half-brother, Lord Hartington, at Harrow, where they maintained the friendship nurtured at Devonshire House, both in ignorance of the blood ties which united them. They were
separated when Clifford joined the Navy at the age of twelve,
there to acquit himself so well as to arouse widespread admiration. Lord St Vincent told Bess he was a 'glorious Boy' . . . the
finest boy he had ever seen or known 'with considerable
abilities, a heavenly temper, and the most generous disposition I
ever met with'.[38] Clifford adored naval life totally, and was to
embark upon an illustrious career which would eventually lead
to a knighthood, a baronetcy, the Admiralty, and a lifetime of
achievement and popularity. He gave no cause for alarm.

Hart was quite a different matter. His obsessive shyness
worried his mother considerably. She once entertained the idea
that Henry Trimmer, a relation of Selina's, should be encouraged to keep the young lord company and help bring him
out of himself, but the Duke of Devonshire would have none of
it. 'You know the peculiarity of the Cavendish temper,'
Georgiana told her mother, but to Selina she had to invent some
kind of excuse for fear of offending her. Selina now could do no
wrong. 'I love you as a very amiable, I respect you as the most
virtuous and valued being I ever knew' were the unambiguous
words she now used in addressing the governess. The older
Georgiana was softer even than the young sprite who had so
often landed herself into 'scrapes'; the generosity of her nature
was ever more warm and affectionate.[39]

But what was to be done with Hart? If Selina was not to be allowed to help, the Duchess must turn to the Duke and make him realise that there was definitely something wrong which ought to excite their anxiety. At the end of 1801, she put her thoughts on paper in a letter to her husband, talking of their son's habits of reserve, seclusion and timidity, and the deafness which by now was plain to all. 'I will allow that I may have spoilt him,' she said, and that he had been indulged for too long by the care of women, which did nothing to ameliorate 'the peculiarity of his temper'. 'He wishes to have his own way', she went on, 'and if he does not he makes it a grievance and gets rather sulky . . . he prefers keeping out of the way or with servants to the mixing with those in whose occupations he cannot take a part.' Hartington, now eleven years old, was driven by his deafness into a moody moroseness as self-protection against hurt. His mother suggested that the society of men might rid him of his sullenness and promote more 'manly habits'. There is no evidence of a reply to this pathetic letter.[40]

Georgiana was also bothered with the pirated publication of her poem on the St Gotthard Pass, which she had written before her return to England in 1793, and which was illustrated with engravings by Lady Elizabeth Foster. Lady Holland was one of the many who congratulated her, but Georgiana, in agony with 'one of my very worst headaches' and still deeply concerned about Hart, could only summon a polite response. 'I cannot tell you how mortified and distressed I have been by its appearance in the newspapers,' she said. 'I am quite sick of the very name and I really have given so few away that I cannot guess in what manner it became so public. . . . I feel how little worth it is to be made all this fuss about . . . at present everything is still gloomy and unsettled – and I feel so unfit for company whilst so anxious that I have been nowhere . . . I should make you ten thousand excuses for such a bore as this letter, but I could not help writing as I *felt*.'[41] The St Gotthard poem appeared in the press with gross printing errors which could only add to the Duchess's annoyance; she had never intended it should be anything but a private indulgence and she was well past the age when she could accept the attentions of newspapers with equanimity. 'I believe I cannot even yet do anything that is not taken notice of,' she complained to Granville Leveson-Gower.

Eventually, combined strains told on her health and Georgiana suffered a series of violent spasms which could only be relieved by swallowing great quantities of opium. 'Farquhar thinks it is gall stones that occasion the pain', Lady Bessborough told Lady Holland, 'and as nothing soothes her when she cannot sleep but being read to, we take it by turns to sit up. This is my night.'[42]

Chapter Eleven

A BETTER HEART NO ONE EVER HAD

Sheridan's famous description of the Peace of Amiens of 1802 as a peace which all men were glad of but no man could be proud of, perfectly judged the feelings of most Englishmen. Years of war with France were at an end – at least for a time, since the politically wise could not indulge a hope that it would last – and even temporary relief was to be welcomed. On a personal level, it meant that old friendships between English and French could be renewed. One of the first French women to arrive in London was the celebrated Madame Récamier, who was naturally received at Devonshire House. Georgiana took her to her box at the opera and presented her to the Prince of Wales, but her appearance caused such a stir that she had to be smuggled out by a back door before the curtain fell. Other visitors included the Duc and Duchesse de Gramont, who were able to see their daughter Corisande for the first time since she was a little girl.

The traffic worked in both directions. Charles Fox and Lady Elizabeth Foster determined for different reasons that they would go to Paris as soon as possible. But first there was a family gathering at Ramsgate to be attended. An assortment of Cavendishes, Ponsonbys and Lambs were gathered, with Lady Melbourne, Lady Bessborough and the Duchess of Devonshire, accompanied by Bess, Frederick Foster, Caroline St Jules, and Corisande de Gramont. Ostensibly the purpose of the assembly was a rest cure from which Georgiana in particular might benefit, but such holidays nearly always concealed an amorous motive; the young could be thrown into each other's company in more relaxed surroundings than in the formality of London society, and a love-match might be engineered. Lady Jersey had precisely this in mind laying careful plans to catch Lord Duncannon for her daughter, Lady Elizabeth Villiers. Lady

Bessborough did not like the idea at all. Neither did Duncannon's sister Caroline, who regarded the 'odious' Lady Jersey as Satan's representative on earth. 'I hope Duncannon will escape from the clutches of that rattle-snake,' she told 'Jarry' (Georgiana Morpeth). 'The finest love is the most concealed, and hers is anything but that.' Caroline might have cause to ponder her own aphorism in years to come.[1] Duncannon, meanwhile, was not remotely interested in Elizabeth Villiers; he pined for his cousin Hary-O, who treated him in return with cold disdain. Bored with all these intrigues, Duncannon escaped to London. Hary-O, now nearly twenty and no great beauty, looked as if she would remain on Georgiana's hands for some time yet. She was, in any case, far too intelligent and sharp for most men.

In the autumn Bess took her children, Caroline St Jules and Frederick Foster, to Paris. The Bessboroughs also went in a separate party. Georgiana stayed at home. This lengthy separation of the two friends afforded an opportunity to renew a correspondence, the fond tone of which recalled the lush outpourings of twenty years before, when they had first met. Bess wrote to Georgiana four times every week throughout the coming months, more often even than she wrote to members of her own family. Sometimes she gave political and social news, describing the effect that Buonaparte had managed over the French, and commenting at one point that 'the lower order are more at their ease and bordering on impertinence'.[2] Sheridan made the rude comment that Lady Elizabeth would faint seven times if necessary to gain Buonaparte's attention. She also reported that Charles Fox's lately declared wife was being snubbed by other English ladies in Paris, including Lady Charles Greville (a daughter of the Duke of Portland, therefore a Cavendish connection) and the Duchess of Gordon. Lady Cholmondeley pretended to have a cold so as to avoid calling upon Mrs Fox until such time as the Duchess of Dorset could offer a lead which others could follow. It was all too silly, in the eyes of both Georgiana and Bess, who never for a moment hesitated in treating the former Mrs Armistead as a friend. For this, in so far as he cared, Fox was grateful.

On the whole, however, the letters to and from Paris in 1802 are a testimony of enduring and remarkable affection.

Georgiana wrote to confess that she no longer had the strength for social life, which tired her too easily, that life was totally without interest for her 'except when I see my children and Ca happy'.[3] Melancholy overwhelmed her. 'I have been fretful and low,' she said. 'Worries about money which return with quarter day, and the unwholesome life I lead put me out of sorts.'[4] This elicited from Bess the plaintive reply, 'My dearest, why are oo gloomy, why are oo vexed, what is the uncertainty about and what are oo worries? I can't bear to have oo so nervous.'

Georgiana's constant headaches and failing eyesight made her letters all but illegible. There is scarcely any pressure on the pen, the writing is small, faint and spidery, and even Bess found it hard sometimes to decipher what they contained. 'I am sorry to say there are words I have not been able to make out', she told her in November, 'and dare not show because of secrets. I put them in every possible position, far and near, high and low, it has not yet succeeded but I shall try till it does.'[5] The Duchess was given to attacks of giddiness as well as acute depressions; sometimes she seemed in the pit of despair. An amanuensis called Gardner was occasionally employed to write her letters for her, but that of course meant they could not be so intimate, so Georgiana preferred to struggle through the page itself, fighting to focus and straining her feeble powers. That she succeeded at least partially in communicating with her friend is attested by the number of erasions and excisions which characterise the correspondence of this period. A passage from Georgiana which appears to tell of her being pursued by a man has been painstakingly scribbled out in different ink, presumably Lady Elizabeth's. Another from Bess begins 'What a beast I am', just visible beneath the scrawl, and ends with, 'cara carissima, t'amo più di mai';* the interim news is quite obliterated. We know that the Duchess wrote to her former lover Charles Grey, and begged him to give her love to her daughter; it is just possible that some contact between them was made at this time, which it was thought better to eliminate all trace of, although she felt free enough to invite Sir Thomas Lawrence, the artist, to meet Mr and Mrs Grey at Chiswick.[6]

Georgiana attempted to be cheerful and amuse Bess with tales of gallantry. 'I must now make you guess what I am about,' she

* My dearest dear, I love you more than ever.

said just before Christmas. 'I am up since 10, and waiting, waiting, for whom? – guess . . . I am to see him this evening . . . I have a good mind not to tell you . . . a person whom it would undo me was it known . . . I should be called a 2nd Duchess of Gordon, a real Bat.'[7]

It was not long, however, before gloom reasserted its pervasive power. Whatever was happening, it is certain that the letters from Paris were a great comfort. 'Oh my love, what dear, dear letters – I am so happy when I receive them,' said Georgiana. And Bess: 'A new year tomorrow. What crowds of thoughts and feelings that day brings to one's mind and heart and soul – may it be a happy one to you and our dear Ca and those I dearly love.'[8] Georgiana spoke of scrapes and worries without being explicit. 'My dearest dear', said Bess, 'we do indeed see by your letters that things have gone wrong, but cannot guess what it has been. My heart aches when yours does.' Possibly, the secrets were explained in other 'private' letters, to which Bess makes occasional reference together with the exhortation that they be destroyed upon receipt. Privacy was sometimes denied Georgiana, having to rely upon her scribe, with the effect that whatever was making her unhappy must remain mysterious to us. At the end of a letter in January 1803, written in another hand, Georgiana adds a postscript, 'God bless you. Guess all I do not say.'[9]

* * *

Although Georgiana was by no means old, longevity was not anticipated then with as much confidence as it is now. There is a sense in which it is true to say that there was precious little 'expectation of life', and each illness was considered potentially mortal. Now a rush of deaths came pelting at the Duchess to remind her that her generation had stayed long enough. First, there was her good friend the Duke of Bedford, who had helped her financially and had never lectured her, a kindly popular man, dying unmarried at the age of thirty-seven as the result of a rupture at tennis. In 1803, Bess was writing anxiously from Paris about her favourite niece, Eliza Ellis, the young and sweet-natured daughter of Lord Hervey who had married Charles Ellis and borne him three children. (The Dowager Lady Spencer had warned Georgiana Morpeth not to be too friendly with her. She had already seen that a Hervey, once introduced, is difficult to dislodge.) She was showing signs of consumption, and growing weaker every day. Bess was frightened, yet allowed herself to be encouraged by the diagnosis of Dr Vaughan who advised that the young woman's lungs were not affected. Georgiana said she was alarmed, but expected some amendment. Alas, since Vaughan did not hold with physical examination of his patients, his opinions were worth naught, and Eliza duly submitted to the disease and died. Bess was deeply distraught. 'In my opinion the attempt at consolation is vain,' said Georgiana.[10]

Only a few months later, Lady Elizabeth's absurd peacock father Lord Bristol, the 'Earl-Bishop', died in Italy, to be conveyed to Ickworth nine months later in a box marked 'antique sculpture'. Much nearer the hearts of both Bess and Georgiana was the departure of their dear friend James Hare, who had been ill in Paris for some time. Hare's death was a terrible blow to both women, for he had been privy to many of their secrets, knew more about the Duchess's debts and Lady Elizabeth's two illegitimate children than did most members of the family, had always been ready to offer sage advice when it was asked, yet never imposed it unsolicited, and had maintained an undeluded respect for both as well as a warm manly affection for the Duke. He was a rare man who understood the true nature of friendship, which he was able to suggest more than demonstrate, and was ever willing to temper his misanthropic wisdom with a sense of humour. His loss was remembered by Georgiana and Bess in poems which reveal honest feeling.

Georgiana herself suffered another serious attack of spasms in September 1803, alarming enough for her sister to be summoned from Roehampton to her bedside. For a week she was in dreadful agony, Harriet sitting up most of the night to read to her, not because she listened but because the humming noise, which was all she could discern, assured her that someone was there. Frequently Lady Bessborough was awakened by the plaintive cry of her sister calling for attention; 'her nurse was, like all nurses, asleep'. Her illness was worrying enough to elicit almost hysterical letters from the Prince of Wales, while Harriet was even in despair of her life. 'You know how I can never love anything *a little*', she told Granville, 'therefore you may judge how I suffer at this moment.'[11]

After passing a huge gallstone, the Duchess recovered and spoke of her gratitude to God for having spared her, but from this moment she was never again to know a full day of good health. She, too, was a spent woman. 'I am unwell. Farquhar must do something for me,' she told the Prince of Wales.[12]

It must be admitted that one of the causes of Georgiana's extreme debility was not medical at all, but consequent upon the resurrection of the crisis in her financial affairs. She fondly hoped that the worries would eventually disappear, as if by consent to make her life more tolerable, but in 1804 they loomed larger than ever. The real problem was not so much the extent of her indebtedness, which was certainly vast, but her fear of the Duke's anger. She was literally scared to death by the anticipation of his reaction, and would do anything to avoid telling him. The humiliating admission that she had learnt no lessons, kept no promises, and had borrowed from all and sundry, including servants, to hide her shame, was more than she could face. 'Oh would to Heaven that once your mind was free and nothing unknown to Ca – how much happier you would be,' wrote Bess.[13]

Not for the first time, Georgiana unburdened her troubled spirit in a long letter to the Prince of Wales, confessing that shame overwhelmed her and that she was so paralysed with terror at facing her husband that she would not even talk about it. 'The idea of conversation with him drives me into tremors that quite destroy me,' she said. And again, 'I do not think I should be able to undergo the explanation with the Duke, good as he is, because there are so many things I could not explain or he listen to.' It was evident that Georgiana woke every morning wondering what new bills would be placed at her feet, what new deceptions she would need to practise, whether she would have to avert the eyes of her husband when he found out. Life was a constant torment for her at this period. 'I have forc'd myself into gayeties and appearance of spirit for the children,' she said, fearing that they might learn from others the bad reputation which hovered over their mother and think ill of her. She tried to explain the impotent remorse of the gambler. 'I believe even in your exalted situation', she told the Prince, 'you know what the sensations are of feeling constant anxiety and humiliation, of knowing one has been to blame for want of caution and getting into bad hands, and yet feeling the impossibility of escaping, and besides the constant and incessant dread of some great alarm and fuss, and shrinking from the idea of being expos'd to the most painful conversations.' She concluded with a frightened plea that her letter should remain unanswered; she dreaded any evidence that she had spoken about the problem to anyone, and begged the Prince not only not to write to her, but never to tell anyone that she had written. 'If I did not think I could depend on you I should go quite mad.'[14]

Lady Bessborough (who mentioned *en passant* that a man had fallen beneath the wheels of her carriage and been killed) determined that she would take charge of everything, tell the Duke the whole sum, and trust that he would not enquire into details.[15] But Harriet was not much wiser than her sister in these matters; far better that a team should be empowered to administer the Duchess's affairs. Charles James Fox and Robert Adair undertook the task, both pleading separately to Georgiana to have the courage to count up *everything*. 'Count up . . . all this mass of mischief as scrupulously and as exactly as if you were making up your account with heaven, and lay the whole before those who are best capable of advising and of saving you,' said Adair, who also reminded Georgiana how often had poor James Hare implored her to make a fresh start. He 'invokes you from the grave to put an end once and forever to that system which has caused you such endless anxiety and alarm'.[16]

The way was prepared for the Duke of Devonshire's discovery of the truth, but while he was expecting to have to settle five or six thousand pounds, the total amounted to well over forty thousand. Harriet, like Bess, knew full well how much Georgiana's sad state of health should be attributed to her nervousness on this account. It is, she said, 'far more than mere relief, but literally a concern of life and death'.[17]

Lady Elizabeth Foster was called upon to use her good offices with the Duke (yet another indication that she was more wife to him now than Georgiana, if she was thus regarded as the person most intimate with him and more likely to persuade him when others dare not even approach him), and it was eventually settled that the debts should be paid off gradually, so as not to arouse the suspicions of the agent, Mr Heaton. Georgiana earned yet another reprieve. 'Meantime I shall have an income of £1000 a year and all my opera and play subscriptions,' she told the Prince of Wales. Never again, she resolved, would she borrow from anyone.[18]

*   *   *

The major event of 1804 was not political or military (notwithstanding the Napoleonic wars raging in Europe), but theatrical. A new young actor called William Betty, the son of an Irish linen bleacher, burst upon the scene with such *éclat* that for months his presence in London literally disrupted all normal life. His most astonishing characteristic was not so much his extraordinary talent but his extraordinary age. He was playing such demanding roles as Hamlet and Richard III at the age of thirteen. Variously known as Master Betty, young Roscius, or simply the Boy, he filled the two theatres of Covent Garden and Drury Lane for months, earning receipts for the management in excess of £40,000, and monopolising conversation in the capital. People willingly changed the hour of dinner so that the Boy should not be missed, and on one occasion Pitt even moved that the House of Commons should adjourn so that members could witness his performance of *Hamlet*.

Lady Elizabeth Foster, who was already famous for her enthusiasms, was naturally won over by this phenomenon. She wrote often and in detail to her son Augustus on the subject, telling him that 'nothing hardly is seen or talked about but this young Roscius', who was even introduced by Sheridan to the Prince of Wales at Carlton House, and acquitted himself with the confidence of an adult. 'His is the inspiration of genius', she wrote, 'with the correctness of taste belonging generally to experience and study alone, feeling far beyond his years, and a knowledge of the stage equal to any performer, and far more graceful; in short, he has changed the life of London; people dine at four, and go to the Play, and think of nothing but the play . . . the Hawkesburys stay in town for this boy's acting all next week . . . as to the applause, the Pit, which is filled with men, not content with applauding, over and over again cry out Bravo!

Bravo! I don't suppose such applause could ever be exceeded.'
Mr Grey also applauded, but as if it hurt his hands.

Three months later, the spell had still not been broken, and
Bess was still writing in ecstatic vein to Augustus. 'I ought to talk
of politicks to you', she said, 'but all conversation begins and
ends with Roscius. . . . When he first rehearsed Hamlet, he had
so worked himself up that when, in the closet scene, he says "On
him! On him! Look how pale he glares!" he fainted in the arms
of his friend. Mr Hough, the prompter, caressed and soothed
him, and said he should rehearse no more that night; and next
day, he said, "What, my dear boy, moved and affected you so
last night?" "Why", he said, "I thought I did see my father's
ghost." Caroline Wortley tells me that his acting Hamlet is the
finest piece of acting she ever saw or can conceive.'

Not everybody was taken in by these publicity tricks. Lord
Aberdeen wrote to Augustus Foster with a different view: 'By the
way, we are to be bored this year by that wretch called the Young
Roscius, who is the greatest imposter since the days of
Mohammed.'[19] And the experienced Mrs Siddons was far too
wary to allow herself to be upstaged by a prodigy; she refused to
act with him, saying he was a clever, pretty boy, but nothing
more. Still, the greater part of London society was swept away
with infatuation and wonderment, and even the Duke of
Devonshire was curious enough to go and see him perform. His
verdict was that Master Betty was 'a deuced good actor'. Fitzpatrick asked, 'Where does the little urchin get all his intelligence?'[20] Georgiana, who shared the general enthusiasm,
persuaded Fox to go and see him, and before the hysteria had
subsided, the boy found himself received at Devonshire House,
where Hart, only a year older than he, tried in vain to amuse
him.

Hart was indeed now old enough to look upon his parents
and their friends with an enquiring eye, and to look upon his
contemporaries no longer as playfellows, but as potential adult
companions. He was curious about his father's relationship
with Lady Elizabeth. When she took him to Hastings in October
1804, he noticed that she received letters from the Duke,
normally a very reluctant correspondent. 'What does Papa write
to you?' he asked. 'He hardly does to anybody!' Bess told
Georgiana that the Duke's attentions seemed to raise her very

much in Hart's esteem, which was a naïve interpretation of an adolescent boy's questioning. Hart rarely confided in anyone, and his true estimate of Lady Elizabeth's position in the house he kept, for the time being, strictly to himself.[21]

Hart was also moving from a fondness for his cousin Lady Caroline Ponsonby to a more mature feeling; she had always been the one member of the family to have patience with his shyness, which she refused to take seriously, and had, with her impulsive exuberance, given him confidence. Where he was painfully aware of himself all the time, there was no one less self-conscious than Caroline. She was, in a way, an example to him. He thought of her as his wife, and assumed that they would one day marry. This dream was quickly shattered in 1805 when Caroline accepted the proposal of Lady Melbourne's son, William Lamb. Hart went into hysterics, and had to be given a sedative by Dr Farquhar.

Caroline never did anything by halves. Not for her a just dose of contentment or orthodox happiness as might arise, with luck, from a marriage arranged for dynastic reasons. She was a creature marked for love, and when love erupted between her and William Lamb, it did so with an intensity which shook the decorous structure of aristocratic self-control more even than had the various entanglements of her mother Harriet, her aunt Georgiana, or Lady Elizabeth Foster. For a long time she smothered her emotion as best she could, knowing that her family did not entirely approve of Lady Melbourne (they took their cue in this from the Dowager Lady Spencer) and that a greater match was anticipated for her. But self-control was not her *forte*, and everyone could see at a glance that she was desperate for William's company. His prospects changed somewhat with the death of his elder brother Peniston, making him heir to the title and estates of Lord Melbourne. 'William must always be handsome', said Georgiana, 'but he never stands upright or sits still. He extends on couches, tables and chairs.'

Eventually, on 2 May 1805, William Lamb proposed. 'I have loved you for four years, loved you deeply, dearly, faithfully', he told her, 'so faithfully that my love has withstood my firm determination to conquer it when honour forbade my declaring myself – has withstood all that absence, variety of objects, my own endeavours to seek and like others, or to occupy my mind with fix'd attention to my profession, could do to shake it.'[22] Though Lady Bessborough was not fully reconciled to the match, it was clear that consent would have to be forthcoming or the highly-strung Caroline might simply go berserk. They all knew that Lady Spencer's agreement was crucial, and so Georgiana voiced the family concern in writing to her mother. 'It has long been evident to me how much she was in love with William Lamb, but till lately she had suppress'd it,' she said. Caroline showed 'such evidence of the most boundless attachment, that I really believe – so does the Duke, that any check would be productive of madness or death'.[23] Confronted with this alarming prospect, Lady Spencer nodded her assent, still not quite happy with the idea that love should enter into the negotiation. 'There seems in the present choice at least the advantage of mutual attachment,' she grudgingly allowed.[24]

The matter was settled later in May. Caro was elated. Lady Bessborough was finally happy, noticing the astonishing change in Caro's behaviour. 'I believe all her ill health, all the little oddities of manner and *sauvagerie* that used to vex me, arose from the unhappiness that was constantly preying upon her,' she told Granville.[25] This was to under-estimate the complexity of Caroline's peculiar temperament, as her subsequent tempestuous career, and her embroilment with Lord Byron, would demonstrate. That is a tale which belongs elsewhere. The marriage took place on 3 June. Separation of mother and daughter was tearful in the extreme. As Caro told her husband, 'Judge what my love must be, when I can leave such a mother as this for you. Girls who are not happy at home may marry without regret, but it required very strong affection indeed to overpower mine.' The couple went straight to Brocket Hall, while the Devonshires, Ponsonbys and Fosters tried to recover from the tornado of events which had snatched away their most original member in a matter of weeks. Augustus Foster, away in Washington, was incredulous. 'I cannot fancy Lady Caroline married,' he told his mother. 'How changed she must be – the delicate Ariel, the little Fairy Queen become a wife and soon perhaps a mother.'[26] Lady Spencer, as wise and canny as ever she was, knew that elation was premature, for none of them had seen the last of Caro's peculiar ways. 'Her nervous agitations will grow to a very serious height if they are not checked,' she counselled.[27]

Other marriages in the family excited less attention by comparison; Caro's brother Lord Duncannon married Maria Fane, daughter of Lord Westmoreland, later the same year, and Lord Tankerville was eventually persuaded to forgo his objections to the marriage of his son Lord Ossulston to Corisande de Gramont. Georgiana cleverly appealed to Lord Tankerville's snobbery by persuading the Prince of Wales to allow it to be understood he would be present at the wedding. Tankerville was, she told him 'the most obstinate and intractable of men, but luckily also the vainest'. Nevertheless, the marriage was delayed until 1806, Tankerville raising every possible objection, and sending dreadful letters to his son Ossulston, which the recipient threw upon the floor in disgust. Ossulston, tired of waiting for his father's permission, eventually went to London himself to get the licence, and Corisande determined to go back to France if the marriage were not permitted. When it did take place, the Duke of Devonshire gave the bridegroom the seat of the borough of Knaresborough. 'Some wives bring their husbands fortunes, but mine brought me a borough,' said Ossulston.[28]

Caro St Jules and Hary-O were now the only ones left of marriageable age (Hart still being too young). As for the Foster boys, Lady Elizabeth was in no hurry to see them swallowed in wedlock; their careers, for the moment, mattered more. Augustus was doing well in Washington in spite of the fact that he did not care for the place and longed to be home. And Clifford was a source of great pride; still only a boy, he was serving in the *Tigre* and had already been part of naval action.

One day in September 1805, Lady Elizabeth and her other son Frederick Foster accompanied the Duke to dine at Fish Crauford's, where they were to meet the hero of the hour, Lord Nelson. Bess was quite overcome with admiration. 'What a wonderful man Nelson is!' she told Augustus. Nelson asked her to share a glass of wine with him. She in turn asked if he would do her the favour of delivering a letter to dear Clifford, with his own hand. 'Kiss it then, and I will take that kiss to him,' replied Nelson. Admiration thereupon gave way to adulation in Lady

Elizabeth's breast.[29] Georgiana, who had not been well enough to dine out and indeed rarely went anywhere now, heard a first-hand account from Bess the same day.

Six weeks later, news of the Battle of Trafalgar arrived in London, together with the awful tidings of Lord Nelson's death. It was Georgiana who had to inform Bess, who was quietly reading Herodotus with her daughter Caroline at Chiswick. Georgiana looked dreadfully pale; she knew that her emotional friend might react dramatically. She did. She flew upstairs, by her own account, and immediately dressed for the journey to London. Georgiana and Hartington, who also admired Nelson with boyish pride, went with her.

There was, she said, a look of gloom in the streets. Crowds assembled outside the Admiralty (where Georgiana's brother, Lord Spencer, had been First Lord) eager for more details of the action, not quite sure whether to be elated or dejected. Georgiana soon ascertained that her nephew, Robert Spencer, had not been involved in the battle. And what of young Clifford? Bess was naturally in a state of great agitation; her beloved love-child might, God forbid, be killed. But no, all was well. Clifford had not been at Trafalgar, and was quite safe.

Georgiana and Bess raced to Devonshire House, where they found Frederick Foster and the Duke. Frederick had informed the Duke, who could scarcely believe his ears and would talk of nothing else. He, too, immediately sought information about Clifford's whereabouts, and was reassured.

Georgiana and the Duke both, separately, wrote lines of verse in honour of the fallen hero. Bess was too distraught to do anything but weep. She went with Georgiana to the lying-in-state, and watched the preparations for the funeral, but could not trust herself to control emotion if she were to attend the funeral itself. 'Nelson was the only person I ever saw who excited real enthusiasm in the English,' she told Augustus.[30] Her own enthusiasm was too ostentatiously expressed in the opinion of Hary-O, who more and more was looking upon Lady Elizabeth's histrionic posturings and lamentations with real distaste. Angrily, she wrote to her sister:

Lady Elizabeth is still in despair for Lord Nelson and really her private affectation is enough to destroy the effect of a whole nation's public feelings, for she has so much grimace about her grief that one can hardly prevent one's disgust of her operating upon one's pity for him. She sobs and she sighs and she grunts and she groans and she is dressed in black cockades, with his name embroidered on every drapery she wears. She is all day displaying franks to Captains and Admirals and heaven knows what – and whilst she is regretting that she could not 'have died in his defence', her peevish hearers almost wish she had.[31]

Nevertheless, Lady Elizabeth was outdone by a certain Miss Bayne, who actually died of hysterics at the funeral.[32]

Early in 1806, two more deaths occurred, one of national importance, the other a painful grief to the family, which seemed to presage an awesome mournful year. On 23 January, Pitt, debilitated by the overwhelming responsibility of leading a country at war and strained by depression brought on by Napoleon's successive victories, at last succumbed to illness and died in the night. The huge sense of shock and fear at losing a man so central to the country's fortunes found expression in the various reactions of the Devonshire House circle. In spite of the long history of political opposition between Pitt and the Foxites, the statesman's shining qualities were well appreciated by Georgiana and her friends. Fox said simply that it appeared as if there was something missing in the world when Pitt died. William Lamb, tears pouring down his cheeks, broke the news to Lady Bessborough, who thereupon tried to hide the emotion on her face; Lamb told her, 'Do not be ashamed of crying: that heart must be callous indeed that could hear of the extinction of such a man unmoved. He may have erred, but his transcendent talents were an honour to England and will live in posterity.'[33]

Georgiana summoned her feeble powers to write at length to Hartington on the subject of Pitt's death and its significance. 'It is awful to the mind to reflect on a death of such magnitude', she said, 'on the death of a man who had so long fill'd an immense space in the universe. It is affecting to behold a life terminating, as it were, in its prime, and it is sorrowful indeed to think that the powerful voice of eloquence, so matchless, so beautiful, is dumb forever. Peace be to his remains.' She went on to eulogise

Pitt's parliamentary fascination, and to point out to her young son that the Opposition, supposedly his enemies, had shown far more genuine feeling at the loss than had his sycophantic friends.[34]

Fox immediately set about forming an administration, after twenty years of powerless barking across the floor of the Commons. His appointments read like a dinner-party guest list for Devonshire House. He placed himself at the Foreign Office, Sheridan at the Naval Treasury, Charles Grey at the Admiralty, Earl Spencer at the Home Office. Lord Grenville was made Prime Minister. As for the Duke himself, he was offered any place that he would care to name, but as usual he preferred the undemanding routine of a ducal existence to the bustle and energy that government required. Not for the first time, the Duke of Devonshire declined the opportunity to work.

While all this activity for the moment diverted Georgiana's attentions and rekindled her interest in politics, she received another blow only a week later with the news that Lady Caroline Lamb had given birth to a premature dead baby. That this 'wild, delicate, odd, delightful person, unlike everything' (to recall Elizabeth Foster's words) was also neurotic beyond recovery, was gradually dawning on poor William Lamb, who did not love her the less for that. She was too nervous a creature for childbirth so young, still too much the naughty intemperate schoolgirl. Protectively, William Lamb extended not merely the arm of condolence, but the warm heart of a healing love. What he did not yet fully realise was that no amount of love would ever be sufficient to satisfy Caroline.

Georgiana was still much exercised with worry about Hartington. He had at last formed a decent friendship with a contemporary, Lord Tavistock, heir to the Duke of Bedford, but the difference in their ages made Georgiana see Tavistock's influence as potentially harmful. He was eighteen and a worthy young man; Hart was yet a boy of fifteen. The memory of her own giddy youth raised fears that by going about with Tavistock to dinners and suppers before he was old enough to cope with them might drag Hart into the 'dissipated' life which his mother knew too well was difficult to resist. 'You must know that in your situation in life ev'rybody will be trying to get acquainted with

you,' she warned him. 'I must insist therefore that all invitations
be refus'd, for they will be endless, and if I have not this security
I must consult with your father.'[35]

There was also the matter of his adolescent infatuation with
Mrs Duff, a relation of the Duke of Rutland, which caused
the Duke much amusement, and worried Georgiana far less
than the threat of dissipation. Hart could not utter a sentence
without making some reference to Mrs Duff, and judged
everything according to its agreeableness to her. He followed
her from room to room. 'Hart continues desperately in love
with Mrs Duff,' said Georgiana, describing it as a 'very serious
passion', but not serious enough, obviously, to warrant parental
interference. Besides, 'serious passions' were by now as much a
part of the fabric of Chatsworth and Devonshire House life as
were the wallpapers.[36]

Wearing glasses shielded with black crepe to temper the effect
of light upon her weak eyes, Georgiana went to tea with Mr and
Mrs Fox in February and gave a brilliant supper for the new
ministers with 46 guests, but the strain of the occasion brought
on more headaches which grew in intensity throughout the
month. It was no longer unusual for the Duchess to be ill, so the
family was not especially alarmed. With hindsight, however, it is
remarkable that two letters of uncommon poignancy were
written during this illness, letters which seem to say far more
than the words which they contain. Bess sent the Duchess a note
which expressed her love as usual, but both its restraint and the
chord of unforced truth which emanated from it were unusual
for Bess. Touchingly, and with a genuineness which no longer
required the gush of former years, she wrote, 'You would not be
hurt if I forced myself sometimes to hold your hand when a kind
or generous action makes you ready to pour out all it holds.'[37]
Nobody, except perhaps Lady Spencer, knew better than Bess
that Georgiana's faults in anyone else would be virtues.

Georgiana herself suddenly and inexplicably felt the need to
struggle with pen and paper in her sick-bed to write a long letter
of advice and endearment to her son. 'Indeed, indeed no
mother ever loved a son as I do you,' she told him. 'I live in you
again.' In a mood of introspective regret, she went on,

I adore your sisters, but I see in you still more perhaps than even in them what my youth was. God grant that you may have all its fervours and cheerfulness without partaking of many of the follies which mark'd with giddyness my introduction into the world. I was but one year older than you when I launch'd into the vortex of dissipation – a Duchess and a beauty. I ev'ry hour, however, thank my protecting angel that all I have seen never weaken'd my principles of devotion to Almighty God or took from my love of virtue and my humble wishes to do what is right. But I was giddy and vain. . . . *I hope to live* to see you not only happy but the cause of happyness to others, expending your princely fortune in doing good, and employing the talents and *powers of pleasing*, with which nature has gifted you, in exalting the name of Cavendish even beyond the honour it has yet ever attain'd. God bless you, Dst Dst Hart. If it will not bore you I have sometimes an idea of sending you a history of your House, from the time of Elizabeth* to the present day, to shew you what you have belong'd to. But believe me, Dst Hart, when I tell you I *do* expect you to surpass them all, all except your Dr Father. He has a mind of most uncommon endowments, a rectitude few others could boast. . . . Dear Hart, banish but indolence, and add but a little activity to this character of your Dr father, and you will bring him back with the only thing he wanted, – *power to conquer idle habits, and to make the virtues that endear'd him to his friends of use to his country.*[38]

Georgiana 'hoped to live'. Is it possible that she knew, what the doctors manifestly did not suspect, that she had only three weeks of life left to her? According to Lady Stafford, she told her family she was going to die.

Feverishly, she sought out the letter she had written to her daughter some years before, and which she now wished to leave as her epitaph. 'One of my greatest pains in dying, my dearest Georgiana', she had said, 'is not to see you again. But I do hope this letter will influence your whole life. I die, my dearest child, with the most unfeigned repentance for many errors. . . . Be dutiful and affectionate to your dear Papa, to your dear Grandmama, and use yourself to treat them with the utmost confidence and to have no secrets from them. Be affectionate to my

* Bess of Hardwick, founder of the Cavendish fortunes.

dear friend Bess. Love and befriend Caroline St Jules. Learn to
be exact about expence. I beg you as the best legacy I can
leave you never to run into debt for the most trifling sum. I have
suffered enough from a contrary conduct.'[39]

Two days after the long letter to Hart, Georgiana was too ill to
finish one to her mother; it was written for her by Caroline St
Jules. Painfully true to form, and poignantly at variance with the
advice proffered to her own daughter, almost her last word to
her mother was a request for money. Having said that she was
very low, and was suffering from jaundice and bilious attacks,
she begged her mother to let her have by return of post a draft
for £100. Not once in her life did Georgiana enjoy the relief of
solvency.

*   *   *

On 14 March the Dowager Countess Spencer confessed to her
daughter Lady Bessborough that she was 'most uncomfortable'
about Georgiana. 'Some horrible difficulty is hanging over her,'
she thought; intuition and experience alike led her to suspect
'her illness is owing to the old and hopeless story of money
difficulties'. The following day her fears were confirmed by the
receipt of Georgiana's pathetic letter asking for £100.
Immediately Lady Spencer again wrote to Harriet. 'I am sadly
distressed about your poor dear sister,' she said. 'I inclose her
letter to me, to which I have been under the cruel necessity of
saying the truth, that I have but 20£ in the banker's hands, which
I had reserved for my journey back from hence, but I can
manage without it, and have sent it to her. Lady Spencer,
afraid that disappointment might render Georgiana weaker
still, sent Harriet a draft for the remaining £80, payable on 3
April, with the request that the money should not be used until
that date and that Georgiana should not be told in advance that
it would be available. Events would show that it was too late to
be of use.

Lady Jerningham heard a version of the Duchess's illness
which supported the impression that money was, if not the root
cause, at least the final straw which broke her will to survive. She
was supposed to have pleaded with the Duke to rescue her once
more from financial worry, and he to have refused in so positive
a manner, declaring that he had already paid enormous sums

and would never pay a penny more, that she fell into a state of lethargic despair and allowed illness, her last resource, to protect her from the awful reality of shame and ruin which she dare not face.[40] According to this account, the Duke thought at first that she was feigning, and realising his error when it was too late, cried out that no sum would be too great to save her life.

Shortly after receiving her mother's £20, Georgiana sank into a deplorable state of semi-coma, interrupted by fits of trembling. For two weeks she was prostrate and inert, all fight having deserted her. A crowd of eminent physicians attended her – Vaughan, David Pitcairn, Matthew Baillie, Gilbert Blane, and of course Farquhar, the only one to see that the Duchess was in danger while the others confidently predicted recovery. Her head was shaved and a blister applied to her scalp. With her sight now almost totally gone, and with strength to speak only in whispers during odd moments of consciousness, the beautiful vivacious Duchess now looked absurd, bald and barely human. It cannot be said the medical profession allowed her to go with dignity. Charles Fox wrote, 'The Physicians think there is now no danger, but those who love her cannot be easy until the fever has entirely quitted her.'[41]

Those who loved her rushed to her bedside on 21 March as her condition worsened. Bess and Harriet kept vigil, comforting each other. Dr Blane suggested that Lord Hartington be sent for, and it was Bess who sent word for the boy, nearly sixteen, to come. Harriet stayed night and day by her sister's bed, occasionally calling for paper so that she could scrawl a note to Granville. 'I rarely quit her room,' she told him. 'Yesterday she was very ill, today much better, but tonight a shivering fit has come on again. I fear it will at best be very lingering! I am very anxious and absolutely pass my life at D.H.' Dr Baillie assured Harriet that the improvement would not be long in coming; Farquhar, he said, took alarm too easily. 'I do not *feel* alarm'd,' said Harriet. 'If I did I should scarcely be able to support it.'[42]

Hartington arrived on 24 March from his tutor's in the country, and his mother, mercifully, was able to recognise him and talk to him. But on 25 March she had another attack of trembling. 'It was dreadful to see,' said Bess. 'We all try to keep up our spirits. If gall-stones, the passing will be painful but will surely relieve her. Lady Bessborough sleeps at D. House. The

Duke hardly goes to bed. I am chiefly by her bedside – yet all will surely be well. . . . Oh, my G.!'[43]

On the night of 25–26 March, Georgiana was shaken by the most ghastly fit lasting seven and a half hours, from 11.30 at night until 7 in the morning, with 'dreadful appearances', as Bess said. At last the medical men woke up to the realisation that their attentions were useless. 'Oh, Good God, what is one to look to, or how to bring oneself to think of her and danger,' wailed Bess.[44]

Such was the fame of the Duchess of Devonshire that there was by now a large crowd hovering at the gates in Piccadilly, waiting for news. No one was admitted. Messages arrived every hour from friends and acquaintances. On the night of 26 March she suffered another fit, lasting one and a half hours, followed by an hysterical sigh as her poor body sank into languour from the effort, then she went into her final agony which endured for three days. No one slept. The Duke paced up and down, Bess and Harriet watched over her, bending over the bed to make out scarcely audible words. There were still odd moments of peace when she could recognise her sister and her friend.

By 29 March the Duke had lost all hope of his wife's recovery. He penned a brief, listless note to Miss Trimmer: 'If the worst should happen I hope you will be so good as to stay at Devonshire House for the present, for I shall not be in a state of mind to attend to anybody, or to receive or give any comfort whatever.'[45] The Prince of Wales made a brief call at Devonshire House.

The next day, 30 March, Georgiana died, and her devoted sister flung herself on the corpse in a paroxysm of grief. It is true to say that Harriet never ceased to visualise those dreadful moments. 'Anything so horrible, so killing, as her three days' agony no human being ever witness'd,' she said. 'I saw it all, held her thro' all her struggles, saw her expire, and since have again and again kiss'd her cold lips and press'd her lifeless body to my heart – and yet I am alive.'[46]

Lady Elizabeth Foster was stunned. 'Saturday was a day of horror beyond any words to express,' she wrote in her Journal. Days passed before she could fully realise what had happened. 'My heart feels broken . . . my angel friend – angel I am sure she now is – but can I live without her who was the life of my existence!'[47] Mrs Fox, who had dined with Georgiana only weeks before, made a simple entry in her diary: 'The Duchess of Devonshire died between three and four in the morning. A better heart no one ever had and her loss will be long and deeply felt by all who knew her.'[48]

Hartington, too young to cope with the responsibility of grief, said very little. Withdrawing into his customary tortured silence, he wrote only to his friend Tavistock, without actually bringing himself to use the word 'Death'. 'Pity me for what yourself have once suffered,' he said.[49] His sister Georgiana Morpeth implored him to take hold of himself and reminded him that their mother had hoped he would learn to be a comfort and a friend to the Duke as well as a son. 'His manner is cold, but his heart is noble and excellent', she said, 'and I am sure that he feels and values any little attentions from you.'[50]

For days afterwards Lady Bessborough and Lady Elizabeth Foster walked through the corridors and rooms of Devonshire House like haunted creatures. The quiet and gloom were oppressive, the impossibility of solace overwhelming. Bess would stay late in the Duke's room, talking and comforting. On the night of 4 April, when she had returned to her own room, there was a knock at the door and in walked Harriet, looking ghostly. 'Don't be frightened', she said, 'but I want to see and speak to a human creature.' Bess was pleased; she was wishing that Harriet would come to her. 'What is this horror that has seized us!' she exclaimed. They went together to the coffin, as they did every night, and knelt beside it, kissed it, and calmed each other. During the day they met in Georgiana's room. Harriet was wounded quite beyond repair. Caroline St Jules saw a look upon her face which seemed to declare that she had lost everything, and told Caroline Lamb that Georgiana's agony 'has deadened her to every enjoyment of life'.[51]

Georgiana had died of an abscess on the liver. It was of little importance now that the physicians had merely observed the symptoms and failed to ascertain the cause. The obituaries were predictably grandiloquent, yet even allowing for the normal exaggerations of such prose, it happens rarely that the death of a public figure should excite unequivocal hyperbolic tributes such as those which grieved over Georgiana. The *Morning Chronicle*, having spoken of her angelic temper and rapturous beauty, went on to proclaim that 'never, we will venture to say, was the death of any human being more universally lamented than hers will be'. It was, as always, the unsolicited personal tributes, written as if by compunction to keep Georgiana's spirit alive, which spoke more eloquently of her extraordinary charm. The Prince of Wales, when he was informed of the death of the woman he used in old days to call his 'sister', simply said, 'Then the best natured and best bred woman in England is gone.'[52] To his friend, the Dowager Duchess of Rutland, he expatiated upon what he called the solid and firm friendship of five and twenty years' standing. 'There is not an hour, a moment, that I do not miss her', he said, 'and every time that she thus shoots across my brain, it brings with it an additional pang. Try to one's utmost either by retirement or change of scene, still nothing will do, for there is always an inexpressible something in everything that is forever recalling her to my imagination and to my heart.'[53]

Months later, the Prince took his brother to see Chatsworth; the revival of fond memories was a painful experience. 'I confess to you', he told Lady Elizabeth Foster, 'it was almost too much for me, the recollection of the several pieces of furniture which I had seen in her room, and which I had so often sat upon in her room when conversing with her, quite overpowered me, for it is enough to have known her as we have, never to be able to forget her . . . such a loss and such a calamity are almost beyond all sufferance; at least it is so to me.'[54]

Elizabeth Foster herself poured out her heart to her son Augustus. 'She was the only female friend I ever had,' she told him. 'Our hearts were united in the closest bonds of confidence and love . . . she doubled every joy, lessened every grief. Her society had an attraction I never met with in any other being.'[55]

Augustus sought to console his mother in the only effective way – by talking at length of Georgiana's unique qualities, combined in such a soft harmony that never again would they be found in one woman: 'You have seen her suffer under long and dreadful pains before her death. It must surely be a consolation to you that all the offices of the purest and most unsullied friendship were performed by you from the first to the very last.'[56] Hary-O, whose antagonism towards Lady Elizabeth for the moment abated, felt her mother's death so keenly that she could not summon the courage to talk about it. A little before Georgiana died, however, her daughter had written her letters of such ingenuous honesty that they must remain the most moving testament of all to Georgiana's unique fascination. 'I never knew thoroughly what I felt for you till I left you', she said, 'and when I think of the happiness of your dear smile, of hearing your beloved voice, I am almost mad with joy. I am sure you alone could inspire what I feel for you: it is enthusiasm and admiration that for anybody else would be ridiculous, but to deny it to you would be unnatural.'[57]

On 5 April, the coffin was closed. The next day it moved away from the courtyard of Devonshire House and through the gates into Piccadilly, in a stately procession which would terminate in the family vault in Derbyshire. Bess and members of the family knelt as it passed. Hartington stood motionless on the steps, watching the coffin as it moved slowly down to be placed in the hearse, not crying, but totally absorbed. 'Never shall I forget Hartington's look,' wrote Bess. Afterwards, Georgiana Morpeth went home. Corisande and Caroline St Jules went up to bed, and quite unexpectedly, Hartington came to Lady Elizabeth's room on the pretext of looking for some ink. There he sat up with her until late at night.[58] The Duke stayed in his room and would see no one.

It was a long time before any semblance of normality could seep into the smitten lives of the family, but of course everyone knew that Devonshire House could never recover its air of gaiety, nor its inhabitants their wonted freshness. The Duke, like his son, suffered inwardly as do those unable easily to release emotion, but one night Lady Elizabeth described him as 'hysterical'; after she had left him in his room, he followed her to hers, dumbly seeking the solace of company. Though he had never loved Georgiana as lovers do, she had brought sparkle to his life, and he had been proud of her.

As for Harriet Bessborough, who felt deeply and did show her emotion, she retreated to Roehampton and locked herself away from the world. In the ensuing weeks, she agreed to see only one man, Charles Fox, and only briefly. The depth of Harriet's grief is best attested not by accounts of her wan looks or even by her own words in letters to Granville, but by a single moving anecdote related by Nathaniel Wraxall. It relates to one day five years later, when Wraxall visited the Cavendish family vault in Derby:

> As I stood contemplating the coffin which contained the ashes of that admired female, the woman who accompanied me pointed out the relics of a bouquet which lay upon the lid, nearly collapsed into dust. 'That nosegay', said she, 'was brought here by the Countess of Bessborough, who had designed to place it with her own hands on her sister's coffin; but, overcome by emotion on approaching the spot, she found herself unable to descend the steps conducting to the vault. In an agony of grief, she knelt down on the stones, as nearly over the place occupied by the corpse as I could direct, and there deposited the flowers, enjoining me the performance of an office to which she was unequal. I fulfilled her wishes.'[59]

With Georgiana's death a precious adornment perished. She deserves to be remembered not for her accomplishments, but for her vital personality, which was so compelling and spirited that even now, two centuries later, it exercises lively fascination. She was charming, and valued charm in others; she was original, and appreciated originality. Spontaneous, impulsive, as sparkling as quicksilver, her whole being was devoted to making life enjoyable, for herself and for others. Although she read widely and involved herself in political affairs, people interested her more than ideas. She exercised influence because she was a hostess, and enabled men of politics and discernment to meet, discuss, and decide in her house. She was a Whig because she knew and liked Whigs, not because she had examined Whig principles in depth. Emotion sprang from her like a geyser, making her demonstrative and excitable, with the result that, while her pleasures were delectable, her sufferings were acute and accumulated to a degree which eventually wore her out. Georgiana knew her faults, and realised that she could not be calmed by self-control; calm came to her in the end through exhaustion.

In all the diaries, journals, letters of the period, there is not one unkind word about the Duchess of Devonshire. This would be a trite observation if one did not pause to reflect how unusual and remarkable it is. She had a strong desire to please, and generally succeeded. Her errors were the errors of the tender-hearted, and it was she who suffered their effect rather than anyone else. Her tragedy was that she, who deserved real happiness, was denied it. She was a romantic in a strait-jacket. Yes, she was adored by her children and her friends, enjoyed a unique confidential relationship with Lady Elizabeth Foster (to which, though, it must be conceded she gave more than she received), but in her most intimate relationship, that with her husband, she had to cope with the dark secretiveness of the Cavendish temperament which achieved its ultimate expression in the 5th Duke of Devonshire, and had moreover to witness the success of her friend where she had failed. Lady Elizabeth Foster could unlock the Duke's reserve while Georgiana remained in awe of it. She was really quite afraid of him. If only she had been able to talk about herself and her problems with her husband, some of the strain of dissembling for fear of causing trouble might have been lifted.

Caroline Lamb began a short story in a rather ornate Commonplace Book dedicated to Georgiana's memory, bearing her initials and coronet on the cover. Though she changed the names of her characters, it is quite clear that one of them is inspired by Georgiana, 'for with everything that might have given her happiness she was surely almost wretched – you will find even under the attempts at pleasantry a certain melancholy that never leaves her'.

The melancholy never obtruded. Nor indeed did Georgiana's rank. The huge popularity which Georgiana and her sister enjoyed would not have endured had either of them thought that to be a Duchess and a Countess entitled them to treat the less fortunate with disdain. 'We have always been fashionable', Georgiana had told her eldest daughter, 'but I do assure you, our negligence and omissions have been forgiven and we have been loved, more from our being free from airs than from any other circumstance.'[60]

Georgiana's greatest fault was of course her incurable passion for gambling. She loathed her weakness and longed to conquer it, but it is the least conquerable of vices and Georgiana's character lacked the resolve even to try. She left Lady Elizabeth in charge of all her papers and personal letters, and there soon began the lengthy sorting and arranging of thirty years' correspondence, together with the irritating (to us) excision and erasure of certain passages. Lady Spencer read them, Bess read them, later on Georgiana's son also read them, and any one of them might be responsible for denying us access to 'secrets'. No one scribbled black ink over the passages relating to Georgiana's debts, however. Shortly after her death, when her financial affairs were scrutinised and the Duke was at last made aware of the corrosive worry which so injured his wife's peace of mind, he was astonished that such despair should arise from so tiny a cause. The amount, to the Devonshire estates, was piffling. 'Was that all?' he cried out. 'Why, oh why did she not tell me?'[61]

EPILOGUE

The months following Georgiana's death were both desolate and awkward at Devonshire House. The removal of the one person who had brought brightness and vigour to a house previously lugubrious now cast it once more into gloom. Hary-O called it simply 'melancholy'. The most distressing aspect of the new situation was Lady Elizabeth Foster's anomalous position there. The Duke clearly could not manage without her company, and she as obviously could not envisage leaving what had become her home. Who can blame her? The Duke of Devonshire had for over twenty years given her security which she now naturally took for granted, and she had in turn given him the affection which he found it so hard to accept from anyone else. They were no longer lovers, but a peaceful middle-aged couple at ease with one another. Unfortunately, the world saw Lady Elizabeth's continued presence in the house with different eyes.

In the circumstances, Bess could have been more tactful. On 8 May she sent a short note to the Dowager Lady Spencer. 'The enclos'd paper is the only thing I *can* take the liberty of asking you to accept,' she said. The paper contained a lock of Georgiana's hair, perfectly curled and golden; it is still there, with its contents, at Chatsworth.[1] The gesture was decent enough, and made with some delicacy, but how could Bess have imagined Lady Spencer would be pleased to receive such a present from such a source? The gift ought to have come from the Duke, but he, as usual, was too lethargic to bestir himself. Coming from Bess, it appeared an arrogant assertion of right.

Georgiana's three children conferred with each other on what should be done about Lady Elizabeth. Of course, they could do nothing – their father was still master in his own house and they would not presume to question his wishes, or even discuss them with him. Hartington, now sixteen, was the most tolerant of the three. 'I only think that as she *has* been calumniated, some little care ought to be taken and difference made at a time when her enemies would talk more,' he told his sister Lady Morpeth. 'If she does that, I shall be the first to pay her every respect and attention.'[2] Characteristically, Lady Melbourne was quick to interfere, proposing a solution to the problem which was absurdly out of touch: Bess should make herself available to the widowed Duke of Richmond. Nothing came of this idea.

Had Bess contrived to efface herself and assume a secondary position at Devonshire House, there is little doubt that a *modus vivendi* suitable to all generations would have been achieved. Her mistake was quietly but firmly to make the children feel that she had taken their mother's place. As little G. was now a married woman and a mother herself, Hary-O ought, according to established practice, have assumed the position as female head of the house at her father's side, acting as the Devonshire House hostess. Instead, she found Lady Elizabeth at the head of the table, Lady Elizabeth fondling with the Duke's dogs, Lady Elizabeth accepting and giving invitations. The Morpeth family planned a visit to London. It was Lady Elizabeth who wrote to say she had chosen their rooms. 'We think, Car and I, that her room will be best, as Laure's will be a dressing-room for Lord Morpeth . . . and then there is the middle room where Corisande sat, for breakfast etc. . . . . I shall tell Mr Hicks to expect the dear children [Lady Morpeth was by now the mother of three] and I suppose they had better dine in the garden room or what is called Clifford's room.'[3]

Most galling of all (and this was hardly Bess's fault), it was Lady Elizabeth who had the ear of her father, to the exclusion of herself.

The atmosphere of the house is depicted for us in scores of little clues in Hary-O's letters to her sister. As soon as Lord and Lady Morpeth had left London, Bess began to lay down the law and show in subtle ways that she felt comfortable. This was quite different from her being allowed to feel comfortable by permission of Hary-O. Bess would pick arguments with Miss Trimmer, making it plain that she expected the servant to defer to her, and choosing always subjects which she knew would provoke the lady so as to give her the opportunity to chastise. 'Lady E. is tiresome and she has power to turn any pleasure into a plague', Hary-O said, and again, 'Lady E. is in perfect humour and quite *obsequious* to me.' This was when Bess sought Hary-O's agreement that they should be seen in society together, thus giving tacit approval to Bess's acceptance within the Devonshire nest. Hary-O would have none of this. So Bess reverted once more to her bull-dozing technique. 'Lady E.F. is very disagreeable in doing the honours instead of me', cried Hary-O, 'which for every reason in the world is painful to me.'[4]

Typical of Lady Elizabeth's ruses was to try to persuade Hary-O to accompany herself and the Duke to Brighton for a month, where they would stay with the Prince of Wales in his Pavilion. The ostensible reason was healthful relaxation, but Bess in her eagerness let slip that she wanted the three of them to be seen at plays and entertainments, parading about together. Hary-O had at all costs to avoid this without being surly. It was very trying for her; she was prepared, she said, for nothing but 'difficulties, vexation and shame'.

More to the point, she suspected that her father was not so content in Lady Elizabeth's company as the woman would have everyone think. There was the suspicion that perhaps she nagged him and pressed her will upon him. When once she fell ill and was thereby removed from his company for a while, Hary-O, suppressing the unworthy thought (to which she none the less admitted) that all would be well if Lady E.F. did not recover, told her sister bluntly that 'my father would be much happier without her. I never saw him in such good spirits, perfectly at his ease and talking so much and so cheerfully.' Even Caroline St Jules noticed the change in him. Of course, Bess could not leave the house now, without Papa reproaching himself for ill-treatment and ingratitude, but 'if she had not rooted herself by all the ties of habit and now almost a sense of duty in his home, he would be ten thousand times a happier person. I was always certain that her character and manners could not suit him, and I am convinced that he is often silent from a wish not to embark in argument and disputations with her.'[5]

Hary-O was sadly wrong in this assessment. In the first place, she was ignorant of the broad fondness which had characterised the relationship between Canis and Bess since before she was born, and secondly, as she was herself still unmarried, she had no comprehension of that tie of habit and regard which makes nagging a welcome sign of attention in couples who have lived together for a long time. The Duke could be relieved and relaxed when the nagging was removed for a short period, but its total disappearance would have been death to him. No one else had ever cared enough to dispute with him over trivia. What Hary-O saw as a sign of irritation was in fact yet another indication that her father and Lady Elizabeth were indisputably linked as an old married couple.

Hary-O could not be expected to understand this. Her position was quite awful in her own lights. She could not very well go and live elsewhere without giving rise to still greater scandal, but equally she felt she could not happily present herself to the world as condoning her father's acquiescence in Bess's supremacy, or accepting her status as a kind of step-daughter. Lady Bessborough was the first to see clearly the only possible solution: Hary-O must marry as soon as possible. With this in mind, she began to take her niece to countless soirées and balls, leaving the Duke and Bess to chat inconsequentially about nothing. Perhaps even now she was contemplating the marriage which would astonish everyone who had any inside knowledge of Devonshire House intrigues.

Lady Spencer behaved, as one would expect, with total control. She contrived to remain on terms of friendly intercourse with her son-in-law while never setting foot inside Devonshire House as long as the usurper held sway, and she found every excuse to have Hary-O to stay with her in Jermyn Street or at Holywell.

Sheridan was the first to say out loud what others had privately suspected. On 10 September, only a few months after Georgiana's death, he found himself talking earnestly to Lady Liz at a small dinner party in Devonshire House. She, he said, cried to him and told him she felt it was her 'severe duty' to be Duchess of Devonshire.[6] The news of this gaffe buzzed about in private letters over the next few days. Bess gave a different version of the conversation. It was Sheridan, according to her, who introduced the idea, and she who replied that she was too distressed even to think of such matters.[7] As it happened, there was another tragedy which distracted everyone's attention from the problems of Lady Elizabeth Foster. Charles James Fox was dying.

It was fitting that the man who had been the political inspiration for the Devonshire House set should bid farewell to life at the Duke of Devonshire's house in Chiswick. He was taken there when he fell ill and his last pathetic days were spent there amidst a crowd of sorrowing friends. However great a man of politics he may have been, it was as a companion with a genius for friendship that he was mourned. Mrs Fox sat on the bed, holding her husband's hand. As he grew more feeble, and could no longer grasp her hand, he laid his palm open so that she could rest hers upon it. Mrs Fox wanted prayers to be said. Fox, who was not religious, did not wish to hurt his wife by refusing, so he consented but took little interest in what was being said. When he tried to talk, his mind would not function with its usual clarity and for the first time in his life he found himself searching in vain for words he simply could not remember. At the last, however, he was able to smile at his wife and summon the strength to articulate. 'I die happy,' he told her. 'Bless you, I pity you.'[8]

Bess was nearby. She saw through the door into the bedroom and noticed that all the men assembled there were wiping their eyes with handkerchiefs. Lord Holland was standing quietly and alone in a dark corner of the room. She then knew that Fox was gone.[9] It was Saturday, 13 September 1806. The grief which followed was extraordinary even for that demonstrative, tearful age. Lord Fitzwilliam was so overcome that he lost all control.[10] Bess immediately returned to Devonshire House to be with the Duke. They sat up until three in the morning, Bess assuring him that no one would think it improper if he were to cancel all engagements. As she left him sitting in his great arm-chair, she noticed that he wiped away his tears with the back of his hand.[11] 'How good and kind he was to us,' said Lady Caroline Lamb of Fox. 'He comforted us for our loss and little thought how soon we should have to lament his.'[12]

Samuel Rogers and Sir Robert Adair were visiting Chiswick some time later. When they entered the room in which Fox died, Adair 'burst into tears with a vehemence of grief such as I hardly ever saw exhibited by a man'.[13] At the funeral, which walked

from Stable Yard, St James's, through Pall Mall and Charing
Cross to Westminster Abbey, ordinary men lined the streets and
they, too, cried like children. Among the mourners walking
behind his coffin was the Duke of Devonshire. George III
forbade the Prince of Wales to attend.

It had indeed been a miserable opening to the nineteenth
century. The hero Nelson and the political marvel Pitt were both
gone. The Devonshire House circle had lost its greatest man in
Fox and its sharpest wit in Hare, as well as its social apex in the
Duchess herself. There was no future to look forward to. It
would have been harmless enough to allow Canis and Bess to
indulge in nostalgia. The trouble was, the younger generation
still suspected that Bess had more ambitious designs, and their
fears were eventually shown to be far from illusory.

In May 1809 Caroline St Jules married George Lamb, a son of
Lord and Lady Melbourne. Thus she became the sister-in-law of
Lady Caroline Lamb, and bore the same name as she. It is from
this time that, to avoid confusion, Lady Caroline was known in
the family as 'Caro William' and the former Caroline as 'Caro
George'.

By September it was widely anticipated that the Duke would
marry Lady Elizabeth, although he would make no clear statement of his intentions. Appalled at the prospect of Georgiana's
name being besmirched in this way, the entire family turned
against Bess. Even Harriet Bessborough, who had been an
intimate friend all her adult life, now admitted that 'she has the
worst judgement of anybody I ever met with; and I begin also to
think she has more *calcul* and more power of concentrating her
wishes and intentions that I ever before believ'd'.[14] There
remained the slim hope that Bess would not use the title, though
how this could be avoided nobody cared to suggest – the wife of
a Duke is a Duchess whether she wants it or no.

The younger generation was far less circumspect. Lady
Morpeth, normally so gentle and tolerant, spoke of the
marriage as 'this afflicting event'.[15] Bess had written to Lord
Morpeth to ask him to prepare the family for news which would
eventually be communicated formally by the Duke, referring to
the harsh incivilities and censure to which she had been sub-
jected, and the determination of the Duke never to be separated
from her.[16] 'I need not repeat to you the details, or arguments

for the change, which her letter contains,' Lady Morpeth told her brother Hartington. 'She says there is to be no ostensible change immediately. . . . Hary-O's behaviour is perfect as it always has been . . . she says she only wishes this to be known to a very few, so pray do not talk of it my dearest Hart – we are the last to wish the sad truth to be known.'[17]

Hartington forgot his earlier understanding of Lady Elizabeth's predicament and now called her a 'crocodile'. He wrote to Caro William about 'this incredible marriage', saying that 'hardly till I see it can I believe that the woman could have the assurance to take that name always so sacred to us, and henceforward to be so polluted . . . I don't see how I am ever to speak to her again with patience'.[18] Furthermore, Caro George had been staying with Hartington for a week, and had never once mentioned the matter, of which no one was prepared to believe she was ignorant.

The most furious reaction came from Caro William. 'However little right I may have to censure that old witches conduct', she told Hart, 'I shall never hear her called by the dear name she has assumed without regret and disgust, a disgust very strong, though I will do all I can to conceal it. Pray tell me how Caro broke it to you, and what that emblem of innocence thinks now of Lady E. Foster? Is it possible she can still be like the Pharisees who had eyes and saw not & ears & heard not, or has she all along cunningly & slyly been aware of the whole intrigue? I detest such petty artifices as Bess employs. If she will be wicked let her be so in the face of day, but when I think of the scene of deceit, plot, iniquity & wiles this serpent has made use of, I shudder at the thought.' Caro went on cruelly to chastise Hart for hypocrisy, saying he had been too gentle with the woman, and had promised her he would not disapprove. She seemed to think that Bess had been preparing for this for almost twenty years. 'This mistress of your papa's knows how to throw her chains about you . . . oh she is a deep one!'[19]

Equally angry was the letter she wrote to Lady Holland about what she called 'this odious tricking business'. 'That pattern of art has written me a note to inform me of an event which ought forever to prevent the request she makes of my continuing to call her by the endearing appellation of Lady Eliz!'[20]

Two days before the marriage, which took place on 19

October 1809, the Duke finally brought himself to inform the
Dowager Lady Spencer in a letter heavy with formality and
strained politeness:

> It is my intention to marry Lady Elizabeth Foster, which I
> have for some time thought of doing, from having been
> informed that it is the opinion of the world, that there is an
> impropriety (which I have not been aware of and which I do
> not yet perceive) in her living in my house upon any other
> terms. . . . I wish you, dear Lady Spencer, not to answer this
> letter, as it must be disagreeable to you to do it, and I shall
> know by other means whether you approve or disapprove of
> my conduct. If I should hear the former, it will be a great con-
> solation to me, but at all events I shall have that of knowing
> that according to my own opinion I have acted rightly.[21]

Canis knew very well that his mother-in-law would disapprove,
hence his poor attempt at justification and his reluctance to face
her or even receive written word from her. Bess wrote out a copy
of the letter, as if to show to posterity that she and the Duke had
behaved correctly in informing the Dowager. She was quite
aware that she would be judged harshly.

Amazingly, the Duke did not see fit to tell his son and heir
what he intended to do. It was not until four days after the
wedding had taken place, when it was already common
knowledge, that he at last wrote from Chiswick to Hartington,
who was at Chatsworth. 'You will have seen by the newspapers
that I was married a day or two ago,' he began. Then, the need to
excuse himself again welled up. 'I intended to have given you the
first intelligence of [the marriage], as I did not intend it should
have been made public for some days, but I see today that the
papers have got the start of me. I shall give you my reasons for
having taken this step when I see you.'[22] Hartington cannot fail
to have noticed that his father was clumsy enough to imply that
his only regret was that the press did not wait for him before they
announced the news; he did not say that he should have consulted Hartington *before* the marriage, only that he wanted him
to be the first to know *after* it. It is no surprise that Lord Hartington's reply is the coldest and most indifferent that the Duke
ever received from one of his children:

I had for some time had reports of the event which has taken place and therefore was not surprised by your letter, which I received last night, and for which I thank and am very obliged to you.[23]

He did not mention the new Duchess – she might not exist; nor did he express any wish for their happiness. Hary-O and Georgiana Morpeth did at least, in separate letters, send good wishes to their father, yet they too contrived to ignore the Duchess and make no reference to a marriage. Rarely can a union have been greeted with such insulting silence. Guilt hovered in the air. The day after the wedding, Lord Auckland wrote to Lord Grenville, 'The Duke of Devonshire has married Lady Elizabeth Foster. There is some puzzle and squabble about declaring it.'[24]

Hary-O's position was now intolerable. It says little for the Duke's sensitivity that he appears never to have considered how his actions might affect her. It was now a matter of urgency that she should marry. In November she became engaged to, of all people, Granville Leveson-Gower, her aunt Bessborough's lover.* The wedding, the third of that year, took place at Chiswick on Christmas Eve. With Hary-O's departure from Devonshire House, it may be said that the world Georgiana created finally came to an end. The remainder was merely a hushed twilight.

Canis and Bess entertained but little. Caro William was suspicious about the silence, writing to her cousin Hart a wicked little rhyme which contained the verses,

> Is the Duchess breeding?
> Tis rumoured everywhere.
> But not such late seeds needing,
> We've got our precious heir.[25]

Similarly michievous in writing to 'Jarry' Morpeth, Caro declared that since her letter would be burnt upon receipt, she would write several secrets at the bottom, such as, 'Lady

---

* Lady Bessborough had since borne Granville a second child, named George Arundel Stewart.

Elizabeth Foster is not good', adding, 'God bless my soul, is that a *secret?*'[26]

The family was fond of quoting Lord John Cavendish's couplet,

> Sure it is as God's in Gloster
> Words of truth ne'er speaks Bess Foster.

Resentment against Bess's wonderful success in capturing the Duke for herself would obviously not abate easily; it continued to exercise the family for many years. Alone of the children, Hartington became reconciled to his stepmother, whom he received at Hardwick at the end of 1810 and whose reticent conduct he applauded. He noted also that his father was as happy as it was possible to be. At this time Hartington was about to undergo an operation for the removal of his tonsils, which is interesting if only because the deafness from which he suffered was thought to be due to them. 'I am deaf alone from their enormous growth,' he told Georgiana Morpeth.[27]

Hartington came of age in May 1811 and immediately received a letter from Thomas Coutts enclosing that from Georgiana which she had directed should be given to Hart at the age of twenty-one, detailing her debts and praising Coutts as her best friend.[28] With the interest accrued from 1791, the total amounted to £28,826. Scarcely did Hartington have time to deal with this problem, than his father suddenly died on 29 July, and he inherited the huge responsibilities of the dukedom of Devonshire. Canis had been ill for a few weeks, yet rallied well enough for all to think there was no serious danger. He died in his wife's arms just before ten o'clock in the evening.

The immediate problem for Bess was to establish where she should live. She assumed the new Duke would allow her to keep Chiswick as a Dower House, and began telling him that she loved him as her own son, to the purpose. When it became clear that this was not to be, she grew difficult and fractious, claiming that Canis had left a codicil in his will declaring that she should have Chiswick for her life, and much else besides. Without these demands, 'Hart' might have been happy enough for her to remain at Chiswick, but she succeeded in antagonising him to such an extent that he deputed Lady Bessborough to tell her in blunt terms that she would have to go. Her mistake was to treat as hers by right something which could have been granted as a favour. Lord George Cavendish had to explain that there was no codicil in the will with any mention about Chiswick, and that she would have moreover to return to the family all jewellery apart from those pieces which she possessed before her marriage to the Duke, or those which he had bought especially for her. 'The curiosity of the public has led, you may have heard, to much unpleasant conversation on the subject of a supposed codicil,' intoned Lord George, adding that she must be made to realise 'the futility of such an idea'.[29] Bess retorted that Mr Heaton must have mislaid or destroyed the codicil.

She was slow to learn. She issued invitations to other members of the Duke's family to visit Chiswick, as if to show the world that thunder and lightning would not remove her from the place. Ever since Georgiana's death she had tried every means to 'legitimise' her position in the family, and had thought that her marriage crowned her ambitions in this respect. She now smarted with indignation at being treated, so she thought, in a cavalier way. She wrote angrily to the young Duke listing what she thought were her deserts. 'After the expectations she has formed anything that I can say will be a disappointment to her,' Hart told his grandmother Lady Spencer. 'Her worst adviser could not have made her do a more foolish thing than write as she has. I shall always feel for her what she deserves but I cannot bear to see art and falsehood employed at such a time.'

Hart then turned to the matter of his half-brother Augustus Clifford. Canis intended to settle £3,600 a year upon him, claimed Bess. Then why did he never mention it to Heaton, asked Hart? Nevertheless, although he would not be pushed by the widowed Duchess, Hart wanted to do right by her and her children. He determined to give Clifford an annuity of £2,000 a year, with more to come if he should marry or leave the navy. 'I only went by my idea and opinion of what *he* [his father] would have wished me to do and of what I think right to one to whom he gave existence, and indeed at times I think I have not done enough.'[31]

At the same time, Hart gave his stepmother a week to pack her bags, and leave the house. 'Thank God I have got rid of the Duchess at last,' he told his grandmother, but he resolved none the less that he would cherish, assist and support 'the poor body in her old age and crepitude'.[32] Good to his word, he increased her allowance from £4,000 to £6,000 a year, and on the recommendation of Hary-O (of all people) he gave her an additional £3,000 with which to buy furniture and fittings for a new home.[33] As his subsequent life would show, the 6th Duke was the most generous of men. He brought tears to the eyes of old Mr Heaton, the family's agent, by making him a surprise gift of £2,000.

Selina Trimmer had waited until the death of the 5th Duke before returning Georgiana's letters, simply because she did not want 'that woman' Elizabeth Foster to get her hands on them. Now she sent them to the 6th Duke with a warm, charitable note: 'They were written by one of the tenderest mothers that ever lived – by one whom I can never think of but with sentiments of gratitude, affection, esteem and tender pity. May you, my dear friend, inherit all her virtues and avoid the errors by which her life was embittered.'[34]

For Bess, the departure from Chiswick was like covering her life with a shroud. Caro George told Augustus Foster that she was busy packing all her things ready to leave the house forever. 'It is a moment I have always dreaded for her,' she said. 'At the time she wants most comfort and care she is obliged to leave her home and the comforts she has been used to all her life. . . . It grieves me to the heart to see her unhappy.'[35] Lord Holland, who was no particular friend of Bess, voiced the widely held feeling that in her devotion to the late Duke she had made up for her betrayal of Georgiana. 'The situation of the Duchess is deplorable', he wrote, 'for whatever faults the man may have had they are expiated by this calamity, for to the Duke she was always affectionate, good, and grateful. And as he was the inducement and cause of her betraying and injuring others, so was he her protector, and now to be deprived of him her only support she becomes an object of very great compassion and pity, and though at no time did she excite any friendly feeling in me, yet from the bottom of my heart do I feel for her present sufferings.'[36]

Bess rented a house in Piccadilly, and endeavoured to recreate the happy atmosphere of Devonshire House in miniature, holding court and giving parties. It was a pathetic attempt, and succeeded only in making her seem an impostor. Nobody could be Georgiana but Georgiana herself.

Worse still, the widow did something which society was bound to consider tasteless; she revealed the truth about the paternity of her two illegitimate children. It was as if she was desperate to grab the status and rank which, in spite of her being a Duchess, continued to elude her. She wanted recognition; she would gain it through her children.

Caroline St Jules had always been in ignorance of her identity. 'I am in my own mind without a doubt that George has opened her eyes,' said Hary-O in 1808, incidentally making it clear that at least she and Georgiana Morpeth knew, even if Caro didn't. But Hary-O was wrong. Even after her marriage, Caro was still writing to her mother as 'my dear Liz', and at Chatsworth there is a scrap of paper in her hand, which bears a touching prayer. It is undated, but the writing is adult. 'I, an orphan in a foreign country', she says, 'without thy goodness might long ago have fallen a victim to my fate, but thy ever watchful mercy has given me parents, ah yes let me call them by so dear a name, for they have been to me the tenderest best of parents.'

If no one else had seen fit 'to open her eyes', then it befell Hart to do so in August 1811, immediately following the death of her father. Caro was taken completely by surprise. To Lady Morpeth she poured out her feelings:

> You whom ignorantly I have always loved as a sister, you from whom I have not one secret thought concealed, to you I must write in this moment of agitation, anxiety, and yet of joy, to tell you I have just learnt I am indeed your sister. That angel Hartington has, with a feeling delicacy and affection no one else could have felt so well, been telling me who I am. You may imagine the various feelings this has caused in me. But love to you all, to my poor beloved *mother* (it is the first time I ever traced that endearing word) is uppermost. I am so happy to be no longer the unconnected being I thought myself. When I am out of spirits, I shall no longer feel that there is not a creature to whom I belong by ties of blood.[37]

Lady Morpeth asked her if she had ever suspected anything. 'I did at times', said Caro, 'but circumstances always put doubts in my mind, particularly an odious picture which for many years I

looked upon as my mother's, and which always deranged my
ideas whichever way they turned.'

As Caro's life was destined to be tragically bereft of the
normal marital joys, the discovery of brother and sisters was
finally to save her sanity; she remained on the closest possible
terms with Georgiana Morpeth throughout her life. But she was
a discreet woman, and was not now about to make a public announcement of her parentage. One's position in society could
be severely affected by an admission of irregular birth,
notwithstanding that everyone in society by this time was
acquainted with the truth. In broadcasting it so soon after the
Duke's death, Bess made a crucial miscalculation; her adultery
by implication insulted the memory of Georgiana, and her later
marriage to the father of her children could not exonerate it.

Bess clearly thought otherwise. In Scotch law they would be as
good as legitimate, she fancied. She went to talk to Harriet
Bessborough about it. 'For the first time she entirely and *cir-
cumstantially* confided to me the account of Caroline and
Clifford's births [and] asked me whether I did not think her subsequent marriage made its being suspected immaterial.'[38]
Harriet was shocked that Bess could not see how distressing this
would be for all who had known and loved her sister. Encouraged by his mother, Clifford claimed at Portsmouth, where
he was waiting to sail, that he should be treated with the respect
due to a Duke's son. Bess even suggested he should be allowed
the Cavendish arms.*

As Bess became more importunate and embarrassing it fell to
the young Duke to deal with her, a task which he undertook with
exemplary kindness. Gradually he became more aware of her
extraordinary place in the affections of his mother as well as his
father, for which he was retrospectively grateful. While other
members of the family continued to counsel keeping her at a
distance, 'Hart' was more disposed to soften towards her, understanding how even the most guileful of women might be
rendered unhappy by the removal of every tie with those who

---

* His son would later take the name Cavendish in addition to the surname
Clifford, and subsequent generations would absorb the name Spencer, though
it is difficult to see what justification there could be for this; Clifford had no
Spencer ancestry, though he was to marry a daughter of John Townshend and
Georgiana Poyntz, the Duchess of Devonshire's cousin.

had rescued her from loneliness and made her life interesting and comfortable. How Hart (who continued to be known as such after his succession to the dukedom) responded to overtures from Duchess Elizabeth may be judged from a letter which Hary-O wrote to him in 1817:

> My fears are on your part the difficulty of ever saying to her 'No, you shall not', and the conviction that short of that she will encounter anything. 'How I long for five months' quiet at dear Chatsworth!' is a speech in character for her, and difficult to be answered by anything but harshness, which does not belong to your nature.[39]

Furthermore, it was Hart who secured the appointment of his half-brother, Augustus William Clifford, as Gentleman Usher of the Black Rod. Bess could not complain that her children, though still illegitimate, were treated as second-class offspring.

Such is the cruelty of English social *mores* that the stepmother of a Duke is considered not nearly as important as the wife of a Duke. The day she became a widow, Duchess Elizabeth was down-graded in the eyes of 'the world', in spite of there being no other Duchess of Devonshire to dispute her pre-eminence in that title. Eventually, she left England to settle in Europe, where she knew she would not be looked upon as a social footnote. First in Paris, where she was friendly with Madame de Staël and Benjamin Constant, then in Italy, where in strange emulation of her curious father, the Earl of Bristol, she dedicated herself to classical studies. Meanwhile, in England, her house on Piccadilly Terrace was rented by Lord Byron; it was there that his daughter Ada was born.

In Rome, Duchess Elizabeth presided over a salon which achieved no small fame. Louisa de Stolberg wrote to her, 'On dit ici que vous régnez à Rome'. Her closest friends there were Mme Récamier and the Papal Secretary of State, Cardinal Consalvi. She became a passionately enthusiastic archaeologist, with a small army of men in her employ digging away at the Forum and in fact discovering some fine objects, some of which she sent back to her stepson Devonshire. She also produced some fine limited editions of classical texts, commissioning translators and illustrators to make her books exceptional. The English

observed all this with unworthy humour, considering it pretentious of the frail old lady to set herself up as a modern Maecenas.

She entered into a correspondence with Sir Thomas
Lawrence, imploring him and eventually persuading him to go
to Rome and paint a portrait of her friend Consalvi. 'You cannot
have a subject of more distinguished merit,' she said, and when
the painting was completed, she averred that it was Lawrence's
finest work. The portrait now belongs to H.M. The Queen, and
hangs in the Waterloo Chamber at Windsor Castle. On the same
occasion, Lawrence found time to draw a charming picture of
Bess herself.

Gradually, her letters lost their chilly formality as she began
to confide in the artist. 'Heaven has kindly given me a love and
taste for the beautiful both in nature and art', she told him,
'which has enabled me to find in the objects by which I am surrounded here first a solace and now an enjoyment.'[40] Still she
could not rid her prose of that calculated refinement, as if she
were sitting an examination for composition, which in the end
does her more disservice than many a lightweight rumour. On
the other hand, Lord Byron wrote seeking her influence with the
authorities to release from house arrest some friends of his, and
had the kindness to say, 'If my acquaintance with your Grace's
character were even slighter than it is . . . I had only to turn to
the letters of Gibbon (now on my table) for a full testimony to its
high and amiable qualities.'[41] She could not, in truth, have
beguiled Georgiana and Canis for so long had she been
entirely false. M. Artaud, 1st Secretary of the French Embassy in
Rome, gave her this epitaph: 'En amitié elle n'a jamais fait
qu'acquérir – elle n'a jamais rien perdu.'*[42]

Sir Thomas Lawrence's drawing of her in 1819 indicates that
she retained her beauty, though she became rather thin. She
likewise retained her fondness for Georgiana and Canis long
after she had lost them both. She wore a locket round her neck,
which contained Georgiana's hair, as well as a bracelet made
from another lock of the same hair. Miniatures of both her
friends were carried with her always. The 6th Duke of
Devonshire was mercifully kind towards her – an estrangement
would have hurt her deeply. They corresponded regularly
throughout her remaining years, he visited her in Italy, she

* She only made friends – she never lost any.

visited him at Chatsworth in 1818 and in 1821. 'I hope you will continue friend to my dear sons', she told him, 'and never quite forget me who loved and adored both your parents with an entire and faithfull affection.'[43] After his visit in 1819, she wrote, 'There is no saying how I miss you, and how much I want you . . . I wish you had not gone so soon.'[44]

The absurd rumours of the Duke's supposed illegitimate birth began to circulate again. He assured Bess that they were contemptible in his view, and could not succeed in their aim of promoting coolness between himself and his stepmother, 'I could never so far forget the obligations I owe to you, and the affection of my parents for you.'[45] There is also one solitary reference to Eliza Courtney, now Mrs Ellice, for whom Bess secured apartments in Rome. 'Pray give her my love' said Hart, 'and appease her just anger at my not writing.'[46] Eliza Ellice was present during the ten days of her final illness.

When she suddenly took ill in 1824, having shrunk to a mere packet of bones, the Duke immediately went to Rome to be with her. George Howard, his nephew, accompanied him. He was at her bedside when she died on 30 March at three in the morning. He would not permit anyone else to see her until a few minutes before her final breath, when Mme Récamier and the Duc de Laval were brought in to say farewell. She asked what time it was. 'Not more than that, not more than that,' she said, then uttered a short scream, and died.

Her death had been caused by a social engagement. She had been invited for the first time to dine at the Borghese Palace. When she prepared to leave, after dinner, she went to the wrong carriage, and was obliged to wait while four other carriages drew up and took their passengers. 'That was in the middle of the colonnade, as you know, betwixt the current of air, that comes from the door of the garden, and that of the Palace,' Pietro Cannucini told Lawrence. Bess did not recover from the chill she caught that evening.[48]

Hours after her death, Hart wrote to Frederick Foster to inform him. 'If you should be unable to pursue your journey you may rely upon my arranging everything with the tenderness and care of a son to her whom we have lost,' he said. Caro George blamed herself for having been absent. 'Why was I not there', she cried; 'that is the pang that never never will go, I

ought to have been with her.' Still, she told Hart that he was the
one person in the world whom she would have chosen to be with
her, 'she loved you so truly, as if you had been her son'.

The Duke honoured her wish that she should be brought back
to England and interred alongside her closest friends. After
lying in state at Devonshire House, her remains were taken to
Derby and put to rest beside those of Georgiana and Canis. The
Duke also saw that the complicated provisions of her will were
carried out to the letter. She left to her sons Frederick and
Augustus Foster all the property which she held from her own
family, the Herveys, while all that she inherited from the late
Duke she left to his children Augustus William Clifford and Mrs
George Lamb. The locket with Georgiana's hair went to
Corisande Ossulston, and the hair bracelet to 'my dear friend
Lady Bessborough – it is her sister's hair – she knows how I
loved her'.[49]

Hary-O received a miniature of her father in uniform. When
she heard of 'the poor Duchess's death', she wrote, 'It has
shocked us very much, she had so much enjoyment of life. It
brings past times to one's mind, and many nervous and in-
definable feelings.'[50]

                    *   *   *

Georgiana's only son, the 6th Duke of Devonshire, did not
marry and had no children, so that Georgiana has no direct
descendants in the male line. But this is a long way from saying
that her personality died with her, for through her daughters she
is the ancestress of more than two hundred people alive today,
including, unexpectedly, the present Duke of Devonshire. While
it would be tedious to enumerate all those who can be traced, it
is none the less interesting to discover who now has some of the
genes of the captivating Georgiana in his or her veins.

LITTLE G.   Georgiana Morpeth became Countess of Carlisle
when her husband succeeded to the title in 1825. They had six
sons and six daughters, and from one of the sons is descended
the present Earl of Carlisle, though he no longer lives at the
grandiose Castle Howard, where Hary-O found the conversation so stultifying; this passed to the grandson of the 9th Earl,
Mr George Howard, who still lives there.

From the Carlisles' daughter Harriet are descended five dukes. She married the 2nd Duke of Sutherland, and her daughters Elizabeth, Caroline and Constance married respectively the 8th Duke of Argyll, the 4th Duke of Leinster and the 1st Duke of Westminster, direct ancestors of the three present holders of those titles. This Duchess Harriet was a splendid, impressive woman, the close companion of Queen Victoria in her early widowhood. There are a number of Leinster descendants in Australia who thereby trace their ancestry back to Georgiana Devonshire, though they are themselves commoners.

Harriet's son was 3rd Duke of Sutherland, whose daughter Florence married Henry Chaplin; their daughter Edith married the 7th Marquess of Londonderry and was the last of the great political hostesses, holding court at Londonderry House even after the Second World War. Through this connection are thus descended the 9th Marquess of Londonderry, and his son and heir, Lord Castlereagh, the present writer's godson, who may count Georgiana as one of his great-great-great-great-great-great-great-grandmothers.

The current Duke of Sutherland is not descended from Georgiana, the title having passed to a distant branch descended from the 1st Duke, in 1963. (Paradoxically, he is probably descended illegitimately from Little G.'s husband, Lord Carlisle.) The Countess of Sutherland *suo jure*, holder of a Scottish earldom dating from 1235, is however directly descended from the union of Georgiana's grand-daughter with the 2nd Duke of Sutherland. Furthermore, the heir to the dukedom of Sutherland is descended from Georgiana, in spite of the fact that his father is not. Harriet Sutherland's daughter Elizabeth, we have said, married the 8th Duke of Argyll; their daughter Edith married the 7th Duke of Northumberland, whose grand-daughter is the present Duchess of Sutherland. In this way the Sutherland heir is descended from Georgiana through his mother. Also, of course, the present Duke of Northumberland is descended from her through his grand-mother.

In fact, were you to be asked to dine with the Duke of Northumberland at Alnwick Castle, and he were to say that it was an intimate family affair with just a few close relations, you may find yourself at table with half a dozen of Georgiana's descendants, including, apart from the connections already in-dicated, his wife the Duchess of Northumberland and his nephew the Duke of Hamilton. This is because the Duchess is a daughter of the Dowager Duchess of Buccleuch ('Mollie' Buccleuch), whose great-grandmother was Caroline, daughter of 'Little G.' Morpeth. This of course means that the present Duke of Buccleuch is likewise a descendant of Georgiana.

As for the Duke of Hamilton, he claims descent from Georgiana, through his mother, another daughter of the 8th Duke of Northumberland, great-great-grandson of Georgiana Morpeth; see above.

To continue the list of Morpeth offspring, there is the present Duchess of Beaufort, niece of Queen Mary. Morpeth's grand-daughter Margaret, daughter of the 1st Duke of Westminster, married the Marquess of Cambridge, Queen Mary's brother, whose daughter married the present Duke of Beaufort.

These, then, are the principal descendants of Lady Morpeth (Carlisle) through her daughters Harriet and Caroline. It is another daughter, Blanche, who brings Georgiana's genes back into the Devonshire line. Blanche married the Earl of Burlington, who succeeded as 7th Duke of Devonshire when his cousin, Georgiana's son Hart, died unmarried in 1858. Thus Georgiana's grand-daughter would have been Duchess of Devonshire but for an early death, and from this connection are descended the present Duke, his late aunt Lady Dorothy Caven-dish, wife of the Prime Minister Harold Macmillan, and their son Maurice Macmillan, M.P. Also among this number must be counted the niece of the world's greatest tap-dancer, Fred Astaire, whose sister Adele married Lord Charles Cavendish, son of the 9th Duke of Devonshire. One must finally mention the present Marquess of Salisbury, whose father, the 5th Marquess, married Elizabeth, daughter of Lord Richard Caven-dish. Strangely enough, the 5th Marquess's sister married the 10th Duke of Devonshire and is the mother of the present Duke, though this might confuse. The Dowager Duchess of Devonshire is *not* a descendant of Georgiana, though her son, the Duke of Devonshire, and her nephew, the Marquess of Salisbury, both are.

HARY-O. Georgiana's ebullience was reflected more in the

lively personality of Hary-O than it was in little G.'s more subdued nature; it is a pity therefore that Hary-O's progeny is less abundant. Her husband, Granville Leveson-Gower, was created Earl Granville in 1833, making her thus the ancestress of the present Earl Granville. Her grand-daughter Victoria married Harold John Hastings Russell, nephew of the 9th Duke of Bedford, and Victoria's daughter is the writer Georgiana Blakiston, whose sharp intelligence and lively wit bring us very close to Georgiana Devonshire, who was her great-great grand-mother. Her grandmother Castalia Granville, Hary-O's daughter-in-law, lived until 1938. Hary-O herself, as Lady Granville, presided over the British Embassy in Paris during part of the glorious Victorian era, and earned her place in literature as one of the finest female letter-writers in the English language.

AUGUSTUS WILLIAM CLIFFORD. The son of Lady Elizabeth and the Duke kept within the circle of his parents. He married Lady Elizabeth Townshend, sister of the 4th Marquess Townshend, by whom he had three sons and four daughters. In 1838 he was created a baronet, and died in 1877. His three sons succeeded him in the baronetcy, namely Rear-Admiral Sir William John Cavendish Clifford, 2nd baronet, Sir Robert Cavendish Spencer Clifford, 3rd baronet, and Sir Charles Cavendish Clifford, 4th baronet. This latter was a Member of Parliament, private secretary to Lord Palmerston, and earned the rare distinction of being elected a Fellow of All Souls College, Oxford. It is interesting that all three baronets of the second generation bore the name Cavendish, thus acknowledging that their grandfather was the Duke. Unfortunately, none of these three sons had any male issue, with the result that the baronetcy was extinct with the death of Sir Charles in 1895. Three of the four daughters of Sir Augustus never married, and none had descendants. The last of the four, Augusta Caroline (so named after her father and her aunt, Caroline St Jules), lived at the family home, Westfield on the Isle of Wight, until well into the twentieth century. However, the blood of Canis and Bess flows in the veins of descendants from their second grandson, Sir Robert, who had three daughters, Rosalie, Rosamund and Marjorie. Of Rosalie (again named after Caroline St Jules, whose middle name was Rosalie), nothing is known. Rosamund married an Italian, Luigi Nessi, and settled abroad. There are presumably Nessi descendants alive today, though efforts to trace them have proved fruitless. The third daughter, sometimes called Marjorie but now referred to as Caroline May, married the 14th Lord Dormer, and her son is the present (15th) Baron Dormer. It is Lord Dormer who has in his possession the journal of his great-great-grandmother, Lady Elizabeth Foster. The Dormers have two daughters.

AUGUSTUS FOSTER. Lady Elizabeth's legitimate son by John Thomas Foster was also made a baronet, in 1831, though this honour too, has since disappeared. There is, however, one quite surprising descendant. Sir Augustus Foster, envoy-extraordinary to the United States, envoy to Denmark, and a Privy Councillor, married Lady Albinia, sister to the 5th Earl of Buckinghamshire. They had three sons – Sir Frederick Foster, 2nd baronet, the Rev. Sir Cavendish Hervey Foster, 3rd baronet, and Vere Foster, the author who edited the letters of his grandmother under the title *The Two Duchesses* in 1898. The 2nd baronet did not marry, and was therefore succeeded by his brother. This Sir Cavendish Foster (so called for reasons which defy investigation, for there was no Cavendish blood in his family) was a rector who married a vicar's daughter, Isabella Todd. They had two sons and a daughter. The eldest was Major John Frederick Foster, a High Sheriff, whose descendants continue. The second, Hervey Foster, died unmarried. The daughter, Jane, married a Mr Heathcote of Chingford, Essex, where perhaps her progeny now thrive. The rector's eldest son, John Frederick, died in 1890 a few months before his father, and so did not inherit the baronetcy. He had in the meantime married and produced a son and two daughters. This son, Sir Augustus Vere Foster, therefore succeeded his grandfather as 4th baronet in 1890. He in turn had a son and two daughters, but as the son died in 1934 at the age of twenty-six, the baronetcy became extinct on the death of the 4th baronet. His daughter Dorothy married Lt-Col. Arthur May, of Ardee, Co. Louth. The Foster line likewise continues through his sisters, one of whom married into yet another church family, Hadow of Uffington, Berkshire. The other sister, Alice, married Major-General Fitzgerald

Wintour, C.B., C.B.E., a Yorkshireman, and they had a son and daughter. The daughter, Cordelia, is the wife of Lord James of Rusholme, a Life Peer and former High Master of Manchester Grammar School, as well as a distinguished academic author, while the son, Charles Vere Wintour, was until 1980 the distinguished editor of the London newspaper, the *Evening Standard*. Thus one of Fleet Street's most eminent figures is the great-great-great-grandson of Elizabeth Foster, afterwards Duchess of Devonshire, and a distant kinsman of the present head of the Hervey family, Lord Bristol.

CORISANDE DE GRAMONT. Her husband, Lord Ossulston, eventually succeeded as 5th Earl of Tankerville, and from this union is descended the present 9th Earl, who lives in San Francisco, California, U.S.A., and has a daughter called Corisande. His half-sister, a daughter of the 8th Earl, is also called Corisande.

Another Corisande was Corisande de Gramont's daughter, who became Countess of Malmesbury, but left no issue. Corisande de Gramont's son, the 6th Earl of Tankerville, married a daughter of the Duke of Manchester, and by her had three sons and two daughters. Two of the sons and one of the daughters died unmarried. The surviving son succeeded as 7th Earl of Tankerville, while the surviving daughter, Louise, married the 13th Earl of Dalhousie, from which marriage descends another line from Corisande de Gramont, including the present 16th Earl and his son, Lord Ramsay. The third son of the 13th Earl of Dalhousie married H.R.H. Princess Victoria, daughter of the Duke of Connaught and grand-daughter of Queen Victoria; she was later more generally known as Lady Patricia Ramsay. Their son, Alexander Ramsay, is therefore not only of obvious royal descent, but the great-great-grandson of Corisande de Gramont. Other sprigs of the same tree now live in Spain and France.

ELIZA COURTNEY. This is very complex. Georgiana's daughter by Charles Grey, named Eliza Courtney, was brought up at Howick by Grey's mother. She was therefore ostensibly Grey's sister. She married General Robert Ellice, a son of Alexander Ellice. As it happened, Grey's legitimate daughter

Hannah Alathea married another son of Alexander Ellice – Edward Ellice, the Secretary of State for War. No wonder that when they were seen together, they were described as 'all mixed up'. Anyway, Eliza Courtney and Robert Ellice had two children, General Charles Ellice and Eliza, who married Henry Brand, Speaker of the House of Commons. Brand was 23rd Baron Dacre by inheritance and 1st Viscount Hampden by creation. From this connection are descended scores of people, including of course the present Lord Hampden and the present Baroness Dacre, wife of the playwright William Douglas-Home. Lord Hampden lives at Glynde in Sussex, where Eliza Brand, Georgiana's grand-daughter, died in 1899.

CAROLINE ST JULES. The Duke of Devonshire's natural daughter by Lady Elizabeth Foster married George Lamb, officially the son of Lord Melbourne, but generally thought to be Lady Melbourne's son by the Prince of Wales. The marriage was not happy. Though George was dutiful and had charm, he had no wish to consummate the union. When Caro first realised that his habit of retiring early arose from a desire to avoid sleeping with her, she confided in Dr Farquhar, who advised that her mother should be told. Caro revealed to Bess that she could never have children, because her husband could not bring himself to love her carnally. Bess was distraught 'to see this lovely and innocent creature chained down to an existence so unnatural, so contrary to the best affection of the heart, that she should never have the blessing of a child like herself . . . doomed to pass her best years with a man who has only the name of husband, to pass a life in short of celibacy'. That George himself did not appear to be worried by his lack of lust was, as Bess rightly perceived, the worst aspect. 'Insensible to joy or passion he is to leave her to her solitary bed. . . . I look upon him as a kind of monster.'

The women conferred amongst themselves and concluded that Hart should not be told, lest his attitude towards George Lamb might become cold. The one woman whom Caro should have kept in the dark was George's mother, Lady Melbourne. 'The mother, which is certainly odd, has been less kind to me, since she has known it, and I have never ceased regretting that she was told.' Caro herself grew philosophical. She knew there was no hope, but she drew comfort from her new-found family 'I sometimnes feel very impatient under it', she told Georgiana Morpeth, 'and am determined not to bear it, but to go off with the first person who will take me.' Nevertheless, the marriage endured in its barren way, with the result that there are no descendants from this line.

REFERENCES

Most of the material for this book is taken from the archives at Chatsworth (5th Duke's group). References to the collection are indicated by the abbreviation C followed by the number of the document. In those cases where the letter has been published in Lord Bessborough's selection from Georgiana's correspondence, this is indicated in brackets with the initial B and the page reference. Where other published sources are used, the reader is referred to the Bibliography for a precise identification of the edition in which the source is to be found.

Chapter One
1. Greville *Memoirs*, Vol. IV, pp. 435–6
2. Walpole, *Letters,* Vol. II, p. 330 *footnote*
3. Granville Leveson-Gower, *Private Correspondence,* Vol. I, p. 312
4. *Lady Bessborough and Her Family Circle,* p. 5
5. John Maclean, *Memoir of the Family of Poyntz,* p. 215
6. C.2014
7. *Lady Bessborough,* p. 8
8. *Lady Bessborough,* p. 161
9. David Cecil, *The Stricken Deer,* p. 234
10. *Hary-O, p. 286*
11. Elizabeth Jenkins, *Lady Caroline Lamb,* p. 13
12. Portland Papers at the University of Nottingham, Pw G. 106–128
13. Alice E Robbins, *A Book of Duchesses,* p. 181; Hugh Stokes, *The Devonshire House Circle,* p. 190
14. Harriet's Journal is reproduced in *Lady Bessborough and Her Family Circle,* pp. 18–30
15. Elizabeth Jenkins, *Lady Caroline Lamb,* p. 14
16. C.12 (B, p. 11)
17. C.12 (B, p. 11)
18. C.12 (B, p. 12)
19. C.14 (B, p. 13)
20. C.15
21. C.36

Chapter Two

1. Walpole, *Letters*, Vol. III, p. 280
2. Brougham, *Lives of the Philosophers of the Time of George III*
3. John Timbs, *English Eccentrics and Eccentricities*, Vol. I, p. 143
4. Walpole, Vol. IV, p. 280
5. quoted in Derek Jarrett, *Britain 1688–1815*, p. 374
6. Portland Papers, Pw G 106–128 (University of Nottingham)
7. C.37.1
8. quoted in Brian Masters, *The Dukes*, p. 174
9. Portland Papers, Pw G 106–128
10. *Hary-O*, p. 222
11. Arthur Griffiths, *Clubs and Clubmen*, p. 236
12. *Dearest Bess*, p. 49
13. *Hary-O*, p. 35
14. *ibid.*, p. 43
15. Iris Leveson-Gower, *The Face without a Frown*, p. 11
16. *Face without a Frown*, p. 20
17. Portland Papers
18. *Hary-O,* p. 249
19. quoted in Robbins, *op. cit,.* p. 173
20. Glenarvon *Memoirs*, Vol. I, pp. 91–2
21. Boswell's *Life of Johnson*, p. 865
22. Wraxall, *Historical and Posthumous Memoirs*, Vol. II, p. 344
23. *Face without a Frown*, p. 132
24. *Lady Bessborough*, p. 31
25. *Face without a Frown*, p. 28
26. C.56
27. C.39
28. C.59
29. C.80 & 85
30. C.93
31. C.62
32. C.62
33. C.65
34. C.19
35. *Face without a Frown*, p. 31
36. C.23, 30, 39
37. C.24
38. *Town and Country Magazine*, March 1777
39. Augustus Hare, *In My Solitary Life*, p. 93
40. David Cecil, *Melbourne*, p. 20
41. *Lady Bessborough*, p. 195
42. C.143
43. quoted in Derek Jarrett, *Britain 1688–1815*, p. 36
44. *ibid.*, pp. 37, 56
45. Archives of Ministère des Affaires Etrangères, Correspondance Politique Angleterre, Vol. 545
46. T. H. White, *The Age of Scandal*, p. 116

47. Historical Manuscripts Commission, *Le Fanu MSS*.
48. Walpole, Vol. VI, p. 70
49. *ibid.*, p. 186
50. Wraxall, *Historical and Posthumous Memoirs*, Vol. I, pp. 113–14
51. *Letters of David Garrick*, ed. Little and Kalire, p. 1035
52. Mrs Delaney, *Correspondence*, Second Series, Vol. II, p. 98
53. Fanny Burney, *Diary*, ed. C. F. Barrett
54. Thornbury and Walford, *Old & New London*, Vol. IV, p. 278
55. Wraxall, *Historical and Posthumous Memoirs*, Vol. III, p. 342
56. Mrs Delaney, *Correspondence*, Vol. II, p. 114

Chapter Three

1. Elizabeth Jenkins, *Lady Caroline Lamb*
2. C.620 (B, p. 83)
3. *Life and Letters* of Lady Sarah Lennox
4. Hugh Stokes, *The Devonshire House Circle*, p. 217
5. Christopher Hobhouse, *Charles James Fox*, p. 120
6. Horace Walpole to Lady Ossory, 9 June 1778 (in Yale edition)
7. Derek Jarrett, *op. cit.,* p. 61
8. David Cecil, *Melbourne*, pp. 83, 193
9. Stokes, *op. cit.*, p. 218
10. *ibid.*, p. 287 *footnote*
11. T. H. White, *The Age of Scandal*, p. 80
12. *ibid.*, pp. 37–9
13. C.666 (B, p. 95)
14. Stokes, *op. cit.*, p. 45
15. B, p. 43
16. *Hary-O*, p. 78
17. C.255 (B, p. 42)
18. C.401.1 (B, p. 54)
19. C.136.2
20. Margery Villiers, *The Grand Whiggery*, p. 24
21. Stokes, *op. cit.*, p. 141
22. C.247
23. Greville *Memoirs*, Vol. II, p. 316
24. *Dearest Bess,* p. 39
25. *Hary-O*, p. 26
26. Granville Leveson-Gower, *Correspondence*, Vol. I, p. 317
27. *ibid.*, p. 237
28. *Dictionary of National Biography*
29. David Cecil, *Melbourne*, p. 48
30. *Glenarvon*, *op. cit.*, Vol. I, p. 151
31. C.74 (B, p. 25)
32. C.103 (B, p. 27)
33. C.109 (B, p. 28)
34. C.126
35. C.134

36. C.130
37. C.141 (B, p. 30)
38. C.162
39. C.151 (B, p. 30)
40. C.1397 (B, p. 224)
41. C.1601 (B, p. 243)
42. C.406
43. Walpole, Vol. VIII, p. 245
44. C.180 (B, p. 32)
45. quoted in Hobhouse, *op. cit.*, p. 5
46. British Museum Department of Manuscripts, Add. MSS. 47570
47. *Speeches* of Charles James Fox, Vol. I, p. 5
48. Arthur Griffiths, *Clubs & Clubmen*, p. 51
49. *Letters* of George III to Lord North, Vol. I, p. 170
50. Archives of Ministère des Affaires Etrangères, Correspondance Politique Angleterre, Vols 542, 543, 545, 548
51. Greville *Memoirs*, Vol. I, p. 267
52. Walpole, Vol. VI, p. 24
53. *ibid.*
54. Hobhouse, *op. cit.*, p. 65
55. *ibid.*, p. 188
56. C.1845 (B, p. 277)
57. C.1789 (B, p. 269)
58. Greville *Memoirs*, Vol. II, p. 344
59. *Hary-O*, p. 17
60. C.52
61. C.39
62. Walter Sichel, *Sheridan*, Vol. I, p. 534
63. C.159
64. Mrs Delaney, *Correspondence*, Vol. II, p. 350
65. C. Box 675, folio 1147

Chapter Four

1. C.217
2. C.232
3. C.233
4. C.235 (B, p. 40)
5. C.234
6. C.217
7. C.223
8. C.236
9. C.237
10. C.219
11. Correspondance Politique Angleterre, Vol. 545
12. *A Lady of the Last Century*
13. C.256
14. C.248, 249, 259, 261

15. C.269
16. C.270
17. C.323
18. C.287 (B, p. 45)
19. C.288
20. C.289, 304
21. C.303 (B, p. 47)
22. C.307
23. C.310
24. C.350 (B, p. 51)
25. C.365 (B, p. 52)
26. C.378
27. C.390
28. C.388
29. C.393
30. C.387.1

Chapter Five
1. C.397
2. C.403
3. C.397, 414
4. Correspondance Politique Angleterre, Vol. 543
5. C.352.4
6. *Dearest Bess*, p. 5
7. C.532.4
8. Vere Foster, *The Two Duchesses*, p. 200
9. Walpole, Vol. VIII, p. 440
10. C.532.4
11. C.397
12. C.420
13. C.422
14. C.423
15. C.485
16. C.568
17. C.460 (B, p. 58)
18. Hugh Stokes, *The Devonshire House Circle*, p. 185
19. C.486 (B, p. 59)
20. C.508
21. C.507.1
22. C.532.2
23. C.534.1, 532.1
24. C.530
25. Correspondance Politique Angleterre, Vol. 543
26. C.494 (B, p. 60)
27. C.508.1
28. C.511
29. C.513

30. C.567
31. C.566
32. *Dearest Bess*, p. 14
33. C.584
34. C.607.2
35. C.576 (B, p. 69)
36. C.594

Chapter Six

1. Walpole, Vol. VIII, p. 469
2. British Museum, Add. MSS. 47570
3. Wraxall, Vol. III, p. 346
4. C.610.1
5. C.613
6. C.610.4
7. *Face without a Frown*, p. 108
8. Correspondance Politique Angleterre, Vol. 548
9. *Face without a Frown*, p. 112
10. Historical Manuscripts Commission, Rutland MSS., Vol. III, p. 88
11. Hugh Stokes, *The Devonshire House Circle*, p. 198
12. C.610.1
13. British Museum, Add. MSS. 40763, folio 250
14. Castle Howard Papers
15. Correspondance Politique Angleterre, Vol. 548
16. *ibid.*
17. *Dearest Bess*, p. 21
18. Stokes, *op. cit.*, p. 230, and *Dearest Bess*, p. 22
19. C.623
20. C.433
21. Wraxall, Vol. V, p. 371
22. C.628
23. C.629
24. Royal Archives, quoted in Christopher Hibbert, *George IV, Prince of Wales*, p. 50
25. C.649
26. C.653
27. C.657
28. *Dearest Bess*, pp. 26, 39
29. C.181
30. C.665.1
31. *Dearest Bess*, p. 24
32. *ibid.*, pp. 25–7
33. C.683 (B, p. 99)
34. C.678
35. C.679
36. *Dearest Bess*, pp. 32–3
37. C.684

38. C.694 (B, p. 102)
39. C.687 (B, p. 100)
40. Hobhouse, *Charles James Fox*, pp. 205–8, and Villiers, *The Grand Whiggery*, pp. 72–89
41. C.716 (B, p. 104)
42. C.737
43. C.744

Chapter Seven

1. Greville, *Memoirs*, Vol. V, p. 308
2. David Cecil, *Melbourne*, p. 50
3. quoted in Stokes, *The Devonshire House Cirle*, p. 239
4. C.1062 (B, pp. 174–5)
5. *Lady Bessborough and Her Family Circle*, p. 146
6. *ibid.*, p. 16
7. Walpole, Vol. VIII, p. 373
8. quoted in Stokes, *op. cit.*, p. 251
9. C.674 (B, p. 97)
10. C.679.1 and 756.1
11. Foster, *The Two Duchesses*, pp. 154–5
12. C.861.1
13. *Dearest Bess*, p. 37
14. C.756
15. Hist. MSS. Comm., Hastings MSS., Vol. III, 8 December, 1786
16. *Dearest Bess*, pp. 14, 41
17. C.993 (B, 160–1)
18. Greville, *Memoirs*, Vol. I, p. 79
19. Granville Leveson-Gower, *Correspondence*, Vol. I, p. 33
20. *Journal* of Elizabeth, Lady Holland, Vol. I, p. 226
21. Correspondance Politique Angleterre, Vol. 545
22. Hist. MSS. Comm., Carlisle MSS., p. 487
23. *Lady Bessborough*, p. 20
24. Andrew Steinmetz, *The Gaming Table*; Arthur Griffiths, *Clubs & Clubmen*; Walter Sichel, *Sheridan*, Vol. I, pp. 145–53
25. C.257 and 164 (B, pp. 44 and 31)
26. Hist. MSS. Comm., Rutland MSS.
27. C.721 (B, p. 106)
28. Walpole, Vol. VII, p. 477
29. Walpole to Mary Berry, 5 March 1791 (in Yale edition)
30. C.607 (B, p. 77)
31. C.769
32. The letters from Georgiana to Comte Perregaux are in the William L. Clements Library at the University of Michigan, Ann Arbor, Michigan, U.S.A.
33. *Correspondence* of George IV, Prince of Wales, ed. Aspinall, p. 533
34. C.802.1 and 782.1 (B, pp. 118 and 114)
35. C.802.2 (B, p. 119)

36. C.813.1 (B, p. 120)
37. C.815.1 (B, p. 122)
38. C.926.2 (B, p. 139)
39. E. H. Coleridge, *Thomas Coutts*, Vol. II, p. 210
40. C.944.1 (B, pp. 142–4)
41. C.945 (B, p. 145)
42. See *Porphyria – A Royal Malady* (British Medical Association)
43. Ida Macalpine and Richard Hunter, *George III and the Mad Business*
44. C.923. 1 (B, p. 138)
45. C.896
46. Countess Granville, *Correspondence*, Vol. I, pp. 178, 300
47. Granville Leveson-Gower, *Correspondence*, Vol. II, p. 300
48. C.892 (B, p. 133)
49. C.894.1

Chapter Eight

1. C.954 (B, p. 146)
2. C.961.1 (B, p. 149)
3. C.961.1 (B, p. 150)
4. Margery Villiers, *The Grand Whiggery*, p. 98
5. Hugh Stokes, *The Devonshire House Circle*, p. 266
6. Arthur Calder-Marshall, *The Two Duchesses*, p. 105
7. *Dearest Bess*, p. 53
8. Stokes, *op. cit.*, p. 266
9. *Lady Bessborough*, p. 80
10. Castle Howard Papers
11. C.991 (B, p. 157)
12. C.994.2 (B, p. 162)
13. C.998 (B, p. 163)
14. C.1034.1 (B, p. 167)
15. C.1052.1 (B, p. 170)
16. C.963 (B, p. 150)
17. C.977.1 (B, p. 155)
18. C.991.1 (B, p. 159)
19. C.998 (B, p. 162)
20. Aspinall, pp. 508, 533
21. C.1044 (B, p. 168)
22. British Museum Add. MSS. 45911, f. 13
23. *Face without a Frown*, p. 166
24. *Dearest Bess*, p. 224
25. Greville, *Memoirs*, Vol. VII, pp. 332–3
26. *Dearest Bess*, p. 54
27. C.1060, 1061 (B, pp. 173–4)
28. C.1062 (B, p. 175)
29. C.1061 (B, p. 173)
30. *Dictionary of National Biography*
31. British Museum, Add. MSS. 45548, f. 79

32. Add. MSS. 45911, ff. 15, 17
33. Add. MSS. 45548, f. 36
34. Add. MSS. 45548, f. 38
35. Add. MSS. 45911, f. 22, and 45548, f. 40
36. Add. MSS. 45548, f. 42
37. Add. MSS. 45548, f. 44
38. Add. MSS. 45911, f. 20
39. Add. MSS. 45911, f. 24
40. Add. MSS. 45548, f. 46
41. Add. MSS. 45548, f. 48
42. Add. MSS. 45548, f. 51, and 45911, f. 32
43. Add. MSS. 45548, f. 12, and 45911, f. 26
44. Add. MSS. 45548, ff. 10, 50
45. Add. MSS. 45911, f. 40
46. Add. MSS. 45548, f. 12
47. Add. MSS. 45548, f. 52
48. Castle Howard Papers
49. C.1137.1 (B, p. 195)
50. C.1129 (B, p. 193)
51. C.1137.1 and 1142.1 (B, pp. 195, 196)
52. Aspinall, pp. 696, 484
53. C.1131 (B, p. 193)
54. Castle Howard Papers
55. *ibid.*
56. C.1175 (B, p. 199)
57. C.1115, 1117, 1118, (B, pp. 187–8)
58. C.1119.1 (B, p. 189)
59. C.1127.1 (B, p. 192)
60. C.1099.2–1127.1 *passim*
61. C.1122.1 (B, p. 190)
62. C.1126.1 (B, p. 191)
63. C.1119.1 (B, p. 189)
64. C.1136.2 (B, p. 195)
65. C.1145.1 (B, p. 196)
66. *Lady Bessborough*, p. 75
67. *Dearest Bess*, p. 69
68. Castle Howard Papers
69. Castle Howard Papers
70. *Dearest Bess*, p. 71
71. Castle Howard Papers
72. Letters from Lady Elizabeth Foster to Gibbon are in the British Museum (British Library, Department of Manuscripts)
73. Castle Howard Papers
74. C.1180 (B, p. 201)

Chapter Nine

1. C.1243 (B, p. 208)
2. C.1190 (B, p. 203)

3. Royal Archives, quoted in Christopher Hibbert, *George IV, Prince of Wales*, p. 126
4. C.1259.3 (B, p. 210)
5. C.1219 (B, p. 206)
6. Granville Leveson-Gower, *Correspondence*, Vol. I, p. 423
7. British Museum, Add. MSS. 45911, f. 44
8. *ibid.*,45548, f. 24
9. C.1256
10. Leveson-Gower, *op. cit.*, Vol. I, p. xxvii *footnote*
11. C.1234.1
12. C.1239
13. C.1448
14. C.922, 941
15. C.152
16. Hist. MSS. Comm., Carlisle MSS.
17. *Hary-O*, p. 277
18. C.1284.1 (B, p. 212)
19. C.1357 (B, p. 220)
20. C.1360
21. C.1364
22. C.1371
23. Leveson-Gower, *op. cit.*, Vol. I, pp. 125–6
24. *ibid.*, p. 142
25. C.1537
26. Walpole to Miss Berry, 15 December 1796 (in Yale edition)
27. Journal of *Elizabeth, Lady Holland*, Vol. I, p. 244
28. C.1198
29. C.1194
30. Castle Howard Papers
31. C.1015
32. C.1191
33. Castle Howard Papers
34. C.1184
35. Castle Howard Papers
36. C.1198
37. Castle Howard Papers
38. quoted in Elizabeth Jenkins, *Lady Caroline Lamb*
39. C.1330, 1331
40. C.1332
41. C.1400
42. C.1379 and Castle Howard Papers
43. C.1388
44. *Hary-O*, p. 174
45. *ibid.*, p. 296

Chapter Ten

1. C.1707
2. Walter Sichel, *Sheridan*, Vol. II, p. 433

3. C.1435 (B, p. 228)
4. Greville, *Memoirs*, Vol. V, p. 367
5. Augustus Hare, *The Years with Mother*, p. 2
6. *Journal* of Elizabeth, Lady Holland, Vol. II, p. 83
7. British Museum, Add. MSS. 40763, f. 250
8. C.1609
9. C.1421 (B, p. 226)
10. C.1463 (B, p. 231)
11. British Museum, Add. MSS. 51723
12. *ibid.*
13. *ibid.*
14. *Hary-O*, p. 185
15. *ibid.*, p. 295
16. Greville, Memoirs, Vol. I, p. 65
17. C.1543
18. British Museum, Add. MSS. 51723
19. Castle Howard Papers
20. C.1554
21. *Dearest Bess*, p. 90
22. C.1562
23. B, p. 238
24. C.1668
25. C.1537.2 and 1567 (B, p. 239)
26. C.1569 (B, p. 240)
27. *Hary-O*, p. 106
28. *Journal* of Elizabeth, Lady Holland, Vol. I, p. 122
29. Sichel, *op. cit.*, Vol. I, p. 177
30. Granville Leveson-Gower, *Correspondence*, Vol. I, p. 286
31. *ibid.*, p. 216
32. *ibid.*, pp. 351–2
33. *ibid.*, p. 427
34. Sichel, *op. cit.*, Vol. I, p. 14
35. British Museum, Add. MSS. 47570
36. *Face without a Frown*, p. 150
37. Vere Foster, *The Two Duchesses*, pp. 173, 182
38. *Dearest Bess*, p. 89
39. C.1397, 1433 (B, pp. 225, 227)
40. C.1611.1
41. British Museum, Add. MSS. 51723
42. *ibid.*

Chapter Eleven

1. Castle Howard Papers
2. C.1659 (B, p. 253)
3. C.1675
4. C.1677.1
5. C.1688

6. C.1677.1; Royal Academy, LAW/1/134
7. C.1686
8. C.1696
9. C.1703, 1708
10. C.1717
11. Granville Leveson-Gower, *Correspondence*, Vol. I, pp. 433–4
12. Aspinall, p. 2287
13. C.1707
14. Aspinall, pp. 2287, 465
15. Leveson-Gower, *op. cit.*, Vol. II, p. 92
16. C.1791.1 (B, p. 270)
17. Leveson-Gower, *op. cit.*, Vol. I, p. 472
18. Aspinall, p. 2287
19. Vere Foster, *The Two Duchesses*, pp. 192, 202, 241
20. *Dearest Bess,* p. 120
21. C.1785.1
22. *Lady Bessborough*, p. 129
23. C.1804
24. *Lady Bessborough*, p. 129
25. Leveson-Gower, *op. cit.*, Vol. II
26. Foster, *op. cit.*, p. 232
27. C.1813 (B, p. 272)
28. Aspinall, p. 2287, and Castle Howard Papers
29. *Dearest Bess*, p. 125
30. Foster, *op. cit.*, p. 252
31. *Hary-O*, p. 133
32. Sichel, *op. cit.*, Vol. I, p. 135: *Annual Register*
33. David Cecil, *Melbourne*, p. 84
34. C.1844 (B, p. 276)
35. C.1815 (B, p. 273)
36. Castle Howard Papers
37. C.1834.1
38. C.1873 (B, p. 279)
39. Castle Howard Papers
40. Stokes, *The Devonshire House Circle*, p. 304
41. *Face without a Frown*, p. 229
42. Leveson-Gower, *op. cit.*, Vol. II, pp. 184–6
43. *Dearest Bess*, p. 141
44. *ibid.*
45. C.1887 (B, p. 281)
46. Leveson-Gower, *op. cit.*, Vol. II, p. 186
47. *Dearest Bess*, p. 142
48. British Museum, Add. MSS. 51476
49. C.1888
50. C.1890
51. *Dearest Bess*, p. 142; *Lady Bessborough*, p. 147
52. Stokes, *op. cit.*, p. 305
53. Aspinall, p. 2165

54. Hist. MSS. Comm., Carlisle MSS., p. 734
55. Foster, *op. cit.*, pp. 281, 286
56. *ibid.*, p. 282
57. Stokes, *op. cit.*, p. 305
58. Castle Howard Papers
59. Wraxall, Vol. III, p. 343
60. Castle Howard Papers
61. *Face without a Frown*, p. 231

Epilogue

1. C.1895
2. C.1892
3. Castle Howard Papers
4. *Hary-O*, pp. 166, 170, 178
5. *ibid,*. p. 262
6. *Creevey Papers*, Mrs Creevey to Mrs Ord
7. *Dearest Bess*, p. 149
8. *Journal* of Elizabeth, Lady Holland, Vol. II, p. 180; *Dearest Bess*, p. 151; Greville *Memoirs*, Vol. IV, p. 115
9. *Dearest Bess*, p. 150
10. *Journal* of Elizabeth, Lady Holland, Vol. II, p. 181
11. *Dearest Bess*, p. 150
12. Castle Howard Papers
13. *Old & New London*, Vol. VI, p. 566
14. Granville Leveson-Gower, *Correspondence*, Vol. II, pp. 345–6
15. Castle Howard Papers
16. *ibid.*
17. C.1955
18. *Lady Bessborough*, p. 194
19. C.1957
20. British Museum, Add. MSS. 51560
21. C.1958
22. C.1960
23. C.1960
24. Hist. MSS. Comm., Fortescue MSS., Vol. X
25. C.1993
26. Castle Howard Papers
27. C.1994
28. C.2000.1
29. C. 6th Duke's group, 25
30. Castle Howard Papers
31. C. 6th Duke's group, 19
32. *Lady Bessborough*, p. 218
33. C. 6th Duke's group, 21
34. C. 6th Duke's group, 22
35. Foster, *The Two Duchesses*, p. 353
36. Howick MSS., Durham University, quoted in Aspinall

37. Castle Howard Papers
38. Leveson-Gower, *op. cit.*, Vol. II, p. 405
39. Harriet, Countess Granville, *Letters 1810–1845*, Vol. I, p. 130
40. Royal Academy, LAW/2/334, LAW/3/219
41. Lord Byron, *Letters & Journals*, ed. Marchand, Vol. VIII, p. 154
42. Royal Academy, LAW/4/210
43. C. 6th Duke's group, 125
44. C. 6th Duke's group, 370
45. C. 6th Duke's group, 305
46. C. 6th Duke's group, 710
47. Castle Howard Papers
48. Royal Academy, LAW/4/222
49. *Dearest Bess*, p. 239
50. Castle Howard Papers

SOURCES AND BIBLIOGRAPHY

Manuscript Sources

Chatsworth MSS. (Papers of 5th and 6th Dukes of Devonshire)
Castle Howard MSS.
British Library, Additional MSS. 47570, 40763, 51723, 51476, 51560
Lamb Papers, British Library Add. MSS. 45548, 45911
Archives of Ministère des Affaires Etrangères, Paris (Correspondance Politique Angleterre, tomes 542, 543, 545, 548)
Royal Academy of Art (Lawrence Papers)
University of Nottingham (Portland Papers)
University of Michigan, William L. Clements Library (Letters to Comte Perregaux)
Northumberland County Record Office (Tankerville Papers)
Richard Page Croft Esq. (Croft Papers)

Published Sources

A. Particular

Georgiana. Extracts from the Correspondence of Georgiana, Duchess of Devonshire, edited by the Earl of Bessborough (1955)
Dearest Bess, by Dorothy Stuart (1955)
The Face without a Frown, by Iris Leveson-Gower (1944)
The Two Duchesses, by Vere Foster (1898)
The Two Duchesses, by Arthur Calder-Marshall (1978)
Lady Bessborough and Her Family Circle, by the Earl of Bessborough and A. Aspinall (1940)
The Devonshire House Circle, by Hugh Stokes (1917)
Private Correspondence of Lord Granville Leveson-Gower, edited by Castalia, Countess Granville (1916)
Hary-O. Letters of Lady Harriet Cavendish, edited by Sir George Leveson-Gower (1940)
Lady Caroline Lamb, by Elizabeth Jenkins (1932)
Melbourne, by Lord David Cecil (1965)
Charles James Fox, by Christopher Hobhouse (1934)
Sheridan, by Walter Sichel (1909)
Speeches of Charles James Fox (1815)

Journal of Elizabeth, Lady Holland, edited by the Earl of Ilchester (1908)
Correspondence of George, Prince of Wales, edited Aspinall
George IV, Prince of Wales, by Christopher Hibbert (1972)
Thomas Coutts, by E. H. Coleridge (1920)
Porphyria - A Royal Malady (British Medical Association)
George III and the Mad Business, by McAlpine and Hunter
Correspondence of Harriet, Countess Granville 1810–1845 edited by F. Leveson-
    Gower (1894)
Letters and Journals of Lord Byron, ed. Marchand (1973–78)
In My Solitary Life, The Years With Mother, by Augustus Hare (1953)

B. *General*

The Greville Memoirs, ed. Strachey and Fulford (1938)
Letters of Horace Walpole, ed. Peter Cunningham
Correspondence of Horace Walpole (Yale Edition)
A Book of Duchesses, by Alice E. Robbins (1913)
English Eccentrics and Eccentricities, by John Timbs
Britain 1688–1815, by Derek Jarrett (1956)
King George III and the Politicians, by Richard Pares (1953)
Clubs and Clubmen, by Arthur Griffiths (1907)
Nathaniel Wraxall, *Historical and Posthumous Memoirs* (1884)
The Age of Scandal, by T. H. White (1950)
Letters of David Garrick, ed. Little and Kalire
Correspondence of Mrs Delany (1861)
Diary of Fanny Burney, edited C. F. Barrett
Old and New London, by Thornbury and Walford
The Grand Whiggery, by Margery Villiers (1939)
Letters of George III to Lord North
The Gaming Table, by Andrew Steinmetz (1870)
History of Brooks's Club (published by Brooks's)

Historical Manuscripts Commission Reports, *Rutland MSS., Hastings MSS.,
    Carlisle MSS., Fortescue MSS.*

INDEX